The IDYLLS of the QUEEN

PHYLLIS ANN KARR

WILDSIDE PRESS
Berkeley Heights, NJ ▼ 1999

THE IDYLLS OF THE QUEEN

WILDSIDE PRESS
P.O. Box 45
Gillette, NJ 07933-0045

CONTENTS

FOREWORD

The setting is Britain in the Fifth Century A.D.—but not a Fifth Century known to any of our history books. It is, rather, an attempt to recreate in modern language the anachronistic, semi-mystical era described by Sir Thomas Malory and his predecessors, when necromancy was as much a fact of life as was the constant need to do battle in the Holy Land, when it was not then as it is nowadays, for "such custom was used in those days, that neither for favour, neither for love nor affinity, there should be none other but righteous judgment, as well upon a king as upon a knight, and as well upon a queen as upon another poor lady." (LE MORTE D'ARTHUR, Book XVIII, chapter 6)

I have sometimes used "Artus" and "Kex," alternate forms in certain old romances for "Arthur" and "Kay," as nicknames.

". . . I, Kay, that thou knawes,
That owte of tyme bostus and blawus . . ."

—THE AVOWYNGE OF KING ARTHUR

Chapter 1
The Poisoning of Sir Patrise

"And when he had eaten it he swelled so till he brast, and there Sir Patrise fell down suddenly dead among them." (Malory XVIII, 3)

When Patrise put his head down on the table beside me and started groaning and twitching, my first thought was: and they call *me* the churl of this court.

Then the bloating became obvious—at least to me; I was sitting beside him. He hunched up with a half-choked cry and collapsed, his face still on the table, and suddenly I guessed that the dark stuff dribbling out of his mouth was not wine.

"Gouvernail," I said.

I suppose, since I did not shout or use sarcasm, the old squire failed to hear the exact tone of my voice. He came and tried to lift Patrise tactfully, assuming the knight had drunk too much. One hardly expects to handle death at a private dinner given by the Queen of the land.

Patrise rolled away from Gouvernail, bumped Safere,

and sprawled on the floor, his mouth still spewing blood.

It happened too quickly. Talk took a few minutes to die away. The last conversation—Pinel's stale speculation on how much of the heat Lancelot might actually have felt when Brumant the Proud was burned to cinders for sitting in the Siege Perilous beside him—went on at least a breath-load of words after everyone else was quiet. (If I had been the one to talk about Lancelot at this particular dinner, I would not have been heard out so politely.)

Gouvernail, bent over Patrise, looked up at me and shook his graying head.

I glanced around at the other tables. Any chance for spiriting the body away as if the young knight had simply eaten and drunk himself into a stupor was gone. Besides, if it had been poison . . . "Gouvernail," I said, "what happened?"

"Internal swelling, I think, my lord. He . . . He seems to have burst inside."

"Poison, then," said Mordred, who sat beside me at my right hand.

At the head table, Her Grace screamed. Gawaine supported her on one side, her cousin Elyzabel rushed up to support her on the other. I fought down a surge of jealousy and looked at the others. Everybody had stopped eating, of course. Pinel of Carbonek took a gulp of wine, then set his goblet down suddenly, as if he wished he had not, and wiped his brown mustache and beard. Ironside and Bleoberis were sneaking the last bite of food out of their mouths. Probably others were as well. Safere, his chair overturned, was standing and staring down with his eyes like eggshells in his dark face. That pious pander Bors de Ganis had stepped aside to let Dame Elyzabel get close to Her Grace. Everyone else was glancing around as if trying to see who would burst next and praying it would not be himself. The dogs had caught the mood, and the only thing you could hear for a moment was their whining and tail-thumping, our breathing, and the Queen's sobs.

"Hand me that apple he was eating, Sir Seneschal," said Mordred calmly.

Patrise had let it roll out of his hand onto the table. I picked it up and handed it to Mordred. Delicately cutting a slice, he whistled to the nearest bitch. She came up, wagging her tail, snuffed up the piece of fruit from Mordred's fingers—and a few moments later was thrashing on the floor coughing up blood into the newly-laid rushes. Astamore started up, one hand to his mouth, and looked for a moment as if he would rush from the room, but got control of himself and sat down again.

"So now," said Mordred, "the question is: was it that one piece of fruit only, or all of them? Brother Gawaine, I believe the bowl was carried back to you. Will someone kindly fetch it here? Gouvernail? Dame Bragwaine? Dame Lore?"

"No!" screamed the Queen. "No, you will not! Bury it—no, burn it!"

"We must learn, dear liege lady." Mordred began sectioning his own pear, so far untasted, and whistled for another dog. The dogs were nosing their dead comrade; a few started to howl.

"No!" Dame Guenevere seized the bowl of fruit, turned, and threw it into the fire. Apples and pears spilled on the floor and table; she snatched them up and hurled them after the others. "Is it not enough? Will you kill them all? All our hounds and brachets, too?"

The fruit sizzled, sending off an odor of roasting juices, laced with something more sickly. Dame

Guenevere turned back to us, the flames leaping in strange colors behind her. "My lords! My good lords—all who have taken any, throw it onto the fire! All of it! At once!"

No one moved. I grabbed the pieces of Mordred's pear, deliberately walked around the room to the fireplace, and threw them into the flames.

My right hand was sticky with pear juice. "Coupnez," I said to the nearest page, "clean water." Coupnez went for ewer and basin, looking, for once, very glad to have something to do.

"That was a foolish deed, Sir Kay," said Mordred. "Come, who else took a piece of it? Will you all play the fool, like our good seneschal?"

Gawaine reached down slowly and picked up the apple he had chosen for himself. His hand trembled. The whole court knew that apples and pears were Gawaine's favorite light food. At this time of year, the large bowl of fruit had obviously been served in honor of the King's favorite nephew, although, with his usual over-insistence on courtesy, he had caused it to be passed around among the other guests first.

"My God!" he said softly. "This was meant for me!" He looked at the Queen, weeping in Elyzabel's arms, at Mordred, back at the Queen. Half-turning, he flung his apple into the flames. Then, in a low voice to the Queen—if the rest of us had not been so silent, we would not have heard him—"Madame, I fear for you."

"True, brother Gawaine," said Agravaine the Beautiful, siding, as usual, with Mordred. "It certainly looks as if it had been meant for you. But as you've just destroyed your own choice of the fruit, we can never know whether it was tainted also, can we?"

"What difference if it was meant especially for

Gawaine?" Mador de la Porte was on his feet now. So were most of us, though not, it seemed, for the same reason as Mador. "Whether she meant to murder one or all, she did not care how many good knights died. And I have lost my cousin, madame, my good cousin and a noble knight, through your treason. A great knight he would have been of his arms in his time! Here I charge you, madame the Queen, with his death!"

Dame Guenevere stared at him, a wild, frightened look in those lovely gray eyes. She moved her lips as if to speak. Jesu! to see her reduced to this!

"Think, Mador," I said quickly. "Twenty-four knights here, four ladies and Gouvernail to serve us, not to mention the cooks and scullions—it could have been any one of us here present trying to murder any other one of us!"

"*I* rather like the idea of someone attempting to murder us all at a stroke," said Mordred, leaning back in his chair and lifting his goblet to his mouth.

"You have not lost a kinsman, neither of you!" Mador shook his fist at the Queen. "I will be revenged for his death, madame—by Jesu and His Holy Mother, I will be revenged! If I must renounce my allegiance to do it, I will prove your treachery with my body!"

Again Dame Guenevere tried to speak, but her cousin had to speak for her. "She will not lack champions, my lord Sir Mador!" Elyzabel looked around at all of us, her temper rising. This was the woman who had once brazened it out with King Claudas of France. "Which of you will champion the Queen, my lords? You do not all believe Sir Mador's lies? Which of you will fight for her? Sweet Mother Mary, must I put on armor myself and prove that Heaven aids the just cause?"

Palomides, who has fought in as many women's quarrels as has Lancelot, and almost as many as Gawaine himself, lifted his knife and drove it heavily into the table before him. "Good Dame Elyzabel, think not that we do not pray for the Queen's innocence and happy deliverance. But it is not for us to fight in her cause." The old Saracen sat down and buried his face in his hands. He was right. Whichever of us fought for the Queen as good as confessed himself her accomplice, a poisoner.

All my life, I have craved and prayed for at least one more chance to fight for Her Grace, hating Lancelot, as I would have hated Gawaine or anyone else who took her battle away from me time after time. And now, when Lancelot was not at hand to take it on himself, when God and Lancelot alone knew where Lancelot had been for the last week, neither I, nor Gawaine, Palomides nor Persant nor any of the rest of us were able to take up her quarrel!

"There is cousin Ywaine of the Lion, of course," said Mordred, glancing around as if to take stock of who was here and who was not. "I rather wondered why he was not among us; dining with the King seemed rather a feeble reason. Or there is Sir Lucan the Butler—he knows food. We might perhaps entice the good Sir Pelleas up from the arms of the beautiful Nimue in their Lake retreat. Or we might send for Mark of Cornwall. As I remember, King Mark once defended himself very ably in an unjust cause."

"Damn you, Mordred," I said. The Queen had fainted.

Gouvernail and three of her ladies carried her away to her own chamber. Dame Lore of Carlisle remained in the small banquet room with us. Maybe she thought to defend the Queen's interests here.

I looked around, counting pages. "Where in God's Name is Grimpmains?"

"Sick, sir," said Clarance, one of the older lads, looking none too well himself.

"All right, Clarance," I said, "go summon the King."

Chapter 2
Of Gawaine's Faction and Lancelot's

> *"Sir, said they, here is a knight of this castle that hath been long among us, and right now he is slain with two knights, and for none other cause but that our knight said that Sir Lancelot were a better knight than Sir Gawaine."* (Malory X, 55)

I sent the rest of the pages out for more clean water. We would all want to wash our hands with greater care than customary. I hoped that her ladies would bathe the Queen, and that the younger pages, who had probably been poking around at the fruit, would remember to keep their fingers out of their mouths.

Mador cleared his own table with sweeps of his sword arm. Safere and Galihud carried Patrise's body over and laid it on the cleared space. Composing his cousin's limbs, Mador set up an Irish keening for him. The rest took their seats again. Here and there a low, uneasy conversation began. Coupnez brought the basin and ewer I had called for, and I began to wash my hands, looking around the tables in their semi-circular arrangement.

Why would anyone want to kill Patrise of Ireland this way? It made far better sense to assume that Patrise had eaten a piece of fruit intended for Gawaine.

Gawaine the Golden-Tongued and Golden-Haired—prince of chivalry, courtesy, manhood, and all the rest of it, who had fought his glorious way through four decades without catching a battle-scar on the face so many ladies loved—now sat with his broad shoulders hunched together, an uncustomary pose for him. God knows Gawaine had been in his share of blood feuds over the years. He might have achieved the Grail if he had been less set, once on a time, on avenging the deaths of his father and mother. But Gawaine always made a point of striking his enemies down in fair fight. The idea that some traitor had tried to burst his insides with poison was going to turn several more of his hairs from gold to gray.

Revenge was not the only reason someone may have had to attack Gawaine the coward's way. It might also have been jealousy on behalf of Lancelot or one of the other few men who might still be considered Gawaine's rivals in glory. Gawaine and Lancelot themselves have always been loyal friends: Arthur's favorite nephew and Arthur's greatest adventurer. But the respective followers of Lancelot and Gawaine are not always so friendly. Bloody at worst and backbiting at best, the factions have plagued us since Lancelot first came across the Channel from France; and if Lancelot had not come, Gawaine's detractors would probably have attached themselves to Lamorak de Galis, Tristram, or anyone else who was on hand.

Those of Gawaine's supporters here present consisted chiefly of his four brothers. I hardly glanced at Gareth Beaumains, the next to the youngest, the favorite (Gawaine's, Lancelot's, and almost everybody else's), the wide-eyed and simple-souled, possibly the nearest thing to a saintly knight Arthur had left, unless you counted Bors de Ganis.

But Mordred, the youngest of all Lot's sons, sitting there now at a nearly empty table, slowly turning his knife as if he were considering licking off the dried juice . . . What in Jesu's Holy Name had happened to Mordred? He had come to court at twenty years of age, honestly and eagerly, been dubbed knight at once and elected to the Round Table after a year, and not solely, like more recent companions, on the strength of his kinsmen and friends. We all thought Mordred was on his way to being the best of the five brothers. The ladies delighted in him—high forehead, graceful nose, delicate lips, gold hair, strong back—handsome as Gawaine and considerably younger.

Then, at twenty-two, he changed overnight. Popular speculation said his brains had been scrambled in the tournament at Peningues, where he fought like a devil and was almost left for dead on the field. But I had been friendly enough with Mordred during those first two, good years. His wit was much like mine even then. And I was one of the few to stay fairly close to him, as close as he allowed anyone to come. It was not his brains that had been scrambled, it was his soul. Tournament fighting alone, no matter how rough, does not do that to a man.

The next to the oldest of Lot's sons, Agravaine the Beautiful, whose face must have made a good number of women jealous, was the only man among us who looked, not grieved or alarmed, but bored. As for Gaheris, who was at least making the effort to look commiserating, he had always seemed caught in the middle in more respects than age alone. Capable, blond, and handsome like all his brothers, he was the only one of them to be embarrassed by a slight deformity. His right arm was overlong. Aside from its length, it was well-formed and shapely, and his mother used to call it a sign that he had been especially formed to wield a weapon. Since her death, he would allow no one else to mention his right arm. But even now, well past the middle of his threescore and ten, he seemed not to have made up his mind whether to veer toward Gawaine and Gareth or toward Agravaine and Mordred. He did not gossip and preen himself like Agravaine, and in his taciturn way he pursued justice as fervidly as Gawaine; but he cultivated none of Gawaine's and Gareth's social graces. Still, perhaps I should have taken Gaheris for my courtly model. He was no general favorite, but, because he kept silent instead of voicing his thoughts, no one spoke ill of his manners, either.

These were Gawaine's brothers and supporters, and one of them, Gareth Beaumains, was more nearly in Lancelot's camp than Gawaine's. Brandiles, the brother of Gawaine's third wife, seemed to stay apart from faction rivalry. The red-haired, six-fingered giant's son Ironside and old, balding Persant of Inde were Gareth's adherents rather than Gawaine's. Persant had never been a vicious man, simply a sporting fellow who fought all comers for the love of it and offered the survivors free hospitality. Ironside's history was not so genial. While besieging Dame Lyonors in her castle, before Beaumains defeated and converted him, Ironside had hanged between thirty and fifty knights in their armor. Which was naturally forgiven him because he had murdered them in fulfillment of a promise made to an old paramour. If Kay the Churl were to mention Ironside's early deeds after all these years of Ironside's good behavior, the whole court would cry shame on Kay's rudeness. But the jolly red giant had also sworn a vow, in those old days, against Lancelot and Gawaine. He had never carried it out, but now Lancelot was missing and Gawaine had barely escaped poison.

Lancelot's partisans outnumbered Gawaine's in the small banquet chamber this afternoon: Lancelot's bastard half-brother Ector de Maris, fathered by King Ban, under the influence of Merlin's magical aphrodisiac, during his stay in Britain; Lancelot's French cousins Lionel of the lion-shaped birthmark, who had once tried to cut down his brother in hot blood; and Bors de Ganis, our last surviving Sir Saint, almost a virgin, the only man to have fully achieved the adventure of the Holy Grail and return alive, who now sat in a posture befitting his reputation, hands clasped, blue eyes closed, and head bowed to show the tonsure-like cut of his grizzled hair; Lancelot's British-born cousins, the twins Blamore and Bleoberis, who looked alike, acted in concert, and probably had the same dreams every night. Lancelot's protégé Breunor the Black-Haired and seldom-washed, otherwise known as Sir La Cote Male Taile or Ill-Fitting Coat—my own name for him; he went on wearing the name as stubbornly as he had worn the filthy, bloodstained coat of his father's until he had avenged his father's murder. Lancelot's less dedicated partisans, Galihodin and Galihud, the princes of Surluse, who had slowly swung to Lancelot's party from Gawaine's, but still maintained friendly relations, at least on the surface.

The Queen's last five guests were harder to place by faction. Palomides and his brother Safere, the lean, scarred, dark-skinned former Saracens, might well end in Lancelot's camp if an open split should ever come, but meanwhile they maintained neutrality. Aliduk, the honorable old fox of a Breton warleader, was another distant cousin of Lancelot; but Aliduk was only marking time with us until his old liege lord Hoel of Brittany called him back from his more or less self-imposed exile. I had objected to Aliduk's election to the Round Table on grounds that when he sailed home to Brittany we would be left with another Tristram situation—a companion permanently absent from his place—but as usual, when my opinion stands alone, it was ignored.

Pinel of Carbonek had returned with Lancelot from the Grail Quest, but had rarely been seen in Lancelot's company since. Elected to the Table on the strength of being a nephew of old King Pellam, the last of the Rich Fishers, Pinel's favorite sport was talking. The only subject he kept quiet about was which of Pellam's three brothers had actually fathered him; maybe he hoped the mystery would make other folk speculate about him as eagerly as he speculated about them. His voice would have been pleasant if it had been less loud. At the present moment, quiet for once in his life, Pinel sat at his table staring down into his goblet like old Merlin reading the future in a bowl of slime.

When Pinel first came to court, Astamore had been one of the first to strike up a friendship with him, and one of the most faithful in keeping to it, although lately he sometimes appeared to be trying to disembarrass himself of Pinel's company. One thing that held them together was their skill with the harp, even if Pinel did seem insistent on playing duets mainly to display his own superior ability. But Astamore was ten years younger, had been at court five years longer, and had finally, acknowledging, but not playing on his own high kinsfolk, won his place at the Table on his own merits.

Astamore's worst fault was a maddening habit of turning his ring round and round on his finger. Although the ring, with its pretentious blue stone set in too much silver, looked more of a size for Ironside's hand than Astamore's, he claimed it did not interfere with his eating or harping; he did, however, hang it on a chain around his neck beneath his breastplate before putting on his gauntlets for battle. I was surprised to see that this afternoon, for once, he was not fondling his ring. Instead, he was prying nuts open with his knife, examining the nutmeats one by one, and then piling them up untasted on the table in front of him.

Gawaine had killed Astamore's uncle, King Bagdemagus of Gorre, during the Grail Quest.

Then there were the principal servers at our small, intimate dinner: Gouvernail, Elyzabel, Lore the Cupbearer, Bragwaine, and Senehauz. Gouvernail was a better man, in everything but might of arms, than his former master Tristram had ever been; and the only one of the four dames whose past might be as spotted as an honest knight's was Bragwaine of Ireland, a silent, dark, aging woman, less handsome now than competent, who might know more than her share concerning plant juices and their use. Senehauz was almost as young as the pages, and as innocent.

As for the pages who had helped serve, I knew them all, both as individuals and as types of the young trouble-courters Lucan and I have helped train through the years. The minds of pages, even when they run to revenge feuds, following the sterling example of their elders, do not usually run to poison. Besides, a page would not have thought of putting the stuff in the apples —he would have put it in the wine.

Had we a new cook or older scullion in the kitchen, anyone over ten years old who had been with us less than half a score of years, I would have wondered whether a spy had slipped in among the servants despite my watching. As matters stood, I knew my kitchen staff better than the pages, better than most of my fellow knights, and I would have fought to prove the innocence of the lowest scullion with as much assurance as I would have fought for the Queen herself . . . though not with a thousandth part of the reverence . . . if I could have fought for anyone in this case.

I glanced at Dame Lore, the one who had remained when the other ladies and Gouvernail bore away the Queen. Lore was standing at the other side of the fireplace, staring around the room. Turning her head slightly, she looked straight back at me.

Moving nearer so that we could hear each other above Mador's wailing, I muttered, "Your opinion, Dame Cupbearer. Which of us poisoned the apple?"

"I have been trying to think which of you it was meant for."

"And?"

Dame Lore is another cousin of the Queen, and her eyes are almost the same noble gray. "I believe it was meant for Her Grace."

"Prove that," I said, "and I'll skewer the whoreson like a pigeon."

"Will you, Seneschal?"

"I will."

"I think not. Remember that poison is more the enchantress' weapon than the knight's."

I stared back into the dying fire, remembering the different colors of the flames when Dame Guenevere had first thrown the fruit into them. "Morgan le Fay again?"

Before Dame Cupbearer could answer, the men nearest the door started standing up. In a moment everyone was on his feet. The King had come.

Chapter 3
The Accusation

"And ever Sir Mador stood still afore the king, and ever he appealed the queen of treason; for the custom was such that time that all manner of shameful death was called treason." (Malory XVIII, 4)

Mador went on keening, eyes closed and back to the door, apparently unable to hear anything beyond the sound of his own grief. Arthur paused for a few moments, looking around at all of us, at Gawaine and myself the longest. Then he went to Mador and laid one hand on the old knight's shoulder.

Mador stopped wailing at last and turned slowly to look at him. "Justice, my lord the King!"

"When have I denied anyone justice?" said Arthur, probably believing it himself.

Mador might have been thinking of the knights whom Lancelot, while half-asleep, had mowed down in their own pavilions; of the murder of Arthur's own sister, Queen Morgawse, when Gawaine had taken revenge into his own hands because the King would not allow

Lamorak de Galis, the wonder of the age, to be put on trial; or of the various grievances which have never been openly brought against Gawaine himself and his brothers because of their kinship to Arthur. But all Mador said was, "Justice, my lord, against your Queen!"

"Old friend," said Arthur, "my Queen would never have done this."

"Was it not her dinner?" Mador struck the table. "Who else could have done this?"

"A different queen," I said. "The sometime queen of Gorre, Dame Morgan le Fay." Not that I quite believed it yet, but Dame Morgan, wherever she was, would hardly notice another treachery or two laid at her door, and it might save Dame Guenevere.

"Yes!" said Pinel of Carbonek. He had never seen Morgan, but he was as ready to theorize about her as anyone else. "Yes, the Fay! Of course—she tried to kill us all, of course—"

"Despite the fact," Mordred said calmly, "that Aunt Morgan has been presumed dead for several years."

"Presumed, not proven," began Dame Lore, but Mador broke in with a shout.

"Liars! Traitors, with the traitress! I claim justice, my lord the King!"

"You will have justice!" Arthur shouted back. "Against the murderer! But my wife is not the murderer!"

"You must admit, Uncle, the circumstances look damning," remarked Agravaine, with at least enough grace not to study his fingernails while he said it.

"Damn you, Agravaine," I said, "don't the circumstances look damning for all of us here present?"

"Not for Sir Patrise," said Agravaine.

"Assuming, of course, that he was shriven before

dinner," added Mordred.

Arthur ignored us. "Mador, you have been my knight forty years and more," he said. "Do you accuse your sovereign lady to my face?"

"I do! And I will make good the charge with my body."

Arthur clenched his fist. "And do you accuse me along with my Queen, Mador de la Port?"

Mador breathed heavily, but did not step back. "You are our King, my liege lord, but in this matter you are no more than another knight like the rest of us—less than the rest of us in that you were not here present."

"By Jesu, when you fight against your sovereign lady, you commit—"

"I do not fight against my sovereign lady!" said Mador. "I keep no allegiance with a destroyer of good knights!"

The Queen had returned. I saw her standing in the doorway, with her cousin Dame Elyzabel. Some of the others had also seen her, but the King had not.

"Do you also renounce allegiance to me, Sir Knight?" continued Arthur.

"To have justice for my kinsman's death," bawled Mador, "I would renounce allegiance to the Pope himself!"

The King pounded the table with his fist. "So be it! Then I will answer your charge with my own body!"

"My lord, no!" cried Dame Guenevere.

Arthur turned and they looked at each other. Tears were quivering on her cheeks. Go to her, I thought, go to her, Artus you idiot! Holy Mary, you didn't realize what you had when you pulled that Sword out of the damn Stone, and you don't realize what you have now! Aloud, I said, "The Queen is right, Sir Arthur. You're trapped. Like all the rest of us."

Aliduk nodded. The dispassionate, scarcely-involved arbiter. "You must serve as judge in this case, my liege lord. You cannot fight as champion."

Arthur sat down, elbows on the table near Patrise's feet, and rested his head on his hands. Dame Guenevere came up behind him and laid her palms on his shoulders, closing her eyes and tilting her glorious head so that the tears slanted backward over her cheeks. "As God is my witness," she said, "I made this dinner for joy and never for harm."

Arthur raised his head and looked around. "Press your charge, then, Sir Mador de la Porte. I may not fight for my wife, but I have other good knights who will." He looked around at us again, as if searching for Lancelot. I tried to catch his attention, but his stare slid over me, uncomprehending, and finally rested on his favorite nephew.

Gawaine started to speak in reply to that gaze.

"Fight for her, elder brother, and you associate yourself with the crime," said Mordred.

"The poison was aimed at *me,*" said Gawaine. "In Jesu's Name, would I have tried to poison myself?"

Mordred shrugged. "Aye, we all know your fondness for apples, brother. And, knowing it, folk will call it rather strange that this time you waited just long enough before eating the fruit."

Gawaine stared at him, then at the Queen. "Madame, I . . . Madame, forgive me!"

He sat again, trapped like Arthur and the rest of us. Whoever fought for the Queen would seem to declare his own guilt. Worse, some of us, her guests, actually seemed to believe Mador's accusation.

I would have championed her myself and damned the appearance. But I was no longer the same man of arms who had struck down the kings of Denmark and Soleise beside the Humber. A righteous cause strengthens the arm of an indifferent fighter—so Gawaine would say—but the Queen needed a champion who could rely on his own arm, righteous cause or not.

Arthur got to his feet and looked around again. "Thank God, we have other knights as good as those here present. Call for your judgment, Sir Mador, but first remember that our Queen may not prove entirely friendless."

"I will prove my charge against Lancelot himself—if he is still in this world," said Mador.

The Queen gasped.

"Name the day, my lord King," Mador went on, with a glance at the Queen. Watching his face, I considered what would happen if Mador stopped living before that day came, and my hand twitched on my dagger's hilt.

"The meadow beside Westminster," said the King at last. "This day fifteen days hence."

"It is not long enough!" exclaimed Dame Lore, behind me.

"It is too long," said Mador. "But have the stake ready and the fire burning."

"The stake will be ready," said Arthur, his voice hard, "and the Queen will have her judgment. All things will be done lawfully."

Mador drove his knife into the table. "I am answered, Sire." If no knight appeared to fight for her a fortnight from now, the Queen could still plead innocent and claim another forty days to find a champion. "But you cannot delay forever in the sight of God and man!" Mador went on. "The traitress will burn before Midsummer."

"See you do not attempt to take your former seat among us, Mador de la Porte," said the King. Then he took the Queen from her cousin and slowly led her away, supporting her against his own shoulder.

Dame Elyzabel looked around at us once more. "God!" she said scornfully, "for a sword and a suit of armor!" Then she followed Dame Guenevere. In the language of courtliness, we were free to go where we would.

Chapter 4
Of Morgan's Duplicity and Kay's Jealousy

"And therewithal they set the queen in a barge into Humber; but always Queen Guenever praised Sir Kay for his deeds, and said, What lady that ye love, and she love you not again she were greatly to blame; and among ladies, said the queen, I shall bear your noble fame, for ye spake a great word, and fulfilled it worshipfully." (Malory IV, 3)

Mordred rose, flipped a scrap of meat from his trencher to the hounds, and left the room. Agravaine shrugged and followed him out, but Gaheris lingered on. Gouvernail, who had returned behind the Queen, cleared the remaining platters off the table where Sir Patrise lay. Lionel and Mador lifted the board from the trestles, carrying the body out as if on a bier. Most of the others followed to watch Patrise laid out decently in chapel. Gaheris joined them, keeping toward the back. In a few moments I was left alone with Lore of Carlisle.

"Morgan le Fay." I shook my head. "It was a beautiful thought, Dame Lore, but—"

"Not merely a thought. A certainty. Have you forgotten her poisoned cloak?"

"No, I haven't forgotten the bloody cloak!" It had been years ago, shortly after Morgan's second and permanent break with her husband and departure from Arthur's court. She had sent the cloak to her brother as a pretended gift of reconciliation; but, on Dame Nimue's advice, Arthur made the damsel-messenger who brought it try it on her own shoulders first. In an instant, the cloth had sucked around her small form and the lining glowed lividly, showing through the seams in the dark outer velvet like raw flesh in a new wound. A few moments of shrieks and writhing, and the girl collapsed, her body melting away like tallow. When it was over, and the cloth was cool enough to pull away, there were her feet, curled up like claws in the cracked leather slippers, and her head, hair singed and features screwed up with pain; there was nothing between but bones turned to charcoal. I hoped Morgan's damsel had been in the plot with her mistress and not merely an innocent messenger, but the stench was not like the stink of Brumant's death in the Siege Perilous or Corsabrin's pagan soul going to Hell—it was plain, scorched human flesh.

"Morgan is as dead as her damsel by now, anyway," I went on.

"You all assume she is dead because we've heard nothing of her for years," replied Dame Lore, "and therefore you say she was not responsible for this. I say that this proves she is *not* dead!"

"She loved her nephews. Why would she try to poison Gawaine?"

"What is her love for Gawaine compared with her

hatred for Guenevere? She means to burn the Queen this time."

Trying not to see the flames leaping up around Her Grace, I thought it over. Dame Lore could be right—Arthur's half-sister might still be alive. But, if so, why had she been so quiet these last several years, since before the Grail Quest?

Dame Morgan's first attempt on Arthur's life had been a complicated scheme involving a counterfeit of Excalibur, sword and scabbard. When that plot backfired and Morgan's own current paramour was killed instead of the King, she had tried to murder her husband Uriens in his sleep with his own sword and, that attempt foiled by her son Ywaine of the Lion, she left court for good and took up residence in various castles of her own, one of them a former gift of Arthur to her. She had gained knowledge of magic somewhere, whether in the nunnery where she was raised or from old Merlin or elsewhere—enough to establish herself as perhaps the most skillful necromancer alive in Britain, as well as the most treacherous. At one time, she had been heart and head of a whole sorority of enchantresses. Yes, this could be the latest of Morgan's periodic attempts to destroy the Queen and court. But . . .

"She had to get the poison into the fruit," I said. "I never heard of any magic strong enough to do that at a distance."

"At what distance? She may be anywhere. Have you forgotten how she turned herself and all her attendants into rocks when she escaped from the King? And how else does poison come to be found in uncooked fruit unless by magic?"

"You poor, silly innocent, for all your silvering hairs," I said. "Do you always look for the magical explanation first? Or do you simply assume that if it's evil, it must be sorcery?"

"The poison was not on the skin of the fruit, Sir Seneschal! Her Grace arranged those apples and pears with her own hands, and did not wash her fingers again before sitting to eat."

"Then Le Fay missed her chance, didn't she? If the stuff had been on the skin of the fruit, it would have gotten onto the Queen's fingers and then into her own mouth with her other food." I threw that thought away from my mind as soon as it was spoken. "A long pin," I went on, "dipped in poison, then inserted through the blossom end or maybe the stem end, slantwise into the meat."

"You seem to understand the process very neatly, Sir Seneschal. Then I will find a way to poison apples without necromancy, too. Suppose they were buried in venomed earth last harvest? Suppose the venom had all the winter to penetrate each piece to the core?"

"Without tainting the peel?"

"Any surface taint would be cleaned off with the dirt when the fruit was dug up. The peel would be left harmful only to the tongue, not to the fingers. And the poison would remain within. You are in charge of seeing the fruit stored each harvest, are you not, Sir Kay?"

"Yes, I am! In whatever place the court happens to be at harvest time. And yes, we were here in London last harvest. But I don't always watch every apple buried individually, and I don't always stand over the servants and order them exactly which pit or bag or tub to go to for the food—or were you aware of that, Dame Cupbearer? This court has made progress through eight different cities since the storerooms were filled here in London last fall, and I go with the court—or had you forgotten that? By God, my lady, when I start poisoning people, I'll know who I'm—"

"You will hardly need any other poison, Sir Seneschal, while you have your tongue!" She stood up. "The earth might have been tainted by a serpent, or by water from a serpent-venomed spring. Such things have happened before now. But since you have chosen to defend yourself where there was no accusation—"

"No accusation!" I was on my feet now, too. "And you call *my* tongue poisonous? What reason would *I* have—"

"Jealousy!"

"Jealousy? Jealousy, in God's Name?"

"Aye, jealousy, Sir Seneschal! You are more jealous of Her Grace and Lancelot than that pitiful fool Meliagrant ever was! Do you think, because the King does not see it, no one else does?"

I don't know whether Dame Lore left then because of her own rage or because of something she saw in my expression. If a tenth of what my soul felt was leaking through into my face, I must have looked fierce enough to give an ogre pause.

I stood there watching her absence until I could be reasonably sure she was not coming back again. Then I sat and stared at the begrimed silver fruitbowl lying sunk in the embers.

Dame Lore was wrong. I am not jealous of Lancelot. You can only feel jealousy toward someone for whom you have some kind of respect or affection. Jealousy is what I feel towards Gawaine. What I feel towards Lancelot is something only the demons in Hell can have a name for, something that should probably frighten me about my eternal salvation, if Lancelot did not deserve every breath of it.

Who should be the King's right hand? Kay, his foster-brother, his seneschal, the man who was raised with him, shared his training (a few years in advance of Artus, too, and for every time I may have played the bully, I smoothed out the way several times for him.) Who was, in fact, recognized as Arthur's right hand? Lancelot. And Gawaine.

Gawaine I can stomach. He is the King's sister's son, and not only is his loyalty above question, but he is usually at hand when needed. When he goes out on quest or mission, he lets it be known in advance. When he aims to kill, he has a reason, he makes sure his opponent is equally armed, and he knows what he's doing. When Gawaine's father rebelled against Arthur, Gawaine came, along with his mother Morgawse and those of his brothers who were old enough, to our side. The decision could not have been easy, especially for a man of Gawaine's scruples and family feeling.

If Lancelot had any deep, noble reason in coming across the Channel to Arthur, aside from personal glory-seeking, he kept it well concealed. He came, was dubbed knight, and left again immediately for his independent adventuring. Lancelot made sure everyone knew what a great warrior he was before he deigned attach himself permanently to Arthur's court. If you can call it permanently when every second or third year he either slips away to go adventuring on his own again, without warning anyone beforehand, or goes out of his mind and runs amok for a year or three. And when Lancelot goes battle-berserk, in or out of a legitimate battle situation, even his friends and kinsmen had better keep out of his way.

We all know what a marvellous man of his arms is Lancelot of the Lake. He goes to any lengths to hammer it home to the world. There was the time he and I spent the night at the same forester's lodging. Lancelot got up before dawn, put on my armor and shield, and rode off while I was still asleep, so that he would have the chance to increase his glory by striking down all the knights who would not have attacked Lancelot but were willing enough to attack a man they thought was Kay. If I had had my good charger Feuillemorte at the time, Lancelot would probably have "borrowed" him, too. Oh, I got back to court in perfect safety. I had no shield but Lancelot's, and his reputation was already such that no one was willing to fight him in love or lightness. For which safety I was expected to be duly grateful to the generosity of the great hero. But any chance I might have had to win a little honor in my own name was gone. One of the few times I have ever been able to leave court for a few fortnights' adventuring on my own, wasted.

Artus may have been the only man to unite Logris, at least as well as it can ever be united. No one denies he is a fine leader in war. When he sits in judgment, so long as he is not personally involved in the case, he has a way of cutting through forms and trivialities, getting to the heart of the matter, and making a decision that endears him to the people. His knights love him because he still ventures his body on the same terms as the rest of us, in an occasional tournament as well as in battle; I suppose the popularity is worth the risk of having a dead or maimed High King and no heir ready. But as for the regular, day-to-day functioning of his kingdom and court, the kingdom runs by the Queen's efforts and the court by my own. Nobody realizes how much. Along with my other duties, I serve as scapegoat for anything that might otherwise dent Arthur's popularity—even Arthur does not quite understand that service. Folk should at least remember what happened in this kingdom when Guenevere's look-alike seduced Arthur and supplanted the true Queen for two years: The country came near to rotting away, and not even the Pope's interdict brought Artus back to his senses. Only the false queen's dying confession woke him up; the kingdom only started to recover when Dame Guenevere agreed to leave her sanctuary in Surluse and come back to her first husband. Maybe the common people remember that interlude more clearly than they are willing to say. I am not sure.

Arthur had been ready to sentence Her Grace to death when he named her look-alike queen. He had been ready to have her hair torn out and the skin peeled from her loving face and gentle hands. If he had done it, I could not have remained loyal to him. I would have given my life to save Dame Guenevere, but Lancelot took it as his natural right to act as her champion. Again. And afterwards escorted her into Surluse to share her banishment while his liege lord played with the look-alike.

I probably owe my own life to the conceited Mirror of All Knightly Prowess. The time Bagdemagus' worthless son Meliagrant accused Her Grace of infidelity, I was the supposed lover he named. I was newly wounded, and there was blood in her bed. There was also blood on the bars of the window, if anyone else noticed it besides myself, and Lancelot answered Meliagrant's challenge with bandaged hands, insisting, as usual, that he and no one else should fight as the Queen's champion. No matter that I had not asked him to clear my name as well as hers—no matter that I was more than willing to have fought Meliagrant myself as soon as I was sufficiently healed to sit my horse—no matter, even, that there was not that much glory in defeating Meliagrant, and Lancelot had to fight with his head and half his body unarmored and his left arm bound in order to win any fresh fame for the encounter.

It was more important to clear Her Grace than to quibble about who the man might have been. But, God! That *he* should have fought to clear me of his own deed —that *he* should have loved the Queen in my place!

Even remembering it, I threw the nearest goblet against the wall, denting it beyond use. No matter, I would pay for the goblet later.

If Lancelot the valorous hypocrite had never come to Britain, *I* might have been the Queen's favorite knight. It's not impossible. Or Gawaine might have been. Either one of us, and it would have been a pure loyalty. Not like Lancelot the seducer, ravishing the Queen and then driving her half mad with his lesser paramours, his Elaines and Amables, and with his habit of risking his life heedlessly on less than no excuse.

At least in the earlier days he had had the decency to keep his dishonesty secret. Even I could not be sure until the Meliagrant affair. But since his return from seeking the Holy Grail, he was more careless of the Queen's safety—trusting, I suppose, that he would always happen to be on hand at the right times to prove the truth was a lie on the field of honor. Someday Arthur was going to believe at last what Morgan le Fay had told him years ago, over and over, about Lancelot and the Queen.

And *this* was the man on whom the Queen's life and safety had depended time after time—on whom it might depend again now!

Suppose Morgan was still alive. Suppose she had captured Lancelot again, even managed to seduce him at last (although, for that matter, we had only Lancelot's word that she had never yet gotten him into her bed, or that all those months he had spent with her on various occasions he had indeed been a totally unwilling prisoner in her stronghold). Suppose that while holding

Lancelot again, whether as prisoner or paramour, she had set another kind of trap for Dame Guenevere—to see her condemned and burned while Lancelot was prevented from appearing in time to fight for her.

Chapter 5
Of a Search for a Serpent

"So when the king and the queen were together . . . Where is Sir Lancelot? said King Arthur; an he were here he would not grudge to do battle for you. Sir, said the queen, I wot not where he is, but his brother and his kinsmen deem that he be not within this realm. . . . What aileth you, said the king, ye cannot keep Sir Lancelot upon your side?" (Malory XVIII, 4)

Someone came in. I looked up to see Pinel and Astamore.

"They're beginning to ask why you haven't come to see Sir Patrise laid out," said Astamore.

"My ears are offended by Mador's banshee wailing."

"It will seem suspicious if you don't come."

"Let it. Maybe he'll come to his senses about the Queen and decide to accuse me instead." If Her Grace were free of Mador's arraignment, it would be a pleasure to fight for once in my own name.

Pinel sat down heavily. "They'll suspect any of us who fail to wake with the body."

"Then you'd better get back before they start to suspect you," I told him.

Pinel shuddered. "I could have no wish to harm Patrise. Why would I have wanted to harm Sir Patrise? Why Sir Patrise, of all of us?"

"Why would the Queen have wanted to kill Gawaine?" I replied. "Maybe age is catching up with Mador. He's not thinking clearly. I suppose he wants everyone to touch the corpse and see who makes it bleed?"

"It's bled several times," said Astamore.

"Only a little, at the mouth. It was the jounce of carrying him." Pinel looked around, found a goblet that was still upright and had a little wine in it, and took a drink. "Bleeding at the murderer's touch only holds good when there's an open, outer wound."

I snorted. "Or when the ghost himself knows who murdered him."

"Even so, the death is too fresh for the test to hold true, I think." Astamore balanced his thin thighs on the edge of the board and began to fondle his ring absently. "We'll return to the chapel soon. I doubt anything will make Sir Mador change his accusation."

"Which may be as well for you, Astamore," I said.

Aside from being slightly too close together, his black eyes were so much like his uncle's that he might have been Bagdemagus' bastard son instead of his nephew. "Your meaning, Seneschal?"

"The poisoned fruit was meant for Gawaine. Not even Mador denies that. And Gawaine killed your uncle Bagdemagus during the Grail adventures."

I am not sure what I hoped to accomplish, or even whether I really believed at that point that Astamore was the traitor. Maybe I wanted to see how he would react, maybe I was looking for ways to divert suspicion from the Queen, or at least spread it out. Maybe I only needed another good quarrel.

"The world knows your tongue, Sir Kay," said Astamore, letting his ring alone for a moment. "And the world knows your insults are meaningless, since you can speak in nothing else. Sir Gawaine killed King Bagdemagus in misfortune, not in treachery."

Pinel rubbed his chubby fingers together, as if limbering them for a lively hour with his harp. "But we don't know that. We have only Sir Gawaine's word for what happened."

Astamore turned his stare from me to Pinel. "And the testimony of both their squires, and that of the monks who tended my uncle in his last moments and buried him in their abbey. King Bagdemagus of Gorre was a generous knight. He did not blame Lancelot for killing his son Sir Meliagrant in fair combat, and his soul can hardly blame Sir Gawaine for the misfortune of killing him in a joust of friendship."

Pinel subsided, muttering, "We don't even know the fruit was meant for Sir Gawaine."

"We know the *fruit* was meant for Gawaine," I said, "especially at this season of the year. We don't know the *poison* was meant for him. But if it was meant for someone else, the poisoner apparently wouldn't have minded getting Gawaine as well."

Astamore started twisting his ring again. "An enemy of Sir Arthur. Some enemy of the entire Round Table."

"No—no enemy of the Round Table," Pinel broke in. "Who but Gawaine would have eaten the fruit so quickly?"

Speculating on all sides of any question at once—except a theological one—was a custom of Pinel. As I had told him to his face, his gadfly arguing was probably the reason King Pellam sent him away from Carbonek. They are said to like singleness of purpose there.

"The question is who would *not* be likely to eat it." I glanced at the dead bitch lying between the tables. "The bowl was heaped. No doubt enough for every man of us to have his choice."

Astamore looked at the bowl in the fireplace. "We don't know that every piece was poisoned," he said carefully.

I thought of the strange colors the rest of the fruit had given the flames for a moment or two. Astamore played with his ring. Pinel rubbed at the short, honey-colored beard he wore to help hide his smallpox scars.

"Maybe they had simply gone bad?" Pinel said at last.

"An adder bit the tree when it was in bloom?" I said. "Or maybe someone pissed into the earth where the fruit was stored? God's Blood, Pinel, go convince Mador de la Porte the fruit had simply gone bad and no one was to blame. I'm going to see if the corpse bleeds at my approach."

Knights who were not even conceived when we fought the rebel kings at Bedegraine and Terrabil have won their shares of glory and sired a new brood of men, and in all those years of my seneschalling, no one has doubled over because of rotten meat or badly-stored food served at Arthur's table. A rotten apple that a man could eat half down without noticing anything wrong until it suddenly burst his guts within a few moments? But first Dame Lore and now Pinel of Carbonek suddenly saw fit to insinuate that the fault was in the storing of the apples. God's Wounds, if they were going to accuse me now, it might at least be of deadly malice, not of incompetence!

Once out of the death chamber, I found Gouvernail and told him to see to having the dog's body burned and the rest of the room cleared and cleaned. New rushes for the floor, and burn the old rushes and all the left-over food along with the bitch.

"The common folk will think it a great waste," said Gouvernail. "Especially in this thin season of the year."

"Give them the scraps, and then when they find out about Sir Patrise, if they don't know it already, the first urchin who gets stomach cramps from wolfing down his food too fast is going to cry poison. No. Burn it all, and scour the dishes with sand."

He nodded and went about his work. Knowing my cooks and scullions, I doubted the remains of our dinner would go to waste. Nothing but the fruit had been poisoned. That everyone except Patrise was still alive proved that. Everything else would probably find its way, gingerly at first but with increasing greed, into some greasy paunches in the kitchen when my back was turned. It did not matter, so long as there was no danger of further scandal because of a few coincidental pains in some commoner's belly. The food would be reported burned, and Artus would be praised for taking care to safeguard his people from all possible danger.

I decided to put off my visit to the chapel a while longer. It seemed more important to beg a private audience with the Queen.

She was closeted alone with Arthur, but I insisted that Dame Elyzabel let me through the antechamber to pound on the door. It has its uses, being the King's foster-brother.

Maybe they were just as glad of a third person. The remains of a quarrel lay heavy in the air. Arthur was poking up the logs in the fireplace. I went and knelt before the Queen's chair.

Her voice was low. "You do not believe me guilty, also, Sir Kay?"

"Madame, I hold you the world's Queen of virtue."

She leaned forward, still twisting a sodden cloth in her left hand, and put her right hand on my shoulder. Command me, madame, I thought. Give me the word, and I'll cleave Mador's lying tongue into his breastbone, skull, helmet, and all. Let me save you again as I saved you on Humber bank, before any of us had heard of your French cock-a-dandy.

"Kay," she said, "find me Sir Lancelot."

"Madame," I said, "the fruit may have been tainted somehow in storage. A viper . . ."

"Find us that viper, then!" said the King.

I nodded, kissed the Queen's hand, and turned to go. Artus joined me at the door. "What ails her, Kay, that she can never keep Lancelot at her side?"

"What ails the rest of us?" I said. "You know him, Artus. Fickle as quicksilver. When has our Lancelot ever chosen to stay at court waiting to be needed when he could sneak away and seek a little more glory on his own? What makes you think it was the Queen's fault he left us this time?"

"Not even his kinsmen know where he is. She's already asked them."

"That's nothing new. Most of the time Lancelot himself doesn't know where he is."

"Kex," said Arthur, "Mador will not believe it was tainted by mishap unless he sees an apple drawn from the earth with a viper still clinging to it by the fangs."

"You have other knights besides Lancelot."

"And most of those who could have hoped to defeat Mador de la Porte were with you at the Queen's dinner." He shook his head and sighed. "If we still had Merlin among us . . ."

More than thirty years and Artus still had not figured out that we were probably better off without the old troublemaker. "Merlin would have given us riddles, not answers. The old gaffer cared more about appearing mystical and mysterious than about deigning to state things clearly." He had also made a few of his cleverly obscure prophecies that could be interpreted as slandering the Queen; and, since for all his supposed foresight he used to have a habit of turning up a day or so too late to save a person's life, I was not sure he would have bestirred his white beard to save Her Grace anyway. "Have you sent out pursuivants to look for Lancelot?" I asked.

Artus shook his head. "See to it, Kex. . . . But Mador thinks his cause is right. He will fight like a mad lion."

"Stall the combat as long as you can. Give her every extra day possible."

"I will do everything in my power. All that the law allows."

"You've twisted the law before. For the love of Jesu, Artus, you won't find another queen like Dame Guenevere. That witch of a look-alike is dead."

I left him and reached the antechamber. Dame Elyzabel was preparing a heavily spiced posset for the Queen. I guessed, by the way she glanced up at me, that she had overheard at least part of what we said. Probably she had also overheard a good deal of the earlier argument between Arthur and Dame Guenevere. "Don't worry," I told Elyzabel. "We'll find that fool Lancelot." I left without waiting for her reply, if she intended to make one.

Another search for Lancelot. Probably more questing-hours have been squandered by knights riding throughout Logris, Cornwall, the North, and the petty kingdoms of Wales looking for Lancelot, and likely as not getting lost themselves in the search, than for any other single cause, not excluding the Holy Grail. But it seemed that, since Lancelot's arrival in this land, no one else must ever be permitted to fight for the Queen. And, curse his hangers, if the Queen's safety was to be ensured, he was the best fighter to ensure it.

I found Gouvernail again and we chose a score of pursuivants to ride out at once and begin combing the country for the Flower of Knighthood, and twoscore more to start in the morning. Marshalling the knights as searchers would have to wait until after Sir Patrise's burial.

I did not intend to stop with scattering pursuivants and knights around like ants looking for the hero of the world. Merlin was gone, but the enchantress who had taken him off our hands, who probably had all his skills and maybe a few of her own besides, and used them with considerably more restraint and less officiousness, was still among the living. Dame Nimue had always been friendly to us; and, since no one knew where Lancelot was anyway, I could just as easily search for him on the way to her Lake as anywhere else.

I returned to the death chamber. The tables were cleared away and the floor was already bare of rushes and swept clean. The fire was blazing up again, higher than before, with young Clarance watching it. "We scraped the dish out of the ashes and sent it to the silversmith, Sir," he reported, "with orders to melt it down completely and rework it. Master Gouvernail said best build up the fire here again and make sure all the fruit was well burned."

"That blaze should do the work. You don't have to put on any more wood when that burns down. Do you happen to know which cellars the fruit came from?"

He shook his head. "No, Sir. Old Rozennik and someone else dug it up and carried it to the Queen. Her

Grace wished to choose and arrange it herself, Sir. And Doran—" (that was Coupnez's real name) "—carried the bowl here after Her Grace had arranged it."

"As soon as your fire starts to burn down," I said, "find Coupnez and bring him to the kitchen. I'll be wanting you, too." Clarance was that rare bird, a reliable page.

I went down to the kitchen and found, as I expected, that everyone from Tychus Flaptongue and Chloda down to the mice had used the tragedy as an excuse to stop work for the more important business of gossip. Two or three scullions had little Tilda in tears, trying to use her kittens as tasters for suspicious scraps of food. Several more were clustered around old, one-eyed Rozennik, accusing her of bewitching the fruit when she dug it up. Grimpmains, who had recovered his stomach with wonderful speed, was sitting like a storyteller in a circle of rapt listeners, and Flaptongue was declaiming, in a voice that he probably hoped would reach the King himself but which in fact hardly carried above the clamor of his own kitchen, that no stew or soup of his seasoning had ever so much as given anyone wind-pains. What other mischief was going on I did not have the chance to see, since most of the noise and confusion stilled at my entrance.

I rescued Tilda's kittens, ordered sound thrashings for her tormentors and those of old Rozennik, and told the entire kitchen staff that if the court went supperless that evening, so would they.

"Nay, then, Sir," said Chloda, who interprets the fact that she became chief cook a few days before I was made seneschal as grounds for questioning my judgment from time to time, "I doubt they'll be in overmuch appetite for supper tonight, nor for livery neither."

"Whether anyone has appetite for it or not, I want

supper on the tables at the usual time, or you'll go hungry tomorrow as well, if I have to brank every one of you myself. Now, what cellar did the fruit come from?"

Chloda folded her arms across her scrawny chest. "Nay, then, how would I know? I told Flaptongue to fetch it, or send folk to do it for him."

"Flaptongue," I said; and Tychus Flaptongue, who has been with us almost as long as Chloda and would probably be jealous if he were less afraid of responsibility, replied that he had sent Rozennik and helpers of her choosing to whatever cellar she liked.

The fruit pits were nearly emptied by this time of year, and it turned out that Rozennik and her helpers, Nat Torntunic and Wilkin, had visited several in order to find what the old woman considered a suitable bagful for Her Grace to choose from. Fortunately, they thought they would at least remember which cellars, if not which exact pits, they had visited. Leaving instructions for Clarance to follow us with Coupnez, we started for the storage cellars.

In the end, we visited all of them, since we found traces of digging in more pits than Rozennik and her scullions remembered. Wherever any ground seemed to have been recently turned, we dug in search of adders or their traces. We found none, but I took an apple or pear from each place we dug, except two pits that seemed completely emptied.

Clarance, pulling Coupnez along, did not find us until we were more than halfway finished with the task. The delay had been occasioned by Clarance's trouble in locating the younger page. Although it was not the usual kind of work for noble-born pages, I set Clarance to digging with the scullions in my place and watching for adder-traces, while I questioned Coupnez.

It was hard work—he seemed to think I was accusing

him of poisoning the fruit, and I had to cuff him a couple of times and threaten him with being locked up alone overnight before I could get anything more than tearful and half-incoherent protests of innocence and pleas not to make him eat any fruit. What I finally learned, if it could be called learning, was that Coupnez had answered the Queen's bell in her own antechamber, taken the bowl of apples and pears ready-arranged from her, and brought it at once to the small banquet chamber, where he had left it on a sideboard; and the chamber had already been full of servants setting things up.

Knowing Coupnez, I doubted he had gone straight from the Queen's apartment to the banqueting chamber without stopping once or twice on the way to gawk at something or put his burden down and run or doze for a few moments. That, however, was his tale, and for once he kept to it. I suspected he was more afraid, this time, of being thought to have had anything to do with a knight's death than of being punished for lying; but you can hardly rack a nobly-born infant, or even threaten him with more than a light whip, so in the end I had to accept his story and let him go without learning where or when he had loitered during his errand.

Having spent the afternoon in an unsuccessful quest for poisonous serpents, I left orders that all rats and mice should be left in their traps and brought to me alive early in the morning, instead of being killed at once. I locked the bag of fruit in my room and then, having already laid myself open to criticism from courtly tongues that would call it the first duty of a true knight to offer his last respects to a comrade's corpse, I went to sup before visiting Sir Patrise in the chapel.

Chapter 6
Of the Blood Feuds of the Sons of Lot

> *"Wit thou well, sir knight, said they, we fear not to tell thee our names, for my name is Sir Agravaine, and my name is Gaheris, brethren unto the good knight Sir Gawaine, and we be nephews unto King Arthur. Well, said Sir Tristram, for King Arthur's sake I shall let you pass as at this time. But it is shame, said Sir Tristram, that Sir Gawaine and ye be come of so great a blood that ye four brethren are so named as ye be, for ye be called the greatest destroyers and murderers of good knights that be now in this realm; for it is but as I heard say that Sir Gawaine and ye slew among you a better knight than ever ye were, that was the noble knight Sir Lamorak de Galis."* (Malory X, 55)

Mordred met me on the way to chapel. "We are gathering together after the burial," he said, cleaning his fingernails with the tip of his knife as we walked. "All those of us who, having been guests of the Queen, share in some degree the suspicion that has fallen on her fair, silvering head."

"I've told you before, keep your evil-meaning tongue off Her Grace."

"Ah, yes. I sometimes forget. We all love Guenevere, but some of us more than others, eh? Mador de la Porte is to be excluded from our meeting, of course."

"Whose inspiration was this meeting?"

"Brother Gawaine's, naturally. Since all of us are prevented from defending the Queen, both because we are all under suspicion with her and because a few evil-minded ones among us suspect her ourselves, Gawaine has had the incredibly novel idea that we should vow ourselves to another quest for our missing Lancelot. Who, sharing no kind of sympathy at all with Her Grace, could not possibly fall under suspicion of sharing any sort of plot whatsoever with her."

Gawaine's idea. As usual, one or other of the great ones had taken the credit before me. "At least this won't be the usual year-and-a-day quest, not counting the time spent coming back," I said.

"I see no reason why it shouldn't. A year and a day have never sufficed before to locate the noble Du Lac. Of course, if he is not found and brought back within . . . I reckon it at fifty-five days at the most that our king may claim custom and postponement . . . even Lancelot will be able to do little except clear the name of a small heap of ashes."

"God damn you to Hell, Mordred!"

"Very likely." It was his standard response whenever I, or anyone else, damned him. "Indeed, I have had it on the authority of a saint that my damnation is a fact already recorded wherever they record such matters. So you see, when I speak of Her Grace as a small heap of ashes, I have good reason to sympathize with that same small heap of ashes." He turned his head to look at me, and for a moment his voice sounded sincere beneath the glaze of witticism. "I would prefer that the Queen not burn. Therefore I will join the new quest with a ready heart. But suppose whoever finds Lancelot is the true poisoner? Will he tell the great hero of the Queen's danger, or will he find means to ensure that Lancelot stays away?"

"We'll go in pairs."

"And thus cover less country, which we would have little enough time to cover singly. Will you join the quest this time, Seneschal?"

"Even if it means travelling with you." If we went in pairs, it would probably come to that in any case. Mordred and I could get along more companionably with each other, most of the time, than most other men could get along with either of us.

He nodded. "There is also the thought that we are misjudging our traitor. A man may wish to murder an enemy, and yet have no objection if another man desires to prevent an innocent dame from suffering for the deed."

"A man could also confess and save a great Queen from taking his blame."

"Ah, but poison is the coward's weapon. Or the witch's, of course. Returning to Aunt Morgan le Fay, have you thought that she may have another secret lover among us?"

"Weren't you the one who reminded us that she's been presumed dead for years?"

He shrugged. "I sometimes wonder if the line between life and death applies quite so strictly to folk like Morgan and Merlin as to the rest of us poor mortals. Who knows? Perhaps, from there beyond the grave, she took a fancy to our handsome young Sir Patrise and summoned him to her. But you haven't been to see him laid out yet, I think?"

"I've had other things to do." Though they had not accomplished much.

"I imagine many of us will watch with the corpse most of the night," said Mordred. "Those of us, especially, who might have an uneasy conscience about his death . . . or might fear being thought to have an uneasy conscience."

I had planned to wake with the body only long enough for decency's sake, but Mordred had a point. By tomorrow or the next day we would have scattered, so this would be one of my last chances to see them all, try to read their souls in their faces. Therefore I spent most of the night in the chapel, in a prie-dieu near the side, watching to see which of the twenty-two passed the longest time with Sir Patrise, and trying to determine who did it for love, who for piety, and who for an uneasy conscience.

Mador, of course, waked the whole night with his cousin's body. So did Bors de Ganis, kneeling almost as close to the corpse as Mador, but more silently. The court would have expected nothing less from the only knight to achieve the Grail and return alive.

Gawaine was there all night, too, or most of it, with Gareth near him. Lancelot's absence and Gawaine's near-escape from death by poison seemed to have brought Beaumains closer to his eldest brother, at least temporarily, than he had been for years. The middle brothers, Agravaine and Gaheris, stayed only long enough to save appearances.

Persant of Inde spent quite a while, but it looked to me as if the old knight had dozed off on his knees, a good trick for a future hermit to learn. Gouvernail did not come until after midnight, probably having sensibly taken some sleep after seeing the remains of the dinner cleared up. When he came, he stayed near the back and I was not sure when he slipped out again—I probably dozed off myself for a few moments. The others seemed to have worked out some arrangement, two at a time for about an hour, then another pair to relieve them, almost as smoothly as monks in choir.

If they had in fact planned their order for watching, they had left me out of the conference. Also, most likely, Mordred. Maybe Pinel, too—he knelt through at least two changes of the watch. But Pinel, coming from Carbonek, was acceptable company to Bors, when he kept quiet (though even Bors seemed to find Pinel's theological theories tedious and unsatisfying).

All in all, I did not make an enlightening study of it. The candlelight and the angles made it next to impossible to read much in any man's face and sometimes the Queen's dinner guests were hidden among other knights, clerks, priests, and dames.

If Patrise had had a paramour, she kept herself well hidden to the last. He had sometimes carried the favor of Dame Lynette, Gaheris' wife; but she was as free with her scarves and sleeves as she was strict with her body. If Dame Lynette's honor had finally cracked . . . but Gaheris would not have attacked his wife's lover with poisoned fruit that his own brother was likely to eat. Besides, King Lot's sons were in the habit of avenging their family's wrongs with lance and sword, and Gaheris was easily better than Patrise in the field.

It still being simplest to assume that mischance had led Patrise to take poison intended for Gawaine, I tried to tally up the various blood feuds Gawaine had been involved in over the years.

The longest and ugliest was that between the sons of Lot and the family of King Pellinore. Pellinore had slain Lot in the battle of Castle Terrabil, when Lot was leading the second rebellion against Arthur. Despite the loss of her newly-born Mordred—for a few years only, as it turned out—Queen Morgawse and her older sons had remained loyal to Arthur and took his part against that of their husband and father; but they could not forgive his death when they had wanted his defeat, pardon, and logical place among Arthur's knights along with King Uriens and other former rebels.

Some of the witnesses claimed that Pellinore could as easily have taken Lot prisoner as killed him. A few even said they thought Lot was about to surrender, or had already surrendered; it was unlikely, considering Lot's character—still, he had enough grievous wounds besides his cloven head, and finishing an enemy without taking time to hear his surrender would have been in keeping with Pellinore's dogged singlemindedness. For all that, Lot's death in battle probably should not have started the feud it did. We interred Lot and the other rebel kings with all honors and rich tombs, maybe a little too much —Arthur could hardly have buried his own foster-father with more dignity—and Pellinore, Lot's killer, was the first to propose Gawaine, Lot's oldest son, for a seat at the Round Table. But Honor must be a shrew of a mistress. Lot's sons waited for years, but at last Gawaine fought it out with Pellinore one day, with nobody else around but Gaheris and the squires. Gawaine saw to it that Pellinore got as fine a burial as Lot, and paid for part of the tomb and a century of Masses. If a rich tomb comforted Lot, it should comfort Pellinore, too.

Pellinore's sons Aglovale and Dorner, and the bastard half-brother Tor, were ready to claim treason and challenge Gawaine and Gaheris; but Lamorak, the best warrior of the group and the only one who could have defeated Gawaine in single combat, acted like a man of sense, or at least it seemed that way at the time, and pretended that he wished to end the feud. Lamorak claimed it had been Sir Balin, not Pellinore, who killed King Lot. Agravaine and Gaheris tried to give him the lie. There had been too many witnesses who testified after Terrabil that Pellinore struck the blow. But in the confusion of battle, and with Lot, Balin, and now Pellinore all three dead and most of the witnesses either dead, scattered, or no longer quite so confident of what they had glimpsed and overheard in the press, who was to say for sure any more? Queen Morgawse at least, poor lady, believed Lamorak. So did Gareth Beaumains. Gawaine did not believe him, but accepted his claim as an honest opinion and agreed to bury the past. As for Pellinore's last known son, Percivale the Pure, he showed himself more interested in baiting me and otherwise maintaining his high virtue than in the rights and wrongs of mundane family matters, and pardoned the sons of Lot out of hand.

Then Lamorak became the Queen's lover, and one dark night in her chamber he struck off her head. Maybe he had planned it all along, or maybe they had some kind of lovers' quarrel. Possibly Morgawse had learned something else about her husband's death, or Lamorak something else about his father's. Maybe it was some foolish jest that turned into a grisly accident. Whatever happened, Lamorak did not return to court at once to report it, but disappeared in the other direction, leaving his confused dwarf to discover the mayhem and gallop back to Camelot.

Gawaine and his brothers, except Gareth, set out in pursuit, but saw nothing of Lamorak until he surfaced again at a tournament in Surluse, in borrowed armor and shield, trying to fight anonymously and bearing away the prize as calmly as if he had not left his paramour headless in her bed. Lot's sons were able to corner Lamorak alone somewhere in the woods after the tournament.

There was talk afterwards that all four brothers must have fallen on Lamorak at once, that he could have defeated Agravaine, Gaheris, and Mordred together, or Gawaine alone, even when Gawaine was in his full midday strength and filled with rage for the death of his mother. No one else was present except two squires Lamorak had picked up at Surluse, full of fresh hero-worship for the hero of the tournament, not well acquainted with what the battle was about, and therefore not overly reliable witnesses. They claimed that one or more of the attackers had killed Lamorak's horse and then, after a battle of more than three hours, another one had cut Lamorak down from behind. The Surluse lads knew Gawaine's distinctive shield, gold pentangle on gules, but the shields of the other three are pretty much alike, lions and bends in various tinctures, so it remained unsure which was the backstabber, not that it much mattered. Gareth Beaumains disowned his brothers for the deed.

Beaumains and the others who say Lamorak could not have been guilty of the death of Queen Morgawse, that something else must have happened to her, have nothing to go on but Lamorak's reputation until then. And Lamorak's reputation, like Lancelot's, was built mainly on the might of his arm, the general opinion being that any man who can strike down ninety-nine out of a hundred other men in battle or tourney must therefore of necessity be a model of honor in every other respect as well. My own opinion was that if it had been Percivale, there would have been some reason to inquire more deeply into what had happened in Dame Morgawse's bedchamber; but, since it was Lamorak,

Gawaine and his brothers could hardly be blamed for interpreting the matter as they did.

Lancelot, though claiming to believe Lamorak innocent, accepted the reasonableness of Gawaine's situation and stepped in to help Arthur enforce a kind of truce between Lot's sons and Pellinore's remaining kindred. Knights with no other interest in the affair than professed concern for honor and justice had a good enough excuse to refrain from attacking Gawaine and his brothers by saying that they were sparing the King's nephews for Arthur's sake. Percivale held gently aloof from the business and at length went away to achieve the Holy Grail and die with Galahad. Gareth Beaumains held haughtily aloof. Dornar managed to get himself killed in a joust that had nothing to do with the old feud, leaving only Aglovale and Tor alive of all Pellinore's known offspring. They did not seem interested in digging up the bones of the old feud with anything but their tongues, from time to time, and neither of them had been at the Queen's dinner. Tor was not even at court, having wintered in his own castle.

Of course, the fruit could have been poisoned by someone else besides those at the dinner, and Pellinore had left nephews and nieces, and maybe a few more bastard sons and daughters not yet identified. Brandiles, Gawaine's wife's brother, was one of Pellinore's nephews, being the son of Pellinore's brother Alain of Escavalon, and Brandiles had been at the fatal dinner.

Nevertheless, the feud between Lot's family and Pellinore's had not led to any new known bloodshed since Lamorak's death. King Bagdemagus' death at Gawaine's hands during the Grail Quest was comparatively fresh. It had not led to any outward demands for justice. All of Bagdemagus' surviving daughters, nephews, and cousins claimed, like

Astamore, to accept it as a simple misfortune of friendly combat. But the honesty of a killing does not always keep kinsfolk from seeking justice or revenge, whichever you call it. Indeed, the more fair-minded we become about refusing to put a man through process of law for killing another in honest accident, the more we seem to force any revenge-seeking relative to work in secret. I liked young Astamore and did not find it pleasant to think of him as a poisoner; but the fact that a father like Bagdemagus could produce a son like Meliagrant showed there was treachery somewhere in the bloodline. Maybe it came from Bagdemagus' parents, had lain fallow in their children, as sometimes happens, and could surface again in their other grandchildren as it had in Meliagrant. Meliagrant had seemed a good young knight, too, at first.

Bagdemagus was not the only man Gawaine had had the misfortune to kill on the bloody Quest for the Grail. There was also Ywaine the Adventurous, the namesake and bastard half-brother of Ywaine of the Lion. Both Ywaines were the sons of King Uriens and cousins-german to Gawaine himself. If it had been Ywaine of the Lion, Morgan's son, that Gawaine had killed, then Le Fay might have had reason to turn her love for her nephew into hate. But Queen Morgan had no reason that anyone knew to love her husband's bastard; and both Ywaine of the Lion and old King Uriens had forgiven Gawaine, more readily than Gawaine forgave himself, for the death of Ywaine the Adventurous. So had The Adventurous forgiven his killer, too, before he died of his wounds.

In the matter of Ywaine's death, we had the testimony of Ector de Maris, Lancelot's half-brother, to second Gawaine's own account. They had been travelling together for a time. Ector de Maris had no apparent reason to gild any tale to Gawaine's advantage. Therefore, when Ector's recital was softer toward Gawaine than Gawaine's own, it was probably the truth.

Gawaine the Golden-Tongued, on the other hand, with his cultivated custom of speaking ill of nobody, might be capable of gilding a tale to the advantage of Ector de Maris or any other rival. And it was at about this point I began to suspect my own head was going unclear with wild surmise and lack of sleep. There were too many possibilities, too many possible traitors—and not enough, if you started with the premise that all of us, in theory, should be too honorable to attack a comrade with poison.

Revenge had to be the key. But revenge of whom? I kept the keys for the King, I wore my own key on my shield . . . why couldn't I find the key to Patrise's death?

Towards dawn, when I woke out of a doze in which I had been mixing up King Pellinore with his brother Pellam, the Maimed Fisher-King of Carbonek, I decided I had thought too much for the time being, and had better take a few hours of real sleep. As I straightened my stiff knees, I glimpsed a similar movement on the other side of the chapel.

Mordred had left the chapel early in the evening, shortly after his brothers Agravaine and Gaheris. He must have slipped back in when I was dozing; it had been some time after midnight that I noticed him again, deep in the shadows on the far left, across from me. Now he rose and followed me out, joining me in the corridor.

"A pleasant game, is it not?" he murmured. "Not that it can save the Queen, of course. Mador will hardly withdraw his accusation on the strength of my surmises, or even yours. Still, it's a pleasant game."

Like Lore of Carlisle in the banquet chamber, Mordred must have been doing much the same thing as myself in the chapel. Why not? He had first suggested it. "All right, King's Nephew," I said, "what pet surmises did you reach?"

"None, as yet. But you may remember my notion—idle, perhaps—that a man with an uneasy conscience might watch the longest at his victim's bier?"

I nodded. "Mador, Bors de Ganis, your brothers Gawaine and Gareth. A saint, a near-saint, the probable intended victim, and the dead man's nearest kinsman. Persant stayed maybe half the night, too. I could hardly have chosen a less suspicious assortment."

"There was one other who stayed most of the night. Yourself, Sir Seneschal."

I thought about it for a moment and decided it was hardly worth the retort I was a little too tired to put into the right words. "And you, Mordred."

"And myself, intermittently. But the Queen has given *me* no cause to use poison."

I might have seized him by the throat, but he moved away. "If we are to play the game, Sir Seneschal," he remarked, "we must begin with all the pieces. Pleasant dreams, King's Brother."

I turned my back on him and walked away without returning the wish. He would come back to the subject later. He might even, eventually, have some thoughts to speak worth the hearing. Beneath that delight in pushing his listeners to the limit, he had a keen mind. If we travelled together seeking Lancelot, we would have time enough to talk things through, assuming we could keep from killing each other on the way.

Chapter 7
The Wife of Sir Gaheris of Orkney

"And upon Michaelmas Day the Bishop of Canterbury made the wedding betwixt Sir Gareth and the Lady Lionesse with great solemnity. And King Arthur made Gaheris to wed the Damosel Savage, that was Dame Linet; and King Arthur made Sir Agravaine to wed Dame Lionesse's niece, a fair lady, her name was Dame Laurel." (Malory VII, 35)

I slept until prime and woke with the idea forming that if all else failed, I could act on one of Mordred's hints and take the blame for the poisoning on myself. It would not be a glorious way to save the Queen, but it would be a surer way than for me to fight as her champion. Mador has kept himself in fighting trim, while, thanks to the other duties that have taken too much of my time, I am no longer the man of arms who killed two kings with one lance beside the Humber. If I fought the Queen's fight against Mador and got myself killed, the only good result would be that I would no longer be there to watch her burn.

In the end, it came to nothing; but for a time the idea of confessing had its charm—the ultimate in secret chivalry, if there can be such a thing as chivalry without glory. For a moment I considered making a confession at once and sparing Her Grace the weeks of doubt and uncertainty. But a mere confession of incompetence would carry no weight without some kind of proof, while the price of an open confession of malice aforethought would probably be death, without recourse, King's foster-brother or not. I have never been suicidal, and the price of suicide is Hell.

On the other hand, if someone would accuse me, if some line of reason or evidence would point strongly enough at me to persuade Mador to drop his accusation against the Queen and charge me instead, then I could fight my own combat cheerfully, win or die. There were still enough folk who remembered Arthur's bastard Lohot, Dame Lyzianour's son, and blamed me for treachery in his death, even though, in the lack of any other witness to the deed, no one quite dared accuse me in open court, especially with the King himself inclined to accept my word. It should not take overmuch to convince some gossipers that this new treachery was also my work. They might be whispering it already.

The chief trouble with the scheme was that, although my taking the blame for Patrise's death would save the Queen this time, it would leave the real traitor at large. Unless Patrise had been the intended victim, and the danger to the Queen only incidental, there would still be someone sneaking around court waiting for a new chance to strike against Gawaine, or Her Grace, or maybe all of us in general. At best, it would leave unpunished a piece of scum who was willing to see Dame Guenevere burned for his own treachery.

We had at least fifty-five days, time enough to reach

Dame Nimue's Lake and bring her back with three fortnights to spare, possibly even time enough to find Lancelot, if we had exceptionally good luck and he was easier to find than usual. I decided to keep my confession as a last measure, with the result that the secret, noble gesture died stillborn.

Nat Torntunic brought me the rats and mice entrapped during the night—not as many as I had hoped, but they proved to be more than enough. I thought of turning the task of testing my bags of fruit over to Mordred, who would have enjoyed it; but he would probably have used cats and hounds instead of rats and mice, and I was not sure I could have trusted whatever results he told me. It occurred to me, rather late, that I should have marked exactly where each piece of fruit had come from; but, as it turned out, it would have made no difference. Not one of the mangy beasts burst its entrails and died from nibbling an apple or pear. The fruit in storage was safe. There had been no viper, no venomed earth. The stuff had been poisoned after being dug up.

I could account for it from the time old Rozennik and her scullery-lads dug it up to the time Coupnez collected it, already arranged in its bowl, in the Queen's antechamber. Gouvernail, Clarance, and others confirmed that there had been servants in the small banquet chamber from the time Coupnez brought in the fruit to the time the Queen and her guests arrived. Therefore, it must have been poisoned between the time Coupnez left the Queen's apartment and the time he arrived in the banquet chamber. The little wretch had either taken it to someone—likely for the bribe of some silly trifle—or put it down somewhere while he played or dawdled. At this point, I was angry enough to have racked the truth out of him, Earl's son or not, child or not, Arthur's and the court's outrage or not—but probably it would have done no good, since the greater chance was that Coupnez had set the bowl down and the fruit had been poisoned while he was not watching. It would hardly have been of much use to question Coupnez straitly if all he could confess was leaving his bowl of apples and pears unwatched for a few moments in a place where we should have had nothing to fear.

I could envision someone creeping up behind Coupnez's back with a long, thin, envenomed pin, or even a bag of ready-poisoned fruit to substitute for the good . . . but I could not envision the traitor's face.

During the burial I tried to watch all my fellow mourners, and thought I saw a few of them watching me, but with no better results than on the former occasions. Suspicious glances darted around like gnats at the meal afterwards, too, but if anyone else had any insights or revelations, he failed to share them with me.

A seat at the Round Table can be empty in a number of different ways: because the man who used to sit there is known dead of battle wounds or sickness and his place has not yet been refilled; because he is presumed dead but nothing can be done about filling his seat until the fact of his death is documented; because he is away on some quest or errand but was alive at last report; because he has chosen to stay away from court at his own castle or on his own adventures, like that noble bladder of half-cooked valor, Prince Tristram of Lyonesse, or like Pelleas the occasional brilliant dabbler in knightly combat; because he is in his own bedchamber or infirmary with a wound sustained in the latest jousting or simply with an ague. The Siege Perilous is empty because Heaven allows no one else except Galahad to sit there, and Galahad only used it a few days before going off again to his Grail and his holy death. That Siege Perilous has been useless lumber for most of its existence, a permanent gap with a golden chain stretched from arm to arm across its seat to prevent accidents. We used to debate whether the chair was deadly in itself or because of its position at the Table—if it were removed, and another chair put in its place, would fire still fall on whoever sat in the new chair at Lancelot's right hand, or would it fall on anyone who sat in the old Siege Perilous wherever that was placed, or would it fall on both chairs, or on neither? But although it is fine and noble to risk a few hundred men's lives at a tournament, it has never been judged worth the risk of one man's life to find out whether, by substituting another chair for the Siege Perilous, we could fill the gap and gain another Companion of the Round Table. (An animal would be worthless for the test. We used to have an old brindled cat in Carlisle that loved to jump up under the chain and nap on the Siege Perilous during our conferences. No one dared put his hand near the chair to touch her, but the dumb beasts are apparently absolved of evil intent in the sight of Heaven.)

Every knight's name appears on his chair in magical golden letters, but only if he is within a mile or two of the Table and acting as a Companion. If, for instance, a companion is alive and in the immediate area but has chosen to take another shield and fight against Arthur's side in tournament, on the grounds that it will enhance his personal fame to fight with the weaker party, then his name will not appear on his chair at the Table. Another example of old Merlin's craft, more showy than practical. If a man's name disappeared at his death, wherever he was at the time, we would not have to wait months or years before electing someone else to his place. Lancelot's name had now faded from the back of his chair, which might mean he was dead, or merely riding around incognito within three or four miles of London.

It had happened before that a seat was empty because of murder and treachery, but the treachery did not often come about by poison. Mador, curse him, was already planning the epitaph for his cousin's tomb, in which he would name Her Grace as a destroyer of good knights.

Gawaine's gathering was to take place two hours after dinner. There was one other person I wanted to see before that: Dame Lynette.

The court has more dames who pretend to sorcery than who can actually practice it. Most of those with any real skill choose to spend the greater part of their time elsewhere. Dame Lynette is the exception. She probably had more knowledge of necromancy than she laid claim to, but, like Dame Nimue, she practiced what she had for purpose rather than display.

I had enjoyed Dame Lynette's company since she first came to court to find a champion for her sister and, on being presented with a kitchen-boy (who knew then that Beaumains was anything else?) very sensibly gave Beaumains, the King, and everyone else a good tongue-lashing. She reminded me of my old nurse.

She was alone in her chamber. Probably she had been at her prayers. "My lord Sir Gaheris has already gone to join his brother," she told me. Since they kept separate chambers, the remark implied that he had been visiting her this afternoon, and that she chose to assume I had heard of it and come to find him.

"I have no use for Gaheris right now."

"Have you any use for Lancelot now? Or did you not know they are planning a new search for him?"

"They won't all make their vows and fly away from London before I join them. I'd like to know if there's any use in starting out."

Lynette whistled one of her brachets to her, took it into her lap, and began slowly stroking its hair. "If I could tell you there was no use in seeking Sir Lancelot, do you not think I would have told my husband?"

"No," I said. "I think you'd rather see him away from court knocking his brains loose on a wild-goose chase."

She smiled. "I will not say you are right. A wife should speak no ill of her lord, even though he deserves it. But I do not advise you to linger with me. Tongues clack, and Sir Gaheris can be jealous even of what he does not prize."

"My tongue can clack as loudly as anyone else's. But call in your pages or your gentlewomen."

"Do you think my lord Gaheris would believe anyone who is devoted to me?" She shook her head. "If you insist on staying long enough for gossip to link us, I would rather it be a private chat."

With more than half of our court dames, that would have been an invitation to bed. With Lynette, it was an invitation to a game of wits. Her nails were long and sharp, her fingers heavy with studded rings that she deftly kept from tangling in the dog's coat, and the small meat-knife at her belt was not strapped into its sheath between meals. Some tongues had even clacked to the effect that her marital troubles with Gaheris were more her fault than his.

"Gaheris aside," I said, "*is* there any chance of finding Lancelot in time to save the Queen?"

"Now Heaven be praised, I have lived long enough to see a wonder. Kay wishes to find Lancelot! Why not champion her yourself, now you have the chance at last?"

"Maybe I will. Let the mightier-than-thou take second place for once."

"Then do not come forward until the last moment, preferably not until the torch is at the faggots. Nothing will bring Lancelot back sooner than news that someone else is to fight for Dame Guenevere." Lynette smirked as if she had hinted at some profound secret.

"If someone else doesn't play Meliagrant's trick and ambush him on the way."

"Meliagrant's prison did not keep him from appearing in time to absolve the Queen of the charge of sleeping with you."

"Meliagrant's mistake," I said, "was leaving Lancelot alive in his prison."

"Have a care, Seneschal. You will involve yourself in the death of Lancelot as well as in that of Patrise."

"Is he dead, then?"

"My opinion would not make him less alive or less dead."

"I'm not asking your opinion, Dame," I said. "I'm asking for a little of your magic."

She rolled the dog over in her lap and began to rub his belly. "Magic is an idle toy. I have put it away with the other toys of my childhood."

"Your old man-at-arms can be grateful you didn't put it away any earlier."

She had sent one of her men, years ago, to attack Gareth when he tried to bed her sister a fortnight or two before they were officially wedded. When Gareth cut his attacker into pieces, Lynette gathered up the pieces, put them back together like a broken crock, and mortared them with a magic salve of hers which restored the man to life.

"What a fool I was in those days," she said, "to think I could keep other folks' morals pure with a few scraps of murder and magic. And the jest of it is that it was Gareth, the purest of the brothers, whom I meant to keep clean. I knew more of death than of life in my youth, did I not?"

"At least you knew your own mind. I suppose you had only so much of that salve of yours to waste?"

"I could have made more. It requires many days and much privacy, but where men devise means of killing, women can perhaps find worse ways to waste their time than in devising means of restoring life."

"Especially if they've been the ones to send men into the fight. Why don't you make more of the stuff, Damosel Savage?"

"If I did," said Dame Lynette, "I might someday have to use it on my lord Gaheris." After giving me a long look, she returned her attention to her brachet, this time fondling his ears. "Did you come to beg my magic salve against the . . . accidents . . . you are likely to meet with? Or did you come to learn where to find Lancelot?"

"I'm not going to meet any accidents, and if I strike a man down, it won't be so that I can help him up again."

"So you think you will find a man you can strike down? Will he be knight or churl?"

"Is that a prophecy?" I said.

She shook her head. "It is mere mortal prediction. I doubt that anyone can gaze into the future. Mage Merlin pretended to, but his prophecies can be interpreted however you will. Nor can I see into the past, except with my own memory. Perhaps Dame Nimue can pick other folks' memories, but I cannot. I can sometimes see what is happening elsewhere at the moment it happens, but most of it is tedious and the rest may be better not to know."

"So, by your reasoning, if Lancelot is dead, it would be better not to know it and squander our time looking for him?" I got up and started for the door. "Forgive me for asking you to interrupt the exciting routine of your monotony with a few moments of tedious magic, Dame."

"Seneschal." She spoke quietly and sarcastically, like my old nurse. I turned back. She went on, "If I were to look for Lancelot in a candle flame or a bowl of still water, as you seem to be asking of me, it would take me many years and much luck to find him and the image would be wavering at best; my magic is not as strong as perhaps you think. Even if I could tell you where he was to be found, he might no longer be there when you arrived. But I will make you a human prediction. Do not waste your time in searching for the hero. Lancelot will come in time to fight Sir Mador."

"Something you know?" I said. "Or something you feel?"

"Lancelot could not bear to let anyone else fight for the Queen, not even his own favorite cousin. And Sir Bors de Ganis has agreed to serve as her champion."

Chapter 8

Of the Start of a Short Search to Locate Lancelot

"My lord, said Sir Bors, ye require me the greatest thing that any man may require me; and wit ye well if I grant to do battle for the queen I shall wrath many of my fellowship of the Table Round. But as for that, said Bors, I will grant my lord that for my lord Sir Launcelot's sake, and for your sake I will at that day be the queen's champion unless there come by adventure a better knight than I am to do battle for her." (Malory XVIII, 5)

"When did this happen?" I said.

"Last night, as I understand it from Dame Elyzabel. The Queen sent for Sir Bors to her chamber."

It must have been after I had left. "Bors was one of her dinner guests, too, damn him!"

"The King was there with them. I gather they both implored Sir Bors, but he was a long time consenting."

Somehow I kept from smashing my fist against the

wall. "Why Bors? Why not me?"

"I assume because Bors de Ganis may possibly be able to defeat Mador de la Porte. Besides, of all you who shared his last meal with Sir Patrise, who can ride above suspicion better than the saint who achieved the Holy Grail?"

The saint who achieved the Grail. Anyone who did not happen to know that story might have mistaken the noble Bors de Ganis for a pander between his glorious cousin and the Queen. "With fifty days to get back into battle trim, I could beat them both together," I said.

"Sir Bors has agreed on condition that no champion 'better than he' appears," Lynette went on. "Shall I ride with you and taunt you back into fighting trim? But you will not have fifty days now. You will have only a fortnight."

"Curse his bloody soul," I said, and left before I destroyed something. What had possessed Artus and Dame Guenevere to go down on their knees to Bors de Ganis? Now? Hadn't I promised we would find their hero Lancelot for them? Why cut the time out from under us like this?

And who was the smug, self-righteous De Ganis to put himself above the rest of us who had been at the Queen's dinner, as if the stink of suspicion that tainted everyone else could not touch him? Saints have fallen into corruption before—Judas began as a holy apostle.

I went on to swear myself to the search for Lancelot—for all the good that would be to us now. Bors had done the Queen no favor. As long as she had no champion, Arthur could grant her the extra forty days to find one. Now that she had Bors pledged to her cause, "unless a better champion appeared," her trial must take place on the earliest day appointed, giving us a fortnight from yesterday to find the elusive Lancelot du Lac.

Of course, Bors and Mador were pretty well matched. It was possible Bors could defeat him—unless Bors had some reason not to want to save the Queen. But Mador's defeat was not the foregone conclusion it would have been with Lancelot; and Mador would have the more battle frenzy to strengthen his arm.

At least I could see who joined Gawaine's search effort and who stayed away. The only excuse a man could have for not joining us was if he believed the Queen guilty, and any fool who could believe that must know himself to be innocent. Therefore, the real traitor would have to be someone who joined the search for Lancelot, either to try to keep the Queen from burning without incriminating himself or else to cover his own escape from court.

Unless Her Grace had been the true target all along, and the murderer wanted to see her burn. Or unless the murderer thought as subtly as I was thinking.

Mordred's "pleasant game." Chances were that we could not save Dame Guenevere this way, but it was better than doing nothing.

As a touchstone, however, the inspiration of counting shields came to very little. Besides Mador de la Porte, and Bors de Ganis, who had already cast suspicion on himself by agreeing to fight Mador, Lancelot's own kinsmen stayed away in a body: Ector de Maris, Lionel, Blamore and Bleoberis de Ganis, as well as Lancelot's old duckling Sir La Cote Male Taile, and Prince Galihodin of Surluse with his brother Galihud. I doubted that they, of all knights, were so convinced of the Queen's guilt as not to seize on this new excuse to locate their glorious and beloved chief of the clan; more likely they were hatching a rival search effort of their own. On this assumption, I was almost surprised that for once Gareth Beaumains had chosen to join his own family instead of Lancelot's, and that we had also gotten the Saracen brothers, Palomides and Safere. Maybe Lancelot's faction was not quite so attractive to them without Lancelot's person at the head of it.

It was also possible that Lancelot's kinsmen knew some secret the rest of us did not about the hero's disappearance after his latest rumored quarrel with Her Grace.

The old Breton fox Sir Aliduk was also absent from Gawaine's assembly, but he was still enough of a stranger among us that, whatever his private thoughts, it was hardly surprising if he remained completely neutral in the business.

But if Gawaine had attracted only half of the Queen's guests, he had also gained a good pick of those who had dined with the King instead of the Queen: his cousin Ywaine of the Lion, Griflet, Bedivere, Lucan the Butler —most of the best of the old guard, who remembered the days before Lancelot crossed the Channel. Also Sagramore le Desirous, Sir King Berant le Apres, Constantine Cadorson . . . and I later learned that old King Uriens and Yon the Wise might have taken our oath too, if Arthur had not requested them to sit with him as judges when the day came. (Yon was good on legal niceties.) We also had a few score non-Companions among us, some of them better knights than some of those who did sit at the Round Table. Not everyone had swallowed Mador's notion that the good Queen could suddenly turn into "a destroyer of good knights."

Gouvernail was there as well, waiting on the fringes, ready to pledge himself in spirit if not in word. I pulled him aside. Someone had to watch over my court duties for me.

He protested. "Is it not more important to save Her Grace?"

"Don't worry. Bors de Ganis is seeing to that. He'd damn well better, after shortening her time from two months to a fortnight."

"The gentlewomen also are pledging themselves to the search," the old squire went on. "I had planned to accompany Dames Bragwaine and Senehauz."

Gouvernail and Bragwaine were a favorite target for the Queen and everyone else who dabbled in matchmaking; but if they had let all this time go by since the deaths of their old master and mistress, the present fortnight was not going to make or destroy their own decision about formalizing whatever relationship they might have. "Gouvernail," I said, "I need someone here I can trust. Someone who can see to the ordinary work and meanwhile keep an eye on any of our possible traitors who stay at court."

He hesitated a moment, then nodded slowly. I put my hand on his shoulder. "I've handed you two jobs. If you scent out the traitor here, get Dinas of Cornwall to take over the seneschalling for a while." Dinas of Cornwall would have been as likely to take the oath with Gawaine as with Ector de Maris and Lionel; so, not seeing Dinas here, I assumed he was keeping his hands clean of the whole affair. I had little use for a knight who would not bestir himself to help his lady the Queen; but Dinas used to be a seneschal himself, for King Mark, and not a bad one.

And maybe, having already heard of Bors' agreement to act as the Queen's champion, Dinas of Cornwall had sensibly decided that trying to find Lancelot this time was too futile to be worth the effort. I would have stayed at court myself, rather than risk not being back by the day of the trial, if my chief motive had been to find Lancelot and not to summon Dame Nimue from her Lake.

It seemed that Bors' decision had not yet been generally known. When Gawaine announced it, as if feeling himself honor-bound to ask for no oath from men who knew less than he did himself, the search lost about a third of the searchers. Even Constantine Cadorson shook his head. "Fourteen nights are not enough. Have messengers and pursuivants been sent out?"

"Last night," I said, "and more this morning. Threescore in all."

"I will send out more, chosen from among the best of my own men," said Cadorson. "And I will ride out myself, for seven days, but I will do so without taking the oath."

"I'll take the oath," said Ywaine. "Futile it may be, but I would rather be bound to the quest than remain here to see such a great lady burn."

"If Sir Bors had not come forward, cousin," said Gawaine, choking a little on the words, "I would have asked you to remain and fight the Queen's battle. I can think of no better man."

"Maybe he should anyway, to spite Bors," I said. "Sir Sangreal promised to step down if a better champion appeared, as I understand it." If I could not fight for Her Grace myself, I would have preferred that one of Gawaine's kin did it than one of Lancelot's.

"Once I would have called myself the better knight of us two," said Ywaine. "But Sir Bors achieved the Holy Grail, and I did not."

"So, at least, Sir Bors informs us," remarked Mordred, who sat whittling one of his ugly serpent rings. "But Bors may have other reasons to know the Queen innocent." Finishing his newest ring, he slipped it on his finger, sheathed his knife, and stood. "Come, brother, if we are to swear this oath, let us swear in God's Name and go to supper."

We swore, agreed to travel in pairs, and went to supper. No one openly brought up the reason for travelling in pairs—so that those of us who were most likely to come under suspicion could watchdog one another. Half a score of the younger knights left that same evening. It was a foolish, half-witted idea, starting out after the time of day when a man adventuring usually begins to look for his night's shelter. They would either get hardly far enough from London to make much difference and then have to settle, likely as not, for bad cheer and a poor night's rest; or travel all night in the dark and sleep for pure exhaustion in the daylight when they could have made better speed. They were idiots, and I envied them. I was ready to have started at once with them.

"Then you must find another travelling companion," said Mordred. "I have work to do here. And I doubt you will find another man fool enough not only to leave here tonight, but to spend his quest in your company, Sir Seneschal."

"I could find another companion more easily than you, Mordred," I said.

"Now, perhaps. Once, of course, I had Lancelot himself as my mentor and companion."

That had been during Mordred's first two years of knighthood, before something happened to twist his soul out of shape about the time of the Peningues tournament. In fact, he had been travelling with Lancelot when they came to that tournament. From Mordred's tone now, I wondered, as I had sometimes wondered before, if the great Hero had played some part in whatever happened to warp King Lot's youngest son.

But Mordred was right in that we could get a more profitable start in the morning, after a decent night's sleep. I found Dame Bragwaine and bought one of her Irish herb concoctions to help me get that night's sleep.

I awoke late—half of the sun was already showing above the horizon—cursed my squire Gillimer for not calling me at first cockcrow, and went to Mass with a headache and a black temper. I did not see Mordred until I was almost ready to leave without him. He found me just in time, waiting in the courtyard with Gillimer, our palfreys, and my charger Feuillemorte. Mordred was still in his tunic and light stockings.

"If you're not armed, mounted, and ready to ride in a quarter of an hour, squire and all," I said, "you can go to the Devil."

"In my own good time, Seneschal. Meanwhile, calm yourself. I've had certain matters to see to before we could leave."

"What 'certain matters'?"

"Matters of some relevance to our game, Sir Kay. I'll tell you of them as we ride. In the meantime, the doubt will give you something to occupy your mind while I ready myself for the road."

Chapter 9
Of Kay's Suspects, of Mordred's and of the May Babies

"Then the king dreamed a marvellous dream whereof he was sore adread . . . Thus was the dream of Arthur: Him thought there was come into this land griffins and serpents, and him thought they burnt and slew all the people in the land, and then him thought he fought with them, and they did him passing great harm, and wounded him full sore, but at the last he slew them. . . .

"Then King Arthur let send for all the children born on May-day, begotten of lords and born of ladies; for Merlin told King Arthur that he that should destroy him should be born on May-day, wherefore he sent for them all, upon pain of death; and so there were found many lords' sons, and all were sent unto the king, and so was Mordred sent by King Lot's wife, and all were put in a ship to the sea, and some were four weeks old, and some less. And so by fortune the ship drave

> *unto a castle, and was all to-riven, and destroyed the most part, save that Mordred was cast up, and a good man found him . . .*" (Malory I, 19; I, 27)

I waited until full midmorning to ask Mordred what were these important matters he had had to see to before we left. He outwaited me, smirking as we rode.

We rode unhelmed, on palfreys, with the squires behind us leading our warhorses. This was not the kind of errand on which a man had time to waste looking for pleasure jousts. We rode for the most part in silence; occasionally, Mordred whistled. Sometimes our squires talked and a snatch or two of their conversation reached us. Once Lovel, Gawaine's youngest son, who was serving as Mordred's squire, found something to laugh at. Maybe something Gillimer said. Gillimer fancies himself a wise wag.

Mordred glanced around at me. "You hear, Seneschal? His father, likely, a poisoner's target and his Queen in danger of the stake, yet Lovel can still see humor in the world."

"All right, Mordred," I said, "what were these certain matters you had to see to before we left? Or did you make them up to excuse your laziness?"

"Accuse your kitchen whelps of laziness, Sir Seneschal. I am not lazy. Merely patient."

"That's another name for it," I replied. "And my 'kitchen whelps' keep your belly full for you."

"Patience another name for laziness? Perhaps. Or for fear. A person can wait with truly astonishing patience fot the unpleasant events of life. I may also lay claim, I think, to a measure of subtlety."

Mordred came close to grinning. He had accomplished something. That much self-satisfaction does not come purely from baiting Arthur's seneschal.

"Out with it, King's Nephew," I said.

"I suppose you have a rudimentary list of them in your mind, Sir Kay—those of us most likely to have been responsible for the poisoned fruit?"

"Ironside," I said. "That smirking Bors de Ganis. Pinel the loudmouth of Carbonek. Maybe even Astamore, though I don't much like the thought."

"This is assuming the poison was meant for brother Gawaine, of course. All us brothers of Orkney share a passion for raw apples and pears, but folk remember it more clearly of Gawaine. You do not honor me on your list?"

"Since you ask me, yes. I'll also include Queen Morgan, if you like." Or Dame Lynette might have been trying to rid herself of her husband Gaheris, but I was not going to share that thought with Mordred.

"Astamore as seeking revenge for his dead uncle, Bagdemagus of Gorre," said Mordred. "Pinel as . . . seeking to avenge King Pellinore, perhaps? Ironside as seeking to fulfill that ancient oath of his at last. Bors . . . I don't entirely see why you include Bors de Ganis."

"General principles."

"Ah. For pure dislike. I *thought* you too clever to include him simply because of the common opinion that any one of us who championed the Queen would implicate himself. But your list seems to me rather short and lacking in imagination. I would add Sir La Cote Male Taile, Mador de la Porte, and the dead Sir Patrise himself."

"But you'd omit Bors de Ganis."

"On general principles. Obviously, the sainted Sir Bors knows where his cousin Lancelot is—assuming the great knight is still in this world—and intends to produce him at the eleventh hour to save Her Grace. Still, I doubt Sir Bors would go so far as to poison a man in order to bring the pair back together."

"Someday, Mordred, you're going to hint a little too much slander in my presence."

"And then you will fight me to save Lancelot's name, as Lancelot fought the unhappy Meliagrant to save yours?"

"I'll fight you for my own satisfaction, when this is over." I had said this more than once to Mordred over the years, and always meant it at the time. For now, I returned to the business of prying his thoughts out of him. "La Cote Male Taile probably still holds his brother Dinadan's death against your family. Why the others?"

"Mador mourns his cousin's death too loudly and seizes too quickly on the easiest explanation, whether it is the likeliest or not. As for Patrise, why should a man not wish to escape whatever Fate holds in store for him?"

"Patrise wasn't that good a man of arms, but what man ever damned himself for a reason like that?"

"If a man were to learn some secret of himself so evil as to make suicide and Hell seem a fair price for cheating Fate, would that man tell such a secret to the world? . . . But you're right, Sir Seneschal. We'll forget Patrise of Ireland. Being dead and buried, he cannot be more than a captured pawn in our game. What of Dame Bragwaine? She presumably knows poisons as well as other herbs."

"More to avoid them than to concoct them, and if she had anything to do with this, she's suddenly become the most accomplished liar since Delilah." I had questioned her when buying my sleeping herbs from her, and, even allowing for the difference in age and experience, the contrast between her open answers and Coupnez's bawling evasions wrote Truth all over Bragwaine's.

Mordred shrugged. "So be it. Let us forget Dame Bragwaine, even as innocent supplier of the poison. Let us also forget Bors, Mador, and La Cote Male Taile for the time, as being beyond our reach."

"Unlike the others?" I said sarcastically. "If all you did last night and this morning was make up your bloody lists to compare them with mine and then say 'Forget them,' Mordred, I may crack your brainpan right now."

"My list was made up long before the burial. Last night I arranged for its testing, in so far as possible."

"A little late for testing, with everyone scattered."

"That was my business this morning—to watch the success of my evening's work. We agreed, you remember, that the poisoner, searching alone, might not want Lancelot found?"

"If the target was the Queen," I said.

"As good a reason as any to travel in pairs. But if the traitor's chief target was Gawaine, and if he were given an opportunity to strike at Gawaine or at one of Gawaine's brothers . . . even if his chief target was one of the younger brothers and he was, by good fortune, given the opportunity to strike cleanly at the one in question—"

"By God, you've set up who's riding with whom!"

"Not entirely to my satisfaction," he replied. "I would have preferred Gawaine to ride with Sir Ironside. But who is the youngest brother to influence the eldest? From the time Ywaine joined us, there could be little doubt—"

"Stop writhing around in circles, Mordred, and just tell me how you've paired them up."

He shrugged. "Gawaine is riding with cousin Ywaine, of course; I could not help that. They are riding southwest. Agravaine is riding due south with Sir

Ironside, Gaheris northward toward Bedegraine with Astamore, Gareth northwest with Pinel of Carbonek, and I westward with you."

"Jesu!" I said. "If one of them is the traitor, you may have marked one of your own brothers for death."

"You understand the game very well, friend Kay, but do you not trust the famous sons of King Lot to defend themselves against their enemies? Ironside's vow, however, was only against Lancelot and Gawaine, and the forty unfortunate knights who happened to come his way in the meantime, of course, not against Gawaine's entire family. The most we can hope there is that brother Agravaine may goad him into extending the feud, which should not be overly difficult a task for Agravaine. As for Gareth . . ." He shrugged again. "Who would include the dearly-beloved Beaumains, everybody's favorite, in an attack on the rest of us? No, I hope for nothing from Pinel. And Gaheris is a match for young Astamore in arms, and suspicious enough not to eat or drink anything Astamore refuses to share with him. Besides, they all have their squires with them. Still, a violent attempt by one of them against one of us might clear the Queen's good name. Would you object to the death of one of Gawaine's brothers, if thereby Dame Guenevere could be saved?"

"Not if the brother who died were you. And how did you manipulate them all according to your own bloody fancy?"

"Your ears are less sharp than your tongue, Seneschal. I think I've already said that I would have preferred Ironside to ride with Gawaine, and Sir La Cote Male Taile with Agravaine. But I could hardly separate Gawaine from good cousin Ywaine, and The Ill-Fitting Coat did not join us last night, though I saw him ride eastward this morning with the good Saracen Palomides and his brother. As for the rest—a word to

Agravaine, a word to Gaheris . . . and Gareth was not unwilling to go with King Pellam's nephew and hear again of the wonders of Castle Carbonek and Lancelot's various sojourns there."

"And your brothers know why you paired them up like that?"

"Agravaine and Gaheris do," Mordred replied. "And I paired Pinel with our gentle Beaumains more for symmetry than for hope."

"I'm surprised you wasted yourself with me," I said.

"I ran out of other suspected traitors. Others, at least, whom I could manipulate to my fancy, as you put it."

"You could have sat in London and watched Mador and Bors."

Mordred snapped off a tree branch that was about to slap his face and examined the new leaves on it. "I can also go with you to find Aunt Morgan le Fay."

"If you want to find Morgan le Fay, we'll have to separate. I'm going to find Dame Nimue."

"I knew you had someone else in mind than Lancelot du Lac." He threw away the first tree branch, plucked a leafier one, and twined it into his palfrey's mane like an early sprig of May. "Yes, we have a better chance of finding the Lady of the Lake than the Queen of Gorre in the allotted time."

"If you don't really expect one of your pawns to make an attack on one of your brothers," I said, "why go to all the work of pairing them together?"

"Why play any game? An attempt on the life of another of Lot's sons within the next ten days would be enlightening, but my chief design was to keep watch on our possible traitors. We've arranged to meet at Astolat three days before the Queen's trial, you see."

"You've arranged that without hearing what I might want to do."

"I assumed you would be interested in the gathering

of murderers at Astolat, Sir Seneschal."

"I'm more interested in saving the Queen," I replied.

Mordred turned in his saddle to give me a look that was half a challenge. "They say that Merlin could cover all Britain in two days," he remarked, "and bring along an army with him if he wished."

"It's the truth. I saw it myself, at Bedegraine. One of the few useful things the old meddler ever did."

"And Dame Nimue of the Lake learned her craft from Merlin, or much of it." Mordred whistled a few versicles of the *Kyrie*. "You are right, Seneschal. Find Nimue, and she can bring us back to Astolat from her Lake within a day or two."

"You're that sure the traitor is one of them?"

He glanced at me again. "Unless it is Aunt Morgan. Or someone else. But I say the fact is not without its meaning that we agreed upon three suspected poisoners, and those three, by coincidence or Fate, the three with whom I was able to pair my brothers."

"I don't take my suspicions as Gospel," I told him. "It could have been the little damsel Senehauz for all I know, and my thinking it was Ironside or Pinel wouldn't change the fact. Nor would your thinking so, for all your subtlety."

"The fair Nimue may even have time to help us find Queen Morgan before we gather at Astolat," Mordred remarked. For a moment he seemed almost wistful. "Yes, I'd enjoy seeing my aunt again. I haven't seen her since I was a boy, you know. Not since she found me at old Sir Antor's castle after the shipwreck and helped restore me to my kith and kin."

That shipwreck had been the result of the worst piece of so-called prophecy Merlin had ever given Arthur under the name of counsel and advice.

Near the beginning of his reign, Artus had a bad

dream one night at Caerleon. Under the circumstances, it was wonderful he did not have nightmares every time he lay down to sleep. We had just quelled the first wave of rebellion, more or less, at Bedegraine, in a battle so bloody even Merlin was disgusted; and even then our victory had less to do with the truce than with the fact that a convenient Saxon attack on one of the rebel kings' cities called them away from our throats for awhile. Our allies at Bedegraine, Kings Ban and Bors, had gone home to Gaul, on the understanding that Artus was to come across the Channel and help them in their war with Claudas. Leodegrance of Cameliard was calling for Arthur's help against Ryons of Norgales, while Ryons was threatening, independently of his broil with Leodegrance, to flay off Arthur's young beard and have it sewn on his mantle beside the beards of eleven other kings he had conquered. None of the recent rebels were asking for help against the Saxons, which was the only call for help that would really have pleased Artus. Queen Morgawse, the wife of Lot, who was one of the leading kings in the first rebellion, had come to our court, gracious and beautiful—Artus was infatuated, and hoped to work out an alliance with King Lot through her as ambassador; but, instead, they yielded to their mutual lusts. They thought they were being very subtle about it, and, in fact, no one could be completely certain how far they had gone, but the gossip was not likely to help the peace effort if Lot got wind of it. Morgawse had picked up old-fashioned ideas about sharing women to cement friendship, but Lot did not share her opinions; and Artus meanwhile, after she was gone, spent several days moping for her like a moonstruck rooster, while the rest of us waited for news that Lot was forming a new rebel coalition.

Being attacked from two or three sides at once,

expecting a call for help from Brittany fortnightly (though as things turned out, we never did get across the Channel until long after Claudas had already defeated and killed Ban and Bors), moping for his latest light-o'-love, and frustrated in his hopes for a truce and alliance with Lot and the other former rebels would have been enough to give any old, seasoned monarch a few bad dreams. Artus was not yet twenty, had not even had a chance to get a few years' experience as simple knight under his belt before jumping from squire (and a rather indifferent squire) to High King, and did not yet know who his parents were—Merlin had stunned him, and me, with the news that my father and mother were not Artus' parents also, but the great mage saw fit to point to the damn Sword in the Stone as the only test and proof that was needed, and save the revelation of Arthur's true parentage for a little later, after several thousand knights had died and the rebellion against a king of unknown parentage, who even feared himself a bastard, was firmly entrenched.

Ordinary, honest, simple-minded folk like my father, myself, and my old nurse did not have to look any farther than the present situation around us to understand why Artus dreamed one night that a serpent came out of his side and destroyed all the land. Every peasant in the country, at least every peasant who knew anything about what was going on beyond his own fields and village, was probably having worse dreams every night. But Merlin, who still had not bothered to tell Arthur or anyone else that he was the lawful son of Uther Pendragon and Igraine of Cornwall and that King Lot was his brother-in-law, now told him his nightmare meant that his own son would cause his downfall and the destruction of the realm.

Merlin then went on to prophesy that the child in question was to be born on May Day. Arthur had been bestowing his kingly body as generously as he could upon the ladies of his realm, to the point where he could not be sure how many lords' children were really bastards of the High King. So, to be on the safe side, when the time came he sent for all the male children born to noble parents in the last sennight of April and the first sennight of May. At first he offered rewards, and when that did not bring in enough baby boys, he threatened death for non-compliance. Then he put all the babies in a leaky ship with a few loose staves in the bottom, and no mariners or adults on board, and sent them out into a stormy sea.

I counseled him against it, to the utmost of my power. Sir Ector, our father (my real progenitor and still the only father Artus knew), counseled him against it. So did Ulfius, Brastias, Baudwin, Hervise de Revel, and Father Amustans, Arthur's confessor, who called it Herod's massacre of the innocents all over again. So did our old nurse. But Merlin the Great had prophesied.

As far as anybody knew, Mordred was the only child who survived when the ship broke up on the rocks; and it was a few years before anybody knew about that, since Sir Antor and his wife, who found him, were understandably shy about mentioning that their new foster-son was one of the May Babies. Probably a lot of the infants on that ship, however, were peasant-born boys who had been substituted for the ladies' own sons, so even if Merlin had prophesied true, Arthur's precaution was as good as worthless. Meanwhile, King Lot, angrier than ever at the murder of his youngest son, had easy recruiting for his new rebel alliance; and Artus, suffering fits of conscience, had his famous nightmare immortalized in a stone carving in Camelot cathedral, to remind himself that he had acted for the ultimate good of the realm.

He had spared his first known bastard, Dame

Lyzianor's son Lohot, because Lohot was born in midwinter; but he loved Lyzianor's son better after Lohot was dead than while he was still alive. Maybe the real reason Artus never had an heir of his wife's body was that he feared Dame Guenevere's son might be born on May Day.

While my mind had slipped into the past, Mordred's had apparently stayed on the business at hand. Maybe that was natural, since he himself had set up the pawns for his game. "Bagdemagus' nephew Astamore; Pellinore's nephew—or possibly bastard—Pinel; Ironside, once sworn to kill Gawaine and Lancelot, and all the sons of Lot and Morgawse." He drew his dagger, flipped it, and caught it by the jeweled handle as he rode. "It should be an interesting gathering at Astolat, Sir Seneschal, even if the poisoner of Sir Patrise is not among us. I rather hope Dame Nimue cannot find out the truth too easily with her crafts."

Chapter 10
In the Castle of Sir Bellangere

"Sir Bellangere le Orgulous, that the good knight Sir Lamorak won in plain battle." (Malory XIX, 11)

We reached Arlan Castle shortly before vespers. I would have preferred going farther; but, as Mordred pointed out, even at our present speed we would easily reach the Lake and return with Dame Nimue to Astolat by the appointed time. He went on to remark that folk speed better by day for having a good supper and warm bed at night. I suspect his real reason for insisting on the hospitality of Arlan was to bait Sir Bellangere, who had not yet rejoined court after wintering in his own castle.

Bellangere the Proud was a protégé of the late Sir Lamorak de Galis, and one of those who believed, on no visible evidence, that Lamorak had been innocent in the death of Queen Morgawse. Thus, Bellangere had less than no love for any of Lot's sons (except, of course, Gareth Beaumains the Guiltless), or for anyone who rode in their company by choice and not simple chance. But as lord of the castle, Bellangere was bound to observe the laws of hospitality and see to the comfort and welfare of any guests, especially brother companions of the Round Table. It did not have the makings of a cozy situation for anyone but Mordred, who seems to relish being hated for the love of being hated.

Bellangere's elaborate care in having us shown to the best rooms and provided with the most expensive robes was little short of sarcasm, and I returned the compliment more than once before he left me alone with my squire to change my clothes. I would rather state my mind and take the consequences than mouth simpering courtesies to fools.

"You should at least temper your tongue to your host, sir," said Gillimer. He thought he was over-ripe for knighthood, and showed it.

"And you should temper your tongue to your betters, if you don't want to stay a squire all your life."

"Maybe I will. Men listen when Gouvernail and Eliezer give good advice." Occasionally Gillimer shows a flash of understanding.

"Men listen to Gouvernail and Eliezer because they're sensible, not because they're old squires. You'd better settle for aiming at knighthood and battering your equals around the field—you're no Eliezer or Gouvernail."

"Neither are you a Sir Gawaine or Sir Tristram, Sir."

"If you ever win the accolade, Sir Wisewords," I said, "you'll find I'm still jouster enough to give *you* a fall."

Before our jolly company was reassembled in front of the hall fire, Dames Lore of Carlisle and Elyzabel had arrived to seek the Hospitality of Arlan. I suppose Bellangere greeted them more warmly than he greeted us. They had taken longer to reach his castle, it seemed, because they had been looking in more nooks and crannyholes for Lancelot. They had made up the time, however, by changing their robes more quickly than we.

"It doesn't make sense for us to cover the same

ground," I said at supper. Gawaine would have prefixed the statement with some flowery apology to the effect that "Delightful as was the company of the fair ladies . . ."

Dame Elyzabel had recovered the talent for courtesy, or diplomacy, or whatever it was that had not helped her sweet-talk her way out of King Claudas' prison some years ago. "It would be a pity to lose your noble company at the day's end, my lords," she began, courteously if insincerely.

Mordred raised his cup of ale as if in a toast. "By all means, my lady, let us keep up the social graces until the very end."

"Or until tomorrow morning," I said. "We could make a more thorough search if we spread out. Why don't you ride southwest, toward Salisbury?"

With so many pairs in the search," replied Elyzabel, "it would be surprising if we did not encounter another couple, whichever way we rode."

Mordred smiled. "And you would prefer to stay near us two for the simple joy of our company. Or have you some other reason?"

Lore of Carlisle looked at me. "Perhaps we are searching the same ground more carefully, we two dames, than you." She had not veneered her manners as carefully as had her dark-haired kinswoman. "Do you really wish to find Sir Lancelot, Seneschal?" Lore went on.

"It cuts both ways, Dame Suspicion. Would Lancelot want to be found by me? Or, for that matter, by anyone?"

"Surely he could not object to being found by the charming ladies," said Mordred. "But you may, of course, have another reason for keeping us in sight, mesdames."

By now, another host would have tried to change the

subject. Bellangere was content to sit and look on, probably hoping Mordred and I would be bested.

"Perhaps my lord Sir Mordred has a guilty conscience," said Dame Lore. "What reason do you think we might have for following you purposely, other than distrust of the care with which you may be searching?"

There were a few moments of silence that no one, not even Elyzabel, tried to fill, while Mordred ate a few bites of veal and wiped his fingers daintily on his bread. Then he replied, "Let us play a small game of trust and mistrust, Dame Lore. Give me a short time alone with mine. Afterwards, we will pledge each other to drain off the contents of our respective cups."

"That wasn't humorous, Mordred," I said. If Bellangere would not stop it, someone else should.

"I did not mean it to be humorous." Mordred shrugged. "Well, if we are not to prove our mutual trust and friendship, we had better speak of other matters. Perhaps our good host can suggest a subject of harmless mirth for the supper hour."

Bellangere tossed a piece of meat to his hounds. "It's been some time, my ladies, since I heard news of Sir Aglovale, or his brother Sir Tor le Fils Vayshoure." He must have been waiting for a convenient opportunity to bring King Pellinore's last remaining sons into the conversation. No doubt he was hoping they had recently done something great that would rankle Mordred when Lore and Elyzabel recounted it.

"Le Fils Vayshoure wintered in his own castle, like you," I said, "doing very little of note."

"The greatest knights of us all do very little, by your account of them, Sir Kay," said Bellangere. "What of Aglovale?"

"Sir Aglovale won honor in the North Downs about Candlemas," said Elyzabel. "Encountering a band of robber knights, he struck down four and routed the others, rescuing a gentlewoman and avenging her lord, whom they had just slain."

"He may have struck down four, but he only brought back two heads," Mordred remarked. "Some wonder if the fair dame's lord was already dead when Sir Aglovale came into the field, or if he survived long enough to help drive off the scoundrels. But, of course, noble deeds must be expected of the brother of the great Sir Lamorak de Galis." Mordred rarely mentioned his mother's lover and murderer, but when he did, you could hear real bitterness beneath his customary sarcasm.

I did not pity our host. Bellangere had brought the implied slur on his patron's memory down on himself. "It does not befit a guest," said Bellangere, "to speak ill of his host's friend beneath his host's roof."

Mordred shrugged. "I attempt to match my geniality with that of my host."

"Let him prattle, my lord," said the Dame of Carlisle. "If an enemy of Mordred's accomplishes any great deed, be sure Mordred and his brothers will always lessen it."

"Which is not that much worse than puffing a small deed into a great one with a lot of brag and boast," I said.

"Each man recognizes his own faults the most clearly in others, my lord Seneschal," said Dame Lore with overwhelming originality.

"Is that the way you recognize Mordred's talent for lessening his enemies' achievements, my lady Cupbearer?" I inquired, wondering secretly why I bothered to defend Mordred.

"Sir Aglovale le Fils Pellinore is not our enemy," said Mordred. "If he were, he and his brothers would have avenged their father and brother on us. But, of course, they realize that the deaths of Pellinore and Lamorak were just."

"That is false!" Bellangere sprang to his feet. "King Pellinore killed King Lot in plain battle!"

"Why, so did my brother Gawaine strike down King Pellinore in honest battle," said Mordred, obviously delighted, in his sleek way, at having goaded his host into so far forgetting hospitality.

"Although Sir Pellinore was his brother of the Round Table—although Pellinore himself had gotten Gawaine his seat!" cried Bellangere.

"Gawaine would eventually have won his seat at the Table without Pellinore's good graces," said Mordred, "or even in despite of Pellinore. And had it not been prophesied . . . how many times? that Gawaine would finally avenge his father's death? Merlin even went about writing it in gold on the tombs of knights who had nothing to do with either Gawaine or Pellinore. What could my brother do but fulfill the prophecy?"

"Merlin and his bloody prophecies," I said. I would have said more, but no one was paying attention to anything except Bellangere and Mordred.

"And what of that noble knight Sir Lamorak?" shouted Bellangere. "Had it been prophesied that you four would close in on him from all sides and cut him down in pure treachery?"

That seemed to checkmate Mordred slightly, but only for a moment. "The old gossip begun by a few silly squires and spread by idle folk who were not there to see it, eh? Yes it's true we searched for the traitor Lamorak together, My lord Bellangere—we were all of us the true sons of Queen Morgawse—but when he was found, Gawaine fought him alone. Would the sons of King Lot repay even a traitor with treachery?"

"Yes, by God," said Bellangere, "I think *you* would,

Mordred—you and your brother Agravaine. But I'll say this for Gaheris—he may be another murderer like the rest of you, but at least he has some sense of honor."

"Credit the rest of us with brother Gaheris," said Mordred. "We were all there to see justice done, but Gawaine fought Lamork fairly, man to man, for more than three hours."

Bellangere snorted. "Gawaine could never have lasted three hours alone against Lamorak de Galis."

Mordred rose to return Bellangere's stare at eye level. "The honor belongs to Lamorak for lasting so long against Gawaine, and it is more honor than the traitor deserved. But if your noble Lamorak de Galis were killed by treachery, it was no more than he merited for cutting down in her bed a woman who trusted him."

"And who is Gawaine to avenge a murdered woman? What of Sir Ablamar's lady?"

That had happened while Mordred himself was a suckling infant, but the story was well known. Gawaine had Ablamar down when the lady ran in between their blades and caught the stroke meant for her lord. Gaheris, who was standing by and watching, blamed Gawaine, a little late, for not showing mercy to Ablamar earlier, but the lady's death itself had been sheer accident.

"My brother killed that dame in the heat of battle and by misadventure," said Mordred. "The great Lamorak killed our mother naked in her bed while she waited for his embrace."

"Lamorak loved Queen Morgawse," said Bellangere, "God alone knows why. He would not have. . ."

Mordred went for Bellangere's throat. I jumped up to separate them. So did Lore of Carlisle. We managed to pull them apart before anyone was hurt, and Lore and Elyzabel got Bellangere seated again.

"All right," I said, "you've both goaded each other into breaking the laws of hospitality. Now sit down and finish your supper."

Mordred pulled away from me. "I will not eat at the table of any man who insults my mother. The duties of a guest do not extend that far."

"Then go to your room and sleep it off," I said.

"No," said Mordred, "I ride tonight."

"Then you'll ride without me. You persuaded me to stop here for supper and a good night's sleep, and by God, now I'm here, I'm going to get them."

He returned my look and smiled crookedly. "I will not breakfast here. Not even if I escape being murdered naked in my bed, like my mother."

"Bolt your bloody door," I told him.

One of the servants got a torch and came forward to guide him to his chamber. Mordred took the light himself and waved the servant away. Fortunately, Lore and Elyzabel seemed to have kept Bellangere from hearing Mordred's last comment, which might have been a challenge to our host. Mordred had sounded almost as if he was looking forward to being murdered in his bed.

Chapter 11

Further Talk of the Deaths of Sir Lamorak and Queen Morgawse, and of the Gossip Concerning Queen Guenevere

"Then, as the book saith, Sir Launcelot began to resort unto Queen Guenever again, and forgat the promise and the perfection that he made in the quest . . . of the Sangreal; but ever his thoughts were privily on the queen, and so they loved together more hotter than they did to-forehand, and had such privy draughts together, that many in the court spake of it, and in especial Sir Agravaine, Sir Gawaine's brother, for he was ever open-mouthed." (Malory XVIII, 1)

With Mordred gone, the rest of us sat back down to try to finish our meal. "Are you not going to beg indulgence for your companion, Sir Kay?" said Dame Elyzabel, as if proprieties had been the principal casualty.

"No," I said. "He and our host can beg each other's forgiveness, if they really want it, but I'm not playing go-between."

Bellangere threw Mordred's food, trencher and all, to the hounds, and ordered one of the servers to pour his ale down the nearest privy and scour the cup with sand. Even that did not calm our host completely. "That they persist in their lie!" he said. "God! Lamorak *loved* the witch—he would have married her, if they had let him. He would never have killed any woman!—"

"Stop talking about it and eat," I said. "Get drunk, if that's the only way you can forget about it."

"Travel with filth and you'll be spattered, Seneschal," said Bellangere.

"Before you start accusing me of dirtying Mordred instead of the other way, Bellangere," I replied, "remember there's more reason to assume that Lamorak killed Dame Morgawse than there is to assume Dame Guenevere killed Patrise of Ireland."

I have never felt especially inclined to worship any man who defeats me in battle as if that alone made him some sort of prince, saint, and model of all knightly virtues. But Lamorak had been the one to defeat Bellangere the Proud, bringing him to Arthur's court and to the infirmary for two months; and therefore, as far as Bellangere was concerned, Lamorak de Galis was the noblest hero who ever lived, with the possible exceptions of Lancelot and Jesu. Our host started up again, with some garbled sounds that seemed about to lead into a comparison of me with Judas, but I cut him off.

"Stop and use your brain, Bellangere, if it didn't all leak out in some head-wound or other. I'm not saying I think Lamorak killed her." (It was what I thought, but I was not saying it.) "But Lamorak was alone with

Dame Morgawse in her Bedchamber that night. All right, maybe, as you Lamorak-worshippers guess, maybe someone else *did* get into Gawaine's castle, find his way to the chamber, swap off her head and get out again, all before Lamorak could get to his sword. And maybe the reason he never came back to Camelot was that he rode off in pursuit of this supposed real murderer, who somehow escaped the attention of Lamorak's dwarf, waiting at the privy postern. But Lamorak's ghost hasn't come back yet to explain it all to us. Patrise of Ireland died of poison in a roomful of people—twenty-three other knights, five chief servers, besides the pages, besides whoever could have gotten to the fruit before the Queen's dinner—which takes in a good part of the court—besides the possibility that Morgan le Fay is still alive and at her old tricks again. But Mador de la Porte immediately accuses the Queen, and several score men and women who pretend to have some sense in their heads are willing to go along with him and see Her Grace on trial. If Mador can accuse the Queen, you can hardly blame Gawaine and his brothers for looking at the circumstances of their mother's death and assuming Lamorak's guilt."

Bellangere sat silent for a moment or two, breathing heavily. Then he said, "Are you for Lancelot and Pellinore's sons, Seneschal, or for Gawaine and Mordred and the sons of Lot?" He might as well have been asking if I were on the side of God or Satan.

"I'm for Britain and the King," I said, "and I'd still be for Britain and the King if Lancelot and Gawaine themselves ever came to blows. Since that's not likely to happen, even if all the rest of you choose to overlook the great friendship between your respective idols, the worst danger is all this bloody rivalry itself between men empty and foolish enough to admire either Lancelot or

Gawaine, or Lamorak de Galis, to the point of blind worship."

Dame Lore of Carlisle decided it was time to treat us to some of the fruits of her profound meditations. "An empty man does better to worship some knight greater than himself than to glory in his own emptiness, Sir Seneschal."

"What great lady do you worship, then, Dame Cupbearer?" I replied.

"Sir Lamorak should have been allowed to defend himself in combat before the full court," remarked Dame Elyzabel, her tact failing for once. Lore and I had almost gotten us clear of that subject.

"Aye, but he was not," said Bellangere. "Gawaine knew he could not defeat him in fair combat. He preferred to defeat him in ambushment with his brothers."

"Lamorak never came back to court to be tried," I said. "And Arthur himself wouldn't permit it at the Surluse tournament. But why don't you charge Lot's sons of their treachery and prove it on them yourself in full court, Bellangere? Defeating Gawaine and his brothers one by one should be easy for the man who almost defeated Lamorak de Galis."

"Maybe you'd be willing to act as champion for your friend Mordred against me, Seneschal?"

"I won't need that excuse to give you a fall, Sir Proud Knight," I said. "After the Queen's name is cleared."

"I wonder you choose the company of Mordred," said Dame Lore, "worshipping our Queen as you do."

"Meaning?"

"Who but Sir Agravaine is behind the gossip? And who but Mordred helps him to spread it?"

"I should have realized that one of your talents is tracing gossip to its source," I said.

"It's a wise talent," Lore replied. "You would do better to cultivate it than to mock it."

"I have other things to do than pry and poke my nose into every idle tale that goes around."

"Sir Agravaine will not rest until he's destroyed Sir Lancelot for pure jealousy," said Dame Elyzabel. "Even if he must destroy the Queen with him."

"The rumors have been going around for years," I said. "Even before the time of that look-alike witch of a false Guenevere. It's a little too easy to charge all the mischief-making to the third or fourth most disliked man at court."

"It might have been better for Her Grace had she refused to come back to the King," said Elyzabel. She stopped just short of adding that Dame Guenevere had been living with Lancelot under the protection of the High Prince of Surluse the whole time Artus was wallowing under the spell of her look-alike.

"You can talk like that, Dame Elyzabel, and then put all the blame for the rumors on Agravaine and his brothers?" I said.

"On Agravaine and Mordred," said Lore of Carlisle. "Never an old tale but they keep it fresh, never a new one but they magnify it, never a chance to lie but they seize it."

"Never a stray morsel of gossip but Dame Lore the Cupbearer follows it back to its source," I said. "Why not charge all five of the brothers?"

Bellangere, who seemed to have been only half-following the conversation while he brooded on the supposed treachery of the sons of Lot, came out of his own thoughts long enough to say, "Slander Sir Gareth at my table and you'll pay for it, Seneschal. Sir Gareth shares in none of his family's sins."

"We all know that Gawaine speaks always in favor of the Queen and of his friend Lancelot," said Elyzabel. "I believe you wrong Gawaine a little, my lord Bellangere. He behaved wickedly towards the good Sir Lamorak, but he was half-crazed with grief for his mother." It was what I had tried to point out, but Bellangere took it more gently and quietly from Dame Elyzabel's lips. "And Gaheris is fair enough to keep his own counsel," she went on. "But how can you close your eyes, Sir Kay, to Agravaine's jealousy and Mordred's malice? You know the King. You know what must happen if he should ever be convinced of his wife's guilt."

Artus has always been slow to anger, but when his temper does break, he listens to nobody. Not even his own laws and customs are safe during one of his royal rages—it seems to be a trait folk admire in their kings. "Well," I said, "if Morgan le Fay was never able to convince him about it, it's not likely he'll listen to his least favorite nephews. Not, at least, while his favorite nephew, Gawaine, is defending the Queen and Lancelot."

In fact, I had spent more effort helping Artus convince himself that the rumors were fools' fancies than in trying to collect and trace them. I was not going to give Lore and Elyzabel the satisfaction of seeing the doubts they had now planted in me—they who blamed Gawaine's brothers for trying to plant doubts in the King. There would have been rumors about Her Grace and Lancelot if Agravaine and Mordred had been killed in their first jousts. If the great Du Lac had never come to Britain, there might have been rumors about Her Grace and the Seneschal.

We did not linger long over supper. But Dame Elyzabel overtook me in the corridor, motioning the torchbearers a few paces farther on.

"Don't tell me you're trying to start a rumor about us, Dame?" I said.

She shook her head. "You are not so bad as Mordred,

Sir Kay. He spreads his poison behind his victims' backs. You at least speak openly."

"My old nurse warned me to beware of flatterers," I remarked. "Suppose you and Dame Cupbearer are right —suppose Agravaine and Mordred *are* behind the worst of the gossip. They can't be behind all of it. Lancelot does a very good job of feeding the rumormongers himself. But suppose Lot's sons are as dangerous as you say —what do you want me to do about it? Cut Mordred's throat while he's asleep? Murder him 'naked in his bed'?"

"Discredit them. Discountenance them. Use your tongue against them, not in their defense."

"The knights *I* discredit have a way of turning into the heroes of court and kingdom. Have you forgotten how Gareth Beaumains and Sir La Cote Male Taile got their start? And that holy fool Percivale?"

"At least do not ride with Mordred," she said. "Don't appear to favor his company."

"I've been frequently assured that I am probably the least-loved man at court," I remarked, "as well as the least appreciated. I should do Mordred's reputation more harm by riding with him than by avoiding him."

That reduced even Dame Elyzabel to falling back on proverbs. "Who touches pitch besmirches himself," she said, echoing Bellangere's earlier witticism.

"Mordred and Agravaine are not much better loved than I am. Why should our noble, intelligent knights and dames listen to their rumormongering?"

"Folk are always ready to hear evil, even from evil tongues. Perhaps they are readier to believe evil tales from wicked tongues than holy tales from saints. Some even repeat the tales as if they were to the glory of Lancelot and the Queen."

"It might be a good thing if you didn't find Lancelot,"

I said. "Bors can probably defeat Mador de la Porte."

"If Sir Bors fights with a good heart."

"Would the hero of the Holy Grail agree to fight with anything else but a good heart?" I said sarcastically. "If you're looking for a source of the rumors, Dame Elyzabel, keep an eye on Bors de Ganis."

"You did not mean it when you hoped Sir Lancelot would not be found?"

"No, I suppose not. I'd rather see him found than Her Grace burned. I'd bring him back myself at sword point, if I had to. And as soon as he splits Mador's head, I hope Lancelot goes to the Devil and stays there!"

We parted, neither of us overjoyed with the other, and I told my torchbearer to lead me to Mordred's room. I was ready to forgive Gawaine's youngest brother a lot, in view of that knock on the head or whatever turned him inside-out at the Peningues tournament—but I was not ready to forgive his gossipmongering about Her Grace.

A time candle was burning in the antechamber, where Lovel, Mordred's nephew and squire, was sleeping as soundly as if he had been drugged. The inner door was ajar. Telling my torchbearer to stay in the anteroom with the snoring squire, I went into the inner chamber.

It was dark, but by the light that came through the doorway I saw Mordred sitting on the edge of his bed, fully clothed. He seemed to be staring so intently at his own thoughts that he could not be bothered to turn his head. I closed the door and we were in darkness again.

"So, was I right?" he said quietly. "But you may find you need a light, if you hope to strike true."

"I didn't take the time to go back to my room for my sword," I said.

"Did you hope to do the work with your knife, then? Or perhaps with a pillow pressed down over my face?"

"You can stop playing the martyr, Mordred. If you haven't recognized my voice, I'm Kay."

The bed cording creaked. Mordred was shifting his weight, maybe turning toward me at last. "Did you come to learn whether I were still in the castle, Sir Seneschal? Or whether I were already murdered by someone else?"

"I came to find out whether it's true that you and your simpering brother have been spreading filth about the Queen."

"Which brother? I have four, and possibly a few bastard half-brothers."

"Only one that simpers," I said. "Agravaine the Proud. Well, is it true?"

"My simpering brother Agravaine, the Proud and Handsome. Yes, I like that. How shall we describe the others? Justice-seeking Gawaine the Golden-Tongued, innocent Gareth of the Clean Hands, Gaheris . . . Gaheris the Dedicated Weathercock, I think."

"And scheming Mordred of the Foul Tongue."

"Can foul deeds be spoken of with a clean tongue?" he asked.

It was as well we were in darkness. My hands ached to strangle him. I might have tried, if I had been closer to the bed. "It's true, then? You confess it?"

"I confessed nothing, I denied nothing. I have invented no tales about Dame Guenevere and her champion. If my simpering brother Agravaine the Proud and Handsome has made up any such lies out of his own jealous fancies, he has imposed on me as well as on the rest of the court."

"Then you *have* helped him spread his poison!" I said.

"Are all the rumors lies? If not lies, then they have a base of truth. Can truth be poison?"

"Damn your stinking souls to Hell, why are you

trying to destroy the Queen?"

"I am not," said Mordred, still with no sound of anger. "I have enemies, Seneschal, and enemies I would like to crush, but the Queen is not among them. I love and respect Her Grace—not as much as you love her, perhaps, but enough, in my way, to want to see whoever has endangered her burned into ashes at the stake meant for her. . . . As for Agravaine the Handsome, he is bitterly jealous of the great Lancelot. A jealousy you should understand well, Sir Kay."

"Tell your brother he can attack Lancelot any other way he dares, but if he goes on trying to drag the Queen down with Lancelot, then by God I'll give his pride a fall he'll never get up from again."

"If all goes well," said Mordred, "you'll see him again as soon as I will, at Astolat. Shall I give you some practice tilts for love as we travel? Once on a time the noble Lancelot himself used to tell me I jousted very well, for a young knight."

"Bad dreams to you," I said, and left him.

Chapter 12
Dame Iblis' Tale of Tragedy in a Pavilion

"And so he rode into a great forest all that day, and never could find no highway, and so the night fell on him, and then was he ware in a slade, of a pavilion of red sendal. By my faith, said Sir Launcelot, in that pavilion will I lodge all this night, and so there he alighted down, and tied his horse to the pavilion, and there he unarmed him, and there he found a bed, and laid him therein and fell asleep sadly.

"Then within an hour there came the knight to whom the pavilion ought, and he weened that his leman had lain in that bed, and so he laid him down beside Sir Launcelot, and took him in his arms and began to kiss him. And when Sir Launcelot felt a rough beard kissing him, he started out of the bed lightly, and the other knight after him, and either of them gat their swords in their hands, and out at the pavilion door went the knight of the pavilion, and Sir Launcelot followed

him, and there by a little slake Sir Launcelot wounded him sore, nigh unto the death. . . .

"Therewithal came the knight's lady, that was a passing fair lady,and when she espied that her Lord Belleus was sore wounded, she cried out on Sir Launcelot, and made great dole out of measure." (Malory VI, 4-5)

"You should not have wished me evil dreams last night," said Mordred next day. True to his word, he had refused to break his fast at Arlan; but, fasting or not, his spirits seemed to have risen on leaving Bellangere's castle behind us.

"My wish took hold, eh?"

"Fortunately, no. Evil dreams can be dangerous, when dreamed by kings and kings' sons. How many infant boys drowned for a nightmare of our liege lord Arthur, that year I was born?"

"Merlin's malicious prophesying had as much to do with that as Arthur's nightmare. Anyway, I never heard that King Lot needed any bad dreams for an excuse to lead his people into war."

"And King Lot's youngest son is never likely to be in a position to make a whole kingdom suffer for the sake of a bad dream, is he?" was all Mordred said to that. He took implied insults against his father much more coolly than those against his mother.

We stopped that night at a convent of white nuns not far from the neighborhood of Malmesbury.The prioress, who had taken the veil on the death of her husband, was a cousin of Lancelot. I judged that Dame Iblis deserved to hear the latest news, such as it was. Since we seemed to have outstripped the rest of the search, it was not likely she had already heard it from anyone else. I also hoped Mordred would be on better behavior in a house of holy women.

Arriving midway through Evensong, we had to wait at the gate with the portress until the nuns returned from chapel. Then an aging lay-sister came to lead us to the guesthouse for knights and other male travellers. I asked for an interview with the prioress.

"Aye, aye," said the lay-sister, nodding."And glad enough she'll be to sup with you, too. Aye, our goodlady loves knightly talk and news of arms."

"A pity,then," Mordred murmured, aside to me, "that she does not have more graceful conversationalists for her knightly guests."

Dame Iblis joined us with the elderly Dame Cellarer as her companion. Aside from the Prioress' ring of office and the Cellarer's ring of keys, they were habited identically; but, whereas Dame Cellarer's white clothes hung on her like a peasant kirtle and cloak,the Prioress wore gown, scapular, and wimple with a studied modesty that came little short of high court fashion.

Mordred was standing at the window, watching the sky darken,his face turned away from the fire, gold hair shining in the firelight. When Dame Iblis first glimpsed him, she stopped in the doorway and gasped. "You!"

He turned to look at her inquiringly. "Yes, madame, I am myself, but what am I to you?"

"Nay, nay, Lady," said Dame Cellarer, "this is not he. I mind the other one well. This is not he."

The Prioress recovered herself and came forward to greet us. "Your pardon, my lord. I mistook you for another. You might be a brother to Sir Gaheris of Orkney."She mentioned the name a bit too casually.

"The family resemblance is strong."Mordred bowed to kiss her hand."Since the sons of Dame Morgawse are known for their beauty, I take your mistake for praise."

"Then you are one of the sons of King Lot and Queen Morgawse. The noble Sir Gareth, perhaps?" She must have been able to see he was too young to be Gawaine or Agravaine. On learning he was Mordred, the youngest, she welcomed him with, "You rode with my kinsman Sir Lancelot for a time, did you not? He spoke highly of your prowess at arms."

Dame Iblis and I had met once or twice before, though she either remembered me, or pretended to, more clearly than I remembered her. I had not thought it especially surprising, at the time, that Lancelot's cousin should retire into a convent upon being widowed by robbers. Now, as she sat conversing with us over richer fare, presumably, than that she usually shared with her sisters in the refectory, all of us saving less pleasant talk for after the meal, I grew more and more puzzled as to why this fine dame had left the world. She might have been widowed thrice over and never found difficulty in getting a new lord. She might even have had several waiting their chance to wed her. Nor was she any landless, dowerless younger daughter to be forced into the cloistered life; even unmarried, she could easily have ruled her first husband's lands. And though she seemed to have a glowing reputation in the neighborhood for good works among the poor and sick, her supper talk was worldly, sometimes worldly enough to make poor Dame Cellarer pay noticeably strict attention to her food, while Gillimer and Lovel laughed and let their serving duties slip. Dame Iblis might be getting along well in her convent—she would probably become abbess as soon as the chief place was vacant—but God had not fashioned her for the cloister, even to rule it.

During the meal we ascertained that Dame Iblis did

not know where her cousin Lancelot might be and had not even heard of his latest disappearance from court, though she took the news, in itself, as no more than a bit of light gossip to sauce her supper. Dame Elaine of Carbonek was dead, Morgan le Fay either dead or quiescent, and what other woman could tempt Du Lac into a prolonged interlude on some island retreat? Clearly, he had not yet grown beyond the stage of riding out in disguise for high-spirited and aimless adventure. We did not tell her of the more serious aspects of the situation until after the meal, when we had sent Gillimer and Lovel to check once more on the horses, and old Dame Cellarer had obligingly fallen into a doze before the fireplace, lending us a measure of artificial privacy.

I did most of the talking, while Mordred twisted floor rushes into little figures and tossed them into the fire.

"So you are searching for either Sir Lancelot to champion the Queen's Grace, or the Lady of the Lake to tell you who is the real Traitor?" said Dame Iblis when she had heard of the Queen's dinner, the poisoning of Sir Patrise, and Mador de la Porte's accusation. "Name me off those under suspicion again, my lord Sir Kay."

"Ironside," I began, "who has yet to fulfill his old vow against Gawaine and Sir Lancelot. Any kinsman of someone slain by Gawaine; Astamore, Bagdemagus' nephew; Pinel, Pellinore's nephew or possibly bastard; Sir La Cote Male Taile, Dinadan's brother—"

"It was not brother Gawaine who killed the lamented Sir Dinadan, of course," said Mordred.

"People sometimes confuse the deeds of Gawaine's younger brothers with the intentions of the head of the clan," I replied. "And, saving your presence, Dame, if any of the rest of us who were there had offered to champion Her Grace, as your kinsman Bors did, the court would have assumed us guilty with no further questions. We can hardly leave out Queen Morgan le Fay, either—"

The prioress waved her hand in a small gesture of impatience. "We do not hear all the news of court and kingdom, but has Dame Morgan ever yet struck at her brother when he himself was not present in the same place?"

I thought for a moment. "Maybe not, but she hates the Queen."

"I speak as a woman, and one woman's hatred for another is not such that she would murder at a distance. A woman can so hate a man that she would kill him across the miles, if it were in her power, but not another woman. The Queen of Gorre is far away from Queen Guenevere, and that will be enough to satisfy her enmity."

"You speak as a holy woman, Dame Prioress," said Mordred. I could easily credit my Aunt Morgan with stronger emotions."

"Then you know little of the strength of women's emotions, my lord Sir Mordred, even holy women's. But name me all who were there, not only those whom you think most suspicious."

I shrugged and refrained from pointing out that one of Morgan's first accusers had been another woman, Dame Lore. "Gawaine and all his brothers; your cousins Sirs Lionel, Bors, Ector de Maris, Blamore and Bleoberis de Ganis; Palomides and his brother Safere; Persant, Brandiles, and the Breton fox Aliduk; Galihud and Galihodin of Surluse; besides the ones I already mentioned. Good men and true, every last man of us—not one in the lot who would commit treachery by poison. Ask anyone. The chief servers were Gouvernail and Dames Lore of Carlisle, Elyzabel, Bragwaine of Ireland, and Senehauz the daughter of Sagramore. Do you want the cooks and pages, too?"

She shook her head. "There was one among you, at least, who would not be above any means of gaining his end. But I do not know what complaint he might have found against poor Sir Patrise."

"There is a strong feeling," said Mordred, "that the poison was meant for Gawaine."

"That is possible . . . Yes, it is possible. In that case, you would know, my lord Sir Mordred, better than I could guess it, what grievance the murderer had."

"For God's sake, Dame!" I said. "If you think you know which of us is the traitor, tell us. Don't play Merlin's old trick of shaking your head and dropping cryptic hints so that whatever truth finally comes out, you can smirk and say, 'I knew it all along.' "

"I do not know who did the deed—I only know one among you who was capable of it." Her glance flickered to Mordred. "In respect of this present company, I will keep my thoughts to myself, with your leave."

Mordred caught her glance and held it until she looked away. "Give us your suspicions, madame. A queen's life may hang in the balance. Which of Gawaine's brothers do you suspect?"

Dame Iblis met his gaze again. "Very well, my lord Sir Mordred. I say that your brother Sir Gaheris is capable of ten such deeds!"

"Gaheris?" Mordred and I said it in almost the same instant. Then Mordred shrugged and sat back, plucking up floor rushes to make another little doll for the fire. "I am a poor Merlin, Dame Prioress. I was prepared to answer you had you named Agravaine or myself. I did not expect you to name brother Gaheris."

"Do you have no defense prepared for Sir Gaheris because you did not expect me to name him," said the lady, "or because you know him too well?"

I noticed that I had been more or less laid aside in the conversation. It tends to happen unless I shout or insult someone. The insults now seemed to be coming thickly enough, although more subtly than when I deliver them. I decided to stay in the background awhile and see if Dame Iblis would explain her reasoning.

"Gaheris is perhaps the most insistent of us all, even including Gawaine, upon justice for rich and poor," said Mordred. "That, however—

"Justice!" The lady's eyes narrowed. "Aye, justice, perhaps—his own kind of justice, according to which Gaheris of Orkney can do no wrong, and therefore, if he sins, it was because others caused him to do so and they, not he, must bear the punishment!"

Her voice woke old Dame Cellarer, who started up. "Eh? Sir Gaheris? let be, my Dame—it's over and done."

"Sleep on, Dame Eldwith. You know the tale, but these noble knights, the companions of my lord Gaheris, apparently do not. It seems he does not always boast of his great deeds and fine justice, even among his kinsmen." The Prioress turned back to us. "How is it noised that my husband met his death, my lords? Mischance in honorable combat? Robbers, perhaps"

The old nun made a second flutter of protest, but Dame Iblis merely rose and stood staring into the fire, waiting for her to subside. After an appeal to us to "Forgive my lady, Sirs—it's over and done, over and done," Dame Cellarer subsided and left the field clear for her prioress, who pressed her palms together, fingers spread, and began.

"I loved my husband, my lords. That may not be fashionable, but I loved my husband, and he returned my love. We had no paramours but one another. Does that shock you? He was quick in his temper and sudden in some of his ways, but he trusted me, as why should he not? Ah, my lords, what sport we had together in our bed! I left nothing in him for any other woman—there was no room in me for any other man.

"We were travelling to one of your King's tournaments. The prize was some circlet of gold or pearls, and he meant to win it for me . . . The first night we found lodging at a hermit's manor, but the second night we slept in the forest, in our own pavilion. Why should we not? We had slept safely and merrily in our pavilion often enough before, and we were to meet my brothers the next morning at Newcross, only a few hours' ride away.

"Our squire and damsel both drowsed, perhaps in each other's arms, and left the pavilion unwatched. It had happened before. But at this time one of your knights found us. Not a renegade knight, no Turquine or Breuse Sans Pitie—such a man might have fallen on us with noise and immediate murder, honest, at least, in his villainy. Not even a common thief sneaking about in the dark, to content himself with our jewels and money, and perhaps leave us dead together, both our throats cut in our happy sleep, our blood mingling in one pool. No, the man who found our pavilion was one of Arthur's noble knights of the Table Round, one of you who are sworn to defend the innocent and bring justice to all, one whose business should have been to ensure our safety. Your brother, my lord Sir Mordred: Sir Gaheris of Orkney.

"We had left food spread on a table. He found it and ate, but he was not satisfied. He found our bed in the darkness, but he did not grope far enough to learn it already held two people; or, if he knew we were there, we made no difference to him. He did not awaken us. Is that your courtesy, to creep into bed with host and hostess without disturbing their slumber? Without so much as awakening their servants to make the presence of a newcomer known? Or perhaps Sir Gaheris hoped that during the night, in the confusion of sleep, I would forget on which side of my husband I lay and turn to my unknown guest instead.

"My lord awakened first. He may have groped for me and reached too far, or he may have heard our visitor's snores. What was he to think? Perhaps he thought it some nightmare. He rose, lit a rushlight, saw another man in bed who was human and no incubus, saw me rolled up close against this other man in my innocent sleep. How was my lord to understand at once that I was innocent?

"He pulled me from the bed to question me. I was newly-wakened, confused, scarcely aware of the other man's presence—able only to see my husband's hurt and confusion, unable to comprehend it or to answer his question. He struck me.

"He had never struck me before, my lords, and if he had been given time to understand, he would have implored my pardon and all would have been well. But Sir Gaheris—your noble companion of the Round Table—woke. Sir Gaheris had gone to sleep with his sword beside him—God knows what treachery our guest feared, or why he had not at least put the naked blade between him and me rather than beside the bed—and he caught up his sword and . . . struck my lord's beautiful head from his shoulders!"

She was silent for a moment, then gave up the struggle, buried her face in her hands, and began to weep. The old nun stirred, but before she could get up and go to her superior, Dame Iblis had wiped her eyes, blown her nose, and looked up again.

"Forgive me, my lords. It has been long enough . . . I thought I could speak of it now without . . . Perhaps I have tried too hard to keep it from my thoughts, so that the wound has stayed fresh beneath the scab.

"Sir Gaheris of Orkney excused his deed by claiming he had seen only a woman ill-treated and was pledged to defend all womankind. Defend! And comfort them too, in the only way such men as he understand, as if they think a woman's entire love is for one part of her lord's body alone, and can be transferred in a few moments to any other man who boasts that part! He seemed surprised—*surprised*—that I should resist him and grieve for my husband . . . my husband who must have died believing me . . .

"In the morning Sir Gaheris insisted I ride with him, leaving my lord's body alone. I had managed to send my damsel and the squire to Newcross for my brothers. They found us shortly after prime. Oh, aye, your knight of the Round Table is a great champion, and strong to defend a woman against her own brothers—especially with the slope of the land to his advantage. He put his spear through my youngest brother's body and then, when he had him pinned half-dead to the ground, struck off his helm and held his sword to his throat until he made me swear to call off my other brothers and be his own true leman forever. *His* leman—the man who had widowed me and an hour later presented his own body for my comfort, now required my vow never to love any other but himself, even after his death!

"I swore, to save my youngest brother, who was hardly more than a boy, knighted only that Epiphany. Sir Gaheris made sure of finding a hermit nearby to nurse him back to life, and my other brothers agreed that the companions of the Round Table were magnanimous and just, that Sir Gaheris was a worthy opponent and would make me a fine protector. Three of my own brothers turned against me, my lords! In that hour I wished that even Gaheris had killed me first. The one who was true, my dear Ewald, lying near death, not to be whole again in less than two months; and the hermit leach, this holy man of God who had once been a knight, agreeing that Sir Gaheris of Orkney, having deprived me of my first lord, now owed me protection in my husband's stead! Cannot God set aside vows extorted by force? Yet this man of God judged that my pledge to Sir Gaheris was binding, and would not absolve me from it.

"Thank the Holy Mother, we came in the evening to this convent. While my new champion dozed over his ale, I told my story to Dame Abbess. By the time Sir Gaheris woke and wanted me to warm his bed, I had taken the veil. Perhaps he had trapped me into being no man's paramour but his—if I could ever have wanted another after my dear, murdered lord—but I could at least cheat him of the pleasure he expected from his treachery."

Dame Iblis paused. I said, "You could have made him bring you to court and appealed to the King."

"And endured his nightly rapes along the way? And when a holy hermit and three of my own brothers had agreed that Sir Gaheris had atoned for his sad mistake, as they called it, and done justice by me, what more could I have expected from the King, Sir Gaheris' uncle?"

Mordred nodded. "Family loyalty can be a burdensome thing, can it not? Yet our good King Arthur knows how to set it aside at need. And you have cousins high in the King's favor, my lady. Lancelot, Bors de Ganis, Ector de Maris, Lionel. . ."

"And Sir Gaheris is brother to Gawaine and Gareth,

is he not? Is even Sir Lancelot higher in the King's affection than your brother Sir Gawaine?"

"No," I said. (At one time, before Lancelot came and when Gawaine was still a squire in Orkney, I had been highest in Artus' affection, which no one remembers.) "But the King is ready to burn his own wife in the name of justice."

"I have learned," said the Prioress, "that justice is one thing for men and another for women. If the King's nephew poisoned those apples, you might save the Queen by proving it—but do you truly think Sir Gaheris would burn in her place? While if you cannot prove certainly that Dame Guenevere is innocent, then God and Holy Mary have mercy on her soul."

Chapter 13
The Tale of Cob the Charcoal Burner

"When thou rest in thy riches, and ride in thy rally,
Have pity on the poor, while thou hast the power,
When bright dames and barons are busy about thee.
As thy body is balmed, and brought on a bier,
They will leave thee full lightly, who now praise thee loudly,
And then nothing helps thee, except holy prayer;
For the prayer of the poor may purchase thy peace."

(The Adventures of Arthur at the Tarn Wadling)

"It would be an interesting situation," said Mordred, when we were alone. "Lancelot torn between family loyalty to his good kinswoman and his love for Gaheris for Gawaine's sake, the King forced to invent justifications for his nephew, our sweet Gareth torn between

Lancelot's family and his own brothers—though that would give Gareth no pause . . ."

"Can't you see people as anything else but pawns to maneuver into your 'interesting situations'?" I said. "The poor dame's already taken the veil—not even Arthur could change that. Leave her here where she has peace."

"What, Seneschal? Even if her testimony would help to save our Queen?"

It would not, and Mordred knew it. At least three times the great Lancelot had played exactly the same sort of bloody mummery as Gaheris in somebody else's pavilion, except that Lancelot had not afterwards tried to make love to the bereaved lady if her lord failed to survive. Dame Iblis' story explained why she considered Gaheris capable of any villainy, but the incident had nothing to do with the poisoned fruit. I grunted. "Arthur would have no trouble inventing a justification. Dame Iblis was right about that. It would simply be said that Gaheris made a tragic mistake, and Lancelot and his kinsmen couldn't very well try to avenge their cousin privately without laying Lancelot open to vengeance for the same kind of mistake."

"But Lancelot would enjoy that, would he not? Unlike some of us, the great hero is always seeking excuses to fight and increase his glory. Still, it is interesting to learn that Gaheris keeps a secret or two from his own brothers."

"Hardly a mystery why," I said. "Gawaine would be scandalized."

"Yes, poor brother Gawaine. He would turn red and white to hear it, read Gaheris a morning-long lecture, then have Masses offered for everyone concerned." Mordred chuckled. "Gaheris had his chance to scold big brother Gawaine years ago, when that poor, witless lady ran in front of Gawaine's sword to save her paramour.

You remember?"

"Better than you do. You were a baby—I think Morgawse had just gotten you back." Gawaine still wore a lock of the slain woman's hair, woven into his swordbelt as a sign of penance for her death and to remind himself, as if he needed the reminder, to honor all women. A few of us have the grace to show sorrow for our accidents.

Gaheris had been acting as Gawaine's squire when it happened, a self-righteous young prig with no accidents of his own to embarrass him yet.

Mordred yawned, stood up, and stretched. "Gawaine would surely have his chance to take revenge for the homily Gaheris gave him that day for the slain lady."

"Gawaine's interested in justice, not revenge."

"Justice, revenge—two words for the same thing, as you yourself have remarked on occasion, Seneschal. And did not Dame Iblis herself refer to Gaheris as twisted by an overstrong sense of justice?"

"The lecture Gaheris would have from Gawaine," I remarked, "is nothing to the tongue-lashing Dame Lynette could give her husband if she heard how he tried to set up a permanent concubine for himself."

"I doubt Dame Lynette would much care. They rarely sleep together, you know. Sometimes I suspect she is grateful to the various paramours who help keep Gaheris out of her bed. For years I've expected her to leave him at court and set herself up as a sorceress, like Dame Nimue or Aunt Morgan." Taking out his dagger, Mordred laid it down with our swords, near the fireplace. "You'll notice that, unlike my brother who sleeps with his sword at his bedside, I go weaponless to my cell."

"Very magnanimous of you, especially in the guesthouse of a convent. You'll be all unprepared if the nuns attack."

* * *

Next day it rained, a heavy, wind-slanted rain that would have kept us guests in the convent for another day if our business had been less urgent. Mordred suggested we leave Lovel and Gillimer behind, to come after us when the weather cleared.

"That's a good way to spoil squires," I said. So they rode along behind us, grumbling at the extra work they would have to do on our armor, even though we rode unhelmed and with oiled cloth covering as much of our forms as possible. Except that Mordred preferred to leave his head completely uncovered and risk fever rather than have the grease from his hood besmirching his golden hair. I think it was less vanity than foolhardiness, as if he were daring the Fates and the weather to injure him; and maybe the Fates appreciate a bold gambler, because he stayed healthy. Of course, Mordred's bare head could not have got much wetter than our heads in their greasy hoods.

Towards afternoon the rain mizzled to a stop and fog set in. We were all right as long as the track was wide enough for two horses abreast, but when it narrowed and forked we had to stop and look for signs that we were still on the road and not astray in the forest.

While we were trying to tell the road from the surrounding forest floor by the bare, deep mud of the former and the moss and weeds of the latter, somebody's cheerful whistling came at us out of the woods.

We hailed the whistler. He hollo'd back, rough and respectful, and soon reached us, his animal clumping after him.

The man was a common fellow, somewhere in the age that usually settles on serfs and peasants by their thirtieth year and keeps them pretty well pickled until their hair goes completely white. His clothes were old and filthy—they could hardly have been clean in this weather, whatever his work—but they were well-mended; at least he and his wife had self-respect, which does not always go with a cheerful whistle in the muck and fog.

But the pack animal he led was a Norwegian palfrey, standing mild and patient beneath her splattering of mud and load of charcoal panniers.

The thought crossed my mind that this was a brash fellow to step out so merrily with a stolen horse; but he spoke before any of us, as if he was used to explaining the situation, and enjoyed it.

"I see your noble worships be wondering at my Beauty. Nay then, she's mine, free and honest." After wiping his hands on his tunic, he dug into his pouch and pulled out a small roll of parchment, which he handed proudly to me—I had dismounted, along with the squires, when we stopped to examine the ground.

I unrolled the parchment, read it, and passed it up to Mordred. It was a simple deed stating that the Norwegian palfrey called Beauty was the rightful possession of one Cob, freeman and charcoal burner by trade, a free gift from the Duke de la Rowse, in restitution for losses suffered by the said Cob through no fault of his own.

I nodded at him. "So you're Cob the charcoal burner."

"Aye, my lord, I be Cob, and this be Beauty." He stroked the animal's neck, and she nudged back in obvious affection. It clearly made no difference to the horse that she was carrying charcoal for a peasant instead of bearing rich gentlemen and dames about their affairs.

"And no doubt you can read this parchment as well, eh, Cob?" said Mordred.

"Nay, nay, my lord, but I know what it do say. My Lord of Rowse read it to me when he put his seal to it, and Sir Gwillim—our priest, Sirs—read it to me again each Lady Day. And when Beauty do give out, Sirs—God and Our Lady grant it be long yet—then I do go back to my Lord of Rowse and give him this parchment, and he do give me another horse and another parchment in her stead."

Mordred rolled the parchment again, tapped it once or twice against his thumb, and handed it back to me to return to the charcoal burner. "And what favor did you do for my lord de la Rowse, Cob, that he should keep you supplied with Norwegian palfreys for your beasts of burden?"

If Mordred meant to test Cob's memory of what the parchment said, Cob passed the test. "No favor I did him, my lord. For the loss I suffered, as it do say in the writing."

"And through whose fault, since the writing says it was not your own, did you suffer this loss? That of the Duke de la Rowse?"

"Nay, nay . . . be ye willing to hear the tale, your noble worships?"

"If you tell it simply and clearly," I said, "and stop wasting our time with your silly hints."

He nodded, seeming genuinely unoffended and not merely forced to swallow his annoyance toward his betters. "It be not a few years back, now, your worships, when my Lord of Rowse were at war with my Lord of Westerwood. I were in the forest, like as today, saving that it was clear weather, when they come by at me with all their din and their clattering, and a strange knight amongst 'em, all shouting and stamping and hacking at themselves with their bright swords.

"When knights do fight—saving your noble worships' presence—it be n't wise to be catched under 'em, for they do tend to trample 'un underhoof, in their fighting zeal and all. So I run, and my donkey run—Nat was my donkey then, and a right strong backed 'un, poor beast—but the rope snaps, and I lose Nat in the woods. And the noise be quiet again, and I come back looking for my Nat, seeing the great lords be finished with their fights and all gone away again, I find my poor Nat half eat up by the wolves, and the coals spilling out of un's broken baskets, and the guts spilling out of un's belly.

"So I be sitting there, trying to save what I can of Nat's poor, mangled hide and my coals, so as to get on a few more days, me and the woman and the young 'uns afore we all go to begging, and while I do kneel there skinning my poor dead beast, and the tears rolling down my face, by here comes the strange knight again, all straight and high on un's great black warhorse, and only a little blood coming out through the metal on one leg, and he stops and asks me my trouble—he stops in his own business, your worships, and asks a poor common man like Cob my troubles—and when I tell him, like as I tell you today, your worships, and how that I needed my poor beast Nat to bring back the charcoals from the woods, and now un's dead I and my family must needs go begging, not having what to buy another—and it be hard to put coin by with the young 'uns to feed, your worships, and that be God's truth—then this noble knight gets down off his fine warhorse, and helps me gather up my coals, and as for poor Nat's hide, he says, leave that, all chewed as it be, and then he makes me climb up on a felled tree and so up onto his great horse behind him, and makes me ride with him all the way to the castle, and there he brings me in before my Lord of Rowse himself, and tells him, 'See here, my Lord of

Rowse, here's a poor man lost his only beast, and all through our fights, and so we've beggared this man with our quarrels and our battles'—but he says it in finer talk, o'course—'and now I've settled your quarrel with my Lord of Westerwood for you,' he says, 'and you've promised me my asking, and so now I've come back to ask it, and all the payment I want, my Lord of Rowse, is that you take and give this poor man a horse from your own stables to carry his loads and earn his bread, and when that horse dies, you give him another, and so he keeps his livelihood and your land keeps its worker and loses a family of poor beggars, and none can say that a Knight of Arthur's Round Table ever beggared the humble in setting right the quarrels o' the high folk.'

"And so I say, your noble worships, I say God and the Holy Mother bless King Arthur and his good Round Table, and God and the Holy Mother bless Sir Gaheris of Orkney, him who stopped to hear a poor man and got me my Beauty and my parchment from my Lord of Rowse!"

"Sir Gaheris of Orkney," said Mordred. "You are quite sure that was the knight?"

"That were he, my Lord. Sir Gaheris of Orkney, and I name him in my prayers morn and night, and the King and the good Queen and all the rest o' the knights, but my Lord Sir Gaheris is the only lord o' them that I know his name, and two or three others."

"We thank you for your prayers, Cob," said Mordred. "We being knights of the Round Table ouselves, you see. This is Sir Kay, seneschal to King Arthur, and I am Sir Mordred, a brother of your Sir Gaheris of Orkney."

"Then God and the Holy Mother bless you twice over!" The charcoal burner started to bend double.

I caught him by the shoulder and pulled him straight

again. "No more of that, Cob. Just point out our way to Rowse Castle."

"Aye, your noble worships, let me guide you there. I be on my way back to the village myself now."

"Yet it seems curious," Mordred remarked, "that Sir Gaheris should not have mentioned any of your story, Cob, even to his own brothers."

"Nay, nay, my Lord, why should he speak of it? Be n't I a poor common man, and you noble Lords helping the likes of us every day? The shame be to me, for not knowing you for his brother, by your hair and your noble face."

Rather than having to keep our pace back to Cob's walk, I insisted he mount behind Gillimer. They rode ahead, leading both my warhorse Feuillemorte and Cob's palfrey Beauty. The arrangement also spared Mordred and me any more of the charcoal burner's gossip.

"Cob the charcoal burner seems to know a completely different Gaheris from the one who widowed Dame Iblis," I remarked.

"Yes. And yet not so different after all, if we assume my brother's passion for just retribution to be the root of his behavior in both cases. Cob was accidentally ruined by a quarrel between noblemen—it was only justice that Cob's fortunes be restored by the same men who had caused his loss. Lancelot's fair cousin was widowed through Gaheris' mistaken zeal to defend a lady—it was only justice that her husband's murderer give her protection in his place, and, since Gaheris was already married to sweet Dame Lynette, his only way of attaching Dame Iblis to his permanent protection was as his sworn paramour."

"If she'd been ugly, of course, he would have contented himself with accompanying her as a chaste and courtly champion. I also notice he insisted on De la Rowse supplying Cob the palfreys, instead of taking the expense himself or sharing it out between De la Rowse and Westerwood."

"In a sense, Gaheris did absorb the expense. The Duke de la Rowse had offered him his choice of gifts in return for his help. By settling the palfreys on Cob, Gaheris gave up his own profit in the matter. And, of course, it will be much easier for Cob to go to his local lord for the animals than to seek out Gaheris again."

"Suppose," I said, "that Gaheris, with his twisted sense of justice—"

"In Gawaine, you would call it an honorable hunger for justice."

"Gawaine has some sense of proportion. He would have gotten Cob a new donkey or two, not a Norwegian palfrey; and he would have allowed Dame Iblis to choose her own course and assign him his penance for her husband's death—not that Gawaine is the type to get involved in these damn pavilion lunacies in the first place." Maybe the difference between justice and revenge was whether it was practiced by a self-questioning man like Gawaine, who confined his excesses to flagellating his own conscience, and a self-righteous one like Gaheris, who inflicted his excesses, for better or worse, on the other folk concerned and then, seemingly, let the incidents slide out of his mind. "Suppose Gaheris decided that for some reason Gawaine deserved to die," I went on. "Gaheris could hardly fight his older brother, especially since Gawaine's the better man in the field. But if Gaheris felt strongly enough about it, might he consider himself justified in using poison?"

Mordred laughed. "Someday, when I'm more of the mood to meet you in battle, I can use that slander as well as any other excuse to fight. You mentioned it, I suppose, to ask if I knew any reason—anything Gawaine may have done—to stir Gaheris to such sublime depths of satisfying justice? No, Seneschal, I cannot supply you any material for your flight of fancy. Gaheris may have his secrets, but I would be much surprised if our breast-beating Gawaine held back any secret sins from kindred and court. We may have learned some interesting facts about Gaheris in these last two days, but we have hardly learned that he tried to poison his oldest brother."

I grunted. "And which of your possible poisoners do you have Gaheris riding with? Pinel, is it?"

"Your memory, Seneschal, provides an excellent argument for the usefulness of books and writing. Gaheris is riding with King Bagdemagus' nephew Astamore. Gareth of the Clean Hands is riding with Pinel of Carbonek, listening raptly, no doubt, to Pinel's tales of life in his uncle Pellam's Castle of the Grail."

Chapter 14
Kay's Views on the Early History of Sir Gareth Beaumains

> *"So thus [Gareth] was put into the kitchen, and lay nightly as the boys of the kitchen did. And so he endured all that twelvemonth, and never displeased man nor child, but always he was meek and mild. But ever when that he saw any jousting of knights, that would he see an he might. And ever Sir Launcelot would give him gold to spend, and clothes, and so did Sir Gawaine, and where there were any masteries done, thereat would he be, and there might none cast bar nor stone to him by two yards. Then would Sir Kay say, How liketh you my boy of the kitchen?"* (Malory VII, 2)

We left Cob and his palfrey at his house in the village, graciously enduring another round of blessings and compliments from the eager charcoal burner. At last I told him to say extra prayers for the good Queen, though without telling him why she needed them, and we rode on through the village to the castle.

The Duke de la Rowse had been Arthur's enemy until Gareth Beaumains won him to our side. I doubt his change of allegiance had ever made much difference in his life. De la Rowse had not been among the active rebels in the old days. He had simply sat more or less at home in his castle, fighting any of Arthur's knights who happened to come by. Though the Duke had offered us battle "for hatred of Arthur," he had been no more violent about it than certain others who offered us battle "for love." Gareth had not even found any prisoners in Rowse Castle, since the Duke used to let anyone who survived a bout with him ride on to challenge Ironside at Dame Lyonors' Castle Dangerous—which amounted to sending them to their deaths, but it was their choice. De la Rowse used to remark that if it had not been for love of his wife and dislike of leaving her a widow, he would have ridden on to the neighboring castle and had a go at Sir Ironside himself. Then, too, he claimed, turning his prisoners free had saved him having to feed them, whether they rode on to Castle Dangerous or not.

The night Gareth had come to Rowse Castle, the Duke was off somewhere, looking for adventures, and the Duchess very politely gave Gareth hospitality in return for his promise to yield himself prisoner to her husband if he happened to come across him somewhere. Gareth graciously gave his word, careful to reserve the right of self-defense if, instead of gently taking him captive, the Duke seemed about to offer him injury. When Gareth met the Duke a few days later, De la Rowse considerately insisted on fighting, thus giving our brave Beaumains the chance to defeat him and send him to Arthur's court. De la Rowse brought his dame and his knights, went through the forms of pledging fealty to Arthur and Gareth, had a pleasant visit, and then they all returned home and went on pretty much as before, except that now De la Rowse challenged Arthur's knights for love and did not need the excuse of saving expenses or allowing them a chance at another local champion in order to let them go. Now it was the King's enemies whom De la Rowse fought for hate, when they happened to come by; but if he defeated them he sent them on to us on their parole, and if they defeated him, as happened now and then, he had kept the fighting-for-hate enough of a formality, and the actual proceedings sufficiently jovial, that his opponents were willing to extend him mercy for the asking and ride on their way.

It was still daylight when we arrived in Rowse Castle. The fog was finally beginning to lift a little, enough to see more than two spearlengths ahead, and the Duke, predictably, proposed a friendly joust or two for old times' sake. Mordred declined, but I was glad of the chance to practice.

"Foolhardy, Seneschal," said Mordred, riding along beside me as I trotted Feuillemorte around the small field below the castle, getting the feel of a lance again while waiting for the Duke to arm.

"An hour's combat with De la Rowse is the safest practice a man can take with unblunted weapons," I replied.

"Unfortunate injuries happen even on the practice field and even with blunted weapons. Should you be killed or maimed—"

"The Duke's an old man. He could have retired honorably from the field years ago, if the old fool didn't enjoy it too much."

"Older knights are the best jousters, of course," Mordred persisted.

"When they're about my age, yes. Not when they're as old as De la Rowse."

Mordred smiled and twisted the serpent ring on his

finger. "Nevertheless, if you should end this evening killed or laid up in bed nursing an improbable wound, do you fully trust me to continue our quest for the Dame of the Lake, Lancelot, and the Queen's salvation?"

"Damn you, Mordred, De la Rowse is hardly worth fighting for the exercise." I closed my visor.

"Then at least hold your blood-red horse back a little," said Mordred. "Feuillemorte's too fast for this fog. Let him run unchecked and you'll be on the duke before either of you has time to aim or avoid."

I put Feuillemorte into a gallop, letting Mordred get out of the way however he chose.

De la Rowse came out, armed and pitifully eager; but his age showed in the way his lance quivered slightly during the first charge. I took pity and aimed my point to glance off his shield, so the first round both of us stayed in the saddle. By the second charge, the old man seemed to have got his palsy under control, but it would have made no difference if my weapon had not shattered at the impact—a perfect strike loses its effect when the blasted lance is flawed and breaks. The dozen or so of the Duke's people who stood around at a safe distance squinting through the mist cheered as if it was their lord's skill and not my bad luck and the incompetence of the lance-maker that unhorsed me. It did not take me long to win back the field once we got to the swordplay on foot. The watchers-on cheered again, this time more politely than enthusiastically; the Duke and I went through the forms of seeking and granting mercy, then his castle folk helped him up and accompanied us inside while the villagers went back down to their own cots for supper.

While helping me unarm, Gillimer took the chance to display his courtly tact. "It's a good thing you waited to joust with a palsied graybeard, Sir. My lord Bellangere the Proud might have killed you in the first fall."

"Instead of making sport of the Duke's beard, you should pray you're half the man he is at that age. If you survive so long. He had experience on his side. And luck."

"You had luck, too. It was luck that his lance didn't hold all the way through your shield and into your side, Sir."

"At least a craftsman made my shield, even if a lazy slackard, probably a kinsman of yours, made that rotten lance I was using."

"You bore your shield very well, Sir," said Gillimer, as if he were an instructor and not a semi-competent student. "Strange, how shield-play seems to stay in a man's arm longer without practice than does skill with a lance."

"When you're forty years older, you might know something of what you're talking about. Until then, keep quiet and hide your ignorance."

"Yet it's odd how even the younger and less experienced knights have such good luck when they joust against you, Sir." Gillimer had begun as a coddled, over-sensitive page. He now had sensibilities of leather.

"Maybe you think you're going to goad me into dubbing you to be rid of you," I said. "Well, don't look forward to that day until you're sure you're ready, because as soon as you're knighted, I'll teach you how to take twenty falls in a row, and it won't be for practice."

He grinned and started whistling as he piled up my armor ready for the next day.

"You may think of yourself as another Sir Cote Male Taile or Gareth Beaumains," I went on, "but at least they kept their tongues respectful until they were safely knighted."

Not that I did not secretly prefer Gillimer's honest

disrespect to the silk-mouthed humility of another Cote Male Taile or Gareth Beaumains, who had sat in the background ashes, meek and undemanding, requesting no special consideration whatever—except that Arthur or Lancelot dub them knight at command, with no advance proof of their skill, training, or blood—and give them, while still untested, the first dangerous quest that offered.

La Cote Male Taile had at least announced at once that he was of good family, though he declined to go into full particulars, and had requested the accolade on the same day he arrived, with a story that he wanted to avenge his father's murder (though, as it turned out, that pressing business had to wait until the new knight could indulge himself in a peripheral adventure or two). Gareth Beaumains, however, had not only come to court refusing to tell his name—which was understandable if all he wanted was to make his own reputation without relying on the fame of his older brothers—but almost insisting on spending a year in the kitchen as a scullion, as if all he wanted was food and drink and a place to keep his toes warm. That was carrying humility a little too far. What Beaumains was in fact doing was preparing a nice soft bed for himself. After starting as he did, he might have turned out a worse warrior than Meliagrant and folk would still have called him a marvel: the scullion who could ride a warhorse and hold a lance, even if to no other purpose than to die like a knight.

Beaumains had had plenty of training and practice at home in Orkney, though he kept quiet about it; he must have known he was good enough with his weapons to have won a reputation without resorting to such tawdry Cinderella tricks.

The rumor started afterwards that Gareth or his mother Dame Morgawse had secretly revealed his identity to his uncle Arthur, or that Gawaine had recognized him and kept the secret, telling only the King. In fact, Gawaine, Agravaine, and Gaheris had not seen their younger brother all the time he was growing to early manhood, and he took care to avoid them as much as possible. Artus let my young knave of the kitchen go with Dame Lynette to rescue her sister because he took a dislike to her and thought it would be a good jest to play on a young shrew. Besides, Lancelot was following to test Beaumains and take up the quest if the scullion proved unworthy. Even so, Artus probably felt a little ashamed of the trick he put on Lynette; at least, he made no attempt to stop me from going after Beaumains and testing him myself before Lancelot caught up with us.

What people overlook is that for every Gareth Beaumains or Sir La Cote Male Taile or Percivale de Galis who comes to us looking like a tatterdemalion and turns out to be a fine man of arms and maybe even a prince in disguise, there are thirty who turn out to be ragged tatterdemalions whose only pretensions to skill at arms is in their daydreams. If we knighted all of them for the asking, we would have a court full of warriors stumbling over their own swords and asking each other the difference between greaves and cuisses, and all going hungry and rusty for lack of enough workers left to till the fields and man the forges. Sometimes the petitioner is so obviously bumble-fingered that Arthur simply laughs and sends him back to his village with the price of a new cow; sometimes Gawaine or Ywaine or Lucan takes the fellow aside and quietly talks him out of it; occasionally, when the would-be knight is more attracted by the ideals than the actual arms, one of the bishops or chaplains recruits him for the clergy. But when the King is in one of his sportive moods, or when everyone remembers Gareth Beaumains, Sir La Cote Male Taile, Tor the bastard of Pellinore, or Percivale Pureheart and decides that the present ragged robin from the ditches looks like another golden champion beneath the mud—and hard work does develop hard muscles—then someone has to speak up and stop the farce. People forget the peasant lads who are sent home by the King or by a council of his knights acting in agreement. They also forget the ones who give up and go home after the seneschal is through with them, whether a tongue-lashing suffices or whether I have to administer a few buffets and bruises as well—sometimes I am the only man at court willing to demean himself by jousting against some ambitious buffoon that a page could unhorse with a toy spear. But the one time in twenty or thirty that the tatterdemalion turns out to be a fighter and gives the seneschal a fall—that, folk remember. Especially since the new prodigy stays around for years as a knight among knights and a constant reminder that Kay made another mistake. Not that Kay tested the candidate and proved him worthy, but that Kay played the churl again and was justly repaid for misjudging his man.

People also forget that for one Gareth Beaumains, the scullion who turned out to be a hero almost as great as Lancelot, the boy who sat in the kitchen for a year, pretending to be busy, making a mess of his work since he was as clumsy with spits and kettles as a true-born peasant is with swords and lances, screwing up his eyes to Heaven and acting like a meek, patient little martyr at every correction, and then turning on me for a bully at his first chance and, like a true mirror of chivalry, leaving me unconscious and bleeding with his lance head in my side while he rode off with my own lance and shield (and I had used to praise him when he showed off his strength throwing stones and bars in the yard, the one thing he proved himself good at during his year as scullion)—for one Beaumains, there are several score clumsy young loafers who never would learn their duties and keep to them without a measure of tongue-basting. The court may have laughed and cheered when Gareth Beaumains got his revenge on the rude-tongued bully of a seneschal; but they would not be so merry if their food came to them spoiled, meager, and badly cooked, their horses and hawks suffered from bad stabling and mewing, their various belongings turned up lost and broken due to bad packing for our moves from city to city, if the furniture was left cracked, records were mislaid, inventories inaccurate, and the court in general falling apart because the seneschal was going around careful to speak courteously and gently to every thick-fingered shirker of a servant who might have his feelings hurt by a rebuke.

Chapter 15
The Opinions of the Duke de la Rowse on Sir Ironside, Sir Astamore, and Others as Possible Poisoners

"So he departed, and by fortune he came to a mountain, and there he found a goodly knight that bade him, Abide sir knight, and joust with me. What are ye? said Sir Gareth. My name is, said he, the Duke de la Rowse. Ah sir, ye are the same knight that I lodged once in your castle; and there I made promise unto your lady that I should yield me unto you. Ah, said the duke, art thou that proud knight that profferest to fight with my knights; therefore make thee ready, for I will have ado with you. So they let their horses run, and there Sir Gareth smote the duke down from his horse. But the duke lightly avoided his horse, and dressed his shield and drew his sword, and bade Sir Gareth alight and fight with him. So he did alight, and they did great battle together more than an hour, and either hurt other full sore. At

> *the last Sir Gareth gat the duke to the earth, and would have slain him, and then he yield him to him. Then must ye go, said Sir Gareth, unto Sir Arthur my lord at the next feast, and say that I, Sir Gareth of Orkney, sent you unto him. It shall be done, said the duke, and I will do to you homage and fealty with an hundred knights with me; and all the days of my life to do you service where ye will command me."* (Malory VII, 32)

De la Rowse was a sensible man. He admired Gareth as a fighter—the better you can consider the man who defeats you, the more honorable it makes your own defeat—but he did not adulate him to idolatry, as Bellangere the Proud adulated his dead conqueror Lamorak de Galis. That, and the fact that nobody considered Gareth of the Clean Hands likely to have poisoned anybody's food, enabled us to discuss matters much more reasonably at Rowse Castle than we had at Arlan. We also managed to put off discussion of the serious news from court until after supper, when we had moved to the fireside in the Duke's chamber, where Mordred, having found a suitable gnarl of wood, began carving another of his ugly coiled serpents. At least I preferred seeing him do that to seeing him make straw dolls and toss them into the flames.

"You were here in the neighborhood during Ironside's career of infamy, Rowse," I said, after explaining the situation at court. "Do you remember any hint, any quirk in his character, any special act of treachery, to suggest the giant's son might be capable of using poison to fulfill his old vow?"

"I'd thought Ironside fulfilled it already, years ago," said the Duke. "Didn't he have a joust and some swordplay with both Lancelot and Gawaine for form's sake before he joined your Table?"

"Yes, he fought them, among others, at the tournament our King held at Dame Lyonors' castle," said Mordred. "But a joust in friendship hardly fulfills a vow of vengeance."

De la Rowse shook his white head. "When Ironside was the Red Knight of the Red Lands, he vowed to take vengeance on all King Arthur's knights for the sakes of Lancelot and Gawaine until he met one or other of those two. And to hang all those he defeated in the meantime, as I recall. I don't remember that he actually vowed to kill Lancelot and Gawaine, but only to hang them when and if he defeated them. Well, he fought them, and he didn't defeat them, but he would have done all he'd vowed simply by meeting them in the field and fighting 'em."

"It was Lancelot he was really after, whether his former leman knew it or not," said Mordred. "She knew that 'the greatest knight of Arthur's court had killed her brother,' but she did not know which of the two greatest knights that was. Gawaine does not ride in disguise. He bears his own shield whenever he can, and he tells his name on demand. He also remembers and confesses very diligently all whom he has fought. Ironside's lady would have known it beyond doubt if her brother had been slain by Gawaine. Since she was not sure, it must have been Lancelot, riding anonymously again, except to let it be known he was Arthur's man, and forgetting one or two of his casual victims among the crowd of killed, maimed, and wounded."

"What matters," said the Duchess de la Rowse, "is not which it really was who killed the brother of Sir Ironside's lady, but that neither the lady nor her knight knew for sure. However, it's all done with long ago. I cannot think that Sir Ironside would decide all at once, after so many years, that his old vow had never been fulfilled."

"It's not unusual for Lancelot to disappear from Court without leaving word," I said, "but it's an uncomfortable coincidence that someone tried to poison Gawaine so soon afterwards. Maybe Ironside's gone back to the side of the Sesnes."

The Duke beckoned a servant to pour him more ale. "Even if Ironside did cast in with his father's people again, or develop a bad conscience about keeping his vow, he'd attack Arthur's right-hand man openly. The only reason for keeping a vow is honor. A man wouldn't use dishonorable means to do it."

"The vow itself included shameful death," said Mordred. "Someone may yet discover our brave Lancelot hanging by his noble neck from a tree, like Ironside's forty conquests at Castle Dangerous. And poison is almost as shameful a death as hanging."

"Maybe the words of that vow left Ironside a way to wriggle out from under it honorably," I said, "but the spirit of the thing obviously meant, 'Kill them.' "

"The words of a vow *are* the spirit," said De la Rowse. For him, no doubt they were. He had yielded to Gareth and shifted his allegeiance to Arthur as genially as he would no doubt have shifted it again to any other lord whose knight happened to conquer him in fair fight.

"Maybe," I persisted, "but there was something very strange about that vow of Ironside. He had made it to his light-o'-love, but he was keeping it at the castle of another lady."

"Ah, you men!" said the Duchess. "And you accuse us women of over-much romancing. Why do you all assume the Red Knight of the Red Lands was besieging Dame Lyonors to make her wed him?"

"As I recall, the Red Giant himself told Gareth so," said Mordred.

"Maybe he said that, knowing it was not like to happen," replied the Duchess, "but the truth of it was that Sir Ironside only set up at a castle to fetch the champions to him there, and he knew they'd come soonest to rescue a besieged, unwed lady. He did not break his heart for Dame Lyonors afterwards, did he?"

"No, but neither did he ever come forward with this former love of his," I said. "A man who would hang forty knights for love of a dame should have loved her enough to go back to her."

The Duchess remained unperturbed. "Perhaps the poor dame died. Or perhaps he would not reveal her to the clacking tongues at court. Or perhaps she would not come, but broke with him of herself when he went over to her enemies."

"Or perhaps," I added, "she was a convenient story to excuse his murders, and never existed at all."

"Why, in that case," said the Duchess, "likely as not he never made a vow against Lancelot and Gawaine, either."

The Duke settled back in his chair. Ironside was no longer his problem neighbor, and his sovereign's court was far away from his own life. "No, no, my lads, you're scenting down the wrong spoor. Ironside was never a bad fellow, when all's said and done. No, not even when he was the Red Knight of the Red Lands besieging pretty Dame Lyonors. He didn't hang those knights up alive, y'know. Used to strangle 'em on the ground if they weren't already dead of their wounds. And he let all their squires go."

"Very generous of him," I said. The executioner would probably slip up, ten days from now, throw a cord around Dame Guenevere's white throat, and strangle her at the stake before lighting the pyre, to be merciful.

Mordred glanced up from his carving. "What do you think of . . . say . . . Sir La Cote Male Taile as a poisoner, your Grace?"

The Duke blinked, leaving it to his wife to ask, "Sir La Cote Male Taile? But what malice would he hold against Sir Gawaine?"

Mordred held his handiwork up, turning it between forefinger and thumb to examine it in the firelight. "Interesting, how because brother Gawaine loves apples and pears, all folk assume the poisoned fruit was meant for him and not for another of us."

"Certain of Gawaine's brothers," I explained, "managed to kill Sir La Cote Male Taile's brother Dinadan in a grudge battle during the Grail Quest."

"Dinadan. Yes, yes, we'd heard he was gone." The Duke was sufficiently saddened to motion for more ale.

"I think, though, that we had forgotten it," said the Duchess. "He's a hard man to think of as dead and gone. So laughing and full of pleasant mockeries."

In my mouth, Dinadan's pleasant mockeries would have been called churlish sarcasm. But Dinadan had been as ready to laugh at himself as at anyone else, and never afraid to refuse a superfluous fight and be taunted for cowardice. "He had some sense," I said. "Something besides long hair to keep his brains from rattling in his helmet."

The Duchess smiled. Being married to a man who had spent his life fighting for the sport of it at every opportunity, she could probably appreciate Dinadan's good sense, though she had only met him the two or three times she and the Duke came to court. "Sir Dinadan would hardly wish to be avenged with poison. He would return to haunt his avenger."

"La Cote wouldn't play the traitor anyway," said De la Rowse. "He'd avenge his brother with lance and sword, the same way he avenged his father."

"We were not all of us so enamoured of Dinadan's character," said Mordred. "Nor has anyone been able to guess why La Cote Male Taile does not attempt to avenge his brother with honorable lance and sword, as he eventually avenged his father. True, he took a very great while avenging his father; but at that time he had to beg his knighthood first and then go in search of his father's killers. His brother's killers he has at hand, ready for him, and he is already a knight to attack them."

"Maybe he doesn't want to attack his fellows of the Table," I said, and added, before it came out more plainly which of Gawaine's brothers had killed Dinadan, or before our host and hostess realized it to their embarrassment, "What about Bors deGanis, agreeing to fight for the Queen after all her dinner guests had been, in effect, disqualified?"

"Can he not fight for her in the name of his kinsman Lancelot, rather than in his own?" said the Duchess.

"He can, but it's a very thin covering," I replied.

The Duke shrugged. "Only a guiltless man would be so willing to accept the appearance of guilt."

"In other words, then," I said, "Bors is letting us know he's upright enough and blameless enough to stand an appearance of guilt which would destroy any of us lesser mortals."

"Calm yourself, calm yourself, Seneschal," murmured Mordred. "We know you would have offered yourself as her champion if you had thought of these things before Bors. And what do you think of Pinel of Carbonek or Astamore of Gorre, your Grace?" he added in a louder voice.

"Pinel and Astamore? Don't believe I know 'em."

"Pinel," I told the Duke, "is a loudvoice nephew of King Pellam of Listeneise. Hence, either a nephew or a bastard son of Pellinore of the Isles. Pellam raised him at Castle Carbonek, and he tagged along with Lancelot back to us after the adventures of the Sangreal, to Pellam's gain and Arthur's loss."

"Pellam the Fisher King?" De la Rowse dismissed Pinel with a wave of his ale cup. "They don't teach 'em vengefulness and poison at the Castle of the Grail, lad. Who is this Astamore, now?"

"The Grail is no longer at Carbonek, by Lancelot's report and Pinel's," said Mordred. "Bors de Ganis adds that it was translated into Heaven along with the soul of Galahad the Pure, to escape the sin and horror of the latter days to come. Astamore is the nephew of Bagdemagus of Gorre."

The Duke and Duchess looked blank. "Gawaine killed Sir Bagdemagus by mischance, during a joust for love on the Grail Quest," I explained.

De la Rowse sighed and tsked.

"The land of Gorre lost a noble king," said the Duchess. "Who rules it now?"

"Officially, Uriens took it back," I said. "He wanted to give it to his legitimate son Ywaine of the Lion, but Ywaine is too happy dividing his time between his own castle with Dame Laudine and the King's court with cousin Gawaine. So Bagdemagus' daughter Dame Clarisin is acting as lady vice-regent."

"Leaving Astamore in the cold, eh? Did Astamore have any claim to the vice-regency?"

I shrugged. "No more than Dame Clarisin, but Astamore doesn't seem particularly ambitious."

"Can't always tell. Sometimes it lies hid, they say. Well, your young Astamore may have complaints against King Uriens and his kinswoman, but I don't see he has any against Gawaine. Chances of combat."

"Yet ambition may twist a man's thoughts into strange patterns," said the Duchess, probably speaking from books of romance and philosophy. Then she glanced at me and blushed. Sometimes news is so scarce in these self-sufficient little castles that old stories stay fresh for a couple of generations. Especially in the minds of the older folk. (I remember how it was in my own father's castle, before we knew we were raising a High King.) The Duchess had obviously just remembered the affair of the Sword in the Stone, and feared her philosophical platitude about ambition twisting men's thoughts would be taken personally by present company.

Yes, when Artus came to me bringing the Sword, putting it into my hands, I probably did develop a sudden overpowering itch to sit in the throne of Britain. But, Sweet Jesu! An untried boy, not yet fifteen years old, who brings his elder brother Merlin's famous Proof of Kinship as if he is completely unaware that the whole gathering and furor all around him—the only reason for us being in London at all—is to see who can pull this same Sword out of its blasted anvil and rock, who seems to think of it as no more than another weapon to use in the tourneying . . . What man would *not* have thought he could make a better High King than this slowheaded squire? And when I remarked on the Sword's importance, when he finally realized what he had done and as good as begged me, like a half-frightened child, to let him slip it back and not tell anyone . . . well, maybe I should have let him do that, instead of trying to pretend I had been the one to draw the Sword; but that would have left us in the same turmoil we had already been in for years. Trying to take the credit myself for drawing the Sword had seemed the sensible thing to do; I was a young fool, too, at the time, not much older than Artus.

"Don't worry, Dame," I said. "You'll have to work harder than that if you want to throw the Sword in the Stone back in my teeth."

"Sir Kay was wise enough," said Mordred, "to see the hollowness of the crown and settle for the office of seneschal instead."

"Where I have most of the work and none of the glory."

"Exactly. The King's invisible but invaluable errand-boy." Mordred put down his knife and held up his right hand to show he spoke in friendly jest. His smirk half belied the gesture. "But we stray from our serious discussion," he went on. "What would you think of, say, Gaheris of Orkney as a poisoner?"

"Nay, nay!" said the Duke. "When you start accusing your own brothers, then it's plain the serious talk is done with."

"True." Mordred rose and sheathed his knife. "And the sooner we're abed, the earlier we can ride in the dawning. Here, Seneschal, I find I've carved this ring too large for my finger. It may fit yours." He tossed his latest serpent ring into my lap.

That night I dreamed someone had found Lancelot hanging from a yew tree, his body cut off at the waist and moss growing in his beard. I was fighting as the Queen's champion against Bors de Ganis. He ran me through in the second or third charge. Artus was screaming at me for a traitor and throwing things at me . . . those strange things you glimpse in dreams and know to be foul, but cannot quite recognize. Then I was at the stake, standing in the middle of the faggots, tied face to face with Guenevere. Her face was horrible, expressionless, as if she had lost her mind and feeling . . . like the face of her false look-alike when Heaven had struck her with paralysis and she took months to decay alive in her bed. Except that this was the true Guenevere. Her face was stiff, but her arms were passionate, pulling me closer to her, into her. I realized Bors' splintered lance was still in my side, piercing the Queen. I tried to pull away, but she held me fast, skewering herself, murmuring that the sword was swifter than the flame. Her lips did not move as she spoke. Holding her tightly to me, I looked around and saw it was not Arthur throwing things at us, but Mordred. I turned back to kiss Guenevere, and her face was already burned away to the skull, only her eyes staring back at me, perfectly round, the gray irises surrounded top and bottom by rings of white beginning to melt down on the blackened cheekbones.

I awoke screaming. I had not awakened screaming at a nightmare for years. Mordred was in the next chamber and heard it.

"And will you not do something to prevent it's coming true?" he asked next day. "As your foster-brother the King did something about his serpent nightmare the year of my birth?"

"I am doing something to prevent it. We've been working to prevent it for the last four days. And I don't have any Merlin at my elbow to interpret every bad dream as a direct prophecy."

"And yet you saw me instead of the King, standing beyond the fire to pelt you with unpleasant things. Well, you might ask Dame Nimue of the Lake to interpret it for you."

"The reason you got into it," I said, "is because I've had to look at your smirking face all day, every day for the last four days and because of that damn serpent ring you tossed me last night."

He smiled. "Yes, I do suffer from a fascination with serpents, do I not? Well, I suppose it must have been a shower of my little serpents with which I was pelting you in your dream."

Chapter 16
The Battle at the Lake

"That is the Lady of the Lake, said Merlin; and within that lake is a rock, and therein is as fair a place as any on earth, and richly beseen . . ." (Malory I, 25)

We pushed ourselves, or maybe I was the one who insisted on keeping up a hard pace, and got to the Lake about sunset that same day.

"It looks like any ordinary lake," said Lovel, standing up in his stirrups as if that would give him an appreciably longer view of its surface.

"Of course it does," I said. "You can drink the water and quench your thirst, row a boat on it and catch fish —or swords, if you're lucky enough—and if you wade in over your head, you'll probably drown. But somewhere beneath that water is a city richer than Caerleon, and if Dame Nimue should deign to guide us there, we'll breathe as easily as up here."

"Will we see the blue sky and the clouds, too?" asked Gillimer. "Or will we see little fishes instead of birds swimming over our heads?"

"Ask Lancelot, if they ever bring him back to court," I said. "He was raised in a Lake identical to this one, over in France."

"One of the oldest pieces of magic on earth," said Mordred, gazing out over the reddened water, with the sun, half-buried in clouds, touching the hills on the far side. "The City in the Lake, ruled always by a lady—sometimes a wicked dame, sometimes a kindly one, always a powerful one. I think the first Lady of the Lake must have been Adam's paramour Lilith. A glamoury older than Merlin. Perhaps the great mage himself was taught by one of Dame Nimue's predecessors, as he in turn taught Nimue and Aunt Morgan. They say that much of the old magic can only be taught to a man by a woman, and to a woman by a man."

"You're waxing poetic this evening," I said.

"Why should I not? I hardly expected ever to see this night."

"What does that mean?" I said. "You knew we were coming here to the Lake."

He turned in his saddle and looked at me. "I admit to some curiosity as to whether you really did mean to come here eventually; but it was a curiosity I curbed, not expecting to be alive when and if you reached our supposed destination."

"What in Jesu's Holy Name are you talking about?"

Mordred waded his palfrey fetlock-deep into the water. "What is your plan, now you've brought me this far?" he called back over his shoulder. "To drown me in the illusory Lake before calling up Dame Nimue? Or perhaps you mean to deal somehow with her to do away with me as she did away with Merlin?"

"Damn you, Mordred, have you gone completely out of your mind?"

He turned his horse, its hooves splashing in the water,

and sat facing me. "Come , Seneschal. The game has almost reached checkmate. Why did you choose to ride with me, if not to finish the work the poisoned apples failed to do?"

"We chose to ride with each other . . . God, Mordred, you've had me on your list of suspects all along!"

"Not quite. I've been all but assured it was you from the beginning. The others were merely possibilities I saw when I tried to examine the situation as an unconcerned scholar. I could not allow my thoughts to stagnate in an obsession with my own approaching death."

I tried to keep my temper, remembering that, after all, I had secretly had Mordred high on my own list of possible traitors all along. "Your brains are even more rattled than we thought. What gave you the idea you were important enough to attract an assassin?"

"Was Sir Patrise important enough to attract an assassin?"

Gillimer said, "But the apples were meant for Sir Gawaine."

"So you were all meant to believe," said Mordred. "Folk remember Gawaine's tastes. The rest of us love fruit, too, but whereas bowls of apples and pears are always brought out especially for Gawaine, his less important brothers must wait their chances. No one would put out a bowl of fruit for Agravaine or Mordred, if Gawaine were not at the same meal. It happens that I have an especial fondness for pears, which were also in that bowl and also, presumably, poisoned—though the Queen and her adoring Seneschal destroyed them before I could make the test. My death, like Patrise's, would have been charged to an attempt on brother Gawaine's life. Clever of you, Sir Seneschal."

Even after he finished his speech, I waited a moment to make sure I could keep my voice steady. Lovel sat pushing his palms along his saddle until the pommel squeaked beneath them. Gillimer had apparently decided he would be safer witnessing the discussion quietly than thrusting more of his own opinions into it.

"Clever and pointless," I said at last. "If someone wanted to kill you, Mordred, what reason would he have for wanting it to look like an attempt on Gawaine? God, don't you have enemies of your own to kill you in open tourney or ambush?"

He seemed to wince, but talked on. "Granted, the need to make it seem an attempt on my brother was not essential. But why should you not use a method so convenient? Why not take all the precautions available against the right questions ever being asked, the truth found out?"

"What truth? If you're talking about your lunatic fancies as 'truth,' they're a pile of dead flies!"

"Then, too, Gawaine would avenge a brother's death, even brother Mordred's, if he could learn the murderer. Convince Gawaine that he himself was the target, and he would be less likely to seek vengeance or even knowledge of who had made the attempt. Certainly he would never believe it of his old comrade Kay, let alone of the Queen. Oh, yes, you were clever. Unfortunate that your plan failed and that the bullhead Mador de la Porte further complicated matters for you."

"And suppose I'd killed Gawaine, too? Suppose I'd killed half the men present? God, the Queen herself might have eaten—"

"Hardly," said Mordred. "Whom are you trying to convince with your bluster, Seneschal? Lovel and Gillimer?"

"You really think I'd risk poisoning the Queen, Gawaine, and a score of Arthur's best knights, only to rid the court of *you*?"

"You risked no more than one or two lives at most," said Mordred. "Patrise proved that. The advantage of quick poison over slow water and a leaky ship. But you should feel heavy for Patrise's death. You might have prevented it, since he was beside you at table. I suppose you were concentrating your attention on me, at your other hand. As for Gawaine, he was in very little danger. The Queen was at his elbow with more competent devices than yours to keep the wrong man from tasting—"

"You're accusing Her Grace!"

Mordred only shrugged. "You had to learn it from someone, the reason I must be destroyed. And you would willingly go to Hell for Dame Guenevere, would you not?"

"Come out of the water and arm yourself," I said. By Heaven, maybe he thought me an incompetent poisoner, but he was going to learn a few things about slandering the Queen in my presence!

Lovel was white and shaky. This was a family matter to him, with Gawaine his father. I doubt he was much help to his uncle Mordred that evening. For once, even Gillimer had the sense to keep his silence while arming me and holding Feuillemorte's stirrup.

If we had been travelling that day fully armed and on our warhorses, I would have gone beserk and charged Mordred in the water. It was as well we were forced to take a few moments to prepare. He had advance warning to be on his guard, but I had a chance to use my battle-rage rather than let it use me, and to study the lay of the land.

Most areas would have been almost too dark for a good fight by now, but the Lake was surrounded by a narrow beach of white sand, even marked by ripple lines. No detail omitted. We charged on the strip of beach.

Mordred's horse stumbled in the sloppy sand at the water's edge, but he got in a lucky hit before he went down. I landed on dry sand, Mordred half in the water. He shook himself like a dog when he stood up, drops flying from his armor. "How does it go?" he called out, drawing his sword. "The son of a mare has failed me, but the son of my mother will not!"

All the same, he stood there waiting, the water hissing against his greaves, and I had to wade in after him.

Mordred might have been feeling suicidal, but he did not let it slacken his arm. We fought everywhere between chest-deep and back onto the grass beyond the beach. Gillimer and Lovel had work once or twice to keep the horses out of our way, and I wondered afterwards if Dame Nimue had already been watching us and guarding us from getting into her Lake over our heads or stumbling off a ledge into the illusory depths. We each left several chips of metal and a fair amount of blood in the water. My entire right vambrace was gone, and I came close to losing the arm with it, before I got Mordred down in knee-deep water and rashed off his helmet.

"Now," I said, "repeat your slander of the Queen."

"Was that not a better way than poison, Seneschal? More satisfying, and less likely to endanger your own salvation. You must take care to shrive yourself of Patrise's death, of course, accidental or not."

I grabbed a fistful of his golden hair in my left hand. The shadow of my shield blocked out what little twilight had still been hitting his face from the western sky, but I could feel where to slice for his neck.

"One last question," he said. "Satisfy my curiosity. Was it you and the Queen alone, or did you act on the King's command?"

"What in God's Name are you talking about?"

"Ah. So the accusation does not enrage you so much

when made against your foster-brother the King as when made against your foster-brother's wife. Whereby I assume that Arthur was behind you in your attempt."

I tightened my grip and shook, my gauntlet rattling against his forehead and scalp. I got nothing but a groan out of him. "By God," I said, "you're going to tell me what you're talking about or—"

"Strike me quickly, Seneschal. Now, while we're both in the mood."

I released my hold. Several of his hairs caught in my gauntlet as I pulled it away. "Come on," I said. "Let's get out of here before our armor rusts off our bodies."

"You're losing your chance, Seneschal. The King will not thank you for this.

"I don't appreciate being played for a fool and goaded into attacking you like another one of your bloody puppets, Mordred. If you want to be murdered on command, you're going to have to tell me why, convince me you're not a madman. Otherwise, you can just lie down, drown, and damn yourself, for all I care."

I turned and began wading to shore. After a few moments I heard him splash up and follow me. Gillimer and Lovel unarmed us and dried us off in silence.

"If you were counting on Dame Nimue to hear the noise and come up to stop us," I remarked, "it seems you would have been out of luck. Maybe she's not at home."

"I assume," he replied, "that a knight seeking the company of the Lady of the Lake should hail her with no less care and courtesy than one seeking admittance to a lesser stronghold."

The squires built a fire on the beach, which they could have done while we were fighting. Nor had they seen properly to the horses; they had been gawking instead at what they could see and hear of the battle. "Then go take care of them now," I said. "We can't count on being welcomed into Dame Nimue's city and stabling them there for the night." Four palfreys and two chargers would keep Gillimer and Lovel out of earshot for some time.

Mordred and I began searching each other's wounds by firelight. "All right," I said, "are you going to tell me now, or will I have to enlist Dame Nimue to get it out of you with her arts?"

"You rely a great deal on your influence over the Dame of the Lake. Do you truly expect her to do your beck and call?"

"I expect her to stand by the King and court," I said. "She always has before."

"Then let us hope she's at home and heard your call." Mordred shrugged, rather lopsidedly because of his wounds. "Very well, then, I'll assume you do not already know the tale, and tell it, to make you regret the opportunity you gave up a few moments ago."

Chapter 17
Sir Mordred's Tale of the Priest in the Woods

"For she was a passing fair lady, therefore the king cast great love unto her, and desired to lie by her; so they were agreed . . . So there she rested for a month, and at the last departed. . . . But all this time King Arthur knew not that King Lot's wife was his sister." (Malory I, 19)

"Have you ever wondered, Seneschal," Mordred began, "why my name is so different from those of my brothers? Gawaine, Agravaine, Gaheris, Gareth . . . the 'g' runs like a badge through the names of the sons of Lot. Only my name is different—the first half of it inherited from my mother. 'Mor'—the Latin sound for Death. None of my brothers shares that sound, not even Agravaine."

"None of them got part of his name from your father, either," I said. "Gawaine was named for his hermit godfather. I suppose your parents simply found they liked the 'g' sound."

"It occurs in our mother's name, also. Morgawse. My brothers inherited the sound of life from her, I the sound of death."

"You think I tried to poison you because you don't have a 'g' in your name?"

"I am more fully our mother's son than any of my brothers. They had two parents—King Lot and Queen Morgawse. Even though they left their father to join their mother in Arthur's party, they still avenged Lot's death. I had only one true parent—Dame Morgawse."

"If you're stalling in hopes I won't make you get to the point when Lovel and Gillimer come back, Mordred, you're—"

He waved me down. "Do you remember when I first came to Arthur's court? I was bright and eager then, was I not? Filled with pure ideals and noble aspirations—too noble, perhaps."

"At least you came more honestly than your sneaking brother Beaumains with his kitchen-boy act."

Mordred nodded. "Truth, honor, and valor. King Arthur had tried to destroy me in babyhood, but I understood and forgave. It was not me, myself, he had tried to destroy, but a prophecy. Let the parents of the other May Babies hold it against him, let the small drowned souls haunt him if they pleased—I had survived by God's good grace, I had no personal memory of the incident, but I could understand our King's fear of Fate, and I forgave. My brothers were serving their uncle with all their hearts, and my mother comforted me when I mourned that all Arthur's greatest wars were behind him, all his deadliest enemies slain or won to his side without my help. 'There will always be the Saxons from over the sea,' she said, 'and the Romans, ever restive. There is the sly King Mark of Cornwall, and war must come someday with Claudas of France. There is still service to do for your uncle, and honor to win.'

"If I had not understood Arthur's fear of Fate before, I would have understood it from the carved stone in Camelot cathedral. The serpent of my uncle's old nightmare terrified me, as if the nightmare had been my own. I never knelt in Camelot cathedral without praying to God that I might help my uncle crush that old nightmare, and I knelt often those first two years of my knighthood."

"Sometimes I thought you were going to turn into another Bors de Ganis," I said.

"I thought, of course," he went on, "that the nightmare had probably been averted, that the serpent had been drowned along with all the other May Babies. But there was the chance that the two warnings—Merlin's prophecy of the child born in May, and Arthur's dream of the serpent coming forth from his own side—foretold two separate dangers. The May child was safely put away, but the serpent might be the King's bastard Sir Lohot, or Mark of Cornwall, Claudas of France, or even Arthur's viceregent in distant Rome." Mordred smiled, the firelight making a gargoyle mask out of his handsome face. "I was very young and very innocent then, aside from being in love with two or three fair dames and damsels at once. A trait I inherited, no doubt, from my royal father."

Or from his royal mother, but I did not mention that aloud.

"You remember that I rode for a time with Lancelot, during my second year as knight," he continued. "The great Lancelot, brother Gawaine's dearest friend and Gareth's ideal. He praised me more than once for knightly work well done. I earned praise from Lancelot, the right-hand man of my King and Uncle, and I was in ecstasy, poor fool.

"We learned of a coming tournament in Peningues. The night before the tourney we stopped with an old vavasour near the castle. In the early dawn we rode into the forest to hear Mass at a woodland chapel our host knew of on our way. The dawn was clear, the birds trilling their morningsong, God was in His Heaven, and there was glory to be won in a few hours in the lists at Peningues."

Mordred had been twisting a branch of driftwood in his hands, harder and harder. It broke, and he threw the pieces on the fire. "Between our host's manor and the chapel, we found an old priest telling his beads at somebody's marble tomb. We would have passed by in silence, not wishing to interrupt his devotions, but my palfrey nickered.

"The old man glanced up. He squinted for a moment at Lancelot and myself. Then he hailed us as 'the two most unfortunate knights who ever lived.'

" 'This does not promise well for the day's tourney,' said Lancelot, who had never lost a battle in his life.

" 'You do not even know us, good father,' I said. 'How do you know our fate?'

"He pointed first at me. 'You are Mordred, son of Morgawse of Orkney and Arthur the King.'

"I thought at first it was some ugly jest—an enemy had pointed me out to the old man in secret and taught him what to say. I tried to hold my anger, like a good, meek Christian. 'I am the last son of Lot the King, old man. Your wits are wandering.'

" 'You are the son of Arthur the King, your uncle. You are the fruit of incest, heinous in the sight of God and man. You are the serpent who has come forth from the side of the King, to destroy him and eat up all his good works. All your fathers have done good in their lifetimes, but you will do more evil than all your ancestors have done good!' "

Mordred's voice broke and he hid his face in his hands. I wondered how much of his last speech Lovel and Gillimer might have overheard.

After a moment he looked up again, smiling crookedly. "Forgive my outburst, Seneschal. An old wound. I jumped down from my horse and began throttling the old man, trying to choke from him a confession that he was lying. I felt Lancelot's hands on me, pulling me away from the priest, but he was too late. In trying to choke his words back down his throat, I had broken his neck.

" 'God!' said Lancelot. 'You've killed him, and he had a prophecy for me!'

" 'Thank God you did not hear yours,' I said. I thought he would go into one of his battle rages and kill me, but instead he rode on with our host. I stayed for some time at the marble tomb with the priest's body. I think I prayed to be forgiven, but already I understood that his prophecy had been true.

"At last I rode after Lancelot and our host, found them in the forest chapel, and perjured myself by eating the Body of Our Lord. I think I hoped that if I were killed in the tournament that day, and the prophecy cancelled out, it would be a sign I was forgiven and might yet hope for salvation. I told Lancelot, 'No doubt his prophecy for you was that you would kill me.'

" 'That would make me a fortunate knight, not an unforturate one,' he said, and rode away from my side. I tried to be killed in that day's tourney—Jesu, how I tried! For a while I thought I had succeeded." He shrugged. "But they pulled me out and nursed me back to life and wholeness of limb, and so it seems the prophecy is indeed true, and I must fulfill it."

"Your brother Gawaine would have laughed it off

like a sensible man," I said. "And he's as faithful to God and Mary as the best of us."

"Gawaine! Always Gawaine! I am not my brother, Seneschal. Gawaine has a very convenient creed—he adores the sweet comforts of holy faith and ignores the threats—he believes in Heaven, but not in Hell."

"That's why he still wears the hair of that poor dame he killed by accident, and the green sash to remind him of the time he was found a little less than perfect," I said. "Your brother, Mordred, has a grain of sense about prophecies. Of course they'll come true—if a man broods on them until he finds his chance to make them come true."

"And that baron—what was his name?—who tried to discredit Merlin's prophecies? You remember him? How he went to the mage three different times and brought back three different prophecies of how he was to die—hanging, drowning, and falling from his horse. Did *he* watch his opportunity to fall from his horse on a bridge and hang upside-down with the reins around his neck and his head beneath the water, merely to prove Merlin right?"

"Accident," I said. "It worked out nicely for the old prophecy monger, but the baron was a clumsy fool. Chances were very good he'd die in some kind of accident, and if any one of Merlin's three prophecies had come true, it would have been remembered and the other two forgotten. Doing evil is not an accident."

"It was accident that I broke the old priest's neck. It was accident that Gawaine killed Sir Ablamar's lady." Mordred shook his head. "When the priest died without retracting his words, and when I missed death in the Peningues tourney, I knew I was fated to fulfill the prophecy somehow, as surely as Judas was fated to betray Our Lord."

"After travelling with Lancelot's example in front of you, it's hardly surprising you went into a rage and killed the old busybody. What is surprising is that Lancelot didn't go into a rage and kill you."

"Exactly. I suppose at the crucial moment he spared me for Gawaine's sake, or Gareth's, or the old vavasour our host's. But it is ever the same tale. At the crucial moment, every man refrains from killing me, or else fails, and leaves me alive to my Fate. Even you, Sir Kay. Even though I am an unnatural birth—a monster."

"Mordred," I said, "neither of them knew they were brother and sister. Merlin relied on the Sword in the Stone to prove Arthur's claim, and never revealed Arthur's parentage until months later. He had never even told my father whose son Arthur was."

"And perhaps even you did not realize he had gotten into her bed? That was her condition, that it be done with secrecy. I know. I asked my mother. She was alive, then. I still would not fully believe the priest's words, you see, until I had heard from her own lips the possibility that I was Arthur's son instead of Lot's. Oh, they were innocent in their incest—but not in their adultery. What could she do? She remembered what Uther Pendragon had done to her mother Dame Igraine—though she did not know that Arthur was the fruit of that sin—and she did not want her husband to die as Igraine's first husband, her father, had died. Satisfying Arthur's lusts in secret seemed the best way to help fashion peace between him and Lot."

"She couldn't have been particularly displeased with Arthur," I remarked. "She stayed loyal to him afterwards."

"Yes. She might have been his queen, after Lot's death, if they had not turned out to be brother and sister, and if it had not been for Guenevere. But my mother's attempt to make peace might have worked, might have saved King Lot, if it had not been for Merlin's prophecy and Arthur's murder of the May Babies." Again Mordred smiled. "I caused Lot's death. Supposing me to be his own son, Lot went to war a second time against Arthur for my murder. Even if you had succeeded in poisoning me five days ago, Seneschal, I might have somehow fulfilled the prophecy and become the serpent of my uncle-father's dream, even in my very death."

"For the last time, Mordred, I did not try to poison you."

"Perhaps you did not know the tale, after all. You heard me out patiently enough. But it's not unlikely that Lancelot confided it to the Queen, and hardly impossible that either he or she confided it to the King. For years I have been waiting for the stroke to fall, wondering whether they would find their chance to murder me, as Arthur's other bastard was murdered for less reason, before I found my chance to play the serpent. Can you blame me for assuming that it had finally come, or for thinking of you as their tool?"

"If you decide you're going to live up to some foul prophecy," I said, "that's your choice. You can cheat it just as well by refusing to take this chance you think is coming to you someday as by trying to get yourself killed in the meantime. But if you're going to ride with me and try to find out what really happened at the Queen's dinner, you're going to stop doubting that Her Grace is innocent."

He smiled and adjusted the bandage on my right arm. "I will, at least, keep my doubts locked in my own brain. As you do, Sir Seneschal. Meanwhile, shall we try to summon up Dame Nimue and gain her hospitality, or shall we sit here until dawn, bleeding into her white sand?"

I stood. "You might at least have accused me back at court."

"To what purpose?" he replied. "Mador would not believe my notions above his unless I were to explain the full reason for my thoughts. Shall we return to court and tell them all my secret?"

"No." He was right. At most, his accusation, without full details, would result in a double trial, him against me and Mador still hot against the Queen. And if Mordred did tell his story to the court, it would seem all the more evidence against Her Grace.

I had finally had my chance to fight for my own good name, beside the Lake with our two squires as witnesses; and it had not done Dame Guenevere a bloody bit of good.

Chapter 18

The Lady of the Lake

"Right so as they sat there came running in a white hart into the hall, and a white brachet next him, and a thirty couple of black running hounds came after with a great cry, and the hart went about the Table Round as he went by other boards. The white brachet bit him by the buttock and pulled out a piece, wherethrough the hart leapt a great leap and overthrew a knight that sat at the board side; and therewith the knight arose and took up the brachet, and so went forth out of the hall, and took his horse and rode his way with the brachet. Right so anon came in a lady on a white palfrey, and cried aloud to King Arthur, Sir, suffer me not to have this despite, for the brachet was mine that the knight led away. I may not do therewith, said the King.

"With this there came a knight riding all armed on a great horse, and took the lady away with him with force, and ever she cried and made great dole. When she was gone the King was glad, for she made such a noise." (Malory III, 5)

* * *

I went to the water's edge. Except for the ripples that caught our firelight, the Lake was almost invisible under the now-blackened sky.

Having given some thought to the matter, I had decided the simplest summons would be best. I cupped my hands and called Dame Nimue's name several times. The water remained black and untroubled, the ripples continuing to lap unconcerned at my toes.

"Sir," called Lovel from somewhere off to my right, where they had hobbled the horses, "there's a boat here on the beach."

"But there's no hand waving a sword in the middle of the Lake," I shouted back. Groping around, I found a couple of good-sized pebbles. I drew back my arm to throw the first one.

"Do not throw it, Sir Kay," said a voice behind me. "Would you put out the eye of one of my hounds or horses?"

I turned and saw Dame Nimue on the grass beyond the sand. She was dressed in white with a little gold embroidery on her sash and the hem of her skirt, and she let her hair flow loose and golden to her waist as if she were still a maid and not a married woman; and, in fact, she seemed not to have aged a year since the time she first took up with Merlin. But she cast no magical glow although that was the effect she gave at first. She walked across the sand to me, seeming to glide rather than step. Mordred rose and stood respectfully as she passed the fire, and I glimpsed Gillimer and Lovel hanging back at a safe distance to watch.

I made my reverence and said, "How did you get there without us seeing you, Dame? Invisibility?"

"Why should I tell you my craft? No, it was not invisibility, which is less comfortable than you might suppose. In part, it was swift travel."

"Oh. Up the far side and around the shore behind us in the darkness, eh?"

"Not in the darkness. In the sunset."

"You've been here that long?"

"Could I hear two brave knights fighting on the shores of my Lake," she said, "and not come up to watch them?"

"Then you know why we come."

She shook her head, her long hair stirring about her shoulders. "I watch the battles of knights, but I do not eavesdrop unasked on their private conversations. I did not even guess the quarrel was in bitter earnest until you stood so long with your sword at his neck."

"Would you have saved him at the last moment?"

"I suppose so," she said. "He is a companion of the Round Table and a nephew of the King. But I was curious to see what you would do. I was reasonably confident you would not strike him down."

At least Nimue had told the truth about not eavesdropping on our conversation. But if she, like everyone else, thought of Mordred as Arthur's nephew, then I began to doubt how much help her craft could be to us. Unless, not knowing I had just learned Mordred's parentage, she were still referring to him as the King's nephew for my benefit. Or unless Morgawse and the old priest had been mistaken—the issue of Mordred's fatherhood was still clouded, in my mind at least. "If you don't know why we've come," I said, "you're a surprisingly long time in asking."

"You would not have come here, stood on the beach calling me, and threatened to throw stones into the streets of my city, if you did not intend to tell me the reason."

"Why not use your arts to find it out?"

"Why should I do that," she countered, "when you will soon tell me yourself?"

"Because," I said, "we come to ask your help in finding out the truth of certain matters. It would help establish your reliability if you could first tell us about the affair itself."

She turned from me and began very calmly walking into the Lake. The water did not even ripple about her legs.

I splashed in after her. "Oh, no, Dame of the Lake—you're not going to walk away from us like this!"

"I have saved your King's life," she said without turning. "I have saved it three times: from Morgan's ploys with the false Excalibur and the fiery cloak, and from the craft of that poor, love-crazed enchantress Annowre. I have played the guardian for Arthur and his court, as Merlin begged me, even though when I first came to your King, when I was but an ordinary maiden with no skill nor magical craft, Arthur laughed at me and only said, as the ruffian Hontzlake of Wentland kidnapped me screaming from the King's hall, that now they would have peace and quiet from my noise. I do not need to demonstrate my reliability at your command, Sir Kay. No, not even at the command of your High King himself."

We were waist deep now, and the water was cold. "It's not guarding us very well, Dame Nimue," I said, "to let the Queen burn for murder while you play in your Lake with your paramour and never bother to find out what's happening in the world above you."

"Sir Pelleas is my wedded husband by the three rites, ancient, modern, and mystical, and I have never had any other love. I have always known well enough when to come and save your King. Would you prefer I hovered constantly about your corrupt court, muttering in the King's ear, like Merlin?"

"So you only come out to save the King, not the Queen."

She was walking as quickly as if we were on dry land. I had to fight the water resistance to keep up with her. It was almost at my chin now. It should have been half over her head, but her voice came up clearly, with no sound of bubbling or gurgling. "Best go back, Sir Seneschal, before you drown."

I shouted, "Dame Nimue!" and made a grab, catching her arm. She whipped up her other arm and I felt her hand on my forehead, pushing me under. The shock was worse than a lance to the helmet at full tilt—I suppose it was like being struck by lightning—I choked in a mouthful and noseful of water and thought for a moment I had died unshriven. Then she was walking back to shore, pulling me out with her. She had the water's buoyancy to help her haul me; I was half floating (it was a good thing we had stripped out of our armor before I tried summoning her). As for herself, she came up perfectly dry.

When we were about thigh-deep, she set me back on my feet and thumped my back a few times. "Very well," she said. "I know all that was in your head, and you should know now why I dislike gaining such knowledge. It was not pleasant for you, and it was still less pleasant for me. To see all the private sins and passions of another in a single moment! If the confessional were a tenth part so revealing, no man would ever turn priest."

I coughed a little more water out of my lungs. "Next time, at least do it on dry land."

"It could have been worse," she admitted. "But I have no desire to search the minds and souls of twenty-two more knights and five chief servers, not though they may be the cream of Arthur's court."

"Then don't read souls. But do *something* to save the Queen."

"Read Guenevere's soul alone? I might find her innocent of the poison in the fruit, and Sir Mador might believe me and drop his charge against her. But perhaps the King would wish to know what else I had found in his wife, and perhaps he would believe me where he has refused to believe his sister Morgan and the gossipmongers of his court."

"Jesu, Dame, there must be something you can do! There's a viper loose in court."

"There are probably several vipers, and the one who poisoned Sir Patrise may be the least dangerous of all. Well, I will join you again in the morning and come with you. Merlin prophesied ill of Guenevere, and if prophecies are reliable, it might be best for Arthur and his kingdom to lose her now—but she's a kind and noble woman, and I will do what I can."

"We'd all have been better off without these damn prophecies," I said. "Aren't you going to offer us your hospitality, Dame Nimue?"

She laughed. "My Lake? You wish to come down into my Lake and drown? Wet lodgings you would have with my mermaids, Sir Knight!"

"We both know your 'mermaids' have no more scales than you do. We're tired and wounded, Dame of the Lake, and you can cancel out the illusion for us."

"It is not my fault you wounded one another in your silly quarrel. And none of your companions, not even the King himself, no one but my Pelleas has ever seen my city."

"Plenty of our companions have seen your counterpart's Lake city in Gaul. Lancelot and his cousins, Phariance and Leonses their teachers—"

"Poor man! Is your curiosity so hot for what you've been denied? And you men put the blame on Eve and excuse Adam."

"Any woman as reluctant as you to welcome guests

must be ashamed of her household. Your famous city must not live up to its reputation."

"Ask Pelleas," she replied.

"If he ever deigns to come visit his place at the Table again, I may." I lowered my voice. "Dame Nimue, if you read my mind, you know what Mordred told me just before I called you."

"Of course."

"You say you're a friend to Arthur's court. Then do something to show Mordred you don't care a stuffed gnat for that priest's prophecy. Welcome us into your city for the night."

"You forget he's not aware that I know of the prophecy. Shall we tell him?" Nimue shook her head. "A man entering his fourth decade is old enough to choose for himself whether or not to bind his soul to a prophecy. You must look for other safeguards against Mordred than coddling him. But I'll send up a pavilion and servants for your needs. Your hard-working squires may rest tonight." She started to leave, then turned back for a few last words. "You might try bullying Mordred into a better state of soul, Sir Kay. That would be more in your style than sweet words and soft treatment."

"I suppose you can see everything that's in my mind now," I said.

"No, thank the Holy Mother! Only what was stored in your mind at the moment I touched you. But I was interested in learning how nearly I could predict your arguments from what I had found out about you. Goodnight now, sweet knight."

She walked away from me into the Lake. I thought I should have been able to hear her footsteps as if she were walking on a paved road; but no one ever heard Nimue's footsteps, unless she walked on dry leaves. I waded back to the fire.

"You must have had a pleasant tête-à-tête," said

Mordred. "Does the Lady's dear husband know?"

"I wish you one as pleasant. She searched my conscience and now she knows I didn't poison anyone. Something like getting your brainpan stirred with a hot poker. It might shake *your* head straight again."

"Well, she may search my head if she wishes. The secret's festered long enough. Having shriven myself more thoroughly to you than ever to any priest, I may as well share it with Dame Nimue, too. Who knows? I may be able to make it common gossip."

I wondered if he hoped that circulation of the story would hurt Arthur as much as himself. But Gillimer and Lovel were now near the fire, pretending to be busy laying out bread, cheese, and ale, so I changed the subject. "Were you really so sure of my guilt, or were you goading me the way you've set up your brothers to goad your other suspects?"

"I would have been very sure of your guilt indeed if you had swapped off my head as I expected."

Gillimer was the first to see Dame Nimue's people coming out of the Lake, carrying lighted torches and walking through the water as if it were not there: seven assorted serving-men, three damsels and four older women, and four laden mules. Four of the men put up the pavilions, one for us, one for the squires, and even one for the horses; two more men and one woman began cooking a small feast; two women, tsking and shaking their heads, unwrapped the bandages Mordred and I had put on each other and began rubbing our wounds with salve—I suppose they might have been surgeons, but Dame Nimue's magic medicines would have made my page Coupnez a surgeon. One of the maidens served us rare wine to help replace the blood we had lost, and the last pair of damsels, with the seventh man, brought out instruments and provided a musical background, while the oldest woman walked around supervising everything.

Five men, including the minstrel, stayed the night through, keeping a watch that may have been more courteous than necessary. The rest of Nimue's folk, leading the donkeys, returned into the Lake half an hour after supper, a bit to Mordred's annoyance. "Dame Nimue may be a chaste witch," he muttered, "but she need not impose her rules on all her pretty damsels."

"Go to sleep," I said. "You'll need your rest for the morning."

"Your pardon, pure Seneschal. It was the carnal appetites of my father speaking. Not all of us can subsist on the idyllic worship of an unattainable lady."

I fell asleep wondering if it was me in particular he was still trying to goad into killing him, or if any murderer would have done.

Chapter 19
The Search for Morgan le Fay

"Then rode Merlin unto Arthur and the two kings, and told them how he had sped; whereof they had great marvel, that man on earth might speed so soon, and go and come." (Malory I, 11)

Next morning Dame Nimue brought up not only her husband Pelleas, but also a priest to shrive us and say Mass before we started out. It being Sunday, we should not have been travelling at all; neither, of course, should we have fought on Saturday after evensong; but Nimue's priest took both matters very lightly. Nimue herself, wearing an intricate silver pendant that seemed to be a cross set in a pentangle, the whole intertwined with some less Christian symbol, partook of the Sacrament with the rest of us.

She had changed her complexion to one more suited for travel. Whereas last night her hair had been pale gold and her skin almost as white as her gown, today she wore her hair chestnut brown and plaited up demurely beneath a thin silk veil, while her skin was close to Spanish olive. She obviously did not intend to ride in a litter, though she could have if she wished. She was bringing along not only the seven men and seven women from last night, but also her priest and his two acolytes, four extra squires, fourteen laden sumpter mules, extra palfreys for herself and her husband, and a white Spanish warhorse in case Pelleas decided to joust on the way.

"I hope you have enough magic," I said, "to get this mob to Astolat by the appointed day."

"Speedy travel was one of my master Merlin's finest arts, whether alone or with an army," Nimue replied. "Queen Morgan le Fay is one of the chiefest of your suspect traitors, is she not?"

"Yes, if she's still alive," I said.

Nimue smiled. "She's alive. How she will receive us may depend somewhat on her mood at the hour of our arrival, of course; but if I had any serious doubts, you may be sure I would not risk my Pelleas."

Pelleas grinned fatuously and stroked his wife's shoulder; and I thanked God that at least I had made my own free choice where to love. The man had, at one time, showed some kind of spirit, though he had never seemed quite sure what to do with it.

"So Aunt Morgan is still in this world, as much as she could ever be said to be in this world," remarked Mordred. Knowing so much, Dame, have you also been able to see her guilt or innocence?"

Nimue shook her head. "The present may be seen sometimes, with the right tools and a knowledge of where to look. Queen Morgan can likewise read the past in her mirror, but I cannot—I can only search the past in memories, and that is scarcely reliable, when two minds remember the same events differently."

"And the future?" said Mordred.

"It is hardly worth reading the future at all. The

greatest skill in the world can see no more than shadowy outlines of what may, perhaps, come to pass, if all the persons involved do what you would expect them to do, if the wind blows favorably when it should, and if the battle is not lost for want of a horseshoe nail. Any competent general, if he can only read the present accurately enough, can also read the future as well as the most skillful mage."

"Merlin made prophecies that came true in remarkable detail," Mordred insisted.

"One or two," said Nimue. "And a great many that are more vague than the Apocalypse, so that future ages can interpret them however they please. And a great many more that are already forgotten. Me for the honest and useful magic that I can control!" Nimue jumped into her saddle like an acrobat, took both reins in her left hand, and snapped her fingers.

Pelleas handed up to her a small arrow, no longer than her middle finger, and attached to a thin chain. The little dart was winged with owl feathers and seemed to have dark threads or strands of black hair bound around its copper point.

"What's that?" I said.

"A kind of lodestone. As ordinary lodestones point to the north, my dart points toward whomever I wish to find. It is fortunate I have some hairs from Dame Morgan's head." Nimue held the dart up by its chain, dangling it at elbow's length. It spun around and pointed northward.

"It seems you could have used an ordinary lodestone as well," I remarked.

"Only as it chances, Sir Kay. Mount, my lords, and prepare to ride."

I mounted, motioning our squires to do the same. Pelleas and the rest of Nimue's people were already in their saddles. Mordred hesitated. as if sensing there would be no more chance for conversation once we were on the way. "How is it Aunt Morgan gave you the chance to obtain a lock of her hair, Dame of the Lake?"

"Mount first, lad, or you may be left behind," Nimue replied. I suppose she had a right to call him "lad." She must have been almost old enough to be his mother, though she still looked to be in her early twenties. She had also kept her clean-shaven Pelleas to some extent from aging, though he was beginning to go silver at the temples.

Mordred shrugged and mounted.

Nimue lifted both her arms slightly, like a bird preparing for flight. "We exchanged locks of hair once, years ago, Dame Morgan and I."

Then she rocked forward in her saddle to cue her palfrey, and we were off. We seemed to be going at no more than a fast trot, maybe a little smoother than most trots—but I found it wiser not to watch the scenery, which was blurring together into streaks of green and brown as we passed by. A few times, glancing behind, I noticed that Lovel was riding with eyes closed and Gillimer looked a little green. Aside from the scenery slurring past, the ride was easy and no more tiring than a normal day's trot, maybe less so. But, once or twice when I tried to shout back to Gillimer, he paid no attention, and a few times I saw Mordred's mouth moving and nothing, apparently, coming out; so I assume we were moving faster than our words, leaving them behind us on the path.

When we came to a stream or river we had to slow down and ford it at ordinary speeds. Occasionally the forest was too thick for us to whir through heedlessly, and we had to wind between the trees no faster than regular huntsmen. And shortly before midday we paused for two hours while Nimue had her people not only prepare dinner, but pitch a canopy for us to eat beneath. Dame Nimue liked to travel in a style befitting the Lady of the Lake. Nevertheless, even with the pauses and delays, we crossed all Sugales and half Norgales in a single day. The entire time we rode, Dame Nimue held her dart tirelessly up at elbow's length, following in the direction it pointed.

As night fell, a bit prematurely because we were in a deep, heavy wood, Dame Nimue's dart began to glow and hum on its chain. Nimue halted the procession once more, glanced around, called for lights, and sat studying her tiny arrow while her people kindled their torches.

"I hope we find Le Fay early tomorrow," I said, assuming Nimue meant to stop here and pitch her pavilions for the night.

"We will sup with her this evening. I know by my dart that she is very near."

"Oh. I thought it was glowing because of the darkness."

"Yes," said Nimue, "that's the reason for its radiance, although we would need more light than this, or even than our torches, to go on at our daylight speed. It's the hum that tells me the Queen of Gorre is near at hand."

We proceeded at a walk beneath the fir trees. Sometimes they grew so close that the torchbearers, who were now afoot, had to be careful not to set the branches afire. If there was a path, I could not see it, but Dame Nimue kept us going in the direction of her dart, and the thing hummed more and more loudly. Now and then, when we had to turn aside for a detour around some thorn thicket or patch of mire, the dart quieted down; but, as soon as we were back in the way it pointed us, it spoke up again louder than ever. By the time we reached our destination, it was humming raucously enough to have frightened every night creature in the woods far away from us, if the torches had not already done that.

We emerged from the trees into a cleared area and saw the castle looming up across the park. It seemed a small fortress, but in the hands of a mere mortal castellan I doubted it would stand a siege, or even a good, enthusiastic attack. But Le Fay, of course, would have her own defenses. Years ago, she had withstood all her brother's men, archers, and siege weapons when he tried to take back Ringwood, the little castle he had given her near the south coast; and none of us had ever seen more than three knights at a time issue out of Ringwood, and maybe six or seven archers on the walls, rarely bothering to shoot.

Besides, this castle seemed pretty well isolated in the woods, far from any strategic importance, probably invisible unless you stumbled across it by accident while out hunting. Maybe Morgan would have kept it hidden from our sight now if Dame Nimue had not been with us to counteract her spells. Or maybe Morgan herself chose for some quirk of mood to welcome us. Lights burned along the battlements and on each of the three towers, and the drawbridge was already down, with torchbearers waiting in two rows on either side.

As we crossed the drawbridge between the double line of torchbearers, half of whom were smiling damsels, I tried to look beyond them into the moat. Something was splashing in the dark water, but I could not see what it was. Only once, when I glanced back, I saw a scaly head resting on the planks between two torchbearers. It was about as big as a cow, resembled a giant snake with ears, and seemed to be attached to a long, gleaming neck. It also seemed to be watching us with friendly curiosity, like a dog. One of the torchbearing damsels noticed it and gave it a shove with her foot to send it sliding back into the water.

Whatever else the creatures were, they must have been excellent scavengers. The moat smelled fresh and slightly perfumed. As we passed beneath the portcullis, I noticed that it seemed to be made of silver worked into fancy shapes, like an ornamental garden lattice. The courtyard was illuminated with maybe a hundred wax candles and hung around with better tapestries than those they weave in Toulouse. To my surprise, one of the tapestries showed Joseph of Arimathea bringing his followers to Christianize Britain.

"Welcome," said Le Fay. She had appeared at the top of a flight of stone steps. The doorway was dark behind her, and she was dressed in black, so she would not have needed any magical invisibility to slip out and watch us for a few moments unobserved before speaking.

"You see, sister," said Nimue, "I have answered your invitation at last."

Nimue dismounted and started up the steps while Dame Morgan started down. They met halfway and exchanged a sisterly embrace and kiss.

"And this will be my youngest nephew, Mordred, will it not?" Morgan went on, gazing down at him. "How like your mother you look, boy!"

He bowed. "Thank you for likening me to her, Aunt, instead of to my father or brothers."

"May I take it, Madame," I said, "that we're here under a sign of truce?"

"Ah, my good Sir Kay of the caustic tongue." Still half-embracing Nimue, Queen Morgan waved one hand and signalled her servants to start seeing to our needs. "If you look for treachery and insist on having it, my dear Seneschal, then I will oblige you. But if you give me your trust, you may sleep here more safely than in

Caerleon. Nor will you wake on a barren hillside. My house and food are substantial, and most of my people are human."

Chapter 20
The Queen of All Dark Magic

"And King Lot of Lothian and of Orkney then wedded Margawse that was Gawaine's mother, and King Nentres of the land of Garlot wedded Elaine. All this was done at the request of King Uther. And the third sister Morgan le Fay was put to school in a nunnery, and there she learned so much that she was a great clerk of necromancy. And after she was wedded to King Uriens of the land of Gore . . ." (Malory I, 3)

The supper Dame Morgan spread for us seemed substantial enough, her plate was better than any we had for the service of the King himself, and her harper had one of the best voices I have ever heard. I was not sure whether her camaraderie with the Dame of the Lake meant that we were safe, or that Dame Nimue herself was not quite so friendly to Arthur as she had always seemed to be. But since our best hope of learning what we could and coming away again safely lay in Nimue's good faith with us and Morgan's willing compliance, I decided to accept her hospitality as cheerfully as I could, not drink too much, and hope the Sign of the Cross would be enough to protect us from being spirited away like old Merlin.

Mordred seemed to be enjoying himself. Lovel remained nervous, despite the efforts of a pretty serving-damsel to flirt with him over the gold platters and flagons they were carrying; Gillimer, on the other hand, relaxed to the point of carelessness. As at the nunnery and in Rowse Castle, we left the important talk for after the meat.

Supper over, Morgan rose and said, "Of course you will want to hear compline, my lords."

"There are other things besides compline we want to hear, Dame," I said.

"You will want to hear compline first. Pray that you will know what questions to ask afterwards, and how to accept the answers. Besides, it is Sunday."

We heard compline. Morgan trooped along to chapel with us, dipped her hand into the font and signed herself with holy water like any good Christian. She had begun her education in a convent, of course; but I had never known her to keep any custom, conventual, Christian, or courtly, which she did not freely choose to keep.

Her black garments were cut very simply. She would even have looked like a nun if she had worn wimple and veil instead of a small gold coronet and thin black silk veil that let her hair show plainly. Her hair was black, too, and she wore it braided and coiled up; but she had permitted it to begin silvering rather heavily though she had not permitted more than a few wrinkles in her handsome face. (I preferred Dame Guenevere's honest ripening, however.) Aside from the coronet, the keys of the castle at her waist, and a few rings on her long fingers, Le Fay wore only one decoration, some kind of silver pendant that hung by a thin chain around her neck. I never could make out the exact shape of that pendant, but while we were in chapel it looked like a cross.

After compline she dismissed the others, including Pelleas, and led Nimue, Mordred, and me alone up into a small round sollar with a half-open roof and a central hearth instead of fireplace and chimney. Motioning us to sit, she poked up the banked fire and added more wood herself, then sat on a chest and started stroking a dark cat that sprang into her lap. The pendant around her neck now looked like a circle.

"Have you arranged your questions?" she said.

"I had somehow fancied, Aunt," said Mordred, "that you would have abandoned Jesu for older gods."

"There is no older and no other god, nephew. Nor is there any goddess but one, though your churchmen would diminish her state. You worship God under one name and call everyone Pagan who uses another name for the Divine, who builds a theology around other aspects, reads other sacred writings, or finds other symbols than those which your churchmen approve. I join myself to God under all His names, explore all His aspects, study all scriptures, choose myself symbols wherever I find them."

"And also choose for yourself which of God's commandments to keep and which to break," I said.

"I thought we would come to the accusations. How shall I reply, Seneschal? That every woman and every man chooses which commandments must be kept and which ones, in her or his own mind, may be set aside with righteousness? Or that appearances lie, and I have kept all of God's commandments more truly than have most men and women?"

"You'd better stick to the first answer," I said. "You'd have a hard time proving the second. Adultery, attempted murder, treason against the King's person—"

"Adultery? Oh, aye. When my sister Morgawse was wed to Lot, King of Orkney, and my sister Elaine to the King of Garloth, they put me into a convent. I did not wish marriage. I wished to be Jesu's bride. My sisters were golden-haired and lovely, like our mother, the Duchess Ygraine; I was dark and blunt-featured, like our father Gorlois, and also very young, and so Ygraine was able to honor my wish. But as I grew older and happier and more learned in my chosen place, I grew too handsome in the sight of the world to be wasted as a bride of Christ, so Uther Pendragon took me from my convent, despite my mother's protests and my own, and wed me to the young king of Gorre, who wished to be the lustiest of the lusty but had not quite enough honest power for it, so that he must stir himself up with various strange and sometimes barely natural couplings.

"There are two ways of joining oneself with the immortal Power: the path of virginity and that of fertility. I would have chosen the first. In order to consolidate a mortal alliance for a few years' time, my mother's ravisher and new lord destroyed my own decision. I lost the path of virginity, and that not even in the arms of a man I loved, or could have loved, but in the arms of one I disliked at first meeting and soon came to hate. One who could not even be true to me, but, in his search for new ways of arousing his lust, pretended that the same meat every night was tedious and that by indulging in a variety of women he could bring himself back to his wife's bed with a fresh appetite and therefore make himself more pleasing to me. The Devils know how he had seed for more than one woman; but, having sown successfully in two beds, he must further advertise his prowess by giving the bastard son the same name as the trueborn. He could not even allow me joy in my child Ywaine without setting before me a constant reminder that that other poor Ywaine was also the fruit of my husband's loins, though not of mine.

"Whose was the adultery, my lords? Uther's, in selling me against my will to such a mate, or mine in leaving Uriens and seeking, now that the way of virginity was closed to me, some gentler paramour for my companion in the way of fertility? Yes, I have had paramours, in the days of my fertility when I needed them—noble and gentle paramours, each one, even the unfaithful one, worth ten such beasts as Uriens. But never more than one at a time, Sir Kay, and I was true to each of them until his death or disloyalty to me."

She looked as if she should still be fertile. But Le Fay could wear the appearance of whatever age she wished. She had still been a young woman in reality when Gawaine saw her disguised as an aged crone in Hautdesert Castle. "All right," I said, "you don't need such an elaborate defense for the charge of adultery. All you had to tell us was, 'Cast the first stone.' "

Morgan smiled. "Nimue could have cast it. So could you yourself, Sir Kay, as I suppose, if only actions are taken into account, and not desires."

"Maybe Dame Nimue knows everything in my past," I said, "but you don't, Dame Morgan. And not every unfaithful wife tries to cut off her husband's head in his sleep."

Dame Morgan never blushed. The cat purred, turned around in her lap, and settled down again. "Who was it told that tale?" asked Le Fay. "Not my son Ywaine, surely. The damsel who brought me my husband's sword? Yes, in a moment of hate and rage I would have yielded to the mortal temptation and cut off his despicable head with his own sword as he slept. If my son had not stopped me, I would have avenged myself like any wronged woman with sufficient resolution—I may even say, like Judith striking off the head of Holofernes. But I acted in that moment as a mere mortal creature in the grip of simple human emotion, not as a sorceress in search of union with the Divine Power. I called for Uriens' sword. I did not attempt to use any sorcery."

"It was the damsel who spread that particular story," I said. "I suppose you *were* acting as a sorceress in search of union with the Divine when you made the counterfeit Excalibur, stole Excalibur's scabbard, sent Artus the poisoned cloak, sent us that lying goblet that supposedly showed which ladies were true to their lords and which were cheating, sent your Green Man with his beheading game, and tried all your other tricks to destroy your brother and the Queen?"

"To destroy my brother?" She shook her head. "My poor little half-brother who made his decisions according to Merlin's prophecies and leaned on other men's magic when he should have been searching for the power within himself. Even Merlin told Artus to call on the magical power of the Sword from the Stone only in the moment of his most crucial need—yet later Artus wielded Excalibur as if he believed that always and everywhere it would lend him its own power. And it was Merlin, was it not, who told the King to prize the scabbard of Excalibur above the blade, since the scabbard would keep whoever wore it from losing his blood. So Artus fought recklessly, relying on the magic of the scabbard rather than on his own battle defenses. A limb or a head may be lopped off, my lords, or a stomach cut open and the bowels spilled out upon the ground though never a drop of blood be lost. At least my charade with the false Excalibur did some good, though it cost me my Accolon—my true paramour who was as good a knight as any of you." She paused for a moment as if her throat had swollen, but the cat in her lap went on purring in sheer contentment. Morgan's hand never faltered nor gave a rough stroke. "After his lesson at that battle," she went on, "did not Artus give Excalibur to Gawaine, who knows how to wield it as a simple, noble blade and an extension of his own arm, without depending on it as a magical wand?"

"And you forcibly weaned Artus away from dependence on the scabbard by stealing it," I said.

"And by throwing it into a deep water." She glanced at the Lady of the Lake and they seemed to exchange smiles. "My sister Nimue could, perhaps, recover it, if she deemed it worth the effort."

"Brother Gawaine, of course," said Mordred, "has his own inbred magic in his strength redoubling from underne to noon."

"Aye. The mystical gift of his foolish godfather," Morgan replied. "And the result of it is that, as other folk notice it through the years, half his victories are credited to his marvelous, mysterious hours of increased strength, and that other men refuse to fight him until after noon, while he, in his chivalry, agrees to fight them at the hour of their choosing. You and the rest of your brothers, Mordred, may thank God you were not given such a christening-gift as Gawaine's."

"For a dame who despises the magical arts as much as you claim to," I said, "you use them often enough yourself."

"Less often now than in my youth. I slowly wean myself away to the better part."

"And your poisoned cloak was an attempt to wean Artus away from magic by easing him away from life, I suppose?" I said.

She shrugged. "I was still young, I was very much grieved and angry for the death of my beloved Accolon, the life of my hated Uriens, and my son Ywaine taking the part of his father and turning from me. I believe I spread a stronger venom on that cloak than I had at first intended." She glanced sharply at Nimue. "Nevertheless, you should have counselled Arthur to throw my gift at once on the fire, not to force it upon the shoulders of my poor, innocent damsel."

"You were my superior in magic," Dame Nimue said mildly. "How could I guess the cloak might be quicker and more powerful than you had meant, sister?" She sighed. "I paid for it soon thereafter when I misjudged the strength of one of my own enchantments."

"Aye, and other women, not ourselves, bore the mortal brunt of our misjudgings," said Morgan. "That is perhaps our heaviest punishment. As for my goblet from which no faithless wife, as the world understands faithlessness, could drink without spilling her wine, did you not consider, Seneschal, that I could not have drunk from it myself? The world had thrown the stone at me, and I threw it back at the world."

"Your lying goblet could have got the Queen burned for adultery if Artus hadn't learned by then what weight to put on your accusations," I said.

"Lying? Well, Dame Guenevere had been the first woman of all to accuse me. As for my dear Green Knight, he was a pretty Yuletide mummery, a toy to help satisfy my little brother's thirst for holiday marvels . . . though it was a pity we could not have sent Artus home again chastened instead of Gawaine."

"Didn't your Green Man himself say you'd hoped to frighten Dame Guenevere to her grave?" I said.

Morgan leaned her head back and laughed. "Did he use some such phrase, my dear Bertilak? And did you all take it for literal truth? Of course it was also devised to give Guenevere a start—but to think I was not aware it would take more than my jovial Green Knight to frighten that woman to death or madness!"

I stood up. "You've hated the Queen for years. You've tried to destroy her time after time. Don't try to pass it all off now as mere light-hearted sports and jesting. Let me tell you, Dame Morgan, you may think of your brother as Merlin's spineless puppet, but he stood on his own two feet and defied Merlin's bloody prophecies when he married Her Grace. If you really did want to make him his own man, you ought to be grateful to Dame Guenevere for helping."

"Unfortunate that he did not ignore Merlin's prophecies more often."

"Why do you hate the Queen?" I insisted.

"I do not hate Guenevere. I no longer hate even Uriens. Does the Earth hate the plowshare that cuts it? How have I tried to destroy your Queen?"

"Dame Guenevere's destruction," said Mordred, "as the world understands destruction, of course, would probably ensue were the King convinced of her unfaithfulness. And you must admit you've done your part to try to persuade him, Aunt, with your goblet, and that shield showing a knight trampling a king and queen that you tricked Tristram to carry in tournament beneath their noses, and so on."

"Lancelot!" I said. "You're jealous of her because of Lancelot. If-Her Grace were out of the way, you think you might yet lure the Mirror of Perfect Knighthood into your bed."

Morgan finally stopped stroking her cat. She gazed at us for a moment, then rose and picked up a lamp. "Come with me. I have made up my mind to show you something I have shown to very few."

Mordred and I followed her out. Nimue stayed behind. The dark cat, which had leaped from Morgan's lap when she stood, sprang up and settled comfortably in Dame Nimue's white skirts instead.

Chapter 21
Dame Morgan's Tale of Sir Lancelot's Pictures on the Walls

> *"Thus as they rode they heard by them a great horse grimly neigh, then were they ware of a sleeping knight, that lay all armed under an apple-tree; anon as these queens looked on his face, they knew it was Sir Launcelot. Then they began for to strive for that knight, everych one said they would have him to her love. We shall not strive, said Morgan le Fay, that was King Arthur's sister, I shall put an enchantment upon him that he shall not awake in six hours, and then I will lead him away unto my castle, and when he is surely within my hold, I shall take the enchantment from him, and then let him choose which of us he will have unto paramour."* (Malory VI, 3)

I did not trust Le Fay, but I followed her. I guessed she was telling us a string of lies and half-truths, probably to try deceiving Artus through us. Nevertheless, I had few doubts remaining as to our personal safety. She would hardly have been so elaborate with her words if she meant we should not return to the world outside.

I imagine she could have walked her castle in the dark. Indeed, if she were able to see in the dark like a cat or owl, the lamp in her hand might have been more hindrance than help to her. But it gave Mordred and me enough light to follow without bumping into the walls, each other, or our hostess. It was not as simple as it could have been to get an idea of the layout of her castle, but we seemed to go from the north tower to the south one, staying inside halls and corridors all the way. We did descend several flights of steps, coming down from the sollar; but I think we stayed aboveground, and we did not pass through any hidden doorways. We ascended stairs again at the end of our expedition and reached a strong door in about what I judged to be the lower third of the tower.

The door was secured by a lock without a keyhole. Dame Morgan ran her fingers over it and muttered some words in a strange language, at which it sprang open. We followed her into a large chamber. At first all we could see were a few shadows on the walls and a window on the other side of the room. The window was barred, but two or three of the bars seemed to be missing.

As Le Fay used her lamp to light wax tapers about the room, the shadows on the wall became paintings. They were crude and probably badly mixed in color (though you can hardly judge color by candlelight); but the painter must have been more enthusiastic about his work than his skill merited, for every foot of the walls from floor to ceiling was worked into a scene. Maybe it was enthusiasm for his or her subject matter that had kept the would-be artist going, despite the fact that the execution was doing more harm than justice to the lofty theme. All the panels seemed to show knightly exploits.

There gets to be a certain sameness about knightly exploits—unless, of course, they are your own—so it took me a few moments to realize that all the scenes within my immediate range of vision had the same champion as hero, whether carrying his own arms, somebody else's, or an anonymous shield. Once I even found him carrying my device, but striking down knights whom, by their shields, I had never unhorsed. To make it obvious that the champion who bore the shield with the golden key was not Kay, the painted knight charged with visor unrealistically raised to show an exaggerated brown beard and mustache extending beyond the edges of the helmet. The hero of the murals was Lancelot.

"The artist probably meant his portraits to flatter the great knight," said Mordred. "Pity he hadn't the skill. They more closely resemble one of the late Sir Dinadan's poetic satires."

"The artist was Lancelot himself," said Morgan. "Who can be sure whether he meant these pictures as boasting or as confession?" She stood at the far end of the room, playing her lamp up and down the panels nearest the window. We went to look.

The first of a set of three panels showed Lancelot kneeling while the Queen—recognizable by her crown, robes, and long white-gold hair—girded on his sword. The King and a dame whom I guessed to be Dame Viviane, the French Lady of the Lake, stood looking on with broad smiles. Obviously this was Lancelot's first coming to court when, as Dame Viviane's protégé, he demanded the accolade from Arthur and the girding from Guenevere, before disappearing on his independent adventures to prove his prowess.

The second of the three panels showed Lancelot presenting the Queen with a scroll, a rose, and a chessboard. The evidence for the truth of this tale was that Her Grace could not win on that board, although she is the best player among us all, while Lancelot could and always did win on it even though on an ordinary chessboard with ordinary chessmen I myself can defeat him easily. Even depicting himself courting the Queen's favor, Lancelot had to include a boastful touch. (And they call Kay the braggart of the Round Table.)

The third panel showed Lancelot in bed with Her Grace.

Morgan put out her hand and stopped me before I could smash that painting with the nearest candle. "You knew, Sir Kay. Do not pretend it takes you by surprise."

"Of course he knows," said Mordred. "We all know except the King, who blinds himself willfully."

"Willfully?" said Dame Morgan. "Or in mere fatuous trust? Perhaps you of the court assume that in his deepest soul Artus is aware of his cuckoldom—for how else than by half-witting choice could any man ignore such clear signs? But, little time as we have passed in one another's company, I know Artus as a sister her brother; and in my opinion, it is not willful choice, but pure foolish, doting, conceited faith that keeps his eyes and ears closed to what the rest of you find so obvious. How could his best knight and his most loving wife betray *him,* the greatest of all mortal kings? His mind will no more accept such a thought than oil will accept water."

I thought of the young squire bringing his big brother the Sword from the Stone, with the idea that I would simply use it in that day's tournament like an ordinary weapon, as if it had never yet penetrated his mind that the entire country was waiting for the one man who could draw that same Sword. Artus is not a lackwit, but he can behave like one at times, whether you call it singlemindedness or stupidity.

"You yourselves realize what is likely to happen should he ever be forced to recognize the truth," Dame Morgan went on. "I tell you that the reason it will happen is the rage of wounded pride. And the longer it is in coming, the worse his rage will be. If he could have seen it years ago, when it was still new and tender, he might have contented himself with shutting her away in a nunnery."

"Maybe he did guess it, about the time that look-alike witch showed up," I said. "Maybe that was why—God! How he would have mutilated Her Grace."

"No," said Morgan, "I think that for a time he utterly believed the false Queen, who simpered on him and flattered him, was the true Guenevere, and the true one the counterfeit. I think he still sincerely believes that those two years Lancelot and Guenevere lived together under protection of the Duke of Surluse, they lived as chaste brother and sister, ever true and devoted to him."

I said, "Why don't you have these bloody pictures painted over?"

"Arthur is bound to see the truth some day. Would it be better that it should happen when he is with his court, the Queen near at hand and fully in his power? Or when he is away from court and Guenevere? Someday, my lords, I hope to have my brother here as my guest, to persuade him by means of Lancelot's own paintings, and to hold him here with me until his rage can be calmed."

"Pardon me, Dame Fay," I said, "if I find it a little difficult to swallow that you're doing all this out of pure regard for the Queen's safety."

"You are partly right in that I have no reason to love Guenevere. She —" For one of the few times, Dame

Morgan seemed momentarily overcome by emotion. Little as I trusted her emotional seizures, I had trouble finding a reason she should treat us to one at this point. "You are aware," she went on, "that my first lover was a kinsman of Her Grace? Guiomar—ah, my Guiomar! He was not a great knight, but he was tender . . . and I needed a tender bedfellow to teach me what love should be. My only knowledge of it until Guiomar had been of my husband's teaching. Had it not been for Guiomar . . . but Lancelot had not yet come among us, Guenevere the Queen had not yet fallen herself, and Guenevere was hotter for virtue than ever Nimue has been. That the men should have their casual paramours outside the court—that Dame Guenevere could not prevent; but they should have no light lovers among the ladies of Guenevere's court. All should be virtuous, from the Queen's own handmaidens to the eldest Duchess whose sour husband might bring her, will-nilly, within Guenevere's influence. And that I, the sister of Guenevere's husband, a queen myself and mated to Arthur's royal ally and vassal, should sin with Guenevere's own cousin! . . . God knows how she found us out, but she stormed, she threatened, she forbade him, by right of her kinship and her queenliness, ever to touch me again, and to be sure of his obedience, she sent him away on a long errand. To his death, it happened . . . though in justice, she could not know that beforehand and grieved as much as I afterwards. But I could guess what it was to be married to my brother, that hot man with his many paramours, and I knew, though not as Merlin pretended to know it in all its details, that someday Guenevere's virtue must fall. I used to think, before Lancelot came, that it would be with you, Seneschal. And that *she* should scorn and chastise me, her elder, who had already gone more deeply than she ever would into the Mysteries, who did what I did more in need than in lust! Yes, I hated her then. I was still young and still in the beginning of my studies, though I thought I was far advanced. That was when I left your court the first time for a while, with Merlin." She smiled. "The old fool had his uses. He did have true power and true secrets, and he was a better teacher than practitioner."

"The knowledge that can only pass from man to woman and from woman to man?" said Mordred. "Aunt, will you teach me some of this knowledge?"

She shook her head. "Nephew, I will not."

"I am the next generation, Aunt. I am a man, to learn from a woman. And we share the first part of a name—my mother Morgawse, you and I."

"And for these reasons I should instruct you in the knowledge and uses of the Power?"

"Do you refuse because of my birth, Aunt?"

"I refuse because of your intent, Nephew. You would use your skill to greater destructiveness than did the Devil's son Merlin."

"Is that a prophecy, Aunt Morgan le Fay," said Mordred, "or a command?"

She stepped closer to him and held the lamp near his face, studying him. "Prove your good intent, then. Bring Arthur here, alone, to be my guest."

He shrugged. "Arthur won't believe your silly pictures, Aunt Morgan, any more than he believed your drinking-horn. He probably won't even believe that Lancelot painted any of them. But I'll find my own opportunity, and I will succeed where you have failed. By the way, how did you persuade the great Lancelot to paint you these portraits?"

"He saw one of my artists painting the life of Aeneas, and that inspired him." Morgan turned to me. "You, then, Sir Kay? For the best service to your Queen as well as to your King, will you find a way to bring Artus here to me? If I can persuade him, I promise I will keep him here until his rage has calmed and the worst danger to Dame Guenevere is past."

"After years of your deeds," I said, "you expect me to believe your words instead? No, I won't deliver Artus over to you."

"And you pretend to love Guenevere."

"And you pretend not to love Lancelot," I replied.

"So you still charge me with hating the Queen for jealousy of her champion." Morgan went to the window. "This room overlooks a garden," she said, extinguishing her lamp and gazing out as if she could see the garden in the dark. "The flowers already show the promise of full summer. . . . I have never loved Lancelot. I have never even, as a mortal woman, particularly desired his body. Guiomar, Accolon of Gaul, my sweet, foolhardy Sir Hemison, the pretty orphan Sir Alisander, who refused me—they were men I could love both as woman and as sorceress. Lancelot I wanted for one reason only. Should not the Earth be plowed by the best and strongest of farmers? And should I not seek the strongest and best of plowmen for myself? Gawaine I could not have, for he was my nephew. Galahad was a greater knight than his father, but to Galahad was given the path of virginity, and I would not have cheated it from him as it had been cheated from me. That left Lancelot. He might have sowed a second Galahad in me—Achilles planting in Diana, Mars in Isis, Llew Strong-Hand in Rhea. Not a Galahad to pass out of this world in a chaste glory of personal fulfillment, but one to follow the way of fertility, to leaven this land, perhaps to reign in it after Arthur. But I would not trick Lancelot into my field, as Pellam's daughter Elaine tricked him into hers, making him think he was with Guenevere when he begot Galahad. For all the enchantments I used to bring him near me, I never clouded his understanding at the moment of choice. He must come to me knowing who I was, or not at all. . . .

"So he lived here for a year and a half, long enough to finish painting the history of his life. I suppose that painting Guenevere reminded him of his love, for one spring day, when the roses had begun to bloom in the garden below, he broke the bars of his window, leaped out, and escaped my castle.

"I am no longer fertile. I no longer need Sir Lancelot, and I never desired him, so what cause have I now to be envious of Her Grace?"

Dame Morgan turned back to us. "And now, my fair lords, what new trouble is it you have come to accuse me of causing?"

Chapter 22

Of Watching the Past in Morgan's Mirror, and of the Spell of Despair

"Lo, said the Damosel of the Lake, ye ought to be ashamed for to murder such a knight. And therewith she threw such an enchantment upon her that . . . well-nigh she was out of her mind." (Malory IV, 22)

"Even if you should be innocent this time," I said, "you don't really expect us to believe you haven't been keeping watch somehow on the court."

She laughed. "You speak as if that were an easier task than scaling fish for supper. Keeping watch on Arthur's court! A single woman or man in the very heart of it can hardly keep all its gossip, true and false, sorted and ready at her or his command, and you expect me to do so at a distance?"

"You claim to be one of the world's greatest necromancers," I said.

"And you used to have spies at court—still do, no doubt," added Mordred.

"And why, do you think, with your overblown notions of the simple, surface tricks of magic, would the world's most skilled necromancer need mortal spies among her brother's folk?" Le Fay laughed again. "Yes, I can keep watch on your doings, but only in a limited way. Well, there was a time when I would have shown no one my secrets save a few trusted fellow-necromancers, but I have mellowed with my advancing years. You may not enter my sanctum, but I will take you as far as my antechamber and we can examine your errand there."

We left, Morgan locking the door to Lancelot's room behind us. She led us down more stairs and along more passageways until, as nearly as I could make out, we ended underground in a semi-circular chamber about twenty paces across, with a tiled floor that showed a snake swallowing its tail. After lighting a triple-wicked lamp on an ancient bronze stand, Dame Morgan went through a curtained doorway in the flat wall of the chamber.

She was gone for several moments, leaving us with nothing to do but examine the antechamber. It was not cluttered. A chest, a chair, two more lamps on their stands, and tapestries on the walls—the furnishings were rich, but hardly mysterious. Once I turned in time to see Mordred starting to lift the curtain to his aunt's inner room, but he dropped the cloth at once, as if it had burned him.

Before Morgan came back out, Dame Nimue and the cat had joined us in the antechamber. I wondered to which of them Le Fay had somehow sent a message. Nodding to us, Nimue lit the room's other two triple-wicked lamps.

At last Morgan returned, carrying an earthenware basin of water. She set it on the chest, drew up the chair and sat before the basin, and made a circular motion with her right hand. "You are free to gather around me," she said.

Nimue hung back, allowing Mordred and me the closest places beside Morgan's chair. The cat, busy washing herself, ignored us. "Now," said Morgan, "when and where shall I look?"

"Why do you ask us?" said Mordred inquisitively.

"I can see the past and the present, but only in one place at a time, and the images move no faster than the reality. It would be impossible for me to watch everything. My spies can give me some imperfect idea of what to watch, rarely more."

"Dame Nimue read my entire life yesterday with a touch," I said, "and Dame Morgan has to use spies like a mere mortal and ask questions like an Oxford clerk."

Morgan glanced at Nimue. "Last Monday," saiid the Dame of the Lake. "The Queen's small, private banquet chamber in London castle, about the hour of . . . shortly after midday."

Morgan nodded. "I know the room." Pressing her palms together, fingers slightly spread, she gazed into the basin of water. After a moment she reached out, not looking away from the water, and took one of my hands and one of Mordred's

Before she touched me, I saw nothing but an ordinary basin of glazed clay filled with water, dark except for the reflection of the nearest lamp's three flames. Once Morgan's dry hand was holding mine, the reflection disappeared, the water seemed to glow from within, and the image of the Queen's fatal dinner appeared on the surface.

It was about halfway over. Gawaine was apparently telling Her Grace a humorous tale. She laughed, while Bors, at her other hand, seemed to smile like a man trying not to show faint disapproval. We could only see, not hear them; and the images were so tiny it was hard to read their faces. Unless Dame Morgan could hear them, and had sharper eyes than ours, I could see that this way of gaining information left even more to be desired than she had hinted earlier.

After squinting at all of us for a few moments, vainly trying to make out which of the guests or servers might look apprehensive, I wanted to tell Dame Morgan she could just as well pass over about the third part of an hour. But for all I knew, speaking might break the spell. So we kept quiet and watched our tiny images aim silent witticisms at one another and lift invisible bites of meat to mouths that looked scarcely larger open than closed. Marvelous or not, leading to tragedy or not, it eventually grew a little tiresome, and I began to admire Dame Morgan's ability to sit gazing at it so intently. Once I glanced around and noticed that the cat had finished washing herself and come back to Nimue, who was quietly petting it without paying any attention to the images in the water.

At last Coupnez brought the bowl of fruit—which was almost too big for him—from the sideboard, knelt awkwardly, and presented it to the Queen. Gawaine turned his head. He seemed to be eyeing the fruit greedily, judging which piece he hoped would be left for him; but I realized I might only be reading into his minute image emotions I had seen in him before when he came face to face with his beloved apples. We watched him instruct the page to carry the fruit around first to the other guests, while Bors, the ascetic who would not eat fruit at this season of the year anyway, seemed to nod approval.

I was so busy noticing who accepted fruit and who waved Coupnez on that I missed seeing Patrise take the fatal few bites. A sudden tightened indrawing of Morgan's breath and a very slight increase of pressure from her fingers told me when she saw Patrise fall. I kept on trying to study the reactions of the other guests. Morgan had apparently realized what was wrong sooner than those of us there present had realized it.

We went on watching until the King had come and gone and the rest of the Queen's guests were beginning to trail away. Then Morgan dropped our hands and leaned forward a little, closing her eyes and resting her chin in her palms. "So it appears that one of your young knights died of a poisoned apple," she said, "and you have come seeking me out to charge me with the deed. Do I interpret the images correctly, my lords? Has Sir Mador de la Porte charged Guenevere?"

"Yes," I said. "It's the general opinion at court that you're long dead, or we might have been able to turn the accusation from Her Grace to you."

"How fortunate you do not know the identities of my poor spies or you might have racked lying confessions from them and burned them at once." Morgan stood to face us. Even before learning magic, she had been taller than most women. "I am hardly flattered that any of you should have taken this for my handiwork, my lords. Does it bear the marks of my infamy? Poison hidden in a piece of fruit! Oh, no, good my lords, if I had done this, there would have been no doubt. I would have given you a marvel—a baby basilisk in the apple, or at the very least a bit of orange smoke and green flame. Doubtless I would have made a test of it: Only the unworthiest knight would have been injured, while the rest would eat with impunity. And it would have happened before the full court, not at a small dinner for a mere two dozen. Have I ever struck when the King my brother was not present? Have I ever struck so purposelessly as this, so over-subtly that it could not be recognized at once for my handiwork, or at least for magic, immediately after the deed? Would I have risked my own dearest nephews? My lords, I am ashamed of you for holding me suspect!"

"Maybe you should be ashamed of yourself for opening yourself up to our suspicion, Dame," I said. "So your poor spies hadn't gotten the news to you yet, eh? When would they have gotten it to you? After the Queen was safely burned?"

"Be careful how you continue to insult my Aunt, Seneschal," said Mordred, "lest she lose her extreme patience and turn you into a toad."

"Dame Guenevere's trial is eight days from now," said Nimue.

"Aye." Morgan sat again, holding out her hands over the basin as if to still the water. "Play my spies, my lords. Where shall we look now? Shall we follow the apples and pears from their storage pits to your table? Or shall we attempt to follow the actions of possible traitors?"

Mordred asked, "You can, then, choose some person —let us say our friend Seneschal here—and follow him from the death chamber to wherever he went?"

"Aye, although as the person moves from place to place, I must either be able to recognize or guess where that person is going, or keep watch by overlapping scenes as a tailor overlaps seams. The passage may become longer in the watching than in the original."

"You see what work we would have to find Sir Lancelot by such means as this," said Nimue brightly. "If you had a bit of his hair or a scrap of clothing he had worn recently, we could find him as I found Dame Morgan. By the way, I can assure you that Sir Kay is guiltless in this matter, and it would do the rest of us very little good to follow his movements."

"I had assumed, by the fact of their seeking me out, that both of them were guiltless," said Morgan, "of this poisoning."

"Try to follow Coupnez—Doran the Earl of Pase's son," I said, and told her, as nearly as I could gauge it, about what time to begin watching the Queen's antechamber for the page's arrival.

"You risk much, Seneschal," said Mordred. "You risk seeing Her Grace envenom the fruit as she arranges it."

"Damn you, Mordred," I began, starting to give him back his vile words in rather too loud a voice for the place we were in—but all at once a sort of incredible melancholy struck me, almost as tangible as a lance. It went through my brain that the Queen scorned me, the court despised me, the very servants obeyed me only out of fear and mocked me behind my back. I had not gone on a real quest for years nor fought in a real battle since the war against Claudas of France, I was useless these days in joust and tournament, I had wasted my life in petty duties that would be forgotten while future ages were singing the glory of careless berserkers like Lancelot and Tristram, and nothing I had ever done or was doing now was to any purpose . . . it was all I could do, for a few moments, to keep from drawing my dagger and plunging it into my heart.

I leaned against the wall and shook my head, aware that the others were watching me and wondering whether to lash out at them and let Le Fay turn me into a toad, or leave them and go throw myself from one of the towers. Then the cloud lifted, and I saw they were looking at me with concern rather than scorn. Nimue, showing the most concern, came forward and touched my shoulder. With an effort, I resisted the temptation to lean forward and sob on her breast.

"Forgive me, Sir Kay," she said. "I had not meant to strike you quite so hard, but I worked very quickly."

"What did you do to him, Dame?" Mordred inquired.

"It is a spell of melancholia, of despair. I judged the time had come that you should stop bickering between yourselves."

"Then why in God's Name didn't you strike *him?*" I said, beginning to recover.

"To what purpose? He had already done his harm. I meant to stop angry words, not to punish them. Besides," she added softly, for my ears alone, "I know your mind and memory and that you could withstand it, at least for a few moments. I do not know what further mischief if would have done to Mordred. Did you not tell me yourself, two evenings ago, to be tender with him?"

We returned to Morgan, still seated before her basin of water with Mordred at her shoulder. "The Queen's antechamber," I said, "an hour before dinner, last Monday."

We saw Guenevere pacing the room, talking to her kinswomen, Dames Lore and Elyzabel. She seemed tense, unquiet—probably worrying about Lancelot and where he had gone this time. Elyzabel opened the door, no doubt in answer to knocking, and took the bags of fruit from old Rozennik's scullions Torntunic and Wilkin.

"Shall I pass quickly over half an hour?" murmured Le Fay, causing only a faint ripple in the picture.

"No," I said, catching myself before I could glare at Mordred, "we'll all watch her innocence."

With something definite to do, the Queen seemed to become herself, cheerful, calm, capable, wise and witty—the wisest and most gracious woman in the world, except where that fool Lancelot is concerned. She chatted happily with her cousins as she picked and chose among the apples and pears, piling the better ones in their silver dish as carefully as a craftsman. She did not have much room for choice; there were no more than thirty pieces of fruit before her. But she scrutinized each one as if she had fifty to choose among, rejecting three. Elyzabel picked up one of the rejected apples or pears (small as the image was, we could not always see which were which) and began to eat it—I wondered why Dame Lore had forgotten to mention that when she propounded to me on how the poison could not have been in the fruit when the Queen arranged it.

When the dish of fruit was arranged to her satisfaction, the Queen rang her bell. She did not slip back into her restless mood, but began to select jewelry for herself, returning once or twice to make some invisible adjustment to her apples and pears. She had arranged the nuts, too, for her dinner, in the gilt wire frameworks of her own design: peacock, cat, hawk, hare, brachet, boar, and two trees; but she had arranged the nuts earlier and sent them to the small banquet room already.

Coupnez came. Dame Lore put the dish of fruit into his arms. The Queen held up one of the rejected pieces, no doubt promising it to the page when he had completed his errand, and sent him on his way. As Coupnez made his exit from the antechamber, Morgan dropped our hands for a moment and the image vanished.

"She *could* have inserted poison on a long pin while she was examining the fruit," said Mordred. This time he at least had the grace to speak cautiously rather than insolently. "We would not have been able to see the pin."

"We might have been able to see its glint," I said, restraining my temper. "Besides, that would make both Dame Cupbearer and Dame Elyzabel her accomplices.

And she had examined that piece Dame Elyzabel ate just as closely as she examined the ones she put in the dish."

Dame Morgan took our hands again, and we saw the door to the Queen's apartment from the other side, the corridor side, with Coupnez turning right. We watched until the page began to disappear at the edge of the basin, then Morgan dropped our hands again and picked them up when she had the next several yards of corridor reflected in her mirror.

Le Fay could not have been with the court in London more than a few times, years ago, but she must have remembered the buildings well, for she was able to follow Coupnez without stopping to consult me as to where he would have gone next. True, there is only one place between the Queens appartment and the small banquet chamber where the corridor divides. The branching happened to come just beyond the edge of the picture, and when Morgan gathered the next image, Coupnez was not there. But he should have been there. Dame Morgan had followed the correct way to the banquet chamber. The other hall led to some little-used stairs to the cellars.

"So that's where the young scoundrel stopped to waste time, or worse," I said.

Dame Morgan shifted the image to the other branching. I became aware that this time Dame Nimue was watching with us, looking over our shoulders and lightly touching Morgan's upper arm.

Coupnez, his gaze fastened greedily on the fruit in his arms, dodged into the less-used hallway. The promise of one piece after his errand had not been enough, because now he awkwardly set down the dish, helped himself to another piece, and rearranged the remaining pears and apples to hide his theft. Then he moved forward several paces, sat on the upper steps, his back to the dish, and began eating.

By my reckoning, Her Grace must have put a few more than twenty-five pieces of fruit into the dish. No doubt she had foreseen this possibility.

We had a side view of the scene, as if one wall of the corridor had been lifted away somehow. I suppose Morgan's magic was tight up against that wall, and the diminished proportions accounted somehow for the long view we seemed to have from end to end. As Coupnez sat munching, no doubt deaf to any sound beyond the fruit in his cheeks, a clerkly figure entered behind him.

The newcomer was in long, white robes, with cowl pulled far down over his face. He stopped a few paces from the dish of fruit, genuflected, and crossed himself. Still kneeling, he pulled a holy-water sprinkler from his robes and sprinkled the fruit thoroughly, making the Sign of the Cross over it as if in blessing. Then he rose, turned, and made his departure. The page never turned his head. The cleric could not have made enough noise to carry over the sound of Coupnez' own crunching.

Dame Morgan sighed and dropped our hands. "Am I absolved, good my lords?"

Chapter 23
The Way of the Tortoise Is Sometimes Inadequate

"But Sir Gawaine had a custom that he used daily at dinner and at supper, that he loved well all manner of fruit, and in especial apples and pears. And therefore whosomever dined or feasted Sir Gawaine would commonly purvey for good fruit for him . . ." (Malory XVIII, 3)

"That could have been one of your spies, Aunt, acting on your orders," said Mordred. "Or, indeed, it could be a mere lie of your own making that you have shown us."

"Had Sir Kay been the one to tell me that, Nephew, you would have threatened him, on my behalf, with being turned into a toad at my hand."

They said that or something like it; for a moment I was only half-listening to their family banter. "That young Satan!" I exclaimed. "He could have come forward and told the court there was no poison in the fruit when he took the bowl from Her Grace!"

"Fear, Seneschal," said Mordred. "Doran Coupnez is

scarcely eight summers old."

"Fear of being punished for stealing an apple? By God, the punishment he would have got fot that is nothing to what he'll get for not telling what he knew and—"

"What did he know?" said Mordred quietly. "Only that the piece of fruit he stole had not been poisoned. What might he fear? Being charged himself, and burned in the Queen's place, or at her side."

"We ourselves do not know that this was the poisoner," said Nimue. "It might have been only what Doran would have seen had he turned: an over-zealous priest stopping to bless a bowl of fruit."

I snorted. "We have too many clerics and not enough work for them if all they can find to do is wander about the corridors looking for stray dishes of food to bless. If he were only a pure-hearted, simple-minded priest, why not bless Coupnez, too?"

"Yes," said Morgan, "this cleric seemed very careful not to sprinkle the child. Still, we do not know but that something further took place between those stairs and the banquet chamber. Do you trust me to continue, my lords?"

If Dame Morgan were manufacturing the images, she could have shown us Guenevere poisoning the fruit; and if the cleric had been one of her own creatures, she need not have shown us the scene at all. "I trust you far enough to watch what you have to show us," I said.

"We will begin with what we have just seen," she replied. "You will know, at least, that I omit nothing."

She brought us back to the scene at the stairs. We watched the clerkly figure go through its sneaking mummery once more and leave. Coupnez finally finished his piece of fruit, jumped up guiltily, as if in sudden fear that someone would notice how long he had taken on his errand, got his arms around the dish, staggered up from his knees to his feet and hurried back to the main corridor, almost overbalancing. Scene by scene, we followed him the rest of the way to the small banquet chamber. Although one step through the corridors is much like all the others, Morgan did not seem to leave any inch of Coupnez' journey unscrutinized. For good measure, we watched the fruit sit on the sideboard from the time Coupnez left it there, with several servants busy in the chamber the whole time, until the dinner was nearing its end and the page brought the dish from the sideboard to Her Grace's table, as we had seen before. There was no other time the poison could have gotten into the fruit.

"But the man may still have been a mere silly, harmless priest," said Mordred. "The poison may have been inserted sometime previously, in one or a few pieces only, and Doran Coupnez been fortunate in choosing one of the unpoisoned pieces."

"For Jesu's sake, Mordred, stop playing Devil's advocate," I said. "Even you can't really believe Her Grace would poison one or two apples on a random whim."

He shrugged. "One thrust of a pin, unseen by her cousins, into one apple so marked that she herself might recognize it again and guide it into the right hand . . . but we can never know, can we, whether all the fruit was venomed or only one or two pieces? Thanks to the Queen's actions, and yours, and brother Gawaine's."

"In my opinion, Dame of the Lake," I said, "you may touch him with your spell of melancholia whenever you please."

Mordred smiled. "I schooled myself long ago in how to fight the demons of melancholia and survive. But how would such a poison be obtained, Aunt, assuming it was indeed in the Priest's aspergillum? Could any person with knowledge of herbs and substances prepare it, or would it require knowledge of the deeper lore and the aid of devils?"

Morgan shrugged. "There are many poisons that can be sprinkled upon food." She bent her head forward, rubbing her fingers through the silvering hair at her temples. "It did not, as far as we could see and at least for a short time, tarnish or discolor the aspergillum, nor did any of you notice marks on the silver dish. It killed almost at once, and blood came up from the victim's mouth . . . that poor young man! He was new to your company, I think? To gain almost the height of your world's ambitions—a place at Arthur's Round Table—and then to die so!"

She must have known Patrise was a companion of the Table by recognizing the rest of us as such. Her remarks may have been only the grieving of a lusty dame for the waste of a handsome young body, but I think that moment, more than anything else, decided me to trust Dame Morgan. At least in the matter of finding Patrise's murderer.

"It may have been a certain preparation," she went on, "called by various names, colorless as water and slightly thicker, and which has other uses than to poison one's enemies."

"Other uses?" said Mordred.

"To name the most frivolous, a tiny drop of it applied carefully with the tip of a pin or fine knife to an eruption in the skin causes the pimple to swell and burst almost at once. The same tiny drop, mixed with certain other ingredients and spread on the chin, is sometimes said to thicken a man's beard."

"Dangerous stuff for vain folk to play with," I said. "But a person could get it without the sorceress knowing he wanted it for murder?"

"In the hands of a skilled surgeon, it can also be used to help heal wounds, cleanse infections, and ease various disorders," said Morgan. "But few of us who can prepare it will sell or give it away lightly, for the mere asking."

"You can answer for everyone who knows how to prepare it, eh?" I said. "Can you name them for us, too?"

She sighed. "It requires no conjurations to prepare, but it does require a deeper knowledge than that of most village herbwives. As for who can make it—my old cohorts the queens of Northgalis and Sorestan, Dame Ysolde's mother of Ireland, Annowre and Hellawes of the Perilous Forest—no, those two are gone now, are they not? Poor, amorous fools. Gwenbaus the brother of the French kings—but he is gone, too. The Duke of Surluse's clerk Helyes, perhaps, and Old Blaise, Merlin's master, writing in his forest in Northumberland, though they have both turned to wiser matters than magic. Dame Seraide and her French mistress Viviane of the Lake, possibly Dame Lynette, and Mark's wise woman of Cornwall, Nimue and myself, Dame Brisane of Carbonek, who has ever held herself aloof from us, claiming the reputation of a 'white witch,' while tricking Lancelot into bed with her young mistress Elaine . . ." Morgan shook her head. "No, once I could have named you the necromancers of Britain, Brittany, and Ireland, with the extent of all their skills. Now I become a recluse, keeping myself more aloof than Dame Brisane of Carbonek, waiting for the events of the world to come to me and letting new necromancers crop up without my knowledge. I cannot name you all who could have prepared the poison. But I can say that very few of us with the ability to learn such knowledge would then dispense the fruits of it without good cause."

"'Good cause' including the deaths of your enemies?" I said.

"I weary of your suspicions, Seneschal."

"I used the word meaning all of you sorceresses and necromancers, Dame Morgan, not you in particular. But take it however it fits."

"I cannot even say surely this was the poison used," said le Fay, "and not some other more easy of manufacture."

"Shall we try to follow the cleric who sprinkled the apples?" suggested Dame Nimue.

We turned our attention back to the basin of water. For the third time, we watched the cowled figure sprinkle the fruit with the poisoned "holy water." This time, when he slipped away, Morgan followed him, again overlapping scenes.

At the earliest opportunity, our cleric descended into the cellars, without benefit of lamp, candle, or torch. "I cannot illumine a picture from the past or present with new light from without, my lords," said Morgan.

"A man who knew enough about the magical arts to obtain that poison and use it," said Mordred, "might be clever enough to guess that someday some unfriendly necromancer would be watching his past actions."

"If he was one of us at the Queen's dinner, he has to come up soon," I said. "And unless he knows those cellars like a rat, he has to stop and strike a fire before he gets lost down there."

"He may very well have taken the trouble to learn the cellars like a rat," Mordred remarked. "He must have planned this carefully, and for some time. Her Grace has given small dinners before. Our poisoner will have been waiting his chance, meanwhile acquiring his clerk's robes and aspergillum, learning his way through the cellars in the darkness, and finding a shadowed corner or doorway where he could wait and watch for a page to pass with food for the Queen's table."

"Assuming he meant to kill Gawaine," I said, "he had to wait for a dish of fruit; and he had to wait for a page who would set the dish down and turn his back. He certainly put his plans at the mercy of circumstance."

Mordred waved away the objection. "We do not know how long our poisoner may have waited, before how many of Dame Guenevere's small dinners he may have watched for his opportunity in vain. In city after city, through all the court's progresses, he may have learned cellars and lurking-places against the day when his chance would come. Or it may have come almost at once. Brother Gawaine is one of the Queen's favorites, she always takes care to have his fruit for him, and pages—despite your firm hand, Sir Seneschal—are well known for stealing moments from their errands. Having taken his chance, our poisoner would probably have discarded his robe and aspergillum in the darkness."

"In that case," I said, "he'll be coming up in his own clothes."

"How many ways lead up from those cellars, Sir Kay?"Dame Morgan said wearily. "I do not know them; I never had cause to go down into them. How many turnings might our cleric have taken? Suppose he, or she, was not among Dame Guenevere's dinner guests and could therefore have waited in the dark cellars for hours, even until night and darkness throughout the castle? Am I to sit and watch the past through every possible hour and at every possible point where our cleric might have emerged?" She shook her head. "It would take more time than you have remaining before your Queen's trial."

"Try," I said. "We might have good luck."

"Ah, so at last you trust me and my magic! But to what purpose if you do? Will Sir Mador de la Porte accept the evidence of what Sir Kay and Sir Mordred have seen in the mirror of Morgan le Fay?"

She was right. We had seen proof that the Queen was guiltless, but it was not proof that Mador would believe. Even if I could make Coupnez confess, Mador, in his bullheaded obsession, would probably say that it only showed Her Grace had not poisoned all the fruit, and the page could thank God he had stolen an untainted piece. It might even make Mador, if he believed any of our story, insist that Dames Elyzabel and Lore be burnt with their kinswoman. If anything, news that Morgan le Fay was the source of what we knew would injure the Queen's case, besides revealing that Le Fay was still alive and possibly bringing Artus here to visit her and see Lancelot's ugly paintings.

"Our only hope is to learn who that cowled devil is," I said. "Confront him with what we know, and work a confession out of him."

Morgan smiled wryly. "You rely more on your skill to extract a confession than our traitor relies on chance and circumstance. But we will try for awhile yet."

She tried. We watched for hours at every way I could remember that led up from the cellars. Dame Nimue curled up with the cat and went to sleep. Some time later, Mordred sprawled out on the floor and went to sleep also. Dame Morgan and I kept our vigil of the past. Unfortunately, those particular cellars were not used either for storage of food or of prisoners, and I was not overfamiliar with them myself. Most of them were used, if at all, for the storage of forgotten old waste lumber that had better have been either refurbished and used, or melted down and burned. Our traitor could probably have left his clerical garb and holy-water sprinkler with the rest of it and they would not have been discovered for years. If we returned to London in time, I would have those cellars searched thoroughly . . . though even if we found them, with some of the poison still in the aspergillum, it could be said they merely showed the Queen had had an accomplice. Meanwhile, our man must have slipped up from the cellars at some egress I did not know about.

Dame Nimue woke up long enough to learn we had found nothing. "Then follow him or her backward through the past," she suggested, "from the time and place where he lurked watching for the page Doran Coupnez to pass with the fruit. As for me, I bid you good-night, if there is any of the night left. My Pelleas is a softer pillow than any here, and you can show me tomorrow anything of interest you may find tonight."

Mordred awakened at her departure, complained that his bones would be stiff from sleeping on the stone floor, and dozed off again. The cat curled up at Morgan's feet. Le Fay and I went farther back in our search, studying the corridors until we found the shadowed corner where our false cleric waited for Coupnez. Morgan apparently could not cause a scene to flow backwards, but had to find the place, watch if for a few moments, then dissolve it and cause it to reform in her mirror at an earlier time. Learning where the traitor had come from to his lurking-place was an even more tiresome business than watching fruitlessly for him to emerge from the cellars . . . and, when we finally traced where he had come from when he began his watch—our long search led us back to the cellars. We watched him coming up, cowl already pulled far forward over his face, and aspergillum doubtless already cradled in his robe, at one of the places where we had earlier watched in vain for him to come up after his deed.

"Whoever this is," said Dame Morgan, "the person seems to know enough of magic to have foreseen the possibility of someone's watching as we watch. No doubt he or she went down into those cellars, having already explored them, put on the cleric's robe—perhaps concealed there even earlier to lie in readiness—came up as we have just seen, then returned, as we have also seen, by a different way. The poisoner may have used four different ways into the cellars; and, it seems, you do not know them all."

"If you could follow him back this far," I said, "you can mount watch on every possible foot of yard and hallway around those cellars and find the door."

"Aye, sometime between now and Martinmass I might, with luck, find the right place and moment to see him or her either going down or coming up without the clerkly disguise, if indeed it was disguise. Meanwhile, Guenevere will be saved by a champion, or burned for the failure of one, within these eight days. And I weary, Seneschal, as do you. More than you. You have but to watch, while I must focus my power to find and hold the images. I cannot do this much longer without rest and sleep."

I tried to reckon up the time. With Nimue's skill in covering distances quickly, we should not need more than three days at most to reach London. Since Watling Street would take us much of the way, we should be able to do it in two. "Four days here," I said. "Maybe five. Luck with us, we'll hit the right place and hour by then. You can have your priests pray for it while we watch. It's our best hope."

Dame Morgan turned her head and stared at me. Even by lamplight, she was white with weariness. I must have looked haggard myself.

"I had thought you wiser than your foster-brother the

King, Sir Kay," she said. "Must you layfolk who know no magical skill always believe that the tools of magic are of necessity better than the tools of reason and mortal effort? Will you depend on my images of the past in a basin of water as Artus depended on the blade and scabbard of Excalibur, instead of looking to your own resources? Oh, yes, you are dogged and determined, Seneschal, and when you are given work that seems sure, you will cleave to it faithfully, ignoring any inspiration that seems more reckless. But though the tortoise may always reach his goal in the end, he may reach it over-late. Sometimes the reckless speed of the hare is better, after all."

She dipped her hands into the basin and brushed them across her face, then stood, leaning heavily on the chest for a moment before straightening her back. "Wake nephew Mordred and bring him up to dinner and a more comfortable sleep. I think we have watched the night through and longer—it must be near midday. We will dine and rest before we talk of these things again."

Chapter 24
Dame Morgan's Tale of Sir Astamore's Boyhood

> "*And at the last he came to a white abbey, and there they made him that night great cheer; and on the morn he rose and heard mass. And afore an altar he found a rich tomb, which was newly made; and then he took heed, and saw the sides written with gold which said: Here lieth King Bagdemagus of Gore, which King Arthur's nephew slew; and named him, Sir Gawaine. Then was not he a little sorry, for Launcelot loved him much more than any other, and had it been any other than Gawaine he should not have escaped from death to life; and* [*Lancelot*] *said to himself: Ah Lord God, this is a great hurt unto King Arthur's court, the loss of such a man.*" (Malory XVII, 17)

In fact, it was after midday when we emerged. We dined lightly, slept until vespers, and supped without much appetite.

"Have calmer thoughts crept into your mind during sleep, Sir Kay?" said Morgan.

"If you mean has my own mind thrown up any sudden, enlightening inspirations at me, Dame Morgan, no." I had realized she was right about the small chance we had of finding the traitor's identity in her bowl of water, or of bringing him to justice on the strength of her pictures; but that only inspired me with a new lack of hope. "It had to have been an enemy of the Queen, or of your nephews of Orkney, or of the Round Table in general," I said. "You were the only enemy of the Queen I could think of who might be active and subtle enough to plan something like this."

"Or it might have been an enemy of *mine,"* said Morgan, sounding slightly amused, "trying to strike at me through my beloved nephews."

"Most folk consider you dead," I reminded her. "Besides, your enemies would have struck at your son Ywaine, not at your nephews. As for an enemy of the court in general, anyone in London might be a spy with a vial of poison; but why sprinkle it on a bowl of fruit and be content with causing at most a few dozen deaths instead of poisoning our water supply or aiming at the King himself?"

"That leaves the enemies of my sister's sons, who are numerous enough to offer you a goodly choice, but not quite so numerous as all London." Morgan slowly twirled her glass goblet by the stem.

"Thank you for including all of us, Aunt," said Mordred. "Most folk would have said an enemy of Gawaine, forgetting his brothers."

"Whoever struck in malice at the rest of you would be striking at Gawaine through you, Nephew. But come—surely you can make me a list of your family's foes?"

Mordred smiled and sipped his wine. "Most recently,

Dinadan's brother Sir La Cote Male Taile, and the kinsmen of the late, lamented Bagdemagus of Gorre. Also, and from old days, Sir Ironside, who had taken an oath of old to the effect of Gawaine's destruction. And, of course, the remaining kin of King Pellinore."

"They suspect others as well," said Nimue. "Sir Bors de Ganis, the dead knight's cousin Mador de la Porte, and Sir Kay has his doubts of Gawaine's own brother Gaheris. Also Sir Kay and Sir Mordred long suspected each other—perhaps, even now, they still do, a little. Mordred, of course, thought the poison aimed at himself, and thus believed, though with deeper reason than Mador, that the Queen, possibly with the King's knowledge and support, was behind the attempt."

Morgan raised one dark eyebrow, in surprise at what part of the information I could not be sure. Mordred's face tightened and he paused very slightly before saying, "How do you know this, Dame of the Lake?"

"Remember, she searched my brain day before yesterday," I said, "without my leave, and nearly drowning me in her blasted Lake in the process."

"That is not quite just, Sir Seneschal," said Nimue calmly. "You baited me until I must assume I had your leave to show you some such power as searching your memory."

"Priests are bound by the seal of Confession for being told less than a tenth part of what you saw," I said. "If your memory-searching doesn't put you under a seal of silence, you could at least blush when you scatter your victims' secret thoughts." She was wearing her lily-white complexion again; she could have blushed easily enough.

"And so you mistrusted me, also, Seneschal?" said Mordred. "Before or after I made you that small confession of mine?" He waved his hand. "No, don't answer. It is hardly worth our friendship to know. Then let me tell you, Aunt, before Dame Nimue or the good Seneschal tells you, of how I have so arranged matters that three of our chiefest suspects—Ironside, Astamore, and Pinel of Carbonek, have been riding these past days with Agravaine, Gaheris, and Gareth, respectively, to meet us again in a few days' time at Astolat."

Morgan raised both eyebrows and nodded. "A dangerous gambit, Nephew, but one that shows imagination. But how, should one of these three strike against your brother, would you find it out and prove it to the court? Do you depend on squires' tales?"

One thing, at least, was clear to me. From what we knew of the poisoner, and from what Mordred and Dame Morgan had reasoned of his patience and plotting, he was too dangerous to leave at large, whether or not the Queen could be saved by her champion. "Maybe you can tell us something about Sir Astamore, Dame Morgan," I said.

"Young Astamore is Bagdemagus' kinsman and therefore suspect; I am Astamore's Kinswoman and therefore may know somewhat of his character, eh? Have you forgot that my husband Uriens and myself are also kin to the late, unfortunate Bagdemagus?"

"We didn't suspect you because of your kinship by marriage to Sir Bagdemagus, Dame Morgan," I said. "You earned the distinction of being suspected entirely on your own merits."

"Hated, feared, and mistrusted." She nodded. "But recognized as a power to be reckoned with. Well, my lords, I could take this chance to cast the blame on my dearly-hated Uriens. It is true that Arthur trustingly acquitted Uriens of suspicion after my ploy with the counterfeit Excalibur, even while driving my Ywaine into exile for a year for no other reason than that he was my son and therefore suspect of complicity in his mother's schemes. But Artus might more easily believe Uriens capable of striking against the killer of his nephew Bagdemagus than he was once able to believe Uriens could let himself be bent to his wife's will. It would not be hard for me to send back with you manufactured proofs and evidences of Uriens' guilt."

"It would be cunning revenge, Aunt," said Mordred, "but Uriens is our uncle as well as Bagdemagus."

Morgan smiled and stroked her cat. "Uriens is uncle to you and your elder brothers by dint of his marriage to me, and I think that his feeling for me as nearly reflects mine for him as his puny soul is capable of. If he meant to avenge Bagdemagus, the beloved son of his brother, he would not hesitate to do so on the sons of his wife's sister. Aye, family loyalties knot and tangle, do they not?"

"Whatever Uriens may be with you and other women," I said, "among men he's a good companion and still a strong fighter, for all his years. You wouldn't convince anyone your husband would stoop to poison."

"Uriens is old, Gawaine still relatively young. Even at the height of his own prime, Uriens could not have defeated his nephew in fair fight. At least, my accusation might make Arthur trust Uriens a little less. But I am not going to accuse my husband or to manufacture false evidences. I merely tell you all this in the hope that, knowing I have refused to turn this to the hurt of the one creature I have most cause to hate in all your court, you will trust my testimony and the true images I have found for you."

"I asked you to tell us about Astamore," I said, "not to give us a long demonstration of your nobility toward Uriens."

"Common blood does not infuse in relatives any instinctive knowledge of one another," said Le Fay. "Did not King Pellinore, in the heat of his quest, once fail to recognize his own daughter, so that she and her wounded knight died for want of the help her father should have given to any folk in such need? I scarcely knew Astamore when I saw him among your Queen's dinner guests. The only period during which I had seen him before was when he was a child of six or seven. Both my husband Uriens and his nephew-regent Bagdemagus were gone from their country on the higher business of attending Arthur, and I took advantage of their absence to return, take the government from Bagdemagus' foolish son Meliagrant, and reign again for a few months as queen in Gorre. The country was better for my governing than for Meliagrant's.

"Astamore was a pretty page and a ready scholar. I helped to instruct him, as I helped to instruct other pages and small damsels, in letters, harping, falconry, and some of the finer gambits of chess. I also taught them a few simple herbs and remedies to ease the pain of wounds and sickness. Most of the lads had little liking for this sort of knowledge, assuming that when they grew to knighthood they would always find surgeons, hermits, ladies and herbwives at need. But Astamore showed greater interest in herbs than in hawks or harping. Aye, he showed somewhat too much interest, pursuing his studies unsupervised. I did not teach my pages the preparation of any poisonous or harmful herbs, my lords, and I warned them strictly against picking and mixing any except those I taught them; but I did take care to point out some of the plants and growths to be avoided with greatest caution. Astamore disobeyed me, preparing infusions of his own device and gathering unknown plants, even some I had specifically forbidden. Once I caught him at it myself, once another boy brought me the tale, and both times I punished my small kinsman, but this alone did not stop his secret studies. The third time he came to me himself, in tears, with a dead brachet in his arms. He had tried out on her one of the deadly mushrooms I had cautioned the children most strictly never to touch. I beat him myself that time, to be sure it was not done over-lightly—but I think that learning I could do nothing, with all my herbs, to bring his brachet back to life again was his greatest punishment.

"As far as I know, Astamore did not meddle unguided with herbs again. But it must have been shortly afterwards that I left Gorre, at news of Bagdemagus' return for the winter. Astamore may have set aside his study of herbs for the more common pursuits of pages, or he may have found another teacher to continue his instruction. I doubt he could ever have found one who would teach him that preparation I told you of, but even as a small boy he had learned enough to kill a person quickly with natural poisons."

I thought of Astamore starting from the table as if about to rush from the room and be sick at sight of the bitch Mordred had poisoned to test the fruit. Strange that the death of a dog had affected him more strongly than the death of a brother knight. Guilty memory of the brachet he had killed as a child? Or fear that a more recent guilt was about to be found out? Or maybe the dog's death had simply driven home the realization of what had happened to the man—what could have happened to any of us there. I did not want to believe Astamore a traitor.

"But would Astamore have wished to use his knowledge?" Morgan went on. "Men and women sometimes change with the years, and I did not know him over-closely, but it seemed to me he was never a vicious nor a vengeful child. And the death of his pet may have so shaken him that he left his knowledge of herbs and posisons to rot away unused in his mind."

Neither was Gawaine a vengeful man, but his sense of justice led to results that could be about the same. Nevertheless, Astamore openly confessed that his uncle's death had been pure misfortune. Bagdemagus and Gawaine had met by chance, two knights questing for the Holy Grail and feeling the need for some of that constant exercise a man must have to keep up his jousting skill. The second time they ran together, Gawaine's spear had struck into Bagdemagus' side and broken short. It had not even been a death in the heat of battle, when a man cleaves the head of an enemy who was on the verge of surrender, as some of the witnesses said had happened in the case of King Lot's death.

"As for your other two," said Morgan, "Pinel of Carbonek is a complete stranger to me; my spies have never considered him important enough to tell me more than that he had come to your court with Lancelot after the Adventures of the Sangreal. And I undoubtedly know nothing of Ironside that you do not know more fully."

"You were not responsible for Ironside's performance before Castle Dangerous when he played the Red Knight of the Red Lands, then, Aunt?" said Mordred.

"You may find it difficult to believe, Nephew, but there is a little evil not of my plotting in the world, and there are a few wicked folk who act independently of me."

Meanwhile, thinking of Bagdemagus' death had led me into another path. Gawaine seemed never to hold back any truth, even if it were unflattering to himself. If his candor had a flaw, it was in leaving out self-justifications and mitigating circumstances. We knew the details of Bagdemagus' death, Pellinore's, and that of

Ywaine the Adventurous. We knew a tale of Gawaine's accidental beheading of Sir Ablamar's lady which was probably even less flattering to Gawaine than if he had told it himself rather than leave it to the only witnesses, his brother Gaheris and the bereaved Ablamar, to tell in their own way. Yet we knew almost no details of the death of Lamorak de Galis, other than that Gawaine and his brothers had been responsible. He had said nothing except that his mother Queen Morgawse was avenged; his younger brothers had added nothing to the statement, and even the squires Lamorak had picked up in Surluse had been surprisingly selective how they told the confused tale that helped feed the rumors and beliefs of Lamorak's kinsmen.

"Dame Morgan," I said, "can you look far enough into the past to see the death of Lamorak de Galis?"

"Lamorak de Galis? My sister's paramour. My spies were never able to tell me quite where it happened, nor have I ever felt the need or desire to learn more than that he was dead."

I looked at Mordred. "You were there, weren't you?"

"I was," he replied with a half-smile. "It happened in the forest somewhere between Surluse and Sugales."

That took in almost as much territory as we had covered between Nimue's Lake and Morgan's castle. "Dame Morgawse's murder, then," I said. "We know where that happened, but, as I recall, there's always been some slight doubt as to who—"

"There was no doubt!" said Mordred. "The traitor Lamorak murdered her as she waited for his love!"

"That has been questioned. I'm not asking you to watch it, Mordred, but if Dame Morgan can show it to me—"

"No!" Morgan rose. "I could find the chamber, and wait for the moment, but to what purpose, Seneschal?

What is important for you to know is not how my sister and her paramour met their deaths, but what your poisoner may believe of the case. If the kinsmen of Lamorak de Galis believe that he was guiltless in my sister's death and that he was killed less than honorably by her sons—"

"The traitor Lamorak met a more honorable death than he deserved," said Mordred. "Even now, the world remembers him as a great knight—the third of the world, after Lancelot and Tristram, if you please—more than as our mother's murderer."

"Leave this!" Morgan waved her hand. I doubt she cast a spell for silence, but the effect was about the same. She sat, calm again, took her cat from its refuge with Nimue, settled it in her own lap once more and began to feed it tidbits from her plate. "You may be interested to know, my lords, that news of the poisoning of Sir Patrise reached me from my spies a few hours ago, while you were sleeping. No, they added nothing to what I learned from you. They are creatures of little imagination; I prefer them so, to send me news uncluttered with speculation. I instructed them to watch, and to try to send me any further information with greater speed. I will learn nothing more from them in time to save Dame Guenevere; but, if her champion saves her, I may be able to learn somewhat to lay the lingering doubts at rest and, more important perhaps, to help you flush out this particular viper from your court. Meanwhile, I will spend the week sitting here staring into my bowl of water in hopes of catching our cleric without the cowl."

"And get the word to us a week too late?" I said.

"I can set up a kind of message link with my sister Nimue to send simple thoughts, like birds, through the air from my brain to hers, in the unlikely event I should see anything of importance. Come, will you trust me, Sir

Kay? I could as easily show you false images here were you to remain, as lie to you about my intent in this."

In other words, she was dismissing us. Well, maybe she was right, after all. "We might as well trust you," I said.

"And in return for my good will in this, you will bring my brother here to visit me?"

I would not. Between the chance that Morgan would convince him with her pictures painted by Lancelot and then persuade him to soften his vengeance and merely banish the Queen to a convent and the chance that he would never be convinced of it at all as things were going on of themselves, I preferred the latter. But, seeing no reason to antagonize Dame Morgan at this point, I said, "I'll consider it."

She sighed. "And you, Mordred? Will you reconsider?"

He glanced at me. "Yes, I'll reconsider also, Aunt. But I doubt he would believe Lancelot's silly pictures."

She wiped the grease from her fingertips and tossed her cat lightly to the floor. "If you will not take Artus my invitation, then say nothing at all to him of me. But I think you would have kept my secret without my bidding, would you not? Well, accept my hospitality this one night longer, and you can set out well-rested in the morning on your way to Astolat. And remember what I have told you, Sir Seneschal. Do not depend on the way of the tortoise. For once, play the hare."

Chapter 25
The Search for Sirs Gareth and Pinel

> *"My sons and not my chief sons, my friends and not my warriors, go ye hence where ye hope best to do and as I bade you."* (Malory XVII, 21)

Thanks to my nap in the afternoon, I lay wakeful for some time, wondering whether the spies Morgan kept among us at court were even human, and musing that I would never again be able to look at hound or brachet, cat or hawk, or even the horses and mules in the stables without wondering which of them were acting as the eyes and ears of Le Fay. After long thoughts, which may have been half dreams, in which owls and turtles lumbered in to Dame Morgan with the news that her servants, their fellow-spies the old bitch hound and the kitchen rats, had been poisoned by Mordred and myself while testing fruit, I at last decided to mull a little of the herbed wine our hostess had left, if we wanted it, to aid our sleep.

When I woke in the morning, my limbs were rested, my head felt somewhat clearer, and I was more inclined to trust Le Fay—with certain reservations. But the prospects of discovering Patrise's murderer in time to save the Queen looked no brighter than before.

Morgan's priests said Mass and her servants set breakfast for us, but Dame Morgan herself we did not see again. Nimue said she was already hard at work searching her images of the past, having risen at matins and gone down immediately after the prayers.

"And where shall we ride today, my lords?" the Dame of the Lake went on cheerfully when we were outside the castle and staring into the woods of Norgales. Dame Nimue was wearing her olive complexion and black hair, ready for travel. "If you had anything at all of Sir Lancelot's," she reminded us again, "a hair, a piece of garment or bandage, the scab of an old wound—"

"Never suspecting I'd have any use for a memento of the great man," I said, "I had better things to do than save up his nail parings and bloody bandages."

"After his experiences with Aunt Morgan," said Mordred, "the noble Du Lac is more careful with the shavings of his beard than with the reputation of the Queen. If such things are what you need, however, I can provide the means of finding whichever of my brothers we might choose."

"What?" I said.

Mordred drew a small, folded deerhide pouch from his cloak. "Here is a lock of Gawaine's hair, a few threads of ravelled embroidery from one of Agravaine's older tunics, a pearl from the sleeve of the Damsel of Whitelands that Gaheris wore once or twice as his token, and a bit of bloody bandage that I believe once wrapped a wound of Gareth's."

"Jesu!" I said. "Do you intend to spellcast your own brothers?"

"A mere harmless pastime of mine," he replied. "*I* would not know how to use these things, nor would I commission any weaver of spells to work to their hurt. But one never knows when such items may prove useful —as, you see, they will now. Come, which shall we choose?"

"If you really expected me to kill you somewhere along the way, why bring along your tokens of your brothers?"

"You would not have known how to use them, Seneschal, any more than myself. You would probably not have been able to guess what or whose they were, even had you found them, though you might have found the pearl a pretty toy. My collection was safer with me than left at court to fall into the hands of God knows whom. What, for instance, might Dame Lynette do with a personal memento of her husband?"

"Dame Lynette could have gotten a piece of Sir Gaheris before now, more easily than you, if only a fingernail full of his skin," I said, "if she'd wanted it."

"More easily than I? Are you really so sure of that, Seneschal?"

"As Dame Morgan could have gotten a memento of her husband years ago, had she wanted one," said Nimue, riding her palfrey between ours. "Come, my lords—the value of such things has been overestimated in some part of the popular mind. They are useful to us chiefly in locating their former owners, and I think my lord Sir Mordred showed admirable foresight in bringing them along. So which shall we use?"

"Not Sir Gawaine's," said Pelleas, with surprising forcefulness. I turned in my saddle to look at him. I had not even thought he was close enough to hear our conversation, let alone take an active interest in it—Dame Nimue's trained lap-husband, riding along with us mainly for the nights and seeming in the daytime, not exactly bored, but as if he had put most of his wits in storage and not kept enough on hand for immediate use to realize that he was bored. "I'd as lief see as little of Sir Gawaine as possible," he remarked.

"There's no need to search out Sir Gawaine in any case," said Nimue. "He rides with his cousin Ywaine, who will hardly be our poisoner, and I understand they are as dear friends as Gawaine and Lancelot himself, besides being bound by blood."

"The more fool Sir Ywaine," murmured Pelleas, letting his palfrey fall to the rear with the squires as he gazed dreamily at the budding trees. There are gossips who say the Damsel of the Lake spoiled Pelleas for the active life, which is also what they said for a while of Dame Enide and her Erec; but from what I have heard about Pelleas' behavior previous to his marriage, he had never been much more than a good strong fighter with a weak head and weak opinions to which he stuck doggedly because he lacked the wit to change them through his own cogitation—ripe to make a mooncalf of himself over Dame Ettard, Dame Nimue, or any other woman with a touch more character than he could boast himself. At least the Dame of the Lake kept him out of mischief.

"Then it will be Agravaine with Ironside, Gaheris with Astamore, or Gareth with Pinel," said Nimue. "The first pair were riding south, the second pair north, and the third pair northwest. That means, unless they have changed their courses, that Sir Gareth and Sir Pinel will be closest to us."

"Sometimes I think you remember my memories better than I do myself, Dame," I remarked.

"I believe I do." She smiled. "Some of them, at least, which I keep sorted and ready on the surface without the weight of emotions to bear them down."

As I thought it over, Ironside, even if he did decide to

turn to treachery, seemed more likely to fulfill his old vow with weapons—a sword in the back in an ill-lit hallway—than with poison sprinkled on a dish of fruit. Besides, the cleric had seemed too small for Ironside, though it was hard to tell in Morgan's tiny images. Astamore, we now knew, could have had the knowledge to prepare the poison himself without relying on a witch or herbwife who might betray him. A young and comparatively small-boned man, he would be no match for Gawaine or Gaheris in the field, nor even, perhaps, in a sneak attack in bad light. The question was whether he might secretly judge the death of his uncle Bagdemagus worth avenging. Dame Nimue could learn that with a touch of her finger to his forehead if she would deign to do it, which she might not without further evidence.

Astamore, also, was travelling with a brother not that much better loved than Agravaine and Mordred. If Astamore felt the need to avenge his uncle strongly enough to have tried poison, he might try striking at Gawaine through one of his brothers. Their family ties are such that Gawaine would feel the murder even of his least-loved brother more keenly than his own, but not many others would mourn Gaheris' death beyond consolation. Dame Lynette might even celebrate her widowhood.

Pinel, on the other hand, was travelling with Gareth Beaumains, the Innocent, the Aloof-from-His-Brothers, the one most likely to be exempted from any blood feud. On the whole, I would have preferred joining Astamore and Gaheris, to prevent further mischief and pick Astamore's brains if we could. And, I suppose, partly because if Astamore were guiltless as I hoped, he would be better company than Pinel the Loudvoice of Carbonek.

But Pinel seemed to be our least-known suspect of the

three; so if he was also the nearest to us in distance, I decided it would be most practical to accept that as a Heaven-sent directional omen.

Mordred sat watching me and patiently toying with his tokens. "All right," I said, "give her Gareth's bloody —which was it?—bandage. Gareth may even have something of his great hero Lancelot's that we can use from there."

Mordred tossed the bandage almost carelessly to Nimue. She snapped her fingers, which seemed to guide it through the air to her hand. Producing her copper-tipped dart, now clean of Dame Morgan's dark hairs, she bound the bandage to its point and held it up by its chain. It jounced for a moment, but Nimue blew on it and it settled down to point southeast.

"Weathercock!" Mordred leaned over his saddle to mutter at my ear. "And we called Gaheris the weathercock of the family, did we not?"

"You also explained him to me as suffering from an over-strong sense of justice." Either Gaheris was guided by the winds of opinion, blowing now from this direction, now from that; or he followed a consistent, if somewhat warped, inner devotion to justice—to me the two attempts at pinning down his character were mutually contradictory.

Mordred, however, reconciled them without blinking. "Gaheris, the Weathercock of the Winds of Justice. Would it not be strange if I were mistaken—if that bloody bandage had once wrapped Gaheris' wound, not Gareth's, so that Dame Nimue's weathercock dart brought us to the weathercock brother?"

"If you're going to keep a collection like that," I said, "you should be very sure you know where every gewgaw came from." I wondered how many more of us Mordred had represented in his collection of mementos. He must have been keeping it almost since the business at Peningues; that lock of Gawaine's hair had not yet showed any silvering. I wondered about other things, too. Meanwhile, we followed Dame Nimue's dart to the southeast, going at her magically-speeded trot.

We soon came to a minor Roman road and took it south to Watling Street, which we followed for a good part of the way even though it veered slightly from the direction of the small arrow. Even Dame Nimue's art of rapid travelling was faster and smoother for having a good road beneath us instead of mud, roots, weeds and rocks. During the day we passed a party of merchants, a few knights—probably from the local castles, nobody whose shields I recognized, at least at the speed we were going—and a number of peasants, none of whom seemed to notice us though sometimes our column had to move closer to one side of the road to pass without touching them. I assume that some spell of invisibility went along with the rapid travelling.

Towards evening, as the dart began to hum again, we left the road for the woods once more. As dark fell, Nimue's servants lit torches to keep the rear of the column together. Nimue preferred no torches near her since her dart had begun to glow and she could see more clearly without further artificial light. So we stumbled along behind her, going more nearly at natural speed because of the darkness. Finally, as the dart's hum reached its loudest, we came out in a clearing where a couple of pavilions were pitched, looking peaceful, with several fowl left unattended on spits over the cooking-fire.

As Dame Nimue's retinue crowded into the clearing behind us, Beaumains and Pinel came out of the nearer pavilion, more or less prepared to adapt their greeting to the company. Gareth carried his shield and had breastplate and swordbelt clapped on over his tunic. Pinel was in full armor and carried his sword drawn, Gareth's squire pushed through after them with his master's helmet ready.

"Did you think we were Saxons, or Saracens?" I asked, dismounting.

Gareth put down his shield and motioned his squire to help undo the breastplate. "We heard a large company coming. Friendly or not, we couldn't tell, but it seemed best to prepare against the worst."

"Well, I don't much blame you," I said. What Saxons had penetrated to this part of the country were cleaned out long ago, but our group could have been a robber-baron's band of cutthroats or even someone like Lancelot with the playful habit of cutting down friendly knights in their pavilions for the pure high spirits of it, before asking names. "Gillimer, go turn those fowls before they burn," I added, seeing that Gareth's squire was occupied unarming the two knights again while, by the sounds, Pinel's dwarf had gone to harness the warhorses in case they were needed and was now busy unharnessing them.

"But how did they hear us coming, Dame Nimue," asked Mordred, "when nobody else we passed today did?"

Nimue was twining the chain around her little arrow. "The charm of escaping folks' sight fades with lessening speed and, not wishing to take our friends by surprise, I lifted what was left of the charm of silence as we approached their camp. But why fret over a few burned fowls, Seneschal?" Flexing her arm and fingers to work out the cramps of holding the arrow up by its chain all day, she motioned to her people and they began finding places for our own pavilions.

"This is Dame Nimue?" Pinel took off his helmet and

stared at her by the fire and torchlight. "The Saxons and the Saracens may be driven back," he said in his richest and loudest voice, "but it seems there are still heathens in these southern woods. What are you doing, brothers, in the company of that Paganess, the Lady of the Lake?"

Dame Nimue stiffened. "Pagan, am I, Sir Knight? It's a proud name, and I do not object when it is given me in respect, but I am not such as your voice implies, Sir Knight."

"You learned your witch's craft from that Satan's son Merlin, did you not?" said Pinel, despite a poke in the ribs from Gareth.

"That's enough, Pinel," I said. "Your King trusted Merlin, and Dame Nimue has been the court's good friend since before you were a page."

"My lord Sir Arthur may have trusted the Devil's son, or pretended to trust him, out of fear. My lord uncle King Pellam has never trusted anything Pagan or devilish."

"Sir Father Petroc," said Nimue to her priest, "it is not too late for evensong, I think?"

"I sang it to myself, my lady, as we rode."

"Sing it again," said Nimue, "for all of us."

"Dearest darling," said Pelleas, "shall I fight him and run him through, or would you rather return to our Lake and leave him to his ravings?"

"Neither, my Pelleas. We will have good Father Petroc sing evensong for the dull soul. Better a good Pagan than a bad Christian, Sir Pinel of Carbonek," she went on.

"I will not attend your Devil's vespers," said Pinel. "In Carbonek, we know that oil and water do not mix."

"Oil is mingled with water during the high mysteries of Easter Eve. Oil burns brightly, though buoyed up by water. And your Fisher Kings blent more of the old ways with the new than you guess, Sir Mudhead."

"Enough!" I said, as Pinel opened his mouth again. "Pay no attention to him, Dame Nimue. He talks to give himself something to think about—half the time there's nothing rattling around in his brain except the sound of his voice, and he himself probably doesn't understand the sense of most of what he says. As for you, Sir Mudhead of Carbonek, you're going to hear evensong with the rest of us, like a good little boy, and hope it does you some good. And you, Beaumains, you could at least show the courtesy to blush for your companion."

"The sword of He-Who-Comes is sharper than your tongue, Sir Kay," Pinel began, but Gareth cut him off:

"For the love of Jesu, Pinel, show courtesy. Whatever her creed, the Damsel of the Lake is a gentle lady and our good friend."

"Show her courtesy, Sir Mudhead of Carbonek," I added, thinking Nimue's name for him as good a one as I could have invented myself, "or she can have her choice of champions against you, and by God, if she chooses me, we'll see whether He-Who-Comes bestirs Himself to save you from my lance and sword."

Pinel glanced around at us and finally sheathed his sword, muttering, "Brothers of the Round Table should not draw iron against one another."

Mordred, who had sat watching it all without taking part, chuckled. "Pinel, if you aspire to take Dinadan's place as the buffoon of the Round Table, you must learn to make yourself ridiculous by choice rather than happenstance."

Chapter 26
Kay's Memories of the Deaths of Morgawse and Lamorak

"Sir Lamorak saw there was none other bote, but fast armed him, and took his horse and rode his way making great sorrow. But for the shame and dolour he would not ride to King Arthur's court, but rode another way." (Malory X, 24)

Nimue's priest sang evensong by torchlight and we patched up a sort of half-armed truce. Probably the fact that Nimue's pavilions offered a lot more comfort than his own helped settle Pinel down. Dame Nimue found a chance, however, to murmur secretly to me, "I could wish that unpleasant knight to prove the poisoner."

"Read his memories," I said. "Maybe he is."

She laughed. "Ah, no, Sir Kay! You must show me clearer reason than your general doubts to make me slip my spirit into that boggy mind."

I think I grinned. "Yes, he's the blustering mudhead you called him. While he was still at Carbonek, the Sangreal probably took one of its flights abroad whenever it heard him coming. Well, if we let him talk loudly enough, maybe he'll dredge up some secret for us from the muddy shallows."

That night I dreamed of Dame Morgawse's murder; but it had not been Morgawse who was killed in her bed by her lover Lamorak, but Guenevere, murdered by Lancelot. I awoke weeping in the darkness, convinced for a time that Du Lac had decided not to fight Mador de la Porte, and chosen a worse way of using his sword to save the Queen from the fire. Even when I remembered which queen had been murdered, I still lay for a while believing it had happened recently and Lancelot had done the deed. I wondered whether Morgan le Fay really loved Lancelot after all, since she had refused to show me the night of her sister's death as if she would protect the murderer.

By morning my mind was more clear, but without much hope. The least slip in my reasoning or Mordred's, and we were chasing idle suspicions of the wrong men completely. Out of an entire court, not to mention the city of London—and there was even the possibility of a witch coming in from the countryside just long enough to work his or her mischief—what was the likelihood that the traitor was one of the three, or half-dozen, or even full score we thought most probable? Only that they had been among the Queen's guests and might have some deep grievance against Gawaine. And it was Mordred who had arranged his chosen company to meet at Astolat—Mordred, who expected the Queen to be saved by the might of Lancelot's spear and sword, or Bors', or possibly Ywaine's; Mordred, who at best regarded this whole expedition as a pleasant pastime to take his mind off a mischievous old prophecy about himself, and whose choice had been further limited to those knights he could manipulate into travelling with his own brothers. Mordred, who said he had considered *me* his chiefest suspect. What hope had we of stumbling onto the truth with reasoning like that? And Dame Nimue, it seemed, for all her magic, could only work with the material we suggested to her.

As for the murder of Dame Morgawse, it had happened years ago, before the Grail Quest, and, as her sons had always believed, Lamorak de Galis probably had been the one to kill her, in a twisted vengeance for the death of his father Pellinore at the hands of Gawaine and Gaheris. Who could blame Dame Morgan, after all, for not wanting to watch the bloody end of her own sister? Not a pleasant sight even for a sorceress like Le Fay. Besides, she was right. Even if Patrise's death had been a freak result of the long feud between the sons of Pellinore and the sons of Lot, what mattered was not whatever really may have happened, but what the sons of Pellinore and Lot believed to have happened, and it needed no magical vigils on the past to know what they believed.

Aglovale and Tor believed as a matter of course, as Dornar and Percivale had also believed when they were alive, that their brother Lamorak could never have done anything so treacherous and unknightly, and, therefore, it was someone else who had murdered Dame Morgawse. Gawaine, Agravaine, Gaheris, and Mordred believed just as firmly that Lamorak had killed their mother in pure treachery. Gareth stayed aloof so as not to anger Lamorak's friends and kinsmen, most of whom, especially after Lamorak's death, were also the adherents of Gareth's idol Lancelot.

A disinterested observer would incline to the opinion of Lot's sons. Dame Morgawse had come down from Orkney, at the invitation of Gawaine and his brothers, to stay in one of his castles near Camelot while the court was there. Gawaine's idea, and Dame Guenevere's (although they had talked of it with very few before the event and never mentioned it at all afterwards, so that most folk forgot it) was to arrange a marriage between the queen of Orkney and her lover, and thus end the long feud. As everyone expected of the paramours, Lamorak, who had let it be believed he was more than willing to wed, took his first opportunity to visit Morgawse alone in the castle by night. He went into the castle alone, leaving his dwarf with the horses at a privy postern, and when Lamorak came out of her room again, she was beheaded.

According to the dwarf's story, Lamorak had returned outside within the half-hour, badly shaken and babbling something incoherent about horror and treachery. He had leaped into the saddle as he was—half-armed and helmless, with only his sword belted around his bare tunic—without even stopping to tighten the girth, and ridden off at the gallop, keeping his seat by pure horsemanship—not back to Camelot, but in the other direction. After a few moments of hesitation between following his master and entering the castle to learn what was wrong, the dwarf had returned to court for help, naturally seeking out Gawaine as the castle's owner. Gawaine and Mordred, finding their mother dead, had gathered their other brothers (excepting Gareth Beaumains, who was absent, fortunately for himself since it spared him a difficult decision) and set out after Lamorak at once, trusting the funeral preparations to me. Unable to find Lamorak that same night, they returned for their mother's burial and then set out again.

De Galis, however, had disappeared from sight. He did not surface again until Duke Galeholt's long tournament in Surluse. Lamorak rode into the lists the third day, disguised in plain armor and a blank shield, but most folk soon recognized him by his size and style of fighting. Arthur had not planned to be at the Duke's tournament, having business elsewhere, so Dame Guenevere was presiding alone over our party. Out of respect for her, Duke Galeholt, and his friend Lancelot, Gawaine insisted the King be summoned. Arthur arrived in two days' time, but, when Gawaine and his brothers tried to appeach Lamorak formally of treason in their mother's death, Arthur refused to bring Lamorak to trial, hopefully attempting to smooth the matter over with words of truce and peace. And Dame Morgawse had been his half-sister, as well as one of his youthful romances. Lamorak loaded himself with tournament honors, fighting as coolly as if he had not been involved a short time ago in his paramour's death, while Lancelot, Palomides, and others who were trying to protect their friend or simply keep the truce prevented Gawaine and his brothers from getting near Lamorak in the medley fighting.

So, after the tournament, Gawaine, Agravaine, Gaheris and Mordred followed Lamorak into the woods. According to the two squires Lamorak had picked up in Surluse, one of the Orkney brothers had killed Lamorak's horse and one of them had finally killed their knight from behind; but the lads did not know the shields of Lot's sons, except Gawaine's, well enough at the time of the battle to say which was which, and they did not speak of the affair anyway, except when they could not avoid direct questions. Maybe they were afraid of Orkney vengeance on themselves, or maybe they were grateful to Gawaine and his brothers for leaving them alive and bringing them on to Arthur's court. Gawaine said nothing about the actual fighting except that Queen Morgawse was avenged, and her other sons said nothing except that Gawaine had fought Lamorak fairly.

Out of respect, as Gawaine said, for the warrior Lamorak had once been, they had refrained from separating the body to bring back the head, but left him buried whole at the nearest woodland chapel, about a mile from the scene of battle. Gawaine even had Masses offered for Lamorak's soul, and when Lamorak's brothers suggested to his face that this showed a guilty conscience, he only replied that Lamorak might have killed Dame Morgawse in a fit of madness rather than in planned malice.

Although Lancelot grieved publicly for Lamorak as a dear friend and a warrior second in arms only to himself and Tristram, he also, at the same time, clove to his dearer and older friendship with Gawaine, maintaining his opinion that by the will of Heaven, justice, however tragic, had somehow been done; and Lancelot's publicly-expressed opinions, as well as the King's affection for his favorite nephew, helped quell the further reprisals and challenges that might otherwise have come from Lamorak's brothers and kinsmen.

Or else the feelings had been driven underground, to fester for years and finally break out in an attempt to poison Gawaine. But why now? Why not years ago, before the Grail Quest, when the killings were fresh? Maybe old Saint Nascien's warning was coming true, and those knights who had gone looking for the Sangreal unworthily, as they demonstrated by failing to find it, really had returned more sinful than when they started.

Meanwhile, Dame Nimue had remembered to ask Beaumains if he had any token of Lancelot's that we could use to find the Queen's champion. He had more than one: a comb and a small dagger Lancelot had given him when he was masquerading as my kitchen knave, the swordbelt and plume Lancelot had presented to him on dubbing him knight, and even a fragment of the first spear Lancelot had broken on him. But all these relics were either back in his rooms at court or laid up in silver caskets at his wife Dame Lyonors' castle. So, since we still had a day before the appointed meeting at Astolat, and Gareth and Pinel had planned their journey cannily enough, we spent that day poking into nooks and crannies at a naturally slow pace and, naturally, finding nothing but a few bees and wasps.

"It's that Pagan woman with us," said Pinel when we stopped for the evening, although he was careful to say it while she and her husband were out of earshot, overseeing the pitching of their large, comfortable pavilions, in one of which Pinel would spend the night.

"If you say such things to a person's face," I remarked, "you're called a churl. If you say them behind the person's back, you're merely called a courtly gossip."

"And if you were merely to think them, never speaking them at all?" said Mordred, lying on his stomach and molding little structures of twigs and earth. "How would you be called then?"

"Probably a model of politesse," I said.

"Aye," Mordred replied, "but is not politesse, then, closely akin to hypocrisy?"

"Aye, sit there and speak lightly," said Pinel, "but I tell you both that Heaven will hardly prosper any search undertaken with the Heathen in our company."

"I notice you're keeping your sweet voice low, Pinel," I said. "Very unusual for you. Afraid the Pagan woman will overhear and make you spend the night in your own tatty pavilion?"

"The vespers of the Pagan woman's priest," said

Mordred, "sounded remarkably like those of our most Christian King's own chaplains and bishops."

"The worst sin of all," insisted Pinel, righteously picking at a frayed place in his tunic, "is to mix true and Pagan practices. It is high heresy."

Gareth put in, "We had no better success in finding Sir Lancelot before Dame Nimue joined us."

Pinel shook his head. "God knows the deeds of men beforehand, and that you would welcome her into our company before the search was over. We understand these things at Carbonek, where the Fisher Kings guarded the Sangreal through the centuries, while the rest of your world outside weltered in heresy and heathendom. Why do you think so few of you found the Sangreal?"

Mordred sat up to face Pinel, not quite seriously. "Ah, and is it true that the Holy Grail is no longer with you, having chosen to leave this sinful world—even Carbonek—forever? Granted that Heaven knows our deeds beforehand, Pinel, and speeds us accordingly; but has Heaven turned Its back on the entire body of searchers because one small, separate group of them, unbeknownst to the others, has taken a woman of questionable creed into its company? Or may it not be that we are, quite simply, looking in the wrong part of the country, and Heaven, declining to bring Lancelot into our way through miracle, has left him wherever he is, to be found by some other searchers?"

"That's right!" said Gareth eagerly. "He may be found already. He may be in London even now to save the Queen."

Pinel shrugged. "Well, and if he is not. . . Yes, Heaven knows all, and will find means to save the Queen if she is innocent."

"She *is* innocent, Sir Mudhead of Carbonek," I said,

tempted to go on and tell him how we knew and where we had watched the poison sprinkled on the fruit. But that might put him on his guard, if he had known anything about it before.

"Innocent of the poisoning, perhaps. Did I charge her with the poisoned fruit? But of some other secret sin. . . Who but Heaven, after all, knows for what sin Sir Patrise was killed?"

"If Dame Guenevere has a sin," I said, "the sin is in being gossipped about by the likes of you. Go out and talk to the common people, De Carbonek. When have they had a better Queen, or one they loved more? Ask the common folk how they knew which was the true Guenevere when that look-alike witch took her place for two years and let the kingdom slide to waste and wrack. By God, if it were legal, the commoners would rise in a body and fight Mador to save their Queen, whether they thought she was a poisoner or not!"

"The commoners also have a high opinion of brother Gaheris," Mordred murmured, "to judge by Cob the charcoal burner. Although good Dame Iblis would disagree with him."

Pinel made one of his rapid veerings to another side of the question. "Even if Dame Guenevere were the most guiltless woman born of the race of Eve, is she not a source of scandal and dissension? You prove it yourself, Seneschal. Might not the Divine Wisdom take her early to Itself for the welfare of our King and court?"

Mordred put his hand on my shoulder just in time to hold me down. "Calm yourself, Sir Kay, calm yourself. Remember that he is but a buffoon, unaware of his own folly." In a louder voice, he said to Pinel. "Is it not strange, knight of God's own country, to maintain that the wicked die for offending Heaven and the good die because Heaven wishes to bring them to their reward, even though both wicked and good die equal in age and equal in agony? Might we not say of Sir Brumant the Proud—you remember, the Gaulish knight who chose to sit in Galahad's Siege Perilous? Of course you remember; we've all heard you talk of him at some length—might we not say of him that, far from punishing his pride, Heaven welcomed him, like the prophet Elias, up to itself in a pillar of fire?"

We did not realize that Dame Nimue had come up behind our circle. Maybe she somehow held our eyes from seeing her until the moment when she said, "And do you really believe, Sir Pinel of Carbonek, that poor Sir Patrise died in divine punishment for some secret sin?"

Chapter 27

Sir Pinel's Tale of the Dolorous Stroke

"And as they were even afore King Arthur's pavilion, there came one invisible, and smote this knight that went with Balin throughout the body with a spear. Alas, said the knight, I am slain under your conduct with a knight called Garlon; therefore take my horse that is better than yours and ride to the damosel, and follow the quest that I was in as she will lead you, and revenge my death when ye may. That shall I do, said Balin, and that I make vow unto knighthood; and so he departed from this knight with great sorrow. . . . Then they rode three or four days . . . and by hap they were lodged with a gentleman that was a rich man and well at ease. And as they sat at their supper Balin overheard one complain grievously by him in a chair. What is this noise? said Balin. Forsooth, said his host, I will tell you. I was but late at a jousting, and there I jousted with a knight that is brother unto King Pellam, and twice smote I him down, and then he promised to quit me on my best friend; and so he wounded my

son, that cannot be whole till I have of that knight's blood, and he rideth alway invisible; but I know not his name. Ah! said Balin, I know that knight, his name is Garlon, he hath slain two knights of mine in the same manner, therefore I had liefer meet with that knight than all the gold in this realm, for the despite he hath done me." (Malory II, 12–14)

Pinel started at her voice and glanced up at her smiling, mischievous face. "Why else, madame?" he said. "Here were apples and pears that any man would have expected Sir Gawaine to taste the first. Yet it was not Gawaine, but Patrise of Ireland who ate of them and died. What else is this but Heaven's making use of the poison at hand to repay Sir Patrise for the sins of his heart, while reserving Gawaine for some other fate?"

"If Sir Patrise deserved to die like that," said Gareth, "what must the rest of us deserve?"

"I've seen worse deaths," said Mordred. "I can conceive worse yet. Why not assume that Heaven in Its mercy chose to translate Sir Patrise, in the bloom of his youth and innocence, from our sinful world directly to bliss and the presence of the Grail? Perhaps Patrise is to be envied. Indeed, why speak of poison at all? No doubt the apple had nothing to do with the miraculous translation, and the bitch I fed with it died of coincidence, or perhaps of an ecstasy of joy at partaking of the relic from a saint's mouth."

I shook my head. "No, no, Mordred. You misunderstand Pinel's parable. The apple represents the forbidden fruit of the Garden of Paradise, and Patrise represents our first father Adam, who ate the fruit and died. It all happened for our instruction, you see."

"Yes, I have thought that, too," said Pinel, and I

swear that, although he had begun to glower as if he realized that Mordred was baiting him, he seemed to take me seriously. "That is the symbolic meaning, of course," the knight of Carbonek went on. "And the Queen represents our first, sinful mother Eve, who gave Adam the deadly fruit."

"How fortunate," murmured Nimue, before I could speak, "that we have one among us bred at Carbonek, where even the simple squires have more understanding of holy mysteries than have archbishops elsewhere, to expound these lessons to us."

Smirking, Pinel inclined his head to her. "Perhaps you are not so very far from the truth, after all, madame."

"I suppose that asking for your speculations on who may have poisoned the fruit would be putting too worldly an interpretation on the facts?" I said.

Pinel shrugged. "In the meaning of the parable, the poisoner naturally represents the Serpent, the Evil One who tempted the woman."

Even though Her Grace knew nothing about it, I thought; but Pinel was prattling on:

"In the punishment of Patrise for his own guilt—for Heaven combines many purposes in a single action: parable, retribution, opportunity for redemption—"

"How thrifty of Heaven!" remarked Mordred.

Pinel glared at him and went on, "In the punishment of Patrise for his own guilt, the poisoner acted merely as the unwitting agent of Heaven, as that unfortunate knight Sir Garlon and the bloody Balin acted in bringing about the Dolorous Stroke."

"Most folk would have called Sir Garlon bloody and Sir Balin unfortunate," said Nimue.

"Most folk in the world know only what that Satan's son Merlin told of the matter," said Pinel.

"And what Balin is said to have told of it on his way from the Waste Lands of Carbonek to his death in the

Lost Isles," said Mordred. "And what information Bors the Pious brought back from his journeyings with the sainted Galahad, Percivale, and Dame Amide. And what half a score of kinsfolk and lovers of Garlon's victims had to tell of it. But let us hear your account of the matter, Sir Knight of Carbonek, since you, of course, know the exact truth, though I doubt your father had yet thought of putting you in your mother's womb at the time."

"You are mistaken in that, Sir Mordred," said Pinel stiffly. "I was already conceived, though not yet born, when the wretched Balin dealt the Dolorous Stroke. But, of course, in your pride you mistake many things."

Mordred began to scratch patterns in the moss with a twig. "Whatever my secret sins, Sir Knight, I am not proud. But let us hear how you saw the adventure of the Dolorous Stroke, from the vantage-point of your mother's womb."

Pinel glanced at his travelling companion of the last eight days. "Sir Gareth has already heard the tale."

"I'll hear it again," said Beaumains. I mused that he had probably heard it, and one or two score of Pinel's other tales, several times over on this journey. Pinel's slight hesitation to go into fuller details of this particular episode seemed unlike his flapping mouth; I realized I myself had never heard Pinel's version of the Dolorous Stroke through from beginning to end—but then, I had avoided Pinel's rigmaroles as much as possible. Of course, Pinel's uncle King Pellam of Carbonek and Listeneise, who had received the Stroke, was Pellinore's brother. I had not credited Pinel with much delicacy before now, but he might be a little reluctant to expound overmuch on his family's history in the hearing of Mordred or any other of the sons of Lot, except Gareth Beaumains.

"You will know, then," said Pinel, "because Sir Bors

tells it with reasonable accuracy, how, many years ago, in his youth, my uncle Sir Pellam, the last of the Fisher Kings and the sixth in direct descent from Josue, the brother of Alain the Great, first guardian of the Holy Grail from the hands of Joseph's son of Arimathea, while out hunting one day, came to the seaside and found the marvelous ship set adrift by the wise King Solomon to ride the waters of the world until the days of his descendant Sir Galahad."

I yawned openly. "Well, we might as well make a full evening's entertainment of it, Pinel. Why not name all the intervening generations between Josue and Pellam, and between Solomon and Galahad, too, while you're at it?"

He squinted in annoyance. "My uncle, King Pellam, read the mystical writing on the ship's side to warn men of weak faith against entering the vessel. Naturally, being firm in the true faith as mortal man can be, my uncle entered into the vessel and found the great sword that had once been wielded by King David, Jesse's son. Uncle Pellam read and pondered the warnings on sword-hilt and scabbard; and, knowing himself to be clean of life, a noble king and descended from noble kings, and the keeper of the Holy Grail, he decided in all humility and holy trembling to make the attempt to draw the sword. Did not Sir Pellam stand a better chance than most knights of being he for whom the blade was meant? How could Sir Galahad himself have claimed the sword if he had not dared try to draw it?"

"So King Pellam drew the sword about a quarter of the way out," said Mordred, "where it stuck fast in the scabbard and would neither come the rest of the way nor go back in. Since, as you say, we know all this from Bors de Ganis, why tell it again? Come straight to the Dolorous Stroke."

"That's asking a horse to leap like a cat, from a crouch, without taking a turn back to get a running start," I said.

"Aye, but after his running start the horse usually leaps clear, while Sir Pinel takes a running start in order to wade ankle-deep through a mire," said Mordred.

Dame Nimue laughed, attracting Pelleas and a few of her other attendants to our group; but Gareth said angrily, "You chastise your kitchen knaves, Sir Seneschal, for showing manners not half so churlish as your own."

"That's right," I agreed. "And you never had the boldness to risk my chastisement for a saucy tongue until you were out of the kitchen and into your knighthood, did you, Beaumains?"

"Oh, hush," said Nimue, still chuckling. "Do you blame poor Sir Pinel for sloughing through a mire and then yourselves raise up a forest of brambles in his way?"

By now, had I been in Pinel's place, I would have left the company, or at least realized that no one was particularly interested in the tale. He, however, straightened his shoulders, rubbed his thin beard, glanced around at us, cleared his throat with dignity, and sloughed on. "Having learned the sword was not to be his, but heartened, by the blamelessness of his life and the fact that he had drawn it partway out, to hope he might escape the threatened retribution for the attempt, my uncle King Pellam left King Solomon's Ship, which began drifting away elsewhere as soon as he was safely ashore. Indeed, for some years his land prospered, in a worldly richness, as rarely before, and the king's daughter, my fair cousin Elaine, grew to young maidenhood.

"Now my uncle's brother, the good knight Sir Garlon, was given the grace to ride through the world invisible, wreaking Heaven's just punishment on sinful knights, whom he knew by the heat of their fleshly lusts or by some other Heaven-sent sign. Balin, that proud knight who gained his sword through sinful enchantment, joined the fleshly paramour of a knight Sir Garlon had righteously slain, and rode in pursuit of Sir Garlon. Balin and his wanton woman came to the castle of Carbonek during one of my uncle King Pellam's feasts of friendship and peace; and, although it was a place and time of friendship, Balin refused to ungird his sword, claiming some custom of his own savage country. The attendants, suspecting no ill-will, decided to allow him his custom rather than mar the peace with quarreling. But when Balin the proud and violent came into the banquet chamber, there in the presence of the king and the other guests, he drew his sword and cut down Sir Garlon in cold blood and treachery, and when good Sir Garlon was dead, the wanton woman thrust her fleshly lover's broken spear through his corpse in mockery.

"My uncle the king called for his own weapon, and when it was brought to him, while Balin and the woman still made sport of their victim's body, Sir Pellam rose up to avenge his brother. At the first blow they struck, Balin's blade, wrought by false enchantments, broke beneath my uncle's righteous weapon. Then the proud Sir Balin fled, deeper and deeper into the castle, paying no heed to private places or sacred, until he came to the Holy of Holies, where the Relics were guarded. Here he saw the hallowed Spear with which the Roman pierced Our Lord Jesu on the Rood. Without stopping to learn what it was, seeing only a weapon and not a holy relic, Balin caught it up and thrust it at King Pellam—and Heaven permitted the proud knight to drive it through both King Pellam's thighs, thus dealing the Dolorous Stroke that punished the good king's one transgression, leaving him a cripple until his grandson Sir Galahad grew to manhood and returned to heal him and restore the land, which had wasted with its ruler, to its prosperity."

"Rather stiff punishment, for an offense as light as you make it out to have been," I remarked.

"So does Heaven punish the sins of Its servants in this life, in order to free them from all punishment in the next. But my uncle, King Pellam, was maimed with the same weapon which had touched the heart's blood of Our Lord Jesu Himself—the highest honor even in the chastisement. Nor did Balin go unpunished for his sins, his pride and impiety. When he touched the sacred relic, the earth quaked and part of the castle fell about him—his wanton woman perished there, as Balin himself would have perished had not the Devil's son Merlin come to save him for a worse punishment: killing and killed at the hands of his own brother, Sir Balan. So did God, for Balin's sins, make him Its instrument of vengeance, and thus allow him to compound his own guilt and bring down further retribution upon his own head, as He allowed the Philistines to triumph for a time over His chosen people for their purification, and afterwards destroyed the Philistines utterly for their greater sin."

"And meanwhile," said Mordred, "King Pellam's folk were left with a blighted land, a maimed king, and a castle to be built up again around the Holy Relics." He shook his head. "And Galahad the Pure was conceived to mend the mischief, as others of us were conceived to make new mischief—all, it seems, by Heaven's design."

"King Pellam's design and his daughter Elaine's had a little to do with Galahad's conception, as well," I said. As nearly as I understood the tale, the crippled busybody of Carbonek and his resident sorceress Dame

Brisane had played the panders to bring Lancelot and Elaine together. According to other reports, also, Pellam's feast of peace and friendship had been closed to any man who did not bring a wife or paramour—maybe to give Garlon the opportunity of finding more "lustful knights" to murder—and Garlon's blood had been needed to heal a victim he had left merely wounded, which explained why Balin and his lady had lingered to "desecrate" the body by collecting blood, instead of making their escape while Pellam waited for his weapon. I had never met either Garlon or King Pellam, though what I heard of them made their brother Pellinore seem more than ever to have been the cream of that generation of the family. But I had known Balin for almost as earnest and well-meaning a young knight as Gawaine himself, though a bit more quick-tempered. Frankly, little use as I had ever had for old Merlin and his symbolic babblings, I had even less use for Pinel's version of the Dolorous Stroke, nor could I see that it told us anything of Pinel we had not known already. Since I was tired of his parabolic interpretations, all I said was, "You should lay aside your weapons and turn hermit right away, Sir Knight of Carbonek. Then you could explain everybody's dreams and histories to your soul's content."

Chapter 28
The Practice Tourney at Astolat

"By my head, said Sir Mordred to the damosel, ye are greatly to blame so to rebuke [Sir La Cote Male Taile], for I warn you plainly he is a good knight, and I doubt not but he shall prove a noble knight; but as yet he may not yet sit sure on horseback, for he that shall be a good horseman it must come of usage and exercise. But when he cometh to the strokes of his sword he is then noble and mighty, and that saw Sir Bleoberis and Sir Palomides, for wit ye well they are wily men of arms, and anon they know when they see a young knight by his riding, how they are sure to give him a fall from his horse or a great buffet. But for the most part they will not light on foot with young knights, for they are wight and strongly armed. For in likewise Sir Launcelot du Lake, when he was first made knight, he was often put to the worse upon horseback, but ever upon foot he recovered his renown, and slew and defoiled many knights of the Round Table. And therefore the

rebukes that Sir Launcelot did unto many knights causeth them that be men of prowess to beware; for often I have seen the old proved knights rebuked and slain by them that were but young beginners." (Malory IX, 4)

We came to Astolat about midafternoon of the next day, it being the tenth day after Sir Patrise's burial, and the day Mordred had appointed for the jolly gathering which he may or may not have expected he would live to see. We were the first to arrive. Our party alone, Mordred, myself, Beaumains and Pinel with our squires, and Dame Nimue with all her people, seemed almost to double the population of the place.

Sir Bernard the Honest, the Baron of Astolat, keeps a small manor with crumbling defense walls, though folk sometimes call it a castle out of courtesy, and depends on the comparative poverty of his town and its closeness to both London and Camelot to guard him from enemy depredations and costly visitations of the court in its progresses. He put a good face on our unexpected appearance and, no doubt, would eventually have been able to lodge us all; but the size of our party, and the news that we expected four more pairs of noble knights with their squires to join us, had almost the same effect on him that a full courtly visitation might have had, and he did not argue when we proposed to set up our pavilions in the meadow between the forest and the fields rather than to take rooms inside the manor itself. Eager to play the good host, however, Sir Bernard had two pavilions of his own brought out and pitched beside ours, one for himself and his sons, one for his daughter and her nurse.

We had Bernard's sons, Tirre and Lavaine, join our own squires and gave them a hasty mock-tournament, with blunted weapons, to help round out their training and take the edge off our wait. Beaumains, Pelleas, Mordred, Pinel, and Sir Bernard formed the knights' party; Gareth Beaumains and Pelleas being recognized as among the top half-dozen men of their arms in the world, each supposedly worth at least three or four ordinary champions, I fought with the five squires, Tirre, Lavaine, Gillimer, Lovel, and Gareth's Villiars—they needed a seasoned man in their ranks, and it was the better exercise for me. A couple of Bernard's men-at-arms waited ready to come in if his old herald, Dame Nimue's musician, and Pinel's dwarf, acting as keepers of the field, judged that either party was too badly overmatched in the melee; but, although Beaumains and Pelleas had pretty much their own way in the individual jousts, once we got to the mixed fighting the squires and I held our own against their party, for all their glowing reputation.

It took our thoughts off our present business, it worked away the afternoon, and it gave Sir Bernard's offspring one of the thrilling days of their lives to date, especially since it was probably the closest thing to a real tournament Asolat would ever witness. The baron's daughter Elaine, still young and almost smooth-chested, enjoyed it as much as her brothers, or maybe more, since she took no bruises, sitting between her nurse and Dame Nimue, clapping her hands and cheering for Lavaine, to whom she had given her second-best scarf as favor.

The keepers of the field seemed about ready to call the action to its close in time for vespers, when Gawaine and Ywaine arrived. At the moment, I had not quite recovered from one of Beaumains' blows to the helm, and Gillimer had been put out of action for the day some time earlier by a blow from Pelleas that numbed his arm and gave him an excuse to shirk his duties for the rest of the evening, so our party was being bested just then. As I began to recover my wits and lift my blunted sword to go to the nearest squire's assistance, I suddenly became aware that a fresh knight was bearing down on me. I had barely time to turn, bring round my weapon, and glimpse the lion rampant of Ywaine's shield before I was rolling on the ground, with Ywaine leaping his horse over to avoid trampling me. By the time I could sit up, Gawaine and Ywaine had the field won for the squires' party, Pelleas and his shield were no longer anywhere in evidence, and the keepers were shouting the end of the medley.

As I finally got the matter sorted out, Gawaine and Ywaine had ridden in, weary from a day of searching for Lancelot (like the champions they were, they had been travelling fully armed and helmed), to find a small tourney in progress. They had realized it was friendly practice; however, counting four virgin white shields against six—as they supposed—blazoned ones, they had also realized it was untested young knights or raw squires against seasoned veterans, and decided to give the youngsters a hand. Since I was not actually striking a blow at the moment, but apparently looking less dazed than I was feeling, Ywaine had assumed from my blazoned shield that I was fighting with the other knights, and accordingly put me out of action before I could fall on the innocents again. Pelleas, meanwhile, recognizing Gawaine's crimson shield with the gold pentangle, had chosen to take offense that Gawaine should dare enter a friendly combat on the side against his, and ridden from the field in a huff.

No one being seriously hurt, and the Astolat folk being unaware of the undercurrents between Gawaine and Pelleas, we picked ourselves up, turned our horses over to the grooms, unarmed with the help of servants and ladies; I managed to kiss and forgive Ywaine with more grace than I felt; and we all washed and went to vespers and then to supper. Gawaine and Pelleas were seated far enough from each other at meat, with enough folk between, to avert unpleasantness during the meal.

Supper over, we danced for a while, to prove we were less bruised and weary than we actually were, and listened to Dame Nimue's minstrel and singing maidens, who know songs and tales no other minstrels knew. Our host's daughter, at least, loved the dancing, and those of us who did not follow the songs and tales with full attention kept our fidgeting to ourselves.

When we separated to go to our own pavilions, neither Agravaine and Ironside nor Gaheris and Astamore had yet shown up.

"All right, it's the evening of the tenth day," I said to Mordred when we were alone. "Where are your brothers?"

"Pacing our borrowed pavilion will not bring them any the faster, Seneschal. I doubt we can look for them, now, before morning."

"Agravaine and Gaheris—the ones you should have had most influence over."

Perhaps no outsider had stated the internal politics of the Orkney clan quite so boldly to Mordred's face before, but he took it in stride. "You flatter me to say that the youngest holds sway over two of his considerably elder brothers. You also seem to credit me with a shade more influence over Gaheris than I actually possess. But if they choose to interpret 'the tenth day' somewhat loosely, shall we lose our sleep, as they probably are not? A simple family rendezvous, after all, lacks the sacredness of an appointment to meet for solemn battle."

"The Queen's trial is in four days."

"And London can be reached from Astolat in one,

even without Dame Nimue's fast travel." Mordred stretched out and pulled up the silken bedclothes Dame Nimue had lent us along with the pavilion. "Has no knight ever been late to an assignation before now?" he added.

"If Ironside or Astamore is the traitor, one of your brothers might be dead!"

"In that case, we will soon know the traitor by his deed. I will hope it is Astamore, as seems not unlikely. Gaheris goes too much his own way to be quite manageable, but Agravaine makes a satisfactory ally."

"A few days ago," I said, "you tried to put all the blame for your slander against the Queen on Agravaine. You said, as I recall, that he must have lied to you as well as to everyone else."

Mordred opened his innocent blue eyes, which had been left slightly bloodshot by the afternoon's tourney, and gazed up at me for a moment. "Can it be that we are mistaken, and it is the elder brother who has the evil influence over the younger? Perhaps Sir Ironside would do us all a favor by dispatching brother Agravaine."

I started to damn him, and decided to go pace outside instead. With luck, he would be asleep by the time I got back.

Light and music were still coming from Nimue's own pavilion, so I walked towards it. The flaps being open, I glanced in. The Dame of the Lake and her consort were not yet abed, but sitting side by side, his arm around her shoulders, listening to her minstrel pluck some soft melody in a minor key.

I stepped inside. The minstrel did not stop playing. Pelleas glanced up and said, "Rude actions as well as rude words now, Sir Kay?"

"Will the flames be polite four days from now, Sir Gentle?" I said. "If you want to be private, close your tent-flaps and blow out your candles. I have something important to talk over with your wife. Do you trust her alone with me for a few moments outside?" Actually, I had nothing to talk over with her that could not have been said in front of Pelleas, but the thought of his moon-face hovering disinterested at the edges of our conference annoyed me.

He shrugged. "Since I would be more than your match with my head and left side unarmed and my left hand bound behind my back, Seneschal, I trust you with her."

Maybe Pelleas was not quite the slaggard wit he usually seemed. He had described, presumably on purpose to nettle me, the way Lancelot had fought Meliagrant when the latter charged Dame Guenevere of sleeping with me. "With your other failings, I wouldn't put you to such an excess disadvantage," I said, "and I'm more afraid of Dame Nimue's weapons than yours."

"Don't be wearisome," said Nimue. She rose and came to the door, signing her minstrel, as she passed him, to keep on with his music. "You must forgive my Pelleas," she went on quietly to me as we stepped outside. "He's out of sorts because of Sir Gawaine."

"He knew Gawaine was going to be here."

"Aye, but do we not all sometimes overestimate our ability to rule ourselves in the situations to come? This is not what you wished to speak of, however."

"We still have two pairs of knights who should have been here today and aren't."

She nodded. "There are a hundred reasons why knights should come late to their appointments. . . but Gawaine's brothers are travelling in company with suspected traitors and enemies to their family."

"I'm glad one other person here besides myself can think with some sense."

"I do my best," said Dame Nimue. "So you wish me to take Sir Mordred's mementos of his brothers tomorrow and search for Sir Agravaine and Sir Gaheris. Would—"

She broke off. Someone was approaching with a strong, healthy stride. Thinking I recognized the sound of his footfall, I turned for a look. Gawaine's gold and silver hair showed up well enough in the patch of light from the pavilion doorway. So did his crimson tunic with the famous green sash making a dark band across his chest.

Chapter 29
The Tale of Pelleas and Ettard

"And she stepped up softly and stole to his bed,
Caught up the curtain, and coyly crept in,
And settled herself full snug on the bedside,
And lounged there at length, to look for his waking."
(SIR GAWAINE AND THE GREEN KNIGHT)

"My lord," said Nimue in a low voice, obviously not badly pleased, for her own part, to see him.

"My lady." Coming up to us, he stopped and bowed. "I do not break in upon you?"

"You don't break in upon an amorous tête-à-tête, Gawaine, if that's what you mean," I said.

"Even so, I still envy you, Sir Kay. The Lady Nimue is known no less for her beauty and wit than for her virtue. Is your lord awake within, madame?"

"He is." She lowered her voice still more. "But I would not try to make peace with him tonight, if I were you."

Gawaine smiled and produced one of his favorite

catch-phrases. "What may man do but try? If you will excuse me now, I'll leave you to your conversation."

As if we were going to be able to finish our own conversation now. After bowing again to the Dame of the Lake, Gawaine went into the pavilion to brave Pelleas. Nimue clutched my arm and we stood and listened. Inside, the minstrel went on plucking his harpstrings.

Pelleas' voice: "This is the night for unwelcome intruders, it seems."

Gawaine's: "I came to ask your pardon, good knight, for my offense this afternoon."

Pelleas: "Oh. So at least you realize you did commit an offense this afternoon."

Gawaine: "Half unwittingly. In the rush and the excitement, I did not at once recognize your device."

Pelleas: "How extraordinary. I knew yours at once."

"Pelleas and his shield were mixed up in the melee," I muttered. I would have gone in to say it to his face, but Nimue held me back.

"Hush!" she whispered. "The quarrel between them is far deeper than an afternoon's mock-tourney."

"We saw it was no more than a practice battle, for love," Gawaine was saying, in response to some statement Pelleas had made while Nimue and I were muttering.

"And you did not recognize even one of our shields?" said Pelleas. "Of five shields, you did not recognize one companion of the Round Table, and two of them your born brothers?"

"Aye, we rode against our brothers of the Table, and we rode in without stopping to change our weapons for blunted ones," confessed Gawaine, "though, with God's grace, no injury was done. I hope at least you will forgive Ywaine, whose offense was the lesser, following my lead. And if you do not find it in your heart to forgive me tonight, I pray you will tomorrow."

"And thirty-three years ago?" said Pelleas. "Was it half unwittingly you betrayed me then? Or was I fair game to you then, not yet being a brother of the Round Table?"

"Jesu!" I exclaimed. I broke away from Nimue and went in. "How in God's Name should Gawaine have recognized your shield, Pelleas? How often have you been around your King's court these past thirty years, to expect people to remember your device? And as for brothers of the Table—"

"Churl to the last!" began Pelleas, and Gawaine tried to catch my arm, but I shook them both off.

"As for brothers of the Table, you were willing enough to let me fight with the squires against you this afternoon. You call *me* churl? I forgave Ywaine a greater offense than you had from Gawaine this afternoon. And as for thirty-three years ago, isn't it about time to let Dame Ettard sleep in peace? And stop that infernal twanging!" I added to the minstrel.

"If you do not hush," said Dame Nimue, who had come in behind us, "I will cast the spell of melancholia over all of you!"

I hushed, not having overmuch taste to experience that again. Pelleas shrugged and sat on the bed, looking as if he believed his little wife had not really included *him* in the threat, but was willing to humor her. I think Gawaine would have remained quiet without the threat. The minstrel finally stopped playing and sat cross-legged, trying to look deaf and dumb.

"It is partly my fault," Nimue went on. "Some memories stay greener than they should, especially in my Lake, where time seems shorter and yet life stays always much the same."

"Pelleas," said Gawaine heavily, "I tried not to betray

you with Dame Ettard. But I cannot blame you for looking at the appearances and believing otherwise."

"It's obvious that your understanding of betrayal in such matters and that of the rest of the world are somewhat at variance," said Pelleas with a sneer.

"Dame Ettard crept from her bed into mine that night, when I was already between sleep and waking. She had done so before, and I had . . . held her in stalemate, trying to work her affections toward you, as I had pledged you my word. That night . . . I am not sure." He shook his head. "She was a very beautiful lady, and my wits were dulled with sleep and wine. I had not meant to betray you. But you have Dame Nimue now. Can we not let the lady whom we destroyed between us rest in peace, as Sir Kay says?"

"The lady whom we destroyed *among* us three," Nimue corrected him.

"Aye," said Pelleas. "When the great Sir Gawaine is the offender, he humbly craves mercy and the forgiving end of the feud. When he is the offended against, he does not rest until he has justice and blood."

Gawaine flinched slightly, but he kept his voice even. "I thank you, Sir Pelleas, for that insight. If you wish at any time to do battle, I will be at your command. . . . My lady Nimue, forgive me for disturbing your evening." He bowed to them both, looked at me and gripped my shoulder—either to thank or forgive me for trying to come to his defense, I suppose—and went out.

"Pelleas," said Nimue, "you will not fight him."

"No. I will not fight Gawaine, I will not fight Lancelot, I will scarcely even come to fight the common foe in my King's battles, though my wife, the Damsel of the Lake, might stand by to keep me from harm! But I tell you this, Dame Nimue, we will not stay here one hour longer where that man Gawaine is also!"

"Fine," I said. "I don't remember asking you to join the company in the first place, Pelleas."

He glared at me, of course. "To be insulted by *you!* To hear the proud Sir Gawaine—'he did not at once recognize my device'—as much as to call me an insignificant knight—'Ywaine but followed his lead'—so he made himself the leader of better men than he—and now to be insulted again by the braggart whom every knight defeats, but who considers himself specially privileged for being the King's foster brother! Dame Nimue, we leave at once!"

I kept my anger under sufficient control to hold back the first remarks that came to my tongue and say instead, "You can go as soon as you like, Sir Most Important, and we'll be glad to see your backside. But Dame Nimue stays."

"My wife comes with her husband, out of this company of rogues and churls." In his anger, Pelleas had apparently forgotten which was the dominant partner in his marriage.

And Dame Nimue humored him. "Of course, my lord. We will leave at once, love, as soon as our pavilion can be raised, and spend the night in some glade far from here."

"For the love of God and His Mother!" I said. "This is a matter of Dame Guenevere's life! I brought you to save the Queen, Dame of the Lake, not to—"

"Let Sir Lancelot save her!" said Pelleas. "Or his kinsman Bors. We will not stay here one moment. Nimue, give your orders and we ride ahead and let our people come after us with the pavilions."

"At least you'll let me finish my conference with your wife?" I said.

He started to refuse, but Nimue cut him off, speaking quickly and gently. "Give the necessary orders yourself, dear love—only leave Sir Gareth, Sir Pinel, and Sir Mordred the pavilions they are sleeping in, rather than take them down about their ears. They have done you no offense." (Gawaine and Ywaine had managed courteously to refuse Nimue's offer to lend them, also, one of her remarkably rich pavilions.) "I will be ready when our mounts are saddled."

She sounded for the moment like the patient nincompoop Griselda, but maybe there was more iron, or magic, in her voice than I could hear, because Pelleas let us go out and off to one side while he went in another direction to start giving his orders to his wife's people.

"I can manage him more easily when we are away from Sir Gawaine," said Nimue. "By tomorrow evensong I'll have him back safe in the Lake, and by evensong of the next day I will have rejoined you, myself alone. That will still be two days before the Queen's trial, Sir Kay."

"And what about Gawaine's brothers and Astamore and Ironside?"

"If Astamore means to murder Sir Gaheris, or Ironside Sir Agravaine, he will probably have done so by now. If not, it is very likely they have been delayed by some natural causes and will join you before my return."

"If Ironside or Astamore meant mischief, four days may not be long enough to find them and their work, let alone two days. Dame Nimue—"

"Can I let my Pelleas go off alone in this temper, ready to challenge Lancelot himself?"

"You might recognize that your husband is a grown man and was considered one of the best young fighters of his time before you ever met him. If Pelleas can't take care of himself for a few days—"

"How much do you know," she said, "of what happened between him and Sir Gawaine for the sake of Dame Ettard?"

I thought I knew as much as anyone needed to know about it. Pelleas, on the rare occasions we had seen him at court, was always close-lipped about it, but we had all heard Gawaine's version, duly if unhappily reported along with the rest of his adventures.

Gawaine had found Pelleas battling ten knights at once in front of Dame Ettard's castle; and, seeing that the young knight was winning easily, Gawaine had refrained from helping him and thus diminishing his glory. He had, however, waited in case the tide of battle turned. To Gawaine's surprise, after defeating all ten hands-down, Pelleas had quietly allowed them to get up, disarm him and bind him under his horse's belly, and take him into the castle. Gawaine began to ride after them to try to gain admittance into the castle, but, learning from the folk of the town that this happened every day and Pelleas was always sent back outside shamed but physically unharmed, Gawaine waited outside the walls instead.

It seemed Pelleas was in love with the lady of the castle and for some reason thought the best way of proving his devotion was to defeat her knights every afternoon, to show he could do it, and then allow them to bind him and lead him before her like a booby, giving him the chance to see her face and enjoy her scorn for an hour. Small wonder she had little use for the mooncalf! If I had been in Gawaine's place, I would have counselled Pelleas that the lady was giving him a rather clear hint she had no use for his company and if he could not forget her and find someone else, he should at least learn to handle his love with a little more dignity and get along alone. But Dame Ettard had refrained from cutting off a few of his fingers or slitting his nose while she had him in her power, and both Pelleas and Gawaine seemed to find this a sign that she secretly nourished some deep affection for her unwanted admirer and might yet be won. Gawaine proposed that he take Pelleas' arms and horse and ride to the castle claiming to have killed Pelleas. If that did not melt Dame Ettard in pity for the supposed defunct at once, Gawaine would linger with her to persuade her gradually into a better state of mind toward Pelleas. Why, exactly, they expected they could coax the lady's love into full bloom by making a fool of her with their interlude I cannot say, but Gawaine was young and green himself at the time. Far from melting in pity at news of Pelleas' supposed death, the lady showed great delight. Maybe she suspected what they were up to; a man who could defeat ten other good warriors for his daily exercise was not likely to have given up his life and armor to a single knight, even a Gawaine, without putting a few new dents in the armor and a fresh wound or two in his conqueror. The charade went still further slantwise when Dame Ettard, like most of the other ladies in Britain who do not choose Lancelot instead, decided she was in love with Gawaine.

It being summer, they set up a pavilion in the meadow. Here Pelleas, wandering around in his impatience one night, found Dame Ettard asleep in the same bed with Gawaine. Those of us who knew of the delicate balance the young fool tried to keep between gallantry in talk and virtue in deed, and the tangles it got him into, like the affair with Bertilak of Hautdesert and his amorous lady, might have stopped to ask whether the situation was exactly as it seemed. Pelleas only knew that he had trusted a gentle-speaking stranger and the stranger had, to all appearances, betrayed him out of hand. So he left his naked sword lying across both their necks and rode home to get into bed alone and announce that he intended to die there of grief.

It was about this time that the Damsel of the Lake came by, found Pelleas, and saw something in him as invisible to me as it must have been to Dame Ettard. So Dame Nimue turned Pelleas' love for Ettard into hate and caused him to fall in love with Dame Nimue instead. They were married and went off to her Lake, with excursions now and then to court to get Pelleas the distinction—which he treats as an honor alone and ignores the duties—of a seat at the Round Table, while Gawaine came home, in his usual state of guilt-ridden despondency whenever he considers his conduct anything short of ideal, to confess he had made a mess of things, testify that Pelleas deserved to be made a companion of the Table, and report that Dame Ettard, on waking to find that Pelleas could have killed her and had not, had finally, too late, conceived a love for him and died of it when he refused her in his turn.

"In his courtesy, Gawaine did not tell the whole truth of Dame Ettard's death," Nimue told me now. "For it was suicide, although I persuaded her priests that she had not jumped, but fallen, from her tower, and so gained her burial in hallowed ground and the Masses sung for her soul. And the reason she jumped was not that she had come of herself to love Pelleas for his noble forbearance, but that I, in my proud triumph, and wishing to make her appreciate the prize I had won, cast on her the same spell of melancholy I cast on you a few nights ago, Sir Kay, mingled with a heightening of whatever small regard she might have had for him. I only meant to tease her a little and then lift my spell, but I was young and still new to my own craft. I must have cast a stronger spell than I had intended, or perhaps, never having read her memories, I had overestimated her strength of will to resist the despair."

The Lady of the Lake shuddered a little, and for a moment I thought I saw wrinkles on her face and silver hairs among the dark brown ones she was wearing at the time, as if for that moment she had let slip whatever spell controlled her agelessness.

She went on, "That is why, though Queen Guenevere's life be at stake, I must consider my own husband the more important for these few days and ride with him to keep him from harm—not only for my own affection, but also for the sake of that love and remorse which poor Dame Ettard felt for him at the last, and which I myself had driven her to feel."

After a moment, I said, "You might try forgiving yourself."

"Though I forgive myself, I must still do what needs to be done." She touched one hand to my cheek. Maybe it was some enchantment to calm me into letting her go without further argument, or maybe I would have let her go anyway by then—I felt nothing in particular at this touch. "If you will hurry and fetch me Sir Mordred's tokens of his brothers Agravaine and Gaheris," she went on, "I will try to look for them on my way back, though I expect to find them already with you when I come."

Mordred was deep in sleep, and feeling out his pouch of mementos from the folds of his cloak was trouble enough without opening it to grope for Agravaine's tunic-threads and the sleeve Gaheris had worn in tournament, so I took the whole bloody pouch to Dame Nimue. Mordred was annoyed when he found out about it in the morning, but confessed he would probably have done the same thing in my place; and, as matters turned out, he finally got his pouch back whole, it having proved of no use to the Lady of the Lake after all.

On my way back again to my own bed, I bumped up against Nimue's minstrel, adjusting his mule's saddle.

"I didn't mean what I said about your twanging," I told him. "You play a good harp, in the right time and place."

"Oh, I wasn't offended, sir," he replied. "But if I had stopped playing when I first should have, I would have been expected to leave discreetly at once, and it's not often we have the chance to see our lord Sir Pelleas in a temper."

He probably winked, though it was too dark to see his face. So much for making apologies.

Chapter 30
Conversations at Astolat

"But thus as Sir Tristram sought and enquired after Sir Palomides Sir Tristram achieved many great battles, wherethrough all the noise fell to Sir Tristram, and it ceased of Sir Launcelot; and therefore Sir Launcelot's brethren and his kinsmen would have slain Sir Tristram because of his fame. But when Sir Launcelot wist how his kinsmen were set, he said to them openly: Wit you well, that an the envy of you all be so hardy to wait upon my lord, Sir Tristram, with any hurt, shame, or villainy, as I am true knight I shall slay the best of you with mine own hands." (Malory X, 88)

I came out of our pavilion next morning to find Gawaine already reassuring Sir Bernard that the reason two of his most honored guests had decamped in the night was in no way the fault of the noble hospitality they had met with at Astolat. I added my reassurances and then left the field to Gawaine before I said the ungracious words about Pelleas that he was carefully not saying.

Neither of the missing pairs of knights had arrived yet, but it was still before prime and probably too early to look for them. I found Gareth alone in the woods a little beyond the encampment, sitting beneath a tree and holding a few crumbs of bread in his hand, outstretched on the moss.

I sat down beside him. "Glad I found you alone. Even you sometimes find Pinel's company a little wearing, eh?"

"I'm alone," said Gareth, glancing at me, "because I hope to entice the birds or small beasts to eat from my hand, and that requires perfect stillness."

I ignored the inference that my company was as unwelcome as Pinel's would have been. "It's no secret you never believed Sir Lamorak killed your mother, Beaumains. Why not?"

The bread crumbs shook a bit in his hand. "Can you find no better way to destroy the peace of the morning than that, Sir Seneschal?"

"I'm glad somebody finds it a peaceful morning. . . . All right, Beaumains, I'm sorry for bringing it up, but this thing's been giving me bad dreams almost every night for—"

"Remarkable it should give *you* nightmares. He was *my* friend, and she *my* mother. What were they to you?"

"A good warrior and a gracious lady. Laugh if you like," I went on, "but I've grown the feeling it's tied up somehow with this present coil."

"It's gossip like yours that keeps the remembrance of such deeds green," he replied.

"It is not gossip to ask someone close to the business, in all seriousness and for serious purposes, what he thinks may really have happened," I said, wondering why I had a reputation for impatience.

"I was not close to it. I was far from court when it

happened. Had I been at hand, Sir Lamorak would not have met his death through treachery."

"If your brother Gawaine had Lamorak cut down in cold blood, it's the only treacherous thing he's ever been known to do in his life."

"I did not say the treachery was Gawaine's," replied Beaumains. "Though Dame Morgawse was his only mother and I believe he sincerely thought Sir Lamorak had killed her. But he should not have allowed that noble knight to be cut down before he could tell what really happened."

"All right, so you think Gawaine didn't strike the teacherous blow himself, but allowed his brothers to do it for him. Any brother in particular?"

"Any one of my other three brothers would have been capable of the deed," said Gareth. "Or all three of them at once. And Gawaine does not disapprove, for he says nothing of what happened when they entrapped Sir Lamorak."

"There are degrees of disapproval," I said. "But who do you think killed your mother, if not De Galis?"

"Perhaps some jealous would-be lover, perhaps one of my brothers' knights who thought to please his lord by striking down Sir Lamorak unawares in bed and by mischance struck Dame Morgawse instead. . ."

"And then compounded his mistake by letting Lamorak get dressed and escape, after all?"

"If you can only mock my opinions, Sir Kay, why do you ask them?"

"I'm not mocking. You just have a habit of taking anything that happens to come from Kay's mouth as mockery. In fact, you may have a point, though I think I've heard the gossips mention it before. It was a very clean blow, but the murderer *could* have struck the wrong person and then been so stunned by his mistake that in his confusion he let the one he'd meant to kill escape. But maybe your brothers and their men had nothing to do with what happened in that room. It might have been one of Lancelot's kinsmen who—"

I'm not sure if he meant to throw his handful of breadcrumbs in my face or if his arm simply jerked and they came my way. "Lancelot! You accuse my lord Sir *Lancelot?"*

"No, you mooncalf, I said one of his kinsmen. Weren't some of them ready to kill Tristram when Tristram's fame started threatening to eclipse the noble Lancelot's?"

"And Sir Lancelot himself promised to kill the first of them with his own hands who dared attack the noble Sir Tristram in treachery!"

"Yes, because he got wind of it in time," I said. "Since I've never heard anyone suggest that's what may have been meant to happen to Lamorak de Galis, obviously Lancelot couldn't have got wind of it soon enough in Lamorak's case. But Lamorak was the only other knight, besides Gawaine and Tristram, who might have been able to win himself more fame than your marvelous De Lac."

"I will not believe that my lady mother died for some jealousy between Sir Lamorak and the men of my lord Sir Lancelot. . . . I have struggled all this time to forget and forgive and tolerate my brothers' company again—why do you come now and open the old wounds?"

"If you don't believe Lamorak killed your mother, Beaumains," I said, "how can you be content to let her real murderer go unknown and unpunished? If not for Dame Morgawse's sake, at least to clear up the doubt on Lamorak's memory?"

"No true man has ever doubted Sir Lamorak's memory." Beaumains rose, quivering slightly. "Since you will not leave my company, Seneschal, I will leave yours."

I let him go. Having as much of his opinions as could probably be of any use—I forgot until too late to question him about Pinel, but I doubt Beaumains would have recognized any unsuccessful attempt on his life even in the unlikely chance one had been made—I believed I could make better progress for a while with my own thoughts.

I did not have long to sit alone with them, however, before I heard horses approaching, and someone hailing me as "Hullah! Good sir!"

I turned to see Ironside and Agravaine riding their palfreys through the forest towards me. They were unarmed, their armor clanking faintly on the mules their squires led some distance behind. Ironside had his right arm in a sling, while Agravaine had one side of his face bandaged from forehead to midcheek. It must have been an extreme annoyance to anyone so proud as Agravaine of his handsome appearance.

"Hullah!" called the red giant again. "It's Kay! And yonder lies Astolat?"

I walked forward while they rode, until we met close enough to talk without shouting. "We looked for you yesterday," I said. "Were you within a few miles, or have you been riding all night?"

"Within a few miles, man," said Ironside, "but half addled out of our wits, the both of us."

"Guessing ourselves to be in the vicinity of brother Mordred's rendezvous with an afternoon to spare," said Agravaine, "we indulged in the foolishness of a friendly joust. When it was over, neither of us was in fit condition to ride further that night."

"You should have postponed your joust until you got here," I said. "You could have joined our little tourney yesterday and, with luck, been mowed down by Gawaine and Ywaine. You could also have been healed by the Lady of the Lake—she was here then, and she closes up serious wounds very cleanly, though she doesn't bother with bumps and bruises since you'll feel them for awhile anyway." Explaining briefly that Dame Nimue had left because Pelleas would not stay after Gawaine's arrival, I looked at the bandage covering half of Agravaine's countenance and added, "Well, don't worry, Fair-Face. Most folk say the scar on Lancelot's cheek improves his beauty."

"Dame Tamsine assures me there should be no scar," Agravaine replied, a little stiffly. "Good dame!"

The squires, chargers, and pack animals had remained half hidden by trees. Now, as she rode forward to Agravaine's call, I saw that one of the two attendants had changed from a squire to a wench or damsel in a plain buff-colored gown.

"Dame Tamsine joined us when we left Florence at Sir Hervin's hermitage to heal his leg," said Agravaine. "Besides making a passable squire, she is an excellent leech and very pleasant company."

I exchanged greetings with Tamsine, who had a pretty smile with a wide gap between her two front teeth, and was probably so flattered at being called "Dame" that she was more than eager to do everything she had ever heard a lady of the court might do. "What happened to Florence's leg?" I said.

"Fell off his horse our third day out and broke his ankle," said Ironside. "Young noddlehead lost count of how many saddle girths he'd tightened and forgot his own."

"We'll hope he's learned his lesson," I remarked. "And which of you two old noddleheads suggested that friendly fight of yours within a few miles of Astolat?"

Agravaine shrugged. Ironside said, "Hardly remember. I suppose I may have done. Grew out of our talk at dinner somehow. Well, all's well that ends well, and a happy thing sweet Dame Tamsine knows her leechcraft, eh?"

I agreed and brought them on to Sir Bernard's manor for morningsong, Mass, and breakfast. By midmorning, when Gaheris and Astamore still had not arrived, Mordred and I went into the woods, found a largish clearing where there was not so much chance of being overheard, and talked the situation over.

"It could have been a stroke aimed to split brother Agravaine's brainpan," said Mordred. "Though I can hardly think why it missed its purpose. Unless, perhaps, Agravaine's helm proved sturdier than his opponent had calculated."

I shook my head. "The helmet wouldn't have saved him. Ironside has too strong an arm."

"Knowing his great strength, he may have reckoned that only a part of it would be enough. Or brother Agravaine may have already dealt his own blow to Ironside's right arm before Ironside's swing. Or it may, after all, have been a mere friendly guileless fight."

"What was Ironside doing swinging at his opponent's head in a friendly fight?" I asked.

"Battle rage and battle chance," said Mordred. "It happens often enough, Seneschal, though you may disapprove of the waste. They may simply have been trying to impress 'Dame' Tamsine. Still, I would like to have seen it."

"I'd like to have heard the conversation that led to it. Ironside may have made Agravaine suggest it himself, to impress Tamsine—though that's more subtle than I'd give Ironside credit for, and I don't think they needed any extra embellishments to impress their little dame. For that matter, with only Tamsine and his own squire to see it, why should Ironside have stopped with one stroke to the helm, if he'd meant to kill? Even if Agravaine had already disabled his right arm, I've seen the giant's son knock out a knight's brains with his left arm and the end of his shield."

Mordred shrugged. "We do appear to be reasoning it into the innocent battle the jovial red giant claims. At the same time, they seem to have been singularly haunted by accidents. Interesting, that such a misfortune should have overtaken Florence. He is usually so meticulous about his horse's harness."

Florence was Gawaine's second son, named for his mother, Dame Floree, and serving out the last few months of a long squirehood under his uncle Agravaine as his younger brother, Lovel, was serving under Mordred. The question of Florence's accident had already occurred to me.

"Falling from a horse doesn't usually result in disabling injuries," I said. "Not in itself."

"Aye, and you should know, Seneschal, having taken so many falls in jousting."

I decided to overlook that comment. "If Ironside had wanted to harm Gawaine's son, he might have found a surer way than loosening the saddle girth. Florence would most likely have come off with bruises. As it is, a broken ankle's not the most serious of injuries, with decent leechcraft. And the accident would have alerted them to be more careful."

"It hardly alerted our guileless Agravaine to beware of entering combat with Ironside, whose own mind, as you yourself remarked, is probably not over-subtle. However, it may have been nothing more than a prank of Ironside's squire. Or even a palfrey subtler than her masters, whose bloating of her belly during the saddling process escaped Florence's attention. I still find it interesting, nevertheless, that Gawaine's son should have suffered a broken ankle and Gawaine's brother a wound in the head while travelling with the man who once swore to have Gawaine's life."

"You might not have found it so interesting if you still held me your chiefest suspect," I said, wondering if, secretly, he still did. ". . . Do you know of any grievance Gaheris might have against Astamore?"

Mordred lifted his brows slightly. "Bagdemagus, of course."

"No. Not what Astamore might hold against Gawaine and the rest of you. What Gaheris might hold against Astamore."

Mordred thought for a moment. "Unless Gaheris has surely discovered Astamore to be our brother's would-be poisoner, I can think of nothing. Although Gaheris does not always proclaim his grievances before taking action to set them right."

"And if he discovered Astamore to be the poisoner, would Gaheris bring him back alive to confess his crime or stand his trial before the full court? Or would he bring back Astamore's head and his own unsupported testimony to convince Mador?"

"I had thought the question in our minds was whether Astamore would allow Gaheris to rejoin us unscathed," said Mordred.

We sat awhile in silence, each presumably pursuing a different line of thought. "King Pellinore's death," I said at last. "Eliezer says Gawaine fought Pellinorc in fair battle; Gawaine doesn't say much more than he does about Lamorak's death. Was the tale of Pellinore's squire true that Gaheris cut Pellinore down from behind while Gawaine was too busy in front to see what his brother was doing?"

Mordred shrugged. "How should I know more of it

than you? Ask Gawaine and his squire. Or Gaheris himself." (Pellinore's squire had died a few years afterwards of the pox.) "But are you not ranging rather far afield," Mordred went on, "if your purpose is to save the Queen?"

"Maybe," I said. "But the key to this coil must be somewhere, even if it's a very rusty key by now."

"And you are the rusty key to find it, eh, Seneschal?"

I gave him a short glare. "Not so rusty I couldn't give you another defeat for all your youth and practice."

I considered asking him whose idea it had been—Gawaine's or one of his brother's—to invite Dame Morgawse to her oldest son's castle beside Camelot. But Mordred's temper inflamed too easily when the conversation touched his mother's death, and I needed his cooperation. "Mordred, when they join us, assuming they do, I want a small, private meeting, just you, your brothers, and me."

His eyes gleamed. "A game of your own, Seneschal? And what shall you do with us when you gather us together?"

"Maybe warn you. Maybe surprise you. And it may not be pleasant. I want to be well away from any curious eyes and ears—say in one of Sir Bernard's cellars."

"Beaumains also?"

"Yes, Beaumains also," I said. "All five of you. We may need our host's invitation to get Beaumains into the party. Can you answer for Gaheris and Agravaine?"

"Agravaine, yes. Gaheris, if he comes."

"And I think Gawaine will join us readily enough at my invitation," I said.

"And who will keep watch on our suspected traitors while we are all six tucked away in the bowels of Astolat manor?"

"I doubt they'll do anything. We'll post Eliezer in the

passage to guard our privacy, and an assassin would have to get past both him and Sir Bernard's folk to try burning us all together or some such unlikely trick. Ywaine and the squires will be at the pavilions, not to mention the two innocent ones of our suspects, if either Ironside, Astamore, or Pinel is our traitor and tries to escape. Which is hardly likely, if he hasn't tried to escape when he was riding in a much smaller company."

I got to my feet, but paused before leaving our glade. "Oh, by the way, I don't think it was Ironside."

Mordred raised his brows again. "Because, having jousted with Agravaine, he failed to deal with him to the uttermost?"

"No. Because just after we realized Patrise had died of poison, and before you demonstrated that the poison was in the fruit, Ironside sneaked the last bite out of his mouth. A man who knew what dish was poisoned, and that he hadn't taken any of it, wouldn't have had to do that."

"Ah, so you've finally remembered that action. Did you notice it at the time or when we watched the tragedy again in Aunt Morgan's mirror?" Mordred grinned broadly. "In my opinion, Sir Seneschal, you are playing as devious and perilous a game as I have ever known you to play, in your open, careful nature."

Chapter 31
Further Conversations at Astolat

"Alas, said Gaheris, that is foully and shamefully done, that shame shall never from you; also ye should give mercy unto them that ask mercy, for a knight without mercy is without worship." (Malory III, 7)

I talked to Gawaine and the baron of Astolat that same afternoon, leaving them to talk to Gareth Beaumains. Mordred, meanwhile, arranged for Agravaine's attendance. I did not specifically ask Ywaine to keep watch on Ironside, Pinel, and Astamore, since the fact that we suspected them rather closely of Sir Patrise's death had so far been my secret and Mordred's, shared only, perforce, with Dames Nimue and Morgan. I was reasonably confident that Ywaine, Gillimer, or one of the other folk about would notice should anyone try to slip away furtively in alarm at a private meeting of Gawaine and his brothers.

I also talked to Gawaine's squire Eliezer, but not solely to arrange for his standing guard outside our gathering. I put to him the same question I had asked

Mordred about the death of King Pellinore.

"My master fought a fair and noble battle," was all the old squire would say at first. "And good a fighter as Sir Pellinore was, Sir Gawaine was a better."

"Tell me Gawaine actually dealt the death blow," I said. As Eliezer hesitated, I pressed on, "The tale of Pellinore's squire was true, wasn't it? Gaheris slipped in from behind and cut Pellinore down while he and Gawaine were busy with each other."

"Gawaine did not need his brother's help," said Eliezer. "But Sir Gaheris was much heated with the old rage against his father's killer, and perhaps he feared he would not have his chance."

The crafty old word-watcher still had not said definitely that Gaheris struck Pellinore a treacherous blow, but if it had been otherwise Eliezer would have said so plainly instead of hedging.

"How have private relations been between Gawaine and Gaheris since?" I asked. "Wasn't it from about that time Gaheris started to veer toward Agravaine?" (Mordred had not yet come to court.)

"My lord loves all his brothers dearly, as befits their common blood."

"Yes, yes," I said, "and if one of them were murdering Gawaine himself, he'd refuse to shout for help rather than let the world see an Orkney with his sins showing. But even if Gawaine doesn't say anything to the world, hasn't he been much less often in Gaheris' company in the years since King Pellinore's death?"

"Among folk less close to my lord Sir Gawaine," said Eliezer, "this would sound very much like idle gossip." He kept his voice soft. He had mastered the art of the mild and respectful rebuke.

"And Pellinore's squire did die naturally, of the pox?"

I said. "You never heard any idle gossip of poison in his case?"

"I try not to hear gossip, sir. As far as I know, the man died naturally. His further talk would not have hurt my lords Gawaine and Gaheris more deeply than it already had."

"I suppose not." All Pellinore's family needed to keep up the feud was their father's death, whether by proven treachery or not. "Would you call it idle gossip," I went on, changing the subject slightly, "to tell me which of King Lot's sons had the idea of inviting their mother to Gawaine's castle beside Camelot?"

"It was Gawaine's own idea," said Eliezer, "to help forward her honorable marriage with Sir Lamorak—he made the mistake of trusting Pellinore's son. He even called his brothers together to persuade them their quarrel had been with King Pellinore alone, not with his family, and had ended with his death."

"Pity Gareth was absent from court. He would have loved that conference."

"Gawaine fully condoned what he thought would be the lovers' rendezvous in his castle, believing it would soon come to marriage," the old squire went on. "He would not want his original motives to be known or remembered now, my lord, for grief and shame at so misplacing his trust and helping bring about his own mother's death."

"The whole court," I muttered, half to myself, "was expecting Dame Morgawse to leave a privy postern open by night for her lover. But her sons might have had some special knowledge."

"My lord would not thank me for speaking so freely of this to you, Sir Kay," said Eliezer. "But the world has put too much blame on him in this matter for too long.

And I think you are not really a bad friend to all good knights."

"Tell me how to know the good knights from the evil ones, Eliezer," I said, "and maybe I'll mend my tongue."

He grinned. "By their deeds shall you know them, sir."

"Fine. And how shall we know their deeds? Well, thank you for telling me as much as you have, Squire Watch-Words, though it was hard enough work getting some of it out of you, and I knew some of it already. But if you think of anything else I should know, don't be so damned cautious about telling me. Preferably before this gathering."

"Why do you wish to bring them together, sir?" he asked.

"I'm not entirely sure yet myself. Maybe to have it out with some of them—not Gawaine, of course—about slandering the Queen. Or maybe to effect a family reconciliation." I put my hand on his shoulder. "Just guard the passage for us when we need you . . . if we need you. If Gaheris and Astamore don't get here by tomorrow, the meeting may never take place."

I spent the rest of the afternoon pacing the woods with my own thoughts, avoiding company and trying to concentrate on the past and the immediate present so as not to see Dame Guenevere with the days running short and Lancelot more likely than not neither found nor returned.

Though Eliezer refused to acknowledge the rift among the sons of Lot, I was sure it existed. So much was obvious from how often the brothers were seen in each other's company. Gawaine and Gaheris had once been boon companions. Almost disregarding—in so far as he was capable—Agravaine, the brother between, Gawaine had even seemed to regard Gaheris as his indispensable Conscience (as if he needed any besides the one in his own head), especially after the accidental murder of Sir Ablamar's lady, which happened when Gaheris was still serving as his older brother's squire. Though other men would resent an exterior conscience, having trouble enough with the inner one, and though the version Gaheris told of the poor dame's death was probably unduly harsh on Gawaine, they remained boon companions, being seen almost as often in each other's company after Gaheris was knighted as when he was Gawaine's squire. Looking back through the years, I was more and more convinced that the time they had ceased to be seen much together dated from their return to court with the report of King Pellinore's death.

The rift with Agravaine and Mordred seemed to date from the Grail Quest and the death of Sir Dinadan, though Mordred himself had largely avoided the company of his oldest brother since the Peningues tournament—since the time, as I now knew, that he had begun to wall himself off from ideas of honor so that he could let the priest's words fester in secret.

Their sins aside, not one of the lot was worthy his oldest brother—Agravaine with his vain and lazy arrogance, whether or not it masked some secret energy for devising schemes like spreading slander about the Queen; Gaheris with his veering moods and his warped oversense of justice; Mordred, who might have been a good knight if he had only indulged a little of Gawaine's heretical skepticism about priests' prophecies. The only possible exception among the brothers was Gareth Beaumains the Beloved, who is about Gawaine's equal —some say his superior—in arms and honor, but who is also a simple-minded dolt. And Gawaine's special love for Gareth was one-sided. Beaumains might have been shunning his brothers' fellowship on principle since the death of Lamorak, but it made little difference in practice; even before Lamorak's death, he had rarely been seen with any others of his family, preferring to puppy-dog around after Lancelot and Lancelot's kinsmen, most of whom had little use for the other sons of Lot, largely because they saw Gawaine as a rival for the fame of their adored Du Lac.

And yet Gawaine called this cocksure, glory-seeking, berserking, unreliable Vanishing Wonder, Lancelot du Lac, his dearest friend. And Lancelot returned the affection, at least ostensibly, all rumors of blood-guilt and treachery in Gawaine notwithstanding. It was, nevertheless, a kind of absentee friendship, holding across the miles, and manifesting itself whenever the two happened to be in the same place at the same time, but not leading to much travel together for adventure. Lancelot was too independent-minded, Gawaine too mindful of Arthur's reliance on him and of his duty to be available, if possible, at the King's need. Or possibly the two Great Ones feared to learn more of each other, finding it safer to keep up their friendship at a distance. No, Lancelot had not crowded out Gawaine's fellowship with his brothers as he had Gareth's.

But though the younger brothers, Beaumains excepted, maintained outward loyalty to the head of the clan and joined him at need—as in running down their mother's murderer—to show the world a united front, within the family circle itself, Gawaine must be alone among his brothers. Maybe Lot and Morgawse had used up all their virtues on their first-born.

If Gaheris and Astamore had not joined us the next day, Saturday, after the arrival of Agravaine and Ironside, I intended to let my plans for gathering the brothers fall by the wayside and start back to London, whether or not the rest of them chose to join me or to wait at Astolat. But the missing pair arrived early Saturday afternoon.

Their reason for being late was that Gaheris had fallen sick their second day out, apparently of drinking bad water from a serpent-infested stream, and it had taken a nearby hermit eight days to bring him out of danger and to the point where he could ride by easy stages. He was still too weak to wear armor, and his squire Melehan, Mordred's oldest son, had to help him off his palfrey. At that, Gaheris was fortunate. When Lancelot had drunk from a serpent-venomed spring one time, he had lost his hair, beard, and fingernails before sweet Dame Amable managed to effect his cure, which took her several fortnights.

Astamore, fully armed on his warhorse, rode in beside Gaheris as if ready to protect the whole party should danger threaten.

"Did you search the stream and find the serpent?" I asked.

Astamore removed his helmet and shook his head. "No. The first thing was to search for help—thank God and Our Lady that Melehan found Sir Alfin's hermitage. But Sir Alfin told us it had happened before in the streams near his house, and he and his folk drank only from their own cistern."

"It was a good thing," I remarked, "that Gaheris was the only one of your party who drank from that stream."

"Aye, thank God!" Astamore's squire Osmond crossed himself. "We had it at our lips! My lord even showed us what leaves to rub our mouths with, in case any of it had already gotten on our lips and tongues."

Mordred and I had our chance to talk it over alone

while Gaheris and his party were resting and being fed. "I think you told me," I began, "that Gaheris was too much on his guard to eat or drink anything Astamore didn't share with him."

"Anything prepared. Naturally, Gaheris would suspect no harm of a flowing spring. And, as I understand, Astamore seemed on the verge of drinking."

"And then knew right away which herbs to pick for rubbing his mouth and the squires'." I shook my head. "No, it seems he hasn't forgotten what Morgan taught him of herb lore."

"And how could he have poisoned the stream?" said Mordred. "Did he also find some chance to put the serpent into it? You tried to blame Patrise's death, also, on a serpent in the food cellars, did you not?"

"Yes," I said. "Brash of Astamore to try the same trick again so soon after the first time."

Mordred stretched out on his cot and began balancing his dagger on his palm. "He must have felt safe, knowing how blame for the first poisoning had been cast on the Queen."

"Cast by that bloody Mador de la Porte. If the rest of the court can really believe it—"

"Try to put your passion aside again for a moment, Sir Seneschal. The brave Sir Mador, whom we all used to love and admire dearly, has, I believe, been an ornament to Arthur's court longer than has Dame Guenevere. If he should win the combat, as is not impossible unless Lancelot appears to replace Bors de Ganis, not only will the Queen's guilt be established according to law—do sit down and calm yourself—but it will also be accepted, however mournfully, in the minds of the court and populace, who meanwhile, we may assume, hardly know what to think. Thus, Mador's victory the day after tomorrow would have effectively masked a second mysterious death by poison from all but a little harmless gossip. Even should the Queen's champion win, the matter of Gaheris' death would have remained sufficiently clouded that the murderer could hope to escape mortal retribution. A serpent-venomed stream in the forest is more plausible than a serpent-venomed apple from Sir Kay's cellars, and brother Gawaine is not another Mador de la Porte, to bring a charge of treachery without better evidence than this, even to avenge a brother. No more is Beaumains, and though Agravaine might bestir himself in the matter of Gaheris' death, it is far from certain."

"And you?"

Mordred managed to shrug without unbalancing the knife on his palm. "Brother Gawaine accepting Astamore's story of a serpent—and though Gawaine can understand blows dealt with sharp steel, he has difficulty understanding blows dealt with poison—he would probably forbid the rest of us to challenge Astamore on nothing but suspicion. Besides, Astamore probably meant to delay his return to court until after the Queen's trial, and possibly, if her innocence were proved and the new death thus laid open to a trifle more questioning, he may have planned to follow the example of the illustrious Lancelot and disappear on some private adventure for a year or three. Or he may have a mind so subtle that he reasons beyond the obvious and trusts that a second poisoning so soon after the first, seeming too foolhardy to be attempted on purpose, should escape suspicion by its very suspiciousness."

"The court doesn't think that subtly," I said. "Mador de la Porte has proved it."

"Ah, but I think that subtly. I even think subtly enough to wonder whether Astamore was secretly dismayed or sincerely gladdened when his victim's squire found Sir—what was his name?—Alfin's hermitage."

Perhaps the fact that I had originally judged Astamore to be a good, honorable young fellow accounted in part for my heaviness now. "Gawaine was the only one of you involved in Bagdemagus' death," I said. "Whatever you expected, Mordred, I didn't expect Astamore to try to avenge his uncle by striking at Gawaine through his brothers."

"But is it not fortunate for Her Grace that he did?"

"God, even Bagdemagus' worthless son Meliagrant was more direct in his aims than this! If nothing else, Astamore would have hurt his chances of getting at Gawaine himself."

Mordred tossed his dagger from his hand and sat up. "Your mind is too honest, Seneschal. Even the business of the late Sir Lohot taught you nothing of traitors' ways. Shall we descend on young Astamore at once and put him to the question?"

"His ring," I said. "That bloody ring with the outsized stone he's always turning on his finger!"

"Yes . . . and so he would not even have needed a serpent for his ally, merely a practised flick of the setting in his ring. Clever." Mordred frowned for a moment. "How shall we best steal that ring to examine it? By night as he sleeps, or at once, this afternoon, by some ruse?"

"Right now," I said, "by going to him and demanding it!" I started up, but Mordred caught my shoulder and held me back.

"Gently, Seneschal, gently! Alarm him with an outright accusation, and we may have to rack him in earnest, knight and king's kin or not, before we have the truth from his lips. There is a better way."

"You have about as long as it takes to say an *Ave* to explain it."

He took a few paces inside the pavilion, less, I think, to aid his thoughts than to get himself between me and the doorway. "Whom can we best trust, and how much need we tell them? A few words to our kind host, a hint to Dame Tamsine or pretty young Dame Elaine of Astamore's thirst for womanly companionship . . . yes, he's fetching enough in person, they'll be ready to stay near him for no other reason . . . Perhaps to hear him harp with Pinel?" He shook his head. "No, best not attempt to include your Loudvoice of Carbonek in the interlude, or he might drive the damsels away even from Astamore . . . but a game of chess, and Sir Bernard will be hovering near, of course—yes, that will hold our Astamore as securely for the evening as would chains and bonds, while we six enjoy our rendezvous in the cellar."

"Don't be too sure of that gathering," I said. "If we can make sure of Astamore's guilt—"

"He knows of our gathering; I've already told Gaheris. And poor Sir Bernard has had his people at work preparing a proper place for us all morning. It would put Astamore more on his guard were we to put off our business now than were we to carry it through."

"Not if we use Gaheris' condition for an excuse," I said.

"A few hours' rest, and Gaheris will be sufficiently recovered from his morning's ride. . . . And we can make sure of my son Melehan, of course; I can trust him to obey me without overmany questions, and as the squire of Astamore's companion, he is very happily situated to be seen about their pavilion, or to raise the alarm in case our man should attempt to fly—which may, after all, be the best way we can hope for him to reveal himself. They will probably engage Astamore in one of the better pavilions, too, leaving my son, with luck, a clear chance to search Astamore's own rather bedraggled quarters—"

"You don't expect him to take off his ring and leave it in his bedding for your son to find?"

Mordred waved his hand. "No, no, of course not. I fear we must wait for Astamore to sleep if we hope to examine his ring without his knowledge. He probably emptied it into the stream in any case, and may not have filled it again. But if Melehan could find some other trace, perhaps a vial wherefrom he fills the ring . . . Should we offer them the use of our own fine, borrowed pavilion? No, best not, it might warn him . . . still, if we offered our host and his family the use of a fine pavilion of the Dame of the Lake's for the evening. . ."

"All right," I said, "we'll play the game by your moves for this evening. But by God, Mordred, if Astamore escapes us, you're going back to London taking the blame for Patrise's death on yourself to save the Queen!"

"If Astamore escapes us, I'll cheerfully promise you that, Seneschal," he replied. "But our family gathering tonight is your move in the game, is it not?"

"It started that way." I tried to force my thoughts back to the gathering of the clan that I myself had called for. "No weapons," I said, remembering Gaheris' pale face and the bandage over Agravaine's left eye. "I don't want any weapons in that cellar with us. Make sure they know that."

Mordred cocked one eyebrow. "No weapons among brothers?"

"None."

"And if we must suddenly rush forth to pursue Sir Bagdemagus' nephew?"

"It won't take us that much longer," I said, "to catch up our weapons on the way from the cellar to the horses.

Meanwhile, we'll have to depend on Ywaine and Ironside, our host, maybe Pinel, and your reliable son Melehan with the other squires to join the chase."

"And what, I wonder, will you reveal to us this evening, or propose to us, or persuade us to promise?"

I realized I had been treated to a sample of Mordred's own powers of persuasion. He looked forward to the gathering of his brothers, and would not be cheated out of it even when what we had just learned of Astamore made it appear superfluous. "Come and find out," I said.

"And will you forbid us even our daggers?"

I would have preferred no weapons of any kind. The Saxons had been known to play unpleasant tricks with concealed daggers at supposedly peaceable gatherings. I hoped we were at least too honorable for that sort of thing; but, on the other hand, daggers are very easily concealed and I hardly wanted to tempt anyone to bring in a hidden blade. "Use your own judgment about your daggers," I said.

Mordred smiled and went out whistling. I suppose, having my promise to go through with my own move, he wanted to give me no chances to renege on my word. He seemed to regard tonight's gathering as a child regards his first wooden sword. I pitied him.

Chapter 32
The Truth of the Deaths of Sir Lamorak and Dame Morgawse

"Sir wit ye well, said Sir Kay, that my name is Sir Kay, the Seneschal. Is that your name? said Sir Tristram, now wit ye well that ye are named the shamefullest knight of your tongue that now is living; howbeit ye are called a good knight, but ye are called unfortunate, and passing overthwart of your tongue." (Malory IX, 15)

Thinking it over, I knew Mordred was right in that openly demanding Astamore's ring would destroy our chance of tricking a revelation out of him; but, unwilling to let it go at that, and unable to wait in idleness, I decided to try the game of subtlety myself. I was not oversuccessful at it.

Leaving our pavilion, I searched until I located Astamore, seated alone on a rock at the edge of the nearest grain-field and thrumming his lute. I strolled up to him, as if casually, and the first thing I noticed, even from a distance, was that the familiar ring was missing from the third finger of his right hand. He had never taken the thing off, as another lutist would have, to play his instrument, only to put on his gauntlet for battle. When I came closer, however, I saw—hardly to my comfort—that the overwrought silver band was still around his finger, but the huge blue stone was gone.

At least this development made it unnecessary for me to use any of the excuses I had been trying to develop for asking to see his ring without arousing his fears. I needed only to ask how he had lost the stone from his ring.

"I gave it to Sir Alfin," he confessed, "in return for his hospitality and Gaheris' cure."

"A hermit asked for pay?"

"No, but it's not a wealthy house, and I gave it to him as a prayer-offering. Gaheris gave him the great topaz from his helmet when he recovered enough to ride," Astamore went on, absently twisting the denuded silver band on his finger in the old way. "It made my stone look rather small. Well, the joy will be in winning another gem some day for the dear old ring."

I went on talking with him for an hour. He might very easily, of course, have thrown away the hollow poison-stone and made up a tale of giving it to the hermit, but you would never have guessed it from his talk. He was either as subtle as Mordred credited him with being, or utterly guileless. He made me doubt my old estimation of Dame Bragwaine, who had seemed equally guileless. He also shook my conviction that he was indeed our poisoner.

Nevertheless, when I got away from his company and reconsidered the three of them, the jolly giant Ironside, Pinel of the Clattering Tongue, and the honorable-seeming Astamore with his early practical knowledge of poisons, I kept coming back to the conviction that

Astamore was the one we had to hold fast.

Mordred's plans for Astamore's entertainment were only partly successful. Dame Tamsine was already rambling with Ironside in the woods, and Mordred sent his son Melehan to spy on them, less for lingering suspicion than for the sake of symmetry. Sir Bernard and his children declined the luxuries of our pavilion, at least until after nightfall, preferring to take advantage of the beauties of the late afternoon and set up their chessboard outside, Astamore giving young Dame Elaine a lesson while her brothers looked on over her shoulder to point out her mistakes as she made them. Ywaine, who was keeping the sword Excalibur in trust for his cousin this evening, sat polishing the gems of its hilt and conversing with the baron of Astolat, while Sir Bernard's old bard provided music in the background. Pinel, who had sustained a long, shallow cut in his left shank in the mock tourney two days before and, since it was far from serious, had refused on principle to let the "Pagan woman" close it up for him with her magic, now pled that it and his other bruises were troubling him and retired to his own borrowed pavilion to drink a bowl of his host's precious wine and take a nap. Keeping up the symmetry of our game to the last, I took Gillimer enough in my confidence to tell him to hover around outside someplace where he could keep a watch on both Pinel's pavilion and Astamore's chess game—but to watch the latter more closely, even to following Astamore if the young knight got up to go answer the calls of nature.

As the time neared, I disliked the thought of the coming conference more and more. What good did I expect might come of it? If Astamore was the poisoner, how would the matter I had to discuss with the sons of Lot help save Dame Guenevere? What connection could it have, after all, with the death of Sir Patrise? I might finally have called it off, but for two thoughts: there might never come another likely chance for getting at the truth of this business, and Mordred would not rest until he had gotten my thoughts out of me anyway.

Jesu! I was made for open dealing, not intrigue—a rude tongue, if you like, but not this bloody business of guarding every word. Well, Dame Morgan had counselled me to try playing the hare for once . . . though, if she were watching, she might not care overmuch for the results her suggestion led me to.

An hour before evensong we gathered beneath Astolat manor. Sir Bernard must have kept his household at work all afternoon to make the cellar we had begged of him fit quarters for our exalted company. A dozen casks of cider stood against one wall, but the cell was cleared of whatever else may have been stored in it, rushes laid down on the floor, tapestries—probably the best the manor afforded—hung on the walls, and six chairs set ready around two tables placed together to form a squarish shape, no doubt the closest the baron could come to approximating a round table using what boards and trestles would fit into the space available. Lamps burned on their stands in every corner and on both sides of the door, and a nine-branched candlestick stood on the table, every sprocket filled with a wax candle or the stub of one, the one in the middle being marked to show the hours as they burned away. An empty bowl waited ready for each of us, and a flask of wine stood at either end of the table; even Sir Bernard's hospitality did not quite extend to pouring the expensive stuff ready for us when there was any chance we might not drink it. There was also a plate of small cakes, crowned with two apples, doubtless our host's last of the winter.

Gawaine was the first to arrive after myself and

Mordred. Noticing the apples, he said quietly, "I would esteem it a great favor, Sir Kay, if you would eat one and leave the core at my place. Our host should not think his hospitality has gone unappreciated."

It did not escape my attention that Gawaine had asked the favor of me rather than of his youngest brother. It did not escape Mordred's attention, either. I more than half expected him to make some comment referring to the possibility or impossibility of these apples, too, being poisoned; but for once he said nothing. He did, however, take the second apple as I reached for the first.

Gaheris came soon after Gawaine, walking well enough by himself, though with the aid of a staff. He sat down heavily and filled his wine-bowl from one of the flasks. Agravaine sauntered in some moments later and leaned against the wall. He was wearing his sword Coup-de-soleil.

"I thought I made it clear we would have no weapons among ourselves," I said. "Or do you expect a sudden invasion of Saracens to reach us down here in the next hour?"

Agravaine shrugged, strolled back to the door, drew his sword and left it propped against the wall in the passage outside, without bothering to ungird his jeweled scabbard. His squire could always wipe off any dampness the exposed blade might accumulate.

Agravaine returned to lean against the tapestry and eye Mordred's apple with something that looked like thwarted greed. I went out to the stairway, where Eliezer had taken up post because the passageway between stairs and cell was too short to accommodate him at a comfortable distance from our voices. "And why, exactly, did you let Agravaine down with his sword?" I said.

"Don't tell me that cock-a-dandy overawed an old hand like you!"

"You never told me to guard against weapons at this meeting," he said evenly.

"God's rage!" I wondered what else I might have forgotten. "And Mordred didn't think to mention it to you either, I suppose. Didn't you suspect anything when you saw the rest of us going down unarmed—when Gawaine left Excalibur with Ywaine, for the love of God?"

"My lord Sir Agravaine wears his sword and scabbard everywhere, for ornament if not for use, and it was not for me to tell him nay on my own authority. And you are all wearing your daggers."

"You're right," I said after a moment. "I'm sorry. No great harm done. . . . Well, we can't do anything about the knives—better open than hidden—but just come and take custody of his blasted Coup-de-soleil, will you?"

"Gladly." The old squire grinned. "I will boast to my great-grandchildren of receiving an apology from Sir Kay."

I returned to the cellar. Mordred had sliced his apple and given half to Agravaine. Gawaine had filled his wine-bowl by now, and Gaheris was refilling his. If Beaumains intended to maintain his aloofness from his brothers, I was ready to open the ceremonies without him—but the Honorable Innocent arrived just in time to be included, having, I suppose, done enough to demonstrate his superiority by appearing only for the business, not for the before-business society.

"I hope, Sir," said Gareth, seating himself and looking at Gawaine rather than me, "that whatever your reasons for calling us together, they will be explained before evensong."

Gawaine had first met Gareth's glance with a hopeful

smile, but at the tone of the younger brother's voice he lowered his gaze to the table. I had thought the two were finally starting to bury their differences along with Sir Patrise. I must have driven the wedge in again by reminding Beaumains of Lamorak's death.

I decided to plunge in with no courtly nonsense. Since there must be hatred in the room, let it be aimed at me. At least for a time. "This meeting wasn't Gawaine's idea, Beaumains," I said. "It was mine. I called you all together to ask you, once and for all, what *really* happened to Sir Lamorak de Galis and Dame Morgawse of Orkney."

I got the animosity I had expected. "That is a singularly crude jest, even for you, Sir Seneschal," remarked Agravaine.

"When I choose to be simply rude," I replied, "I can find plenty of reason at hand, without going back years into the past."

"Sir Kay," said Gawaine, "you know as well as the rest of us here how they met their deaths."

"Don't lose truth in courtliness, Gawaine," I said. "I saw Dame Morgawse's body—I never saw Lamorak's."

"He may know as well as some of you how our mother died," said Beaumains, for once playing my ally, "but neither Sir Kay nor I know the full truth of Sir Lamorak's death."

"Gareth," said Gawaine. "Gareth. I know you have never believed it—you will not think evil of any good knight, save of your own brothers—but Sir Lamorak murdered our mother. . . . Perhaps it was a short fit of madness that came upon him, perhaps, in his right mind, he did truly love her. But he did not deny it when we charged him with her death. In all justice, we had no course but to give him battle—"

"Four against one," said Gareth.

Gawaine faltered. "I gave him battle fairly, trusting to God and Our Lady to—"

"Four against one!" said Gareth. "By Jesu's Cross, brother, I think I could forgive your seeking vengeance, but I cannot forgive the lie that you alone outmatched Sir Lamorak de Galis!"

"Then perhaps it's time you learned the truth, poor innocent," said Mordred. "You and our good, curious seneschal. Yes, Gawaine could have outmatched your noble Lamorak de Galis in the end—your oldest brother is a better man than you and some of your Lancelot-worshipping friends take him for. And yes, Gawaine did offer Lamorak fair fight—too fair a fight for that murdering craven. It was I who rode up from behind and put my sword through the traitor's back, and I would do it again!" He smiled and swung one leg around to sit astraddle his backless chair, getting his body at an angle that enabled him to lean part of his back against the table. "Now, is that what you wished to hear, Sir Kay?" he asked, looking up at me. "Confessions and self-accusations? Have I not immolated myself nicely? And what will you do now with your knowledge—bring me to trial for sending a treacherous cur to the Hell he deserved ten times over?"

No one spoke for a moment. It was Agravaine who broke the silence. "Well, perhaps it's just as well. Some of the rumor-mongers have always said it was Gaheris or myself, or all of us together."

"Maybe you threw in those last few remarks to make me think you were lying, Mordred," I said, "but I believe your confession. You might have spoken up before and spared your brothers some of the blame they've been carrying around for your sake. Probably none of Lamorak's kin would care to charge you in open court before the King, any more than they've ever charged

Arthur's nephews formally as a group. If definite word gets out, of course, some of them might hunt you down alone." And you might enjoy that, I added in my thoughts. "But as long as Gawaine's refrained from charging you openly," I continued aloud, "so will I. You thought you were justified. Gareth, of course, can keep the secret or speak as he chooses."

I looked around at them again: Gawaine across from me, Agravaine at his right, Gaheris at his left, Mordred at my right, lounging against the table to gaze up at me half-insolently and half-whimsically, Beaumains at my left, with his chair drawn a little distance away from the table and more towards me than towards his brothers.

"However, I don't think you were justified, Mordred," I said. "Not in striking him down from behind, not even in offering him fair battle. It goes against the grain to say this, but I now think Gareth, with his foolish, unreasoning hero worship, has been right all along. Lamorak did not kill Queen Morgawse."

Gareth sighed. Mordred's body stiffened, drawing back from the table's edge. Gawaine stared at me unmoving, and Gaheris stirred only a little from his weary posture of resting his head in his hands. Agravaine said, "Now I know why you demanded we leave our swords outside, Seneschal. You feared we might draw them against you."

"No," I said, "I feared you might draw them against each other."

"Explain yourself," said Mordred, taking the game seriously at last.

I looked away from Mordred, directing my gaze at Gawaine. The youngest brother might be in most need of whatever sympathetic support I might be able to offer, but the oldest brother deserved it most. Not that I have ever known how to put any kind of sympathy into my words. "Anyone who blames you for looking at the appearances and assuming Lamorak killed your mother is a fool. But there have always been a few things that didn't ring quite true. For instance, why did Lamorak wait until that night, in Gawaine's own castle? They had met often enough before, in her castle, in his, probably in forest or open field. Maybe, as Gawaine has said, it was a passing fit of madness. Or maybe Lamorak thought it was somehow more fitting vengeance to kill her in the castle of the son he most blamed for Pellinore's death. Maybe Lamorak had a sense of honor that made him open the way himself to being chased down for the deed—though, in that case, why run at all? —Or, maybe, he did not plan the deed to his own best safety and advantage because he not only never planned it at all, but never committed it."

"Go on," said Mordred.

I went on. "But if someone else did it, why didn't Lamorak attack his lady's killer, or at least ride back to court and declare what had happened? Why did he even refrain from declaring his innocence when you four found him alone? Did the horror of seeing his love killed almost in his very arms addle his wits that badly? But he was sane enough to turn up in borrowed armor and carry off his full share of honors in the Surluse tournament. His actions don't seem to fit either an innocent man or a guilty one.

"Gareth thinks your mother's murderer was either a jealous would-be lover, or some man of your own who thought to please you with Lamorak's death and struck Dame Morgawse instead, by mistake. Those are possible explanations, but in either case the murderer should have tried to finish the job and strike Lamorak while Lamorak was still naked and unarmed. Of course, the traitor might have decided to make his escape before

Lamorak could reach his own weapon—in fact, Lamorak could have ridden out into the night in pursuit of this traitor. Lamorak's dwarf had not seen anyone else go in or out by the privy postern, but the traitor could have been hiding somewhere in the castle before Lamorak arrived, and he could have got out by some other way, while Lamorak returned to the gate where he'd left his horse."

"I fail to see where this is leading us," said Agravaine, "except to display your brilliant intellect for our admiration, Seneschal."

"It wouldn't lead us anywhere," I said. "I probably wouldn't even bring it up now, but for another strange thing. We visited your Aunt Morgan le Fay in her castle, you see, Mordred, Dame Nimue, and myself—yes, your aunt is still alive, though I wouldn't mention the fact too widely abroad and I'm not going to tell you where we found her. Dame Morgan has the ability to see the past in a basin of water, and to show it to others at the same time."

"I'm not surprised," said Beaumains. "She is mistress of all the evil arts."

"Maybe not quite so evil as you think, Beaumains," I said. "Maybe not quite so powerful, either. She has to know exactly where and when to look in order to summon up her images. Now, she was very cooperative about helping us search for Sir Patrise's murderer, in so far as we could guess the whens and wheres. We actually watched the fruit being poisoned—"

"What!" cried Gawaine, starting up. "Then why—"

"The poisoner was too heavily robed and cowled for us to see who it was," I said. "We know how the poison got into the fruit, but we don't know enough to save Dame Guenevere, even if what we do know were believed. It would only be said that the poisoner was one of the Queen's creatures."

Gawaine fell back into his chair.

I went on, "My present point is this: When I asked Dame Morgan to show me what happened in your mother's chamber that night, she refused. Flatly. She claimed that seeing it would be of no use to us, pointing out that if it had any connection with the presumed attempt to poison Gawaine, the connection lay not in whatever really happened, but in what the poisoner believed to have happened. She was probably right in that. But why so reluctant to let me see the truth? It would only have taken a few moments. She knew exactly where and almost exactly when to look—that much is common knowledge. I think she tried to imply that she herself had chosen never to witness her sister's murder, which I would not believe if she had actually sworn it on a fragment of the True Cross. However ugly it might be to watch, Morgan le Fay would have wanted to know the truth of the deed as soon as she learned of it, and be sure she has her ways of learning news, even if the word sometimes takes a week to reach her. I can understand she would find it distasteful to see a second time—but not quite distasteful enough to explain her manner of refusing to let me see it. And she surely couldn't have been tender about *my* stomach! No, I think she refused to show me what happened because she was shielding someone. Who? Not her sister, hardly her sister's memory. She could have done Dame Morgawse more honor by letting us see the truth—know certainly that your mother had been avenged if Lamorak killed her, or give her the chance to be avenged if someone else had done it. Someone dear to Morgan herself, then?"

"One of Morgan's own creatures did the deed, then?" said Agravaine.

"Our aunt has always been a destroyer of good

knights," said Gaheris, without lifting his head.

"Has she?" I replied. "Has she destroyed any more good knights than Lancelot or Tristram or some of the rest of us who ride around wasting each other for the sport and glory of it instead of conserving our strength to serve the King? No, I do not believe that Morgan ordered Lamorak killed."

"You have fallen under that evil woman's spell," said Gareth.

"Maybe. But Le Fay has no special quarrel with the family of Pellinore. If she's never made another attempt after that first one on the life of her husband Uriens, whom she hates, it's hardly likely she would have made an attempt on the life of Lamorak, against whom she had no particular grievance."

"Unless she knew ahead of time that he planned to kill our mother," said Agravaine.

"So she sent her man, or her magic, against Lamorak that night, missed, and killed her own sister?" I shook my head. "Even if Lamorak had gotten out of the castle with his skin afterwards, there wouldn't have been enough of him left to fight by the time of the Surluse tournament, let alone enough for you to find, living or dead. No, Dame Morgan had nothing to do with what happened in her sister's chamber that night, nor did she have any knowledge of it before the fact. But she does know the truth of it now, and the only reason she might have to withhold her knowledge is to protect someone. Not Lamorak—she'd have no cause either to protect or to damn Lamorak's memory, and besides, those who believe him innocent would hardly change their opinion on the strength of the tale of what Kay saw in Morgan's mirror. So she was protecting someone she, or Dame Morgawse, or both of them, had held dear, or at least felt some kind of loyalty to, despite his deeds."

I glanced around at them again. I had made such a long explanation of it in the hopes he would have betrayed himself by now, listening to me.

Gawaine sat watching me as if in stunned, unwilling belief. Mordred's stare as good as told me that if I were having some sport with them my fate would make Lamorak's look pleasant. Gaheris was still staring down at the table, his head propped up on his right arm, the arm that was slightly too long. Beaumains seemed confused, as if unsure whether to try to sneer at what I was saying or to applaud me for accepting his hero Lamorak's innocence at last. Agravaine was cleaning his fingernails with the tip of his dagger.

"I think you'd better give me that dagger, Agravaine," I said.

He glanced up at me and returned his attention to his manicure. "I think not, Seneschal."

"Then the rest of us had all better draw our daggers, too," I said. None of them did it at my word, but Mordred moved his right arm a little to let me see that his dagger was already in his hand, beneath the tabletop. I decided to leave my own blade sheathed. All I wanted was their continued attention and at least a little willingness to believe what I was saying.

"If Lamorak did not kill Dame Morgawse, the likeliest person to have tried to attack him in her bed was someone who already had some grievance against him. Also, in all probability, someone very familiar with Gawaine's castle, which more or less excludes any of Lancelot's or Tristram's kinsmen who might have been growing uneasy that Lamorak was a threat to their cousins' glory. Probably our man was someone who not only knew the castle, but was a familiar and trusted sight around it—although I suspect that this time he came between nightfall and Lamorak's arrival, and avoided being seen by any of the castle folk. Someone who could have seen his chance at the first suggestion that Dame Morgawse come to spend some time in her son's castle when her lover was nearby."

Agravaine stopped cleaning his fingernails. Mordred brought his right arm up to the top of the table, turning the blade slightly to make it gleam in the candlelight.

I pressed on. "The man who tried to surprise Lamorak in Dame Morgawse's bed, and by mischance struck the lady, must have been one of her own sons."

To my surprise, Mordred sat unmoving. Beaumains shook his head, Gawaine crossed himself, Gaheris gave no sign of having heard me and I wondered whether he was really feeling his recent illness. Agravaine shrugged. "Small wonder you wanted to get this blade out of my hands. Or are you actually trying, for some reason, to goad us into killing you? We are still brothers, five against one."

"Let him speak," said Gawaine. "Sir Kay, I guarantee your safety."

"Aye, Seneschal, speak," said Mordred. "Which of us do you charge? Or do you charge us all?"

"Mordred," said Gawaine, "you will lay down your weapon. You also, Agravaine."

Agravaine put his dagger on the table, gave it a spin, and folded his arms across his chest. Mordred tightened his fist around the hilt. "I will have my blade in my hand, older brother," he said without turning, "as he makes his accusation."

Gawaine rose. "You will lay it down."

Mordred looked at him then. They stared at each other for a moment, and finally Mordred drove his weapon into the tableboard and turned back to me. "Now, Seneschal, speak."

"First, Mordred," I said, "I am not going to accuse

you. Nor Gawaine—if he had felt any grievance against Lamorak for being Pellinore's son, he would have eased it in honest battle, not concealed it under a show of friendship. Nor was it Beaumains, for obvious reasons. That leaves Agravaine and Gaheris."

"I grant you Gawaine and Gareth," said Agravaine, "but most men, having gone as far as this, would have accused brother Mordred along with Gaheris and myself."

"Mordred loved his mother too much to have risked her life in such an attack," I said. "He would have lain in wait for Lamorak somewhere between the postern and the bedchamber." I did not add my other reason for excluding Mordred from suspicion, but he added it for me.

"And what quarrel did I have with the sons of Pellinore?" Mordred demanded, turning on his brothers. "Let the rest of you carry on your feud against the family of Lot's killer—the king of Orkney was not *my* father! I am a bastard, do you understand me? The unnatural bastard of another King, a King who used his power to ravish the Queen of Orkney—Dame Morgawse was my only true parent! I had no quarrel with Lamorak de Galis until the night he butchered her!"

"Except, of course, that he did not butcher her," said Agravaine. "As Sir Kay has been expounding to us, that unfilial deed was done by either Gaheris or myself."

"And I doubt you take anything seriously except yourself, Agravaine the Handsome," I said. "Besides which, when you do have any energy to spare, you prefer making trouble with your tongue. No, I don't think it was you."

I should certainly have had some outcry from the only brother left by now, but he still sat with his right hand propping up his head, and for a few heartbeats no one else spoke. Finally Gawaine stated the obvious. "Then you charge our brother Gaheris with the death of our mother, Sir Kay?"

"The accidental death. Seeing what he had done, he was naturally too horrified to prevent Lamorak's escape. But, afterwards, he realized he could still accomplish Lamorak's death, simply by letting the appearances speak for themselves and convince Gawaine that Lamorak had murdered Dame Morgawse." I hurried to finish my speech before their faces sank too deeply into my soul. "Both you and your brother Gaheris thirst a little too strongly for justice, Gawaine. The difference is that while you insist on seeking justice with honor and in due proportion, Gaheris will take—or give—an eye for a tooth, and by any means he can find."

"Gaheris," said Gawaine, in the same tone he had used to command Mordred to lay down his dagger, "is this true?"

Gaheris finally lifted his head from his hand and straightened his back. "Not entirely. He mistakes in one point. I did not aim at Sir Lamorak and strike our mother by mischance. I accomplished the stroke I had intended."

Mordred screamed, snatched his dagger from the table, and lunged at Gaheris. I had just time to catch him, knock the blade from his hand, and hold him back, while Gawaine held Gaheris, who had shaken off some of his weakness and reached for Agravaine's dagger.

"He had ensnared her!" said Gaheris. "He had trapped her soul with his cursed youth and grace—his strong, perfect body. That he was her paramour was a disgrace to God and our father—that he should become her husband—the son of our father's murderer to wed the woman who gave birth to King Lot's sons—that the seed of Pellinore should be lawfully planted in the same womb that gave us birth! Aye, I killed her—I freed her from his snares—and I spared him that night so that you should be cured of your meekness toward Pellinore's accursed son, so that you should take your part in the honor of his death!"

"And Lamorak must have kept the secret because Dame Morgawse had loved you, Gaheris," I said. "Poor, silly Lamorak with his own overblown ideas of honor."

"Jesu!" said Gawaine. "Ah, sweet, holy Jesu—we have murdered an innocent man!"

"Lamorak?" cried Mordred. "God! brother, you fret for Lamorak when this—when our mother—Cry Jesu mercy on Dame Morgawse's soul, Gawaine! I was the one who killed Lamorak, let me cry mercy for that in due time!"

"I permitted it." Half-staggering against the table, Gawaine gave up his hold on Gaheris to Agravaine, who had for once bestirred himself to come around the table. "Our mother is at peace," Gawaine went on. "We cannot avenge her death without slaying this pitiful, mad son she loved. . . . No, we will not injure him—Gareth—Kay—Agravaine—let there be no more blood shed here, no bloodshed among brothers . . . but I, if I stay here longer, I may—let me make my peace with Lamorak's ghost," he ended, walking a little unsteadily to the door.

Maybe I should have stopped him. But I assumed he was going to Sir Bernard's chapel, to find a priest, shrive himself, and buy more Masses for Lamorak's soul. Besides, I was busy holding Mordred from Gaheris' throat.

Chapter 33
The Poisoner of Sir Patrise

"The knight spoke with strong cheer,
Said, 'Ye be welcome, Sir Gawaine, here,
It behooveth thee to bow. . ."
(THE GRENE KNIGHT, Percy Ms. version)

Hardly was Gawaine gone and the door closed behind him when Mordred, who had remained comparatively quiet for a few moments, tried to break from my grip and reach Gaheris. Having outguessed him, I held him fast, so he used his tongue instead.

"You—She loved you best, Gaheris Longarm! By God, I'm the bastard—the son of rape and incest—but you are a more unnatural son than I! To kill the dame who bore you—the mother who loved you, nourished you, trusted you—"

"I killed her because I loved her too much to see her the love-toy of Pellinore's son!"

"God!" cried Mordred. "You killed her for jealousy! You would have—"

"Quiet!" I exclaimed. "Quiet, the both of you, before we tie you down and brank you!"

"Incest?" cried Gareth suddenly. I had hoped that word would go unnoticed in the rest of Mordred's ravings.

"A distant kinsman," I said. "You don't know him—neither of them knew they were related until—"

"Liar!" screamed Mordred. "The truth, you say—you bring us together to teach us the truth of ourselves, and you lie? Aye, to protect your noble foster-brother! It was the King! It was your great, noble, beloved ruler Arthur that you follow for the love of God and glory! Aye—all you others, you're only Arthur's nephews—I am Arthur's own son! Do you not envy me for it? I am the son of a brother who forced his own sister—and before Heaven, I charge that this trueborn Gaheris is a more unnatural monster than I!"

"Oh, God!" said Beaumains. "But they knew—surely they knew—"

"You were too young, brother," said Agravaine, who did not seem particularly taken aback by Mordred's revelation. "We knew they cast admiring glances on one another, but none of us knew their relationship, because Merlin, for reasons best known to himself, saw fit not to reveal who was our King's mother until some time after he had demonstrated his own might by settling Arthur safely on the throne without benefit of parentage."

"And the lady was not quite so unwilling," I said, "God rest her soul."

Beaumains sat and buried his face in his hands. Mordred strained in my arms and went on shouting at Gaheris, who answered him back in kind. Agravaine shouted to me above the noise, "I liked your suggestion, Seneschal, of binding them—but would it not be simpler to strike them a few good blows to the head?"

Le Fay and her advice to play the hare! I thought for some reason of Cob the charcoal burner, blessing

Gaheris and the whole Round Table for his Norwegian palfrey. "And some day they're going to remember us as the cream of chivalry!"—I think I muttered it aloud. Then something else came into my head—Gawaine with the green sash and the lock of a dead woman's hair that he always wore to remind himself of his sins and failings —Gawaine going out, with this fresh load of undeserved guilt, to "make his peace with Lamorak's soul" . . . a cowled, priestly figure sprinkling poison out of an aspergillum as if in benediction . . . and Pinel of Carbonek taking a drink of wine between the moment Patrise died and the moment Mordred proved where the poison lay. . .

"Pinel!" I shouted. "Pinel of Carbonek—Lamorak's closest living kinsman!"

"What?" asked Agravaine.

"King Pellam's nephew—Pellinore's nephew, too, maybe even another of Pellinore's bastards! Right under our noses and we forgot it the whole bloody time! And Gawaine's gone—"

"What are you talking of?" said Gareth, lifting his head from the table.

"Keep them apart—lock them away from each other —or let them get at each other if they can't come to their senses!" Normally I would have wanted Mordred at my side, but not in his present state. "We've got to get up there!"

"Have you gone raving, too?" inquired Agravaine.

"Idiots! Pinel is the poisoner—it was revenge for Lamorak's death, and your silly, noble brother's gone back up to give him another chance!"

Gareth got to his feet. "It could not be Pinel—not a man raised in the sanctity of Carbonek—and on Sabbath eve?—"

"Beaumains, if you have any love at all for your

brother, stop babbling and come with me now—or at least hold Mordred for me—and if I'm wrong we'll laugh about it later!" But if I was right, Gawaine might already be dead.

Gareth stood there gaping, babbling something more about the Sunday truce. I let go of Mordred and made for the door without looking back or listening to their din. They might kill each other for all I cared at that moment, and deserve it.

Eliezer was still standing his post, holding Agravaine's sword and staring watchfully towards our cell. The noise carried loudly enough even to the stairs, but I didn't stop to ask how much of our shouting the old squire might have understood. "Did Gawaine tell you where he was going?" I demanded.

"No. Should I have—"

"Yes! Come on!" I grabbed the sword from him and led the way. Unlike the knighted fools in the cellar, Eliezer followed without asking questions. We didn't talk. I saved my breath for running, with the image in my mind of how Gawaine must have looked years ago, kneeling in the snow before Morgan's Green Knight, putting honor before sense to the last, waiting, true to the rules of a ridiculous game, to lose his head. But Pinel, unlike the Green Man, might really swap it off.

As we neared Pinel's pavilion, we saw his white warhorse standing ready-saddled in front of it, gold in the setting sun, with Pinel's dwarf holding its head. At the sight, Eliezer sheered off from my side to head for Sir Bernard's chess party, far away on the other side of the pavilion and apparently unaware of anything amiss. I ran on towards the closed doorflaps of Pinel's pavilion.

I brushed past the gaping dwarf and threw back the flaps. My guess had been right. Gawaine was kneeling in front of Lamorak's cousin. Pinel had his sword raised ready to split his enemy to the collarbone.

I shouted and rushed into the tent. Pinel looked up, saw me, and hesitated an instant, then took a hasty swing at Gawaine while he still had the chance. His aim went wide, missing Gawaine's head and cutting into his right shoulder—but in the moment I spent making sure Gawaine was still alive, Pinel got past me and outside. By the time I got back to the doorflaps, Pinel had his foot in the stirrup and was swinging up into the saddle.

I shouted. The dwarf glanced at me, let go the charger's head, and started to run. I suppose he saddled his donkey and escaped into the woods, planning to meet his master again when he could, or else get back to Carbonek on his own. I never learned whether he reached home safely, nor how much in his master's confidence he had been. Meanwhile, other folk were finally running toward Pinel's pavilion through the lengthening shadows.

I heard a groan and looked around. Gawaine had somehow gotten to his feet and managed to walk as far as the door, holding his shoulder together and gushing blood in every direction. "Kay. . ." he said, and crumpled.

"Just keep your arm on your fool body!" I said. Dame Tamsine, back from the woods, had almost reached the pavilion by now, with Astamore and Sir Bernard's sons closing in from the other side, and I left Gawaine to their care while dashing for my own tents.

Eliezer, seeing Pinel's warhorse saddled, had realized there might be a chase; and, reasoning that, whatever was going on, I could better do without him in the pavilion than without a mount if I needed one, he had hurried on, after a shout to the chess players, to bring my steed. Between Eliezer and Gillimer, Feuillemorte was ready for me, and I blessed them for him. There was no time to put on my armor, but Pinel hadn't had time to arm himself, either, beyond sword, lance, and shield. Without stopping to change Agravaine's sword for my own Tranchefer, I caught my shield from Gillimer, threw it round my neck, vaulted into the saddle, snatched up my lance from Eliezer, and managed to join pursuit just before Pinel was out of sight.

For some reason—maybe because he thought he could make better time or because he had stopped using his brains—he had chosen to cut across the fields and the long meadow, keeping more or less to the open, rather than galloping at once into the woods, where I would have lost him right away in the twilight.

Pinel's mount was good—a better horse than he deserved—but my blood-red Feuillemorte is as fine and fast as ever Gawaine's own old Gringolet or Tristram's Passe-Brewel were in their prime. I came within jousting distance quickly.

Pinel saw he had no other choice but to turn and fight. Or maybe what decided him to start charging while I was still a spearcast away was the fact that, with my lance in my right hand and Agravaine's sword in my left —since I hadn't taken time to mess with belt and scabbard—I had not been able to pull my shield around from my back and get it into place.

I charged without shield, trying to get my own point home while forced for lack of armor to twist away from Pinel's weapon—a maneuver I defy the almighty Lancelot himself to accomplish without more than his share of good luck. Without armor, also, it somehow seemed, beyond all reason, more like a boy's training ride at the quintain with a blunted lance than like deadly earnest. Maybe that was why, despite my intentions of aiming for Pinel's chest, my point instinctively hit his shield instead. At least it was a solid hit—and the blasted weapon broke to splinters, so Pinel kept his seat, while I fell. It wasn't Pinel's lance itself that toppled me—it was twisting away from it at the last moment that got me off-balance—though if his aim had been better in that charge, I doubt I would have escaped unwounded to remount and ride after him again.

This time he got into the woods, but it was a narrow strip of woods, coming out on the road. I caught up with him again in the bowshot-length of cleared ground bordering the paved way.

By now I had gotten the sword into my right hand and my shield in place on my left arm, and I shouted at him to stand and draw—expecting, I suppose, that a man who had tried to poison his enemy and then taken advantage of the said enemy's conscience to strike him down unarmed, not to mention letting the Queen take the blame for his deed, was suddenly going to follow the rules of honorable combat at this point. Pinel's lance, having missed me the first time, was still whole. He lowered it and bore down on me at full speed.

I did the only thing I could do—tried to turn his point with my sword. It's been done, and with my own Tranchefer instead of Agravaine's Coup-de-soleil in my hand, I could probably have done it again. As it was, in the failing light and with the unfamiliar blade, I missed. But the effort laid my side open just long enough for Pinel's lance to get in and stay there.

I remember falling with a broken lancehead in my ribs. I remember lying there on my stomach, feeling the point wedge deeper and the weeds under me get wet with my blood while Pinel galloped away, his horse's hooves shaking the ground less and less. I think I pounded the earth with both fists until I lost consciousness.

Ywaine and Astamore found me. Ywaine rode on after Pinel while Astamore staunched my bleeding and waited for Eliezer and Gillimer to catch up to us and take me back. I awoke in a bed in Astolat manor. It still seemed to be shortly before sunset. Gawaine lay sleeping in another bed on the other side of the room, and Mordred sat between us, with an ugly cut and welt on his forehead, blackened left eye and scratched cheek, and other assorted bruises over his face and throat, but seeming his usual calm self again.

"Pinel!" I said. "Did they—"

Mordred shook his head. "Neither Ywaine, nor Ironside, Astamore, Melehan, our host and his sons and yeoman, nor anyone else have found his trace. Unfortunately, I and my brothers, those of us left fit to ride, were unable to join the chase until later. Don't worry, though. Dame Nimue should soon be back among us."

"Why aren't you on your way to London?" I demanded. "God, man, the Queen's trial is in two days!"

"The trial is tomorrow. It is now Sunday evening—did you think the sun had been rolled back in the sky? But what, exactly, would we tell the court in London? What proof have we of Sir Pinel's guilt?"

"Sweet Jesu! He nearly succeeded in splitting your brother's head, he fled the moment he was caught in the act—not to mention giving me my death wound!"

"None of which actually proves he was responsible for the death of Sir Patrise, whatever else it may prove. Oh, and the leeches say there is a chance you may not die, nor brother Gawaine either."

"What more proof does Mador want? It's better proof against Pinel than anyone can produce against the Queen!"

"Peacefully, peacefully, Sir Seneschal, unless you are determined to prove your leeches wrong. The Dame of the Lake should be here again before morning."

Gawaine groaned in his sleep, but did not waken. I

made the effort to calm myself. It did not help the pain in my heart, but it made the hole between my ribs feel a little easier, "Who else but Pinel, with his upbringing at holy Carbonek, would have thought to use an aspergillum and sprinkle poison like holy water, asking a blessing on his treachery?" I said, putting into words what I suppose must have gone through my head the evening before without my realizing exactly where the certainty had come from. (Morgan's hare.) "Who else but Pinel would have justified himself, when his poison killed the wrong man, by assuming that Patrise must have had some hidden sin that Heaven chose to punish this way, while reserving his intended victim for another vengeance? God, Pinel must have taken it as a sign from Heaven when Gawaine walked into his pavilion and meekly offered himself up!"

"Nevertheless," said Mordred, "we must look at this as Mador would look at it. Granted, Pinel did try to take vengeance for his cousin's death when Gawaine came to him yesterday evening, and then he quite understandably fled when you came bursting in on them like a crazed demon. But that does not in itself prove the poisoning, and Carbonek does not invariably breed such sinners as you make Pinel out to be."

"What about Pellam and his daughter seducing Lancelot on the justification that Galahad must be engendered?"

Mordred clucked his tongue. "Do you compare self-justification for murder with self-justification for love, Seneschal?"

"Pinel never said which of King Pellam's brothers was his uncle," I persisted. "It must have been Garlon, the only one with a bad reputation in the world outside Carbonek. Remember how Pinel justified Garlon in that version of the Dolorous Stroke he told us?"

"Oh, for myself, I fully believe it, that Pinel is our traitor," Mordred agreed. "And no doubt he obtained the poison from his uncle's sorceress Brisane, on the pretext of using it to thicken his beard, as Aunt Morgan explained to us. But Mador de la Porte will not believe it. Come, will you follow Gawaine's example and take an herbed posset of young Astamore's preparation to help you sleep?"

"No." Tired of his constant references to the hopelessness of saving Her Grace with what he had learned, I said, "What about Gaheris?"

Mordred set his jaw and stared at his brother, as if to make sure Gawaine was still asleep. "The traitor," he said in a completely altered tone, "is our own blood, and our mother's murder is our own to avenge or forgive. And brother Gawaine, in his sweet and infinite mercy, has decreed that the madman must be forgiven, 'for he knew not what he did.' So let it be for now. But I will destroy Gaheris. I will destroy him, no matter whom else I must destroy in doing it."

I awoke in the night from evil dreams that may have been partly delirium and found Dame Nimue sitting by my bed, wearing her white-gold hair, almost as lovely as Dame Guenevere's, and a delicate glowing nimbus around her entire body.

"Congratulations," I said. "I half expected you to stay with Pelleas, after all."

"I have already healed Gawaine," she replied. "He will be able to ride tomorrow, though he will of course remain too weak to do battle for some time yet. Now sleep again, and I will heal you."

"You missed the best part of the game. You should be very happy to learn that the traitor was Pinel of Carbonek."

She chuckled very softly. "I know. I returned here earlier than you may think. This morning, in fact."

"And you spent the day trailing Pinel?"

"It was quite simple," she said. "Sir Pinel had left behind a whole pavilion bestrewn with his possessions."

"That's why it took you so long to get around to healing us. But why didn't they tell me?"

"Didn't they?" she asked, and I realized that Mordred had, twice, although I had assumed he meant she would soon return from escorting her husband back to their Lake, not from tracking down Pinel.

"So you found him," I said. "You did bring him back?"

"No. I did better than that." She smiled, beatific as a stained glass saint. "I touched his forehead and saw all his memories. It was very easy to get close to him; I wore my hair red, my face sunburnt and freckled, my clothes in tatters—he did not know me. And when I had seen beyond question that he was indeed the poisoner, I cast the spell of melancholia over him. The same spell I cast on you once, and on poor Dame Ettard, except that I do not intend ever to lift it from Sir Pinel of Carbonek." She chuckled again, a little louder. "He has a very ugly mind for the charm to feed upon. I doubt he will reach Carbonek again before he kills himself."

That was news worth having gone through the spell myself to hear. I considered asking Dame Nimue to put it on Gaheris, too. But I thought again of Cob the charcoal burner and his palfrey. And if Dame Nimue were to start meting us our deserts on one another's wish, how many among us, from Artus himself on down, would deserve to escape? Thinking it through once more, I might almost have asked her to lift the despair from Pinel . . . but it might well be too late by now anyway. And he had left Dame Guenevere to face his stake.

"All this is good to hear," I said, "but it doesn't do the Queen much good. You should have brought Pinel back to make his confession before the court."

"Ah," she replied, "but the court, and even Sir Mador, will take the word of the Lady of the Lake."

As it turned out, not even the word of Dame Nimue would have been needed to save the Queen. The great and noble De Lac had been lying snug at old Sir Brastias' hermitage in Windsor Forest the whole time, a secret shared only by Lancelot, Sir Brastias, and Bors de Ganis, who had been bringing his cousin the news and who had only agreed to say he would champion the Queen on Lancelot's own instructions, with the understanding that Lancelot would ride in at the eleventh hour and take the field. It was a brilliant coup for Lancelot, who defeated Mador easily. No matter that Dame Guenevere had been kept in torture for a fortnight.

We arrived in time to ride into London on the great champion's tail. Dame Nimue remained in disguise until after Lancelot's victory, allowing him, for the sake of her French sister-in-magic who had raised him, to play out his little game and collect his glory before she came forward to share her knowledge with the court. Her testimony had at least the good result of getting the false damnation of the Queen erased from Sir Patrise's monument, to be replaced by a true statement of the matter. The rest of us said little about our own parts in the search, and what little we said seems already to have been forgotten, or merged into Dame Nimue's fame.

She also healed both Lancelot and Mador of their wounds. It takes you about as long to get back your full battle strength as after ordinary leechcraft, and, even with Dame Nimue's mending, your wounds, though they have disappeared, still tend to itch a bit; but at least it spares you the worst part of your knightly life—lying in the infirmary waiting for your flesh to close up and your bones to knit again. Mador wasted no time making his apologies and being welcomed back to his allegiance to Arthur and his seat at the Round Table. I hope I managed to impress on Coupnez the duty of telling the full truth when asked for it, and so the book was closed and bound on the whole unhappy adventure. Gouvernail had kept things pretty well under control for me, and I soon let it be known I would take no nonsense from anyone, from Chloda and Titus Flaptongue on down, on account of the lingering weakness of my recent wound. Especially with the new work to be done.

Epilogue
Of the Queen and of Sir Kay

"And that time was such a custom, the queen rode never without a great fellowship of men of arms about her, and they were many good knights, and the most part were young men that would have worship; and they were called the Queen's Knights, and never in no battle, tournament, nor jousts, they bare none of them no matter of knowledging of their own arms, but plain white shields, and thereby they were called the Queen's Knights." (Malory XIX, 1)

Dame Guenevere has a small, private garden within the walls of London Tower, which she loves and where she can sometimes sit alone for a while with her thoughts. With all the rejoicings and festivities that marked Lancelot's rescuing her and Dame Nimue's freeing her name from any last suspicions Lancelot could not have laid at rest by force of his arms, it was late afternoon of the third day following her trial before she was able to seek her garden. And there I intruded on her solitude. I had been waiting too long for the chance to kneel at her feet and beg her forgiveness to let it pass, even at the cost of disturbing her peace.

"I would forgive you gladly," said Her Grace, "but what is your offense, Sir Kay?"

"Failure, your Grace. If you had depended on my efforts alone, you would be a heap of ashes now."

"But did you not summon good Dame Nimue?" The Queen, at least, has never forgotten that. "And did you not free the court of a dangerous man who would still be among us, unknown, for all of Sir Lancelot's skill? And, unless I mistake, were you not actually in London with the Lady of the Lake very soon after Sir Lancelot? You would have been in time to save me, even if he had not come."

And by waiting to come forward until after he had won his victory, endangering both himself and the outcome of the trial—however slightly—in the chances of battle, we had made ourselves no better than the glory-seeking Du Lac. "Dame Nimue left us for a time at Astolat," I said. "It was Heaven's good grace she chose to come back in time. I should have stopped her from ever going."

Dame Guenevere smiled and covered my clumsy hands with her own. "I will not have you still kneeling before me, Sir Kay. And I will not have you, of all knights, meek-tongued and self-accusing. It does not become you. Sit and speak a few unpleasantries, and let us laugh as in the old days."

I rose and sat on the bench facing her bower, already covered with new, budding spring vines. I should have said, "I can only speak unpleasant things in unpleasant company," or "I would rather have your laughter, Madame, than another woman's praise," or some such thing; but the courteous replies never come to my mind quickly enough, only the cutting ones. So, having what

I might consider her leave to speak, I tried to obey her. "Will you have an unpleasant speech, Madame? Then I'll say to you, Send your cock-a-dandy Lancelot about his ways."

She sat very still for a moment, plucking at a new leaf, while the westering sunlight made a halo of her hair. "And the next time I needed Sir Lancelot's arm?"

"You see? For all your kind comfort, Madame, I was no use to you—it was Lancelot who saved you. But with his wanderings and his adventures and his two-year absences, he might not be here anyway, should you ever need him again as you have this time, which God and Our Lady forbid! And if he is here, he himself may be the very cause of your danger."

She raised her head. I could see no tears in her lovely gray eyes, though God knows I had already said enough to put them there. "You know, then, Sir Kay?" she said.

"The entire court knows, Madame, with the all-important exception of Artus."

"And have we been so very . . . careless?"

"*You* have not, your Grace. But your cocksure fool Lancelot as good as boasts of it in public."

"Boasts? Or simply maintains his aloofness from other women?" As I started to reply to that, she held up one hand and went on, "No, Kay. I have tried, sometimes, to break with him . . . and he with me . . . although never at the same time. When he would be free, I hold him, and when I would be free, he holds me, though I am not sure we could long remain apart even if we should ever try to break free both at once. But even if we could accomplish so much, would it be of any use, now? Would our past not be as great danger to us as our present, should my lord ever learn of it? . . . And if we were able to break our long custom now, would not the King himself chide me yet again for failing to keep Sir Lancelot at my side?"

I rose. "Forgive me, Madame. I came to try to unburden my guilt, not compound it by disturbing your peace."

She rose also, standing in the path between me and the door. "You would not be Kay if you could not speak out your mind to the rest of us. If only it were possible for the rest of us to be so honest!"

"But preferably not quite so churlish in their honesty, eh?"

She took my hand and led me to another arbor, where we could sit facing one another across the chessboard she keeps always on its own pedestal, ready for play. The sun was touching the high garden wall now, but there was still daylight enough to see the moons of her delicate fingernails as her hand rested on the black and white squares.

"They say that the Saracens of the East each keep more spouses than one," she said, "though Sir Palomides and his brothers abjured the custom even before they were christened. Perhaps, Kex, I should have been born a heathen Saracen."

"Would there have been room among your spouses for more than two?" It seemed, at first, that for once I had thought of the courtly response at the right moment; but if I had used my brain before my tongue, it would never have been said.

"You never chose a lady, did you, Kex?" she asked softly.

"I chose a lady, Madame, long ago. The most gracious in the land. Should I have made a fool of myself, like Palomides weltering in his love for Ysolde when she already had Mark for a husband and that feckless gadabout Tristram for a . . . favorite?"

"What unkind words to speak of poor Sir Tristram!" The Queen smiled. "And what fitting ones. So you are still the same old Kay, after all. I had feared a little for you, when you first came to me here this afternoon."

"I was a Queen's Knight before I was a companion of the Table, my lady," I said. "I am still more proud of the first honor."

"Then you should not be." For the third time she took my hand, and this time pressed it for a few moments. "But I think I am more proud of my company than the King of his."

Letting go my hand at last, she opened her box of chessmen, took out a white pawn and a red one, shook them in her cupped palms and then separated her hands, holding out her fists for me to choose. "Now come, Sir Kay," she said, "I think we have time for one short game before evensong."

"Wherefore I liken love nowadays unto summer and winter; for like as the one is hot and the other cold, so fareth love nowadays; therefore all ye that be lovers call unto your remembrance the month of May, like as did Queen Guenever, for whom I make here a little mention, that while she lived she was a true lover, and therefore she had a good end." (Malory XVIII, 25)

Printed in the United States
6480